The Last Roman: Vengeance

by

Jack Ludlow

Magna Large Print Books
Long Preston, North Yorkshire,
BD23 4ND, England.

British Library Cataloguing in Publication Data.

Ludlow, Jack
    The last Roman: vengeance.

    A catalogue record of this book is
    available from the British Library

    ISBN   978-0-7505-4366-8

First published in Great Britain by Allison & Busby Ltd. in 2014

Copyright © 2014 by David Donachie (writing as Jack Ludlow)

Cover illustration © Nik Keevil by arrangement with
Arcangel Images Ltd.

Published in Large Print 2016 by arrangement with
Allison & Busby Ltd.

Magna Large Print is an imprint of Library Magna Books Ltd.

Printed and bound in Great Britain by
T.J. (International) Ltd., Cornwall, PL28 8RW

THE LAST ROMAN: VENGEANCE

During the sixth century of the Byzantium Empire, corruption is rife. The country is in turmoil and Flavius Belisarius expects to join his father's cohort to help protect the border of the Eastern Empire. Flavius's father Decimus is the Governor of Dorostorum city, and has two goals: to keep out the Sklaveni barbarians and to expose the deep roots of secular corruption. Seeking to prevent a Sklaveni raid, Decimus asks the powerful magnate, Senuthius Vicinus, for help. But treachery leads to the death of Flavius's family. Swearing vengeance on the man that betrayed his father, he begins a journey from which there is no way back.

THE LAST ROMAN: VENGEANCE

To Lucy & Jeremy
two lovely people
of whom we don't see enough

CHAPTER ONE

The tension easily penetrated the walls of a schoolroom only just beginning the functioning day: running footsteps, occasional raised voices, followed by a full-throated shout of the kind that hinted at major alarm. This made life awkward for the pupils seeking to concentrate on the subject of mathematics, never one to hold the mind of a group of boys on the cusp of manhood, youngsters who hankered to be outdoors playing games or doing military training, rather than ingesting the other three pillars of imperial education: Latin, Greek, and rhetoric.

The sounds of commotion made it seem necessary for everyone in the class to make contact with the others, and in this they were as one – not always the case. As in any group of a dozen adolescents there were as many rivalries as friendships and even the odd relationship founded on jealousy or deep antagonism, not least by an interest in the opposite sex that had gone from indifference, though interest, to the start of rivalry. These were all now set aside by intense inquisitiveness added to an opportunity for exchanged whispers and excessive shuffling.

Rendered impatient by the distraction displayed by his pupils he might be, but their teacher was too kindly a soul to inflict what others might have imposed on an inattentive classroom: Beppolenus was not one to wield a vine sapling, and besides, he could not be other than inquisitive himself. He might well be fearful for he was a timid soul, noted for a vivid imagination that saw danger in mere shadows.

Not that it was unusual to be rendered fretful living on the very edge of the Eastern Roman Empire. It was a region subject to unremitting threats from barbarians, made doubly insecure by the instability presently disturbing the whole Diocese of Thrace, the causes being the onerous taxation decreed by an avaricious emperor and the imperial decision to endorse a dogma so at odds with the strongly held beliefs of the local population that insurrection was in the air.

It was from the north that danger was more often anticipated: the River Danube, which formed the border, was not visible from the windows of the Belisarius villa but beyond that, from the upper floor on a clear and crystal day, the hills that hemmed the lands of the barbarian Sklaveni were clear to the eye, dark green and forbidding, rising in time to the distant mountains that held their caps of snow even into the height of summer.

Behind the Sklaveni and beyond those mountains stood a more serious threat, the nomadic Huns and Alans, tribes many times more numerous and as much a menace to the people who bordered the empire as they were to those on the southern bank of the river. Although these more distant barbarians had not recently caused trouble it was within living memory what had come from that quarter on the last occasion they had mounted a serious incursion: death, mutilation and wholesale destruction only alleviated when, sated by the wealth they had plundered, they withdrew in the face of an approaching Roman army.

Schoolroom order had barely been restored when a loud military bellow caused Beppolenus to look anxiously towards the stout oak door that did little to muffle the sound. His pupils naturally threw their teacher another surreptitious glance to see how he would react, none more curious than Flavius Belisarius, the son of the house. If there were some kind of emergency it would involve his father, who commanded the under-strength cohort that was all that was available in these times for border security in what had, in the distant past, been a proper legionary outpost.

A new sound overrode that from within the walls, this time coming in through the open casements overlooking the street, a cacophony of alarm – horns mixed with the babble of men and women on the move, punctured by the wailing of fractious infants. A ripple of whispers crossed the room to report that the citizens, many bearing bundles, were hurrying towards the old citadel of Dorostorum which, though it was in less than perfect repair, offered better protection from a marauding horde than the indifferently repaired walls of the city.

No regional uprising could be the cause of such abandonment of homes and most of their possessions; there had to be a barbarian raid and a serious one to produce general panic, which had Flavius wondering at how such an incursion could have been mounted without any prior warning from those who, by habit or instruction, were best placed to advise of approaching danger.

The possibility of such an event was a subject often speculated upon by him and his fellow pupils, friends and rivals alike, as well as the way they would, with their yet to be appreciated fighting abilities, help their seniors to counter it. They knew themselves to be heroes in the making and were prone to vocal frustration that, given no forays of any magnitude had happened for years, the chance to show their martial prowess seemed destined never to arrive. Had it done so now?

Flavius, an avid student of anything military, put himself in the place of the barbarians to speculate on how they would have made the crossing in a way that achieved surprise. They must have sealed the northern bank of the Danube long enough to keep hidden their preparations, the gathering of boats plus men in numbers. Had they made their crossing in darkness? The previous night had been one of heavy cloud that had obscured the moon, which would allow them to move in serious numbers without discovery.

Or had they then launched those boats way upstream in broad daylight, to avoid any sight of their presence being reported by the farmers who tilled the southern flood plain? The meandering current would carry them slowly downstream and it would take little in the way of steering to make an unobserved landfall at the right time and at a suitable place.

Such imaginings were rudely interrupted as the schoolroom door was thrown open in a way that made the teacher cower in foreboding, the gap filled by the imposing frame of Cassius, Flavius's eldest brother, dressed in breastplate and greaves, sword at his side, his helmet under his arm, the sight of him immediately followed by a peremptory command.

'Pack up your lesson tablets and make for the citadel.'

The sibling reply, a rasping one, was addressed to a man already turning away. 'Do they not go to their families first?'

Cassius swung round, the look on his face one of mild impatience. In his voice there was just a hint of weariness at being questioned by a much-loved younger brother, who was also capable of being, at times, a sore trial.

'Their families, if they have any sense, they will find already within the walls.' He chucked over a set of large keys, swiftly caught. 'Now you, Flavius, go to where the servants are gathering in the atrium and do what your father requires of you. Take them to safety.'

'It is serious then?'

'We shall need every man we can muster to put a check on what we face. A messenger has already gone to seek support from the forces camped north of Marcianopolis in case we cannot.'

'Can I not fight alongside you?'

'You're too young,' Cassius snapped, as those he reckoned wiser heads were already pushing past him, their teacher well to the fore.

'Not by much.'

The response was delivered over a departing shoulder. 'By enough.'

Soon there were only three pupils left in the room, Flavius and his two closest companions,

Asticus and Philaretus. Both matched him in age and attitude, if not in height, boys eager to know what their friend would do: obey his brother's command or flout parental authority, a pattern of behaviour to which age was making them all particularly prone? There was no doubt that Flavius was tempted but he could not meet what was their clear hope.

'If you decide to follow your father and join in the fight we could do so with you.'

Looking at Asticus, with his eager expression, Flavius had to shake his head. He often took the lead in their adventures and he was being asked to do the same now, as a sort of cover for what would be seen as wrongdoing even if they acquitted themselves well: just as often he got the blame if matters went awry, obliged to accept whatever came of their misdemeanours. In the background the sounds of activity within the walls were fading, meaning there was little time to make up his mind, and it was with an air of resignation that the moment arrived.

'No, I must obey.'

'Flavius?' Philaretus hissed, disappointment obvious through the tone in which the name was used. 'How long have we prayed for a moment like this, a chance to show our mettle?'

'There's no one else to carry out the task my father has set me, Phila, and what will happen to you if you do not do as my brother commanded?'

'My father was not present to hear it.'

'He will hear of it and out will come that staff of his.'

That brought forth an obstinate look and a

squaring of the shoulders. 'Which I do not fear.'

That was, if not an outright falsehood, close to one; Philaretus had a parent easily driven to anger and a level of chastisement not visited upon his friends, both of whom had seen too many times the way he sought to avoid punishment as well as the stiffness brought about by the failure to do so. The true extent became very evident when they bathed after fighting practice or bouts of wrestling, great blue and black weals all over Phila's body.

'If we are to go,' Asticus said, clearly accepting Flavius's argument, 'we'd best move.'

'If you insist...'

Flavius cut off the disenchantment with a quick embrace. 'Time will grant us the chance we need.'

'Till then,' added Asticus, moving forward to hold out his arm, to be clasped in turn by both his companions in the prescribed Roman manner. Then they were gone.

Left on his own, Flavius went to look down at the crowd milling along the road in search of safety, which underlined to him, if his brother's response had not already done so, that it must be a very significant attack. Raids were a regular part of life in this part of the world but they had tended towards pinpricks, incursions low in numbers and effect; a few small livestock stolen, a few bodies taken into slavery and very rarely a man killed or a woman defiled.

Four whole years had passed since anything occurred which might cause the population of the city to seek the security of the citadel; he could recall quite clearly being taken there by his mother at the time. With a mind still churning on how it had come about, as well as how it would be countered, he turned away to carry out his father's instructions, though he resolved to go by his quarters to don his own set of armour and collect his sword. If he could not be a fighting soldier he could at least look like one.

Citizens of the region were prone to fright but that was as nothing to the fear of the slaves and servants, the fact made plain to Flavius before he ever clapped eyes on them. The sound of the wailing filled the atrium, near loud enough to drown out the clattering sound of horses' hooves and stamping feet as their master led his men away to do battle, this overlain with the barking of the family hounds that would run ahead of them.

It did nothing to quell their anxieties that the youngest of their master's sons should appear before them dressed in a decorated leather breast-plate, with a sheathed sword at his side. Try as he might, Flavius could not command silence with the kind of tone that would have come easily to the other male members of his family. His voice was yet to fully break so his instruction came out as a croak and being that was utterly ignored.

Thankfully Ohannes, his father's *domesticus,* had the ability to replicate the order and be heard to do so, which if it did not bring calm at least dimin-ished the howling so that the young master could issue his instructions and, once heard, lead what he thought of as a flock no better than goats out of the double gates of the villa, locking them behind him.

Each of the servants, twenty in number and varying in age, had their bundle in their arms, within which would be laid their meagre possessions. Flavius could not help but wonder if there was some of the family's property in there too, such an alarm being a perfect time to pilfer. If the barbarians made it to the Belisarius villa and sacked it, who was to say what they had taken, against what had been secreted away beforehand? If after all the barbarians did not reach the villa, any stolen object could be later replaced.

'They would not dare,' Ohannes snapped, when Flavius quietly suggested the possibility, added to the notion that they might be searched.

Looking up at the old man's face, mostly the prominent nose and the jutting jaw – it was half hidden by his long greying hair – Flavius had to smile; this old soldier was too faithful to his master himself to see a lack of that in others. The notion that he should order those bundles examined was, on consideration, an instruction Flavius declined to issue and in this his years were once more against him. If it turned out he was wrong then it would be he who suffered the wrath of his family for the resentment caused; aggrieved servants, even if most of them were slaves, had many subtle ways of exacting revenge on those they served for perceived slights.

The presence of Ohannes was telling; would he not have set off at the side of his master if there had been anyone to shepherd the servants bar Flavius? True, Ohannes was past his prime and perhaps not fit enough for a hard march followed by fighting. Yet he was held in high regard by the head of the house so he might have been expected, at the very least, to be left to protect the Belisarius property, which could not be left empty. A gentle enquiry regarding that duty established the task had gone to another.

'Would you not then be more contented riding to do battle?'

'I have done enough of that in my time, Master Flavius, which my scars would tell you.' That was followed by a derisive snort. 'And what makes you think I rode? Folk like me used our feet and my bones are a mite rigid for too much of that now.'

The steps Ohannes was taking gave something of a lie to the assertion; slightly stooped by his years, he was long in the leg and his footfall was extended and seemed firm. A Scythian recruit to the armies of Byzantium, he had ended up on the Moesian border and on retirement had taken service with the man who had been his last commander. It was a position in which he clearly felt comfortable, appreciated and of some value; if Ohannes was heard to moan, and that was not uncommon, it was not about the tasks he was asked to perform. His complaints were aimed at the uselessness of the servants who also tended to the Belisarius household, at their lack of application and any sense of discipline.

'Time to use your elbows, young sir,' he growled.

The street that formed the approach to the fortress had become increasingly crowded, turning to a pushing and shoving throng, which did not diminish as they flowed out onto the old parade ground that lay before the gates. Streams of fleeing citizenry, coming from several directions, were melding into one heaving mass, each person seeking advantage so that the sound of disputes rose to a crescendo as men and women jostled to get themselves and their possessions to safety.

Even if his voice could have carried, it would have been useless for Flavius to try to shout out and state that panic was unnecessary, to say the Sklaveni were not on their heels and the garrison, soon to be joined by the men retained by the local landowners to protect their own property, had set out to impede any advance on Dorostorum. The mood had taken hold and could not be controlled and what was before them now was getting dangerous: a melee in which to stumble risked being trampled.

'Let us hold back, Ohannes,' Flavius croaked.

'Your charges won't wait, Master Flavius, better you draw that sword on your hip and force your way through by a bit of belabouring or we will lose them.'

The noise of the crowd made it equally impossible for Flavius to impose a check on the servants who, already wracked with anxiety, had picked up on the general air of alarm. Pushing forward despite his rasping command to halt they became mingled with the terrified citizenry. He had stopped, while Ohannes, by his side and hearing his order, had done likewise. There they stood, watching as matters ahead of them descended into chaos, the crowd around them shoving to get by, while by the double gate itself it was clear people were being crushed.

'This should have been done with more calm.'

'Easy to say, young sir, hard to manage when terror takes hold.'

'It is enough for me, I have done my duty as requested.' Those words being met with an expression of enquiry, Flavius added, 'The servants are either on their way to safety or in a place where, even if it is dangerous, I cannot aid them.'

The look he got from the taller man clearly begged a question, which he answered with a puffed-out chest. There was a sense that in declining the requests of his school friends he had diminished himself, something circumstances now allowed him to redress.

'I intend to ride to join my father.'

'Which will be against the expressed wish of that very man, if I know his mind.'

'It is my hope he will applaud my willingness to stand by his side.'

'More likely he'll tan your hide.'

'Not if I prove my worth, which I am determined to do. Take these keys and look after them. I will see you Ohannes, when I have helped to rout the barbarians.'

'You will see me by your side, young sir, for I fear to face your father for what you propose if I do not accompany you.'

'Can you ride?'

The implication of the question was obvious; Flavius would go to join his sire on horseback and the thought of doing likewise, judging by the furrowed brow, was not a welcome one to Ohannes, albeit the old mercenary replied in a firm voice. 'I can hold my seat if it's not at the gallop, though I would not care for jumping of any kind.'

'You will not consent to my going alone?' That got a very firm shake of the head, accompanied by a glare of determination. 'Then let us find you a mount.'

Ohannes did not enquire as to where such a thing might be found; a citizenry fleeing on foot would have left what horses they owned in their stalls, but he clearly felt the need to point out a possible transgression. 'We will be required to steal it.'

'Borrow,' Flavius croaked happily. 'And what cur would deny those set to protect them the use of their mounts?'

The retracing of steps was done through streets thinning of people until they were actually deserted, though no doubt the dishonest elements of the citizenry would be busy pilfering where they could. Without telling the older man why, he went by the houses of both Asticus and Philaretus only to find them securely locked and abandoned, and while there was disappointment in that there was also a bit of pleasure to be had, for he would render them jealous when later they were told of his exploits.

Stables were easier to enter than any of the houses, and as he suspected, many had been left unsecured. Folk running for safety had done so without much care and on foot, abandoning their animals, including their goats, pigs, donkeys and horses. Flavius having his own mount, the task was to find something suitable for Ohannes, the kind of cuddy on which a non-rider could keep his seat, for the old man was adamant anything skittish would likely throw him off.

They visited several before finding a comfortable-looking mare, one that was calm enough to give them no more than a lazy glance on entry and a creature that made no attempt to avoid their attention as they got her bridled and saddled. The reluctance of Ohannes to actually mount was clear; on the way back to the Belisarius villa he was content to stay on foot and lead the animal.

They found the family stable open, which had Flavius looking sheepish, for though it had not been stated to him, it had been his responsibility to secure the property and, assuming some servant would lock these gates without being asked, in that he had failed. It mattered not, since it seemed nothing was untoward, allowing him to breathe a sigh of relief.

That did not last: having only just begun preparing the youngster's stallion, they heard a crashing sound from the main house, followed immediately by another, an indication that someone unwelcome might be within the walls. Ohannes's silent gesture that the youngster should stay still and let him investigate was ignored; Flavius, sword out, was dogging his heels as the Scythian slipped in through the kitchens and headed for the family quarters.

The centurion Decimus Belisarius could not go into battle with the family valuables or his military treasury, but as had already been established, a soldier had been left behind to guard both. They found his body in the main hallway, leather helmet split open and blood oozing from his raggedly cut throat. His unused sword was still in his hand, while from within the nearby room that Flavius's father used as his bureau came the sounds of both cursing and crashing as the men who had done the killing sought to smash their way into the huge padlocked chest that held everything the centurion considered precious.

CHAPTER TWO

'You must stay here,' Ohannes insisted in a hushed whisper as he picked up the sword from the murdered guard.

The reply was just as hushed, but terse. 'This is my house.'

'Then go fetch help.'

'From where?' Flavius said, making for the open doorway until a strong flat hand hit his chest, stopping him dead, but doing nothing to dent his determination. 'There's no one about and my father is half a league away.'

'Then stay behind me,' Ohannes hissed as another set of curses and thuds came through the open doorway.

So great was the noise that the pair, swords at the ready, eased unseen through the doorway, until Flavius, possibly through nerves, certainly through a lack of experience, allowed his weapon point to touch the stone of the wall and send out a metallic warning. The men intent on robbery spun round, one holding the axe with which he had placed several deep woodcuts around a lock set in stout oak. The other villain had a short spear and somewhere on their person both must have had knives.

Killers already, they knew they were confronting death and it was inevitable that faced with an old man with greying hair, bony and scarred from many a battle, set against a young and fresh-faced youth, they should make Flavius their prime target. The spear point was aimed at his breastplate within a blink, the hand holding it drawing back to thrust, the youngster too rooted to the spot to react properly. Ohannes saved him by rushing forward and closing with the spearman before he could cast his weapon, a thrust-out and fully extended sword taking the surprised thief in the upper part of his chest.

That exposed Ohannes to a blow from a now raised axe and he was badly placed to avoid the swing of it, while Flavius was not close enough to counter what was bound to be fatal, so when he threw his sword it was in panic rather than any real hope. Mere luck had it spin point forward to take the axeman in the face, cutting his nose and cheek deeply and imposing enough of a check on his swing to allow Ohannes the time to extract his blade from the spear carrier. That did not entirely save him, for the axe had been raised again, ready to come down at a speed that would split the old man's skull.

Flavius had followed up his weapon and, charging past Ohannes, he hit the axeman's legs just below the hips with every ounce of his weight. This was enough to drive his body back onto the chest, over which he collapsed, the swinging blade missing the old man by a whisker. Sword now freed, Ohannes was swift to employ it once more on his opponent, a man wounded but still dangerous. The blade sliced down on his neck as the spearman thrust out awkwardly with the fore part of his weapon to parry the blow.

Not that Flavius saw much more than movement in the corner of his eye; the axe that had threatened the Scythian was now about to be employed on him and all the youngster could do was thrust up his own arm to try and ward it off. He soon found out that while he was able to impede the speed of the blow, an adult had the kind of strength he could not match. His head was down and he was sure he was going to die when the sword swished past his crown with such energy that he felt the wind of it on his flesh; he also heard the arm bone break.

'Your sword,' Ohannes yelled. 'Get the damn sword and finish him off.'

That command had to be executed by a very rapid scrabbling on hands and knees. Once the hilt was in his hand Flavius made to stand up, only to find he lacked the time to do so. Added to that he was, once more, fighting one to one, Ohannes being involved in a to-and-fro wrestling match with his wounded opponent. The axeman might be twice injured, but he was still able to threaten Flavius, having transferred the axe to his good hand. The inability of his adversary to swing with real potency saved his young victim, the arc of the left arm being wide enough to avoid by Flavius throwing his body sideways.

From that moment instinct driven by terror took

27

over. Those same pupils with whom he studied in the classroom, the sons of his father's officers and senior rankers, as well as the offspring of some of the moneyed citizenry of the city, all undertook military training, albeit with wooden swords and blunted spears. For all the lack of threat in the weapons used, the intent by their instructors was that they would be taught as if they were real, so each one carried a leather crop that was used to painfully chastise any youngster who made a false move or employed their arms so badly as to leave themselves uncovered.

Now on his knees Flavius realised that to seek to rise would be to leave himself utterly exposed: time would not permit it so, gaining as much balance as a split second permitted, he thrust out hard, sending the point of his sword right into the gonads of his attacker, propelling with all his might to seek to get to the stomach. The scream that his assault produced was horrible but that had to be ignored; he was required to use his other hand, fully extended, to catch hold of the arm holding the axe, this while he sought to withdraw his weapon from what was bone-free flesh.

The knee that took him in the face might have been the act of a desperate man but it was effective; Flavius recoiled, immediately aware of the taste of blood in his mouth. Thrown onto his back he might have died at the hands of a fellow who was himself fatally wounded had he not kicked out frantically to put him off balance. One hurriedly placed boot caught the man below the knee and checked him, and this gave the youngster the time he needed to swing his sword low and hard at a bare ankle. He did so with such force that the blade went right through the back to the bone.

One leg gone and already off balance his assailant collapsed, which allowed Flavius to spring up from his static position and deliver the killer blow insisted upon by those who had trained him, albeit he had never employed it for real: a cut to the soft join of the head and neck, a swipe that produced a fount of misty blood as his sword edge severed the main artery. Ohannes, up against a much younger man, had survived because of the first wound he had inflicted, which had sapped the strength of the fellow he was fighting, but he must have had to go at it hard to still be engaged.

That contest ceased when his adversary finally lost the grip on his spear, leaving it in the hand of a fellow who knew how to use it. Ohannes spun it round so the point was aimed at the man's face, to then draw it back and plunge it into the exposed gorge below a head thrown back as the victim sought to avoid what was coming. The gurgling that followed from both ruptured throats was the only sound that could now be heard: no words came from either Flavius or Ohannes, both sucking in much-needed air.

After a lengthy pause, in which silence took over, Ohannes kicked at the now comatose bodies to ensure they were dead. That established, the two unlikely victors looked at each other with wonder for several seconds before the old man grinned and spoke, his breath heavy and panting.

'God in heaven, I had forgotten the joy of a damn good fight.'

'It would be better to thank God for the good

29

fortune we have just enjoyed. We were lucky!'

Flavius croaked that response as he wiped the blood from under what was an obviously broken nose, aware that he was shaking badly in reaction to what he knew now to be a fear suppressed by the need to act. Then he sunk to his knees and his shoulders began to heave as he felt tears well up in his eyes while at the same time he wondered why his mouth was entirely devoid of saliva. There was soon a hand on his back, patting as softly as the spoken words.

'Wait till your papa hears of this, eh? He will not be minded to leave you behind from his battles in future, I'll wager. Now come, it is time to wash that blood from your face and those tears from your eyes.' The tone was firmer, intended to lift his spirits as Ohannes added, 'You are, Flavius Belisarius, no pretend soldier now.'

It was common knowledge that Flavius was stubborn; it was the way of late children to be so for he was overindulged. With three sons already, the youngest five years his senior, the oldest seven, his parents had seen him as a gift from heaven, a late indicator of their continued regard for each other, and when conceived, a genuine surprise. He had come into the world from the loins of a man well past his prime and through the womb of a matron held to be too old to survive such a conception. If the arrival had been noisy from both mother and child, it had been achieved with surprising ease.

Named after an old companion of his father, he seemed to combine within himself all the best traits of both sides of his family: bonny as an infant and attractive as a growing boy, scamp enough to get into all the usual scrapes but with the charm to avoid too serious chastisement for his frequent transgressions.

Flavius was good at his schoolwork, which he took from his mother, and showed natural grace as he grew both in physique and his combative manner, traits shared by his brothers and inherited from their soldier father. Only recently had puberty begun to put some of his features out of balance, giving him a head a mite too big for his body as well as a small eruption of spots that went with the passage to full maturity.

He was, quite simply, the apple of his parents' eye and it was not just his father and mother who were given to indulgence; two of his brothers, Cassius and Ennius, the eldest and nearest in age, were equally ready to forgive an increasing precocity. This manifested itself in a ready tongue that was, at times, too clever by half, overly sharp and critical for his years.

Flavius made no secret of the fact that he was the clever one in the family and that severely irritated Atticus, the middle of the senior trio. Being much slower of wit than his siblings, he lacked the patience of his close brothers: he would fetch Flavius a quick clip for being cheeky when he was sure no one was looking.

When small, this had ended in tears that inevitably saw Atticus punished. That had long since ceased and in an odd way it was Atticus that set the example, for he took his chastisements without complaint and with utter indifference to any pain inflicted; the youngster had learnt like him not to cry, steeled himself to avoid any sound if he and his brother came to what were blows or a wrestling match between a pair totally unmatched in size and weight, contests in which Flavius was a constant loser even when he got close to his elder's height.

In part his silence was for the sake of his pride, the reluctance to admit being bested. Yet added to that was the influence of one of the emperors of Rome he truly admired, a fighter as well as a philosopher, held in high regard by his father, a paragon he had studied assiduously both within the schoolroom and without, the stoic Marcus Aurelius. That was not the only reading in which he indulged; anything regarding Rome or Ancient Greece he studied with a passion, for instance Diodorus Siculus, who had written of the campaigns of Alexander.

Another favourite was the *Commentaries* of Julius Caesar and his conquest of Gaul. If the library of Dorostorum was far from comprehensive it did contain volumes of imperial history and given the nature of the empire much of that was a story of conquest: Scipio Africanus fighting Hannibal and the final conquest of Carthage. The same story of the very province in which Flavius now lived, taken from Macedonia by the Roman legions and held against constant barbarian attempts to repel them.

There was the narrative of Mark Antony versus Octavian, of campaigns all along the Rhine and the Danube as well as the conquest of Britain by the lame Emperor Claudius. All the Belisarius sons were imbued with their father's love of things Roman, though the last of the litter was the most affected. Steeped in his reading he held it as unmanly to show either hurt or to let his parents know that anything untoward had occurred when he and Atticus fought. Being active at robust games as well as regularly taking part in military training and wrestling bouts against his peers, there was little need to explain the appearance of sudden bruises.

That streak of stubbornness came to the fore now: Ohannes's attempt to imply they had done enough, that the duty was now to stay and protect the house ran into a wall. Flavius, once the flow of blood from his nose had been stemmed, was even more adamant that his place was alongside his relatives on the field of battle, which left the *domesticus* in a quandary for he lacked the standing to order this youngster around.

Thus he was torn between the requirement to protect his master's goods, set against the need to ensure that this much-favoured son, having just survived a dangerous encounter, did not now get himself into any scrape that might prove fatal. In the balance of value there was no other conclusion.

'Then I must accompany you.'

'I would not impose that upon you, Ohannes.'

'You're not laying it on me and if you knew me better, had you seen the marks on my back, you would also know that few folk have ever got me doing anything I don't want.'

'I could not be unhappy, after what has just taken place, to have you by my side.'

33

Flavius blushed then; that statement sounded and was sententious. The knowledge that such a view was shared seemed obvious by the jaundiced look the words received, added to a derisive snort.

Ohannes insisted on one last act before departing, which was to drag the bodies of the now dead thieves, as well as that of the murdered soldier left on guard, to be left at each entrance to the house; one outside the kitchen entrance, another by the gate to the stables, both relocked from the inside, the third outside the main atrium doorway, it being hoped this would give pause to anyone else thinking of robbing the place. That complete, it was an unenthusiastic old soldier, now with sword, spear and an axe in his belt, who got himself astride a less gentle mare, a mount made unsettled by the smell of so much blood.

Flavius needed to breathe deep to contain his mirth as he watched the equine struggles: having been taught to ride almost as soon as he could walk, he sat easily in his saddle, even on an energetic beast a mite oversized for a lad his age and build. His horse was a stallion to grow into, an animal that pawed at the ground and loved nothing more than to run, requiring a firm hand to keep it in check, never more than when, out on a ride, Flavius turned for home and the lure of food took hold.

Now he hoped to test him in battle and with Ohannes in his wake, holding the reins tight, he went in the direction taken by the imperial cohort, easy to see by the rising smoke from burning farms now high in the sky. Outside the city they came across one of those farmers and his family, trundling along as fast as they could go, a cart bearing their possessions, having abandoned their home to head for what would now be a very crowded fortress.

Being mounted and wearing Roman armour they asked him for information he did not possess; his assurances that they had little about which to worry when it came to survival failed to gain much traction.

'Fighting men will have gathered all over the district. Once all available forces are gathered the barbarians will have a choice to flee or be slaughtered.'

'Rumour is they are in their thousands.'

Tempted to scoff – the Sklaveni could not muster such numbers – Flavius had to rein that in as much as he was needing to do with his skittish horse. 'At worst we must hold them until aid comes. You should be safe to return to your farm.'

The answer was a glare, before the farmer smacked the rump of his plough horse to move it and his family on, the children taking their cue from their sire to add their own baleful look. There was a moment when he considered telling them who he was and to whom he was related but that died as he recalled his age; that would be against him, even if he did feel his advice to be sound.

Armed men would now be rushing to his father's aid from all over the district, the *limitanei* – those able-bodied men who could be quickly mustered to fight alongside him – necessary given he led a unit under-strength for the length of border he was tasked to maintain when serious trouble

35

threatened. If imperial taxation was high, none of the proceeds seemed to be employed in paying for the soldiers needed to secure the borders, which left many of the men who had served in the armies of the empire to seek private employment.

It was from these that support would come; a decent-sized local farm would run to a quartet of fighters, some bigger landowners to as many as ten. If it sounded good in theory it was less so in practice; Decimus Belisarius had to rely heavily, despite his reluctance to do so, on the men mustered by the greatest local magnate, a senator whose landholdings and wealth dwarfed those of anyone else in the borderlands.

If Flavius had not been at his studies he would have heard his father cursing the very name of Senuthius Vicinus as soon as he was informed of the raid; not that the son was unaware of the antagonism between them or the reasons for it, their differences – from religious dogma to conduct – being a frequent parental refrain.

Given his numerical weakness Belisarius senior was adamant that only by peaceful cooperation could he hope to effectively fulfil his duties. He worked assiduously to maintain relations with the tribal chieftains across the Danube and by doing so he hoped not only that they would restrain their more excitable young bloods, but that he would also be forewarned of any incursions into their lands by the tribes to the north.

Senuthius was the exact opposite; too often he acted like a man poking a hornet's nest with a stick and with no regard for the consequences. He provoked the Sklaveni by sending raiders across the river: livestock his men would merely butcher, crops they would burn; it was slaves Senuthius sought, fit young men, women and children who could be sent on to the markets where such unfortunates were sold, all the way to the rich buyers in Constantinople if the younger ones of either sex were fair of hair and comely enough.

Nor did he respect anything of a religious nature; if the men who carried out his bidding came across a temple or a sacred burial site, pagan or Christian, it would be razed to the ground or desecrated, further antagonising the Sklaveni elders, while at the same time firing the desire for revenge among the younger tribesmen.

Decimus Belisarius was convinced that most of the Sklaveni, certainly the older members, were content to live in peace, and given they had as much to fear from Alans and Huns as did the citizens of the empire, they should be counted as potential allies, not as enemies or a source of ill-gotten profit.

'Who can blame them if they respond in like manner?'

His father would always splutter this protest when the subject came up, which it too frequently did, usually following on from some rapid vengeful response that, coming in reprisal, he was called upon to contain.

'Taking good citizens from farms I struggle to protect, using those they kidnap as a means to bargain?'

Not that Senuthius was willing to trade those slaves he had acquired; able, given the number of fighting men he could muster, to protect his own property, it mattered not to him that others suffered from small and revenge-driven raiding parties, citizens taken from their destroyed dwellings to a life of servitude well north of the Danube, for the Sklaveni would not keep them in an area from which they might escape; they passed them on to the Huns or Alans.

Pleas for mercy were left to Decimus Belisarius, who had only insufficient coin and his own honesty to offer in exchange. His coffers were far from full and not every tribal elder trusted his protestations of non-collusion. Too few of those taken ever came home, while attempts to curtail these activities fell on the stony ground of private support.

Senuthius was a senator, and if that was a moribund body that met rarely, if at all, he was still a leading citizen of the empire with well-placed friends and one high-ranking relative at court. It was doubly a problem that he had an ally in Conatus, the too willing to be bribed *magister militum per Thracias*, based in Marcianopolis. When Decimus complained to his military and gubernatorial superior, Conatus did not even deign to respond.

His cousin Pentheus was likewise a senator, a sly courtier in the imperial household, so even bypassing Conatus produced no results, the functionary being well placed to dismiss or rubbish any written submissions from Decimus Belisarius detailing the Senuthius misdeeds, while praising him as an upright citizen, a man who paid substantial taxes without complaint into the imperial treasury and was continually rated as honourable by the military governor closest to him.

Nor, unlike many of the citizens of the Thracian diocese – and this counted as much as any other factor – did he question the emperor's right to set the codes of Christian belief that his subjects should follow. These factors had made it impossible to either chastise the swine or to have him indicted for his blatant transgressions.

The person of Gregory Blastos, the local bishop and a close associate of Senuthius, compounded such difficulties, the cleric being a blatant pederast and corrupt priest who was held in the Belisarius household to be a disgrace to his calling. Blastos was a man who saw his Christian duty, which stood above that of looking after his flock, as lining his purse and slaking his carnal desires. Worse, he was a trimmer, a man willing to bend to any prevailing wind to maintain his position.

The empire had been locked for decades in discussions over two competing dogmas concerning the human and divine nature of Jesus, a matter supposedly resolved at a convocation called the Council of Chalcedon. It was not: the dispute simmered on despite the passing of much time, in excess of sixty years, given the bishops of Armenia, Syria and Egypt fought hard to overturn the conclusion. They held on fiercely to a different set of beliefs to that which had been agreed.

Blastos had come to the Diocese of Dorostorum preaching the doctrine as decided at Chalcedon, only to switch when Emperor Anastasius announced his personal endorsement of the Monophysite interpretation and took forcible steps to see it implemented throughout his domains. It was not hard to fathom his reasons, even if many wondered at his principles. Bishops who stuck to the Chalcedonian interpretation and defied Anastasius were, by imperial decree, being dismissed from their diocese and the thought of that Blastos clearly could not abide.

Such suppleness gave him, too, a sympathetic ear in Constantinople; a patriarch who seemed either blind or indifferent to his faults as reported, as long as the revenues he anticipated were forthcoming and the doctrine the emperor insisted upon and he preached was being spread. Any attempt to blacken the Blastos name tended to rebound on the complainant and had done so more than once; the Church, of whatever persuasion in dogma, did not take kindly to accusations that its priests were anything less than saintly!

The citizenry were not blind; if a man of the rank of Senuthius could do as he pleased and their bishop could flaunt his catamites as well as his peculations with impunity, while trimming his principles to suit himself, then why should they too not behave as they wished? The transgressions this caused led, with the wealthier citizens, to furious confrontations and threats of legal redress rarely taken to a satisfying conclusion. With the poorer folk it manifested itself as many a severe whipping, none of which were imposed with any great pleasure, for crimes, many of which were misdemeanours.

The public peace had to be maintained and Decimus Belisarius, even after six years in post still an outsider to this part of the imperial lands, was the man tasked to maintain order – the result being that he was not loved in the first instance as the agent of a state seen to be tax greedy as well as over-intrusive, and he was also resented for his palpable probity, as well as for being the overseer of any physical chastisement of wrongdoing.

CHAPTER THREE

Rising ground overlooked the Danube as well as the flat, sometimes flooded plain bordering its waters, land that produced abundant crops, wealth for a few, a good living for many and labour for droves – in all a tempting prosperity. In cresting the ridge Flavius was presented with a panorama of an unfolding military engagement and one that seemed to favour the Roman side, as well as elicit admiration from the observer. Instead of riding to drive back the raiders his father, as indicated by the position of his distant banner, had succeeded in getting between them and the riverbank, thus cutting them off from their boats.

It was a deadly manoeuvre and very obviously a surprising one: the youngster could see the enemy milling around in apparent confusion, noting they were exceedingly numerous, several hundred in number, he reckoned, which made what was already unusual truly exceptional, for in such numbers they could not all be Sklaveni. By closer examination they looked, judging by their distinctive helmets and armour, to be not Sklaveni, but mainly Huns.

'How did they get to here without anyone knowing?' Ohannes asked, when Flavius made the identification.

'Why would the Sklaveni stop them if in doing so they put their own folk and farms at risk? Best to stand aside and let them do their worst to us.'

'They won't all be Huns.'

'No,' Flavius acknowledged; too many of their close neighbours, seeing a chance of both plunder and revenge, would have joined in. 'Though from what I can see they are all in a bind, from wherever they hail.'

Between the barbarians and a city full of fearful citizenry stood the local militia, now seemingly fully assembled, and they would match their enemy in strength. They were under the authority of Senuthius, who with his senatorial rank was deferred to and acted as the militia commander. Added to that, he could muster more fighting men than the imperial cohort.

Flavius imagined him to be salivating at the prospect of how many prisoners he could take to sell, for these raiders were likely to be the fittest of their race and he would have a good chance of mass captures. Present too was the Bishop of Dorostorum, his ecclesiastical banner, bearing a golden cross on a white background, raised high to inspire the faithful to deeds of valour that would elevate them in the eyes of God.

For the youngster the problem was obvious: between him and his family, for all three of his brothers were with his father, stood not only the forces of Senuthius but also the raiding barbarians, now no longer burning homesteads and

42

stealing what they could but working out, he surmised, a way to extricate themselves from what had become a trap.

'I could ride round them, Ohannes.'

'Take too long,' came the gruff response.

'Only if I had to abide by your pace.'

That got a Scythian glare, for in getting this far Ohannes had enjoyed little comfort. Nor was he unaware of what the youngster was implying, that he could ride much faster on his own and perhaps be able to join his sire before battle was commenced.

'And who's to say those swine from over the river will let you pass?'

'They have more to concern them than one lone rider.'

'One lone rider who happens to be the son of the imperial commander.'

'That they do not know.'

'How can you be sure, young sir? There's bound to be Sklaveni hotheads in that lot. It may be that you will be recognised even with your swollen snout. Even if they are Huns to a man, you're well mounted and wearing the clothing and armour of a Roman, so they will seek to kill you anyway.'

Ohannes then proved that although he had been a mere footslogger, he could still see plainly what was what. 'And if you're recognised by the Sklaveni they will use you to bargain. A good way to get by your papa, don't you think, and back to their boats, offering your head for their freedom.'

'They won't capture me, Ohannes,' Flavius responded with a false laugh.

'They're not going to get the chance, for I will be forced to stand in your way.'

Whatever good humour or kindly feeling Flavius had towards this old man disappeared quickly, to be replaced by a growl made more telling by the state of the boy's pubescent throat.

'You do not have the right.'

The spear came up slowly until it was couched on his shoulder and ready to throw. 'It is a right I will take, as well as what comes of it.'

'You would harm me?'

Ohannes actually grinned, or was it a grimace? 'No need, young sir, but this spear will do for your horse and even you are not mad enough to seek to join your father on foot.'

The pair stared at each other, Flavius seeking and failing to impose his silent will on the older man, whose lined and weather-beaten face had settled into a bland and calm look that was somehow more telling than belligerence. The spear was still held in the cup of Ohannes's hand and Flavius knew he could use it, just as he knew there was no need for his horse to be killed; a wound to its breast would suffice. The stand-off was broken by the sound of blowing horns from the riverside, a sign that Flavius's father was about to advance.

'Too late now,' Ohannes said, lowering the spear.

'My father will hear of this,' Flavius snapped.

For all the force with which that was delivered, in his heart he knew he would say nothing. Angry as he was there were two reasons not to, the first being it was unbecoming for a Roman to go telling tales, but it was the other truth that was more unsettling: the fact that Ohannes was more likely to be praised in the Belisarius villa for his restraint of a headstrong youth than chastised. In an endeavor to regain his lost dignity, Flavius made a very obvious attempt to concentrate on what was unfolding below.

On a wooded plain, broken by a maze of small plots of farmland interspersed with hedgerows and woodland, it was far from easy to see every part of what was happening, but there was no doubt the imperial cohort was pushing forward; the urgent blowing of horns Flavius took to be a signal for the forces of the local landowners to likewise advance so as to squeeze their enemies between the two. Soon came the sound of distant battle, of screeching men and the occasional clash of metal on metal loud enough to carry in the clear early summer air.

'They're not moving,' Flavius exclaimed, pointing to the static banners of local *limitanei*, by far the more numerous of the two Roman forces. 'Why are they not moving?'

Ohannes did not reply; there was nothing he could say. Both he and his young charge, from such an elevated position, could see as plain as day the way the battle was unfolding. The raiders needed to get back to their boats and cast them off so they would live to fight another day, therefore they had to attack the imperial troops standing in their way, men who could hold them at bay so the local militia could come up on their rear and destroy them. But if they did not engage...

'They must advance,' Flavius cried, when the inactivity continued, spurring his mount and heading off the crest of the hill.

Wild thoughts filled his mind as he hunched over the withers, having no need to urge on his stallion, rarely using the reins and giving the animal very much its head, trusting it to look out for them both. There was no time to worry about obstacles, be they holes in the ground, ploughed loam or rush fences, as well as hedges enclosing the fields of wheat, which the steed, in combination with a rider who knew how to let him leap, cleared with ease.

He was soon within the rear ranks of the militiamen, some of whom were required to move aside sharply to avoid being mown down. As he made for the banner of the bishop, under which stood both Blastos and Senuthius, his ears were assailed by many an angry curse.

The way he brought his mount to a halt, the manner in which he kept his seat as it reared up, hooves flying, would have excited admiration in an arena. All it produced in the most prominent citizens of this part of the province, the men gathered round that banner, was the kind of alarm that made them scatter too, their ears filled with a rasping demand as to why they were not advancing.

Unlike his shocked companions Senuthius had not moved, his corpulent frame, encased in expensive armour over garments of silk, remaining stock-still as he looked with disdain at the youngest of the Belisarius clan. He only deigned to respond as the boy made a repeated shout that the men he led should advance immediately, the reply, delivered to the very obvious sounds of battle in

46

the fields to the fore, rendered odd by the nature of his voice, high-pitched and utterly unsuited to his imposing physical appearance or his rank.

'Am I to be commanded by a child?'

'You must support my father.'

'I must do that which I think wise,' Senuthius replied, as the men who had scattered for fear of Flavius's hooves reconvened to gather around him and glare.

'He cannot fight the barbarians without support. You will not be able to see from here but they are Huns and too numerous for my father to contain alone.'

'Huns!' was an alarmed cry that issued from several throats, though it had less effect on Senuthius, who replied with what was almost a scoff in the piping voice. 'Then it is a pity the emperor does not see fit to provide us with more men.'

'But–'

That changed the tone; Senuthius snapped at him. 'If they are indeed Huns then I and my fellow landowners will advance when we consider it prudent, for there will be no recompense from Constantinople if we lay down our lives for a few peasants of little worth.'

It had taken Ohannes a great deal longer to get to the same point, but it was just as well he arrived. Flavius had drawn his sword and was loudly threatening Senuthius with the removal of his head if he did not go forward with his men. Some of his retainers moved to protect their master, just as the mare Ohannes was riding waddled in between the boy and those who might harm him.

The youngster had no eyes for them or the

threat they represented; he was glaring at Senuthius and beside him again the bishop, who was as ever eying the youngster, flowering yellowing bruises and distended nose notwithstanding, as if he were a tasty meal waiting to be consumed, his lips wet from the salivating.

'Put up that sword, boy, or I will order my men to kill you.'

'Do as he says, young sir,' Ohannes said in a low growl. 'You cannot overcome such numbers.'

The turmoil on the face of Flavius was a mirror of his tumbling thoughts; was this an accident, an act of caution for fear of the consequences, or was Senuthius deliberately leaving his family exposed? If he was doing so he was being aided and abetted by every man who had brought a sword to this fight, as well as the cleric who brought no more than his crucifix.

Why that should be he was struggling to comprehend, for if he knew there was no love lost between his father and these two men, and a residual dislike of authority in the rest, he could not fathom the depths of the politics involved.

The sounds of fighting, which had filled the air, much louder now he was close to the action, had begun to seriously diminish; the battle was moving away from this position and that could only mean one thing. He spurred his horse once more and aimed it straight at Senuthius, ignoring those who stood in his path, his dark-brown eyes boring into the pale green of the older man, orbs set in a fat, round face topped by thin strands of hair.

The men Senuthius employed tended to be ex-

48

soldiers and so they knew how to deal with such an assault. As a terrified Blastos jumped away for a second time, one grabbed the bridle and hauled hard while a second shoved his spear shaft between the horse's forelegs, to set Flavius shooting forward as the mount stumbled.

Having fallen off ponies and horses many times the youngster was quick to clear his feet out of his stirrups. He also knew that to fall under the horse would lead to him being crushed, so rather than fight the motion he enhanced it, throwing his weight outwards and launching his body into the air.

If he could save himself from harm in that fashion there was no way to avoid the pain that came from landing on rock-hard ground and he felt the shock as his left shoulder made contact, as well as the immediate pain of a joint that had possibly been dislocated. His mount was over on its side, legs kicking in the air as several men sought by holding its head to keep it still. He did not see Ohannes slip off his mare to come to his aid but he did hear Senuthius order his men to leave Flavius be, his voice ringing out as he said to all assembled:

'Never let it be said that a man of my standing makes war on children.'

The hands that began to lift him were gentle and Ohannes's solicitous voice was in his ear asking him how badly he was injured.

'Not hurt, not hurt,' came the reply, which had about it a snuffling sob that gave a lie to the words, made more so by the fact that his nose was once more bleeding copiously.

'You,' Senuthius called. 'I take it you are a servant of the family Belisarius?'

'I am, sir.'

'Then take this young miscreant away from here before I find I cannot restrain men he has so insolently insulted from slicing his gizzard.'

Helped to his feet, one hand holding a right arm now feeling numb and useless, Flavius lifted his head and glared at Senuthius. If the fleshy senator saw the look of pure hate it did nothing to affect his demeanour and his voice was steady as he spoke to those who now surrounded him.

'Time for us to sound the advance, I think.'

It was a much-chastened Flavius Belisarius, needing one good arm to support the other and with the taste of blood still in his mouth, who eventually followed in the wake of the advancing militia, men who did so without the need to raise or employ a weapon. The raiders had made it to their boats and were now out on the river, there to jeer and bare their arses as the first of their enemies came to the bank or to hold up as trophies the shields and armour they had taken from their soldier victims.

In moving forward the militia had passed the mutilated bodies of the men of the imperial cohort, few of whom had survived. If they had they were now on the water, destined to be thrown out midstream to drown or to be taken north as slaves. Flavius and Ohannes found the bodies of the centurion and his three sons in a tight cluster not far from the riverbank and it was only later, in a visualisation that would come

50

back to haunt him throughout his life, that Flavius realised how his siblings had sought to protect their father, putting their persons before him in a bid to keep him alive and in control of his cohort and the battle.

It was a dream that would recur often at night, but also a vision that would come to him unbidden during many a day as he recreated time and again the scene, without ever being sure he had the right of it. He would remember with clarity that all four were covered in blood and had multiple wounds, deep cuts to arms and body, so that it was impossible to know which blow was the one to prove fatal, while around them, in ground made soggy by so much gore, lay a dozen corpses of the men they had slain, evidence that they had not been cheaply overcome; the barbarians who had escaped would be jubilant but on this spot they had paid a heavy price to kill the men of the Belisarius family.

Flavius fell weeping to his knees and if he had suffered mental turmoil before this moment it was as nothing to what he was going through now, that jumbled up with the seeking of a reason why this should have happened. Being alive for fourteen summers did not prepare anyone for this, the sudden realisation that all the pillars that supported his life, barring his absent mother, were gone.

'We must get a cart, young sir, and take their bodies home to be laid out for burial.'

Ohannes's soft injunction took time to penetrate the troubled mind of the kneeling youth and when it did that brought forth an image of the slimy, pederast bishop Gregory Blastos overseeing the funeral rites, a thought at which Flavius rebelled.

If Senuthius had betrayed his family then he had done so with the blessing of a man who did not deserve the ecclesiastical title he wore. Added to that, Blastos would say Mass according to the Monophysite creed, an interpretation of gospel and the nature of God to which his father had never subscribed.

Decimus Belisarius had worn his Christian faith as a badge of honour and that permeated his family. That said, he had been sure that if salvation existed there were more routes to grace than the one solely provided by a church that was so often corrupt, with prelates and priests who seemed to care more for their own comfort than that of God's flock. It had also become more Eastern and mystical, less the pure faith into which he had happily been subsumed as a young man.

Proud to call himself a Roman he had allowed himself no truck with the way the empire leant towards the Greek in both language and behaviour, refusing to allow anyone to address him as *kentarchos* instead of centurion, quick to remind any person unwise enough to use that military title of the nature of the domain of which they were part. It was not a Greek polity even if a high proportion of the population were of that race; it was Roman and had been, whether pagan or Christian, before the dawning of the Augustan age!

Descended from barbarian stock himself and raised outside the Christian faith – he had first taken the Eucharist as a soldier – Decimus had embraced the empire and its doctrines with a full heart and mind, to become more Roman than the citizens of the ancient city itself. It had become a creed, if not an obsession, to be seen so, to show those over whom he held sway that there was a better way to act, a true Roman way.

It was that which coloured the bereaved youngster's thinking as he finally replied to Ohannes, his voice a hiss. 'I wish them to be left here.'

'What!' Ohannes replied, clearly shocked that the boy could consider such a thing for his loved ones. 'So the crows can peck their eyes out?'

With some effort and still on his knees Flavius scrabbled forward to ensure their eyes were closed and to kiss each blood-coated cheek in turn, his father the last and longest, mouthing as he did so a quiet prayer, before whispering a wish based on many intimate moments he had shared with the object of his supplications.

Decimus Belisarius had never ceased to remind his offspring of their birthright as full Roman citizens, a gift, to his thinking, beyond price and that included the rituals of what had been a pagan society, one he had refused to condemn as worse than its Christian successor. Added to that was an oft-expressed wish to die like one.

'I want them to have a proper Roman funeral, it is for that my father would have wished, something of which he spoke many times.' Ohannes was confused as Flavius continued, a fact made obvious by his silence. 'I will remain with them and pray for their souls. You I would ask to return to the villa – the servants will come back as soon as they know the threat has receded. Fetch the males to this place and bring with them saws and axes.'

'In God's name, why?'

The reply was firm for the first time since the boy had fallen to his knees, forced through his troubled larynx. 'So they can be given the funeral rites of Romans. Fetch pitch too, and oil as well as terebinthus. I intend that a pyre should be built and that they should be laid upon it and cremated.'

'Am I allowed to say, young sir, that such a thing is blasphemous and is forbidden?'

'Say nothing to anyone!' Flavius rasped. 'Bring what I ask here for this is where I want their ashes to remain. As for blasphemy, is not the bishop who resides in his basilica the very living expression of that sin? I would not have that swine say a single word over their bodies, for any prayer from him is a profanity.'

'Sir, I–'

The youngster cut across Ohannes and he did so looking him hard in the eye, though his voice lacked any note of censure, being gentle.

'You must do as I ask, for I am master of the house now and though you are a freeman, you're still a family retainer. I cannot command you as I would a slave to obey but I can ask you, as one who was loyal to my father and his sons, to do for him what I insist he would have wished.'

'You could be consigning them to hell.'

'God, I am sure, will forgive me, and how can he place against their salvation an act of which they have no part? Better he be entreated over by those who esteemed him than a man he thought an apostate.'

All around them the militiamen were moving enemy bodies, having first searched them for booty, before carrying them to the riverbank and throwing them into the flowing waters, which would take them downriver to rest on some sandbank as carrion, perhaps even to be carried all the way into the Euxine Sea as food for the fish. The soldiers Decimus had led were being piled up like slaughtered cattle. One group approached Flavius to remove those killed by members of his family and, that completed, hinted they would help with the four bodies over which he was mourning, only to recoil at his glare, as well as his grating command to get out of his sight.

There he knelt praying quietly as the sun began a slow, shadow-making descent. He was obliged to take from his relatives anything of value they had carried into battle, rings and personal talismans, most tellingly his father's keys. Even without any of the twelve books to hand, the oft-memorised reflections of Marcus Aurelius came forth, to remind him of the transience of existence, that death comes to us all and what comes from nature will return to it.

Normally a source of consolation, even such a wise voice failed to ease his feelings now and he wept until no more tears would come.

CHAPTER FOUR

As he made his way back to the villa, Ohannes passed men digging a long trench, which he assumed to be a communal grave, for the raiders had indulged in much casual slaughter of any citizens they had come across. As he strode along he reasoned that with so many farms now without owners or folk to occupy what houses still stood, there must close by each be a pile of already cut timber.

On arrival at the family villa he found that the household slaves had indeed returned and they were first ordered to cast into the road the bodies of the two thieves, as much to see if anyone would claim them as to clear the entrances, this while the poor guard who had been murdered was laid out in the servants' quarters, there to remain until his relatives, if he had any, came to claim him.

That done he led the male staff, freedmen and slaves alike, back to where their master had met his end, gathering on the way such timber as they came across, carrying it to a spot near to where Flavius still knelt, before sending them to scour for more. The wood, both gathered and cut down, was raised into a decent pyre onto which, once it was soaked in inflammables, the four bodies were laid, Flavius, unable to take part in any lifting, only able to watch.

An ex-soldier never went anywhere without his

flints and it was Ohannes who gathered the long, dry grass and kindling that allowed him to ignite some straw then make that into a proper fire. One cloth-covered pole was soaked in oil and resin and this was handed to Flavius who stood in silent prayer before setting it alight.

Devotions complete he walked to the edge of the pyre where he thrust the torch into the heart of the timber. The soaked brushwood at the base showed an immediate flame, then the first of the logs ignited and soon the blaze began to spread and lick upwards, this as the sun dipped out of sight in the west, leaving a clear sky and a gilded edge to the horizon, that disappearing by the time the pyre was fully alight.

The darkness, aided by a palpable wind, made the flames appear furious as with red and orange flicks they began to wrap themselves around the quartet of bodies, sparks emerging from any un-seasoned wood to fly into the night air. If the flames appeared angry, that was as nothing to the feelings of Flavius Belisarius, who saw in the shapes created the faces of the men who had betrayed his family, and there and then he swore two things.

He would erect here an obelisk to his father and brothers inscribed with their names and the manner of their demise. The second vow was even more heartfelt and filled his thoughts as he made his way, with a heavy tread, back to the Belisarius villa: the creatures that had caused their deaths would suffer a worse fate.

On his return home, the silence drove home the

loss in an even more telling way than either the sight of the mutilated bodies or the act of cremation. From a busy and raucous household-cum-military-headquarters it was now as silent as what it had become, a graveyard if not of actual corpses, certainly of hopes, aspirations and activity. Just the day before the building had resounded with the sound of endless callers: soldiers seeking orders, citizenry in search of advantage or more often justice; now those who came would do so as mourners.

His family had been a noisy presence, their needs catered to by people who no longer bustled about the rooms and corridors but crept around in near-total silence, giving Flavius on any encounter a quick and sad look, before ensuring that apart from that first fleeting glance they avoided his eye. Their bickering, an ever-present part of life, was utterly muted now, while the schoolroom remained empty, so the daily noise of the pupils coming and going was likewise absent. When Flavius wandered from room to room it was as if it was already a place of ghosts, which in a sense it was; lacking an imperial centurion it had lost its function.

Exhaustion had got him through the first night; the next, even if he was just as tired, was very different. Sleep seemed impossible and when it finally came he was troubled by wild dreams. The advent of first light and awakening was a moment of confusion, turning to dread and disbelief, slowly maturing into the realisation that what had happened was true; Flavius was on his own and only the need to act as his family would have wished kept him from breaking down completely.

Ohannes tried for a certain level of normality, though there was a forced quality to his actions; he must have the physician look at his shoulder, fortunately not as badly damaged as at first feared, though a sling was advised. Flavius had to eat, to bathe and to be presentable for the callers who came to proffer their condolences, as well as the widows and offspring of his father's dead soldiers, who were wondering how they would be able to keep body and soul together now that the stipend they were supposed to receive through imperial service – it was often late or absent – was no more.

Nothing was harder than maintaining a decent composure in shared grief, to which was added his ignorance of what reassurances he could with honesty provide. Even with his fellow pupils, especially his closest friends, a mask of acceptance must be maintained. There were duties to perform: word had to be despatched by a trusted messenger, one of the older servants, to Illyria, to his mother, who had gone to the place where he had been born to visit relatives of what, on her side, was a significant and extended family. How would she cope with the news?

The chest over which he had so recently spilt blood, with the bright, fresh cuts of the axe a stark reminder of how close he too had come to death, had to be unlocked and the contents examined. He had quickly found and read his father's last testament, which made him well up again as he saw the names of his brothers listed above his own, each to be given equal shares of what was a constrained inheritance, but only what remained upon the death of their mother.

The document included within it not only his wishes for his posterity, small gifts to certain religious institutions who would be asked to pray for his soul, a stone to be carved in Latin and placed on a wall outside the city with his full name, his title and a list of his battles, but also such mundane instructions as to which slaves should be in receipt of manumission. It was the accepted way to reward long service upon death and it would be another manifestation of his father's desire to be seen as nothing less than a proper citizen of the empire.

Flavius was familiar with most of the contents of a chest in which he had occasionally been allowed to rummage as a child: silver tableware and decorated goblets that were laid out on special occasions, one brightly polished silver salver held up in his hand to show him the now dark, yellow-tinged bruises under both his eyes, framing his swollen nose.

There was jewellery too, the property of his mother, and a mass of saved communications from both parents relating to friends and relatives, as well as the official despatches between the court and the centurion, too many demands for overdue money which had him look into the smaller chest containing the funds his father had control of, no great amount of coin, that went with the office he held.

He came across only one object on which he had never before set eyes, a tightly sealed and tied oilskin pouch. Unravelled with one hand and his teeth, it revealed a set of rolled-up papers, once opened contained a series of letters. A quick perusal showed they were copies of those sent to, as well as replies from, Constantinople. The former were in an inelegant hand he knew belonged to his father; the replies were properly composed and laid out with a fine hand, and given the elaborate broken seal, they appeared official.

That his father had written any letters was unusual for he was not fully gifted in the art, having been taught late in life by his spouse. Normally when communicating with palace officials he had used a trained scribe, a fellow well versed in flowery hyperbole, who knew how to set out communications in an acceptable manner, which required not only that the subject be presented clearly and properly but had the added requirement that certain people be addressed with a degree of flattery alien to a mere soldier.

The very first missive sent by his father was dated less than a year past and it was to an old friend. Decimus Belisarius had, in his youth, been a boon companion of Flavius Justinus after whom he named his fourth son. It was an oft-repeated tale of how he, Justinus and two other companions had fled an Ostrogoth invasion of Illyria to arrive in Constantinople without money and with little food, their minds full of dreams of riches, which would surely come the way of such a deserving set of hearty fellows.

The truth, if it was sobering at the time, became a humorous tale in later life and one oft referred to. The streets of the imperial capital were not paved with easily gathered gold, nor were the citizens, be they high or low, in any way impressed by

61

these ragged, illiterate individuals from a far-flung province who spoke an incomprehensible tongue between themselves, a bit of rough Latin, and barely knew ten words of decent Greek.

It was fortunate that the empire always required soldiers, for they would have starved had it not. It was a world to which they took with a whole heart and varying success, given two of the original four had died in battle. Flavius Justinus had fared the best; through his own exploits and not a little luck he had risen to high imperial rank, that being common knowledge in the Belisarius household.

The beautifully executed reply to his first letter told Decimus that Justinus had been elevated yet again to the post of *comes excubitorum*. That was certainly a piece of news that had never been disseminated, strange given that the exploits of Justinus and the parental association had been the object of some pride. As Count of the Excubitor he was commander of the Imperial Palace Guard, which made him the most trusted military officer in the capital.

Flavius was slow to realise why his father had written his part of the correspondence, but he got the point the further on he read: these communications concerned a matter he had wished to keep to himself and perhaps even from his own relatives. Flavius could recall no mention of it and if his brothers had known they had been as silent as their sire. Had his mother knowledge of it, for they shared everything as a couple? There was, at present, no way to find out.

Laid out in date order, it was the next copy of a parental letter that revealed his father's reticence and need for secrecy. First he reminded Justinus that he had served the empire as a faithful soldier, campaigning in every theatre of war from Illyria to the Persian frontier, putting down local insurrections, seeing off barbarian incursions as well as fighting the enemies of the empire. If the position he had achieved as commander of an under-strength unit in a far-flung outpost was not so very elevated, he wished to assure his old companion that his reputation for probity was as important to him now as it had ever been.

He referred to the present disordered state of the whole Diocese of Thrace brought on by the imperial religious decrees, being open that his conscience would be troubled if he were called upon to take part in any uprising designed to restore the Chalcedonian dogma. General Vitalian, camped with the rump of an army north of Marcianopolis, was insisting upon a reversal of the imperial policy, he being a one-time commander of both men and a man Decimus still admired. More on that dispute and the potential ramifications followed but it was of little interest to the youth.

The real crux of the communication was to point out his local difficulties: that the depredations of the leading citizen with whom he had to deal, aided by the local bishop, were undermining all his attempts to keep order in his area of responsibility. More importantly they stood against his endeavours to broker peace with the Sklaveni tribal elders and there was much written outlining his efforts in that regard, as well as a roll of those with whom he had dealt.

All his efforts had failed in the face of the most

powerful man in the district and those who backed him, not least the *magister militum* Conatus. The offences committed by Senuthius, both alleged and known as facts, were listed, those of Blastos being broadly outlined, as well as the twin layers of protection that ensured they were never sanctioned. The crimes that could be laid at the door of Senuthius shocked even a young man who knew the object to be corrupt, for there were laid out acts of thievery the nature of which he was unaware.

This letter received a sympathetic reply, added to a reserved position on Vitalian and any proposed insurrection, but no real hint that Justinus would act regarding Senuthius and Blastos. Reading it several times, the words intrigued Flavius. The youngster got a strong impression that Justinus was agnostic on the dispute regarding dogma, though the letter was so carefully worded as to be open to several interpretations. While asking his father to reiterate his complaints it seemed also to contain some kind of gentle admonition, hinting to Decimus that he could not take them any further unless the centurion avoided all reference to religion.

Decimus had taken the hint; he duly rewrote his original complaint and was rewarded by a more positive reply. Justinus, having unfettered access to the throne he was tasked to protect and to oblige an old friend, had bypassed the court officials, especially the protective relative of Senator Senuthius, and taken these critiques directly to the emperor himself, where they were seen as matters requiring more information, for instance the names of potential witnesses prepared to testify, this duly provided in that crabbed and inelegant parental hand.

Dated as being no more than a month past, the last missive from Constantinople carried within it a notification that an imperial commissioner with plenipotentiary powers would soon be despatched to investigate both named miscreants – it would include an imperial confessor to question Gregory Blastos – one that would bypass and keep in ignorance the Patriarch of Constantinople and the provincial government as well as certain unnamed but obvious palace officials.

Flavius conjured up an image then, of his father's elation as he read something that would lay to rest years of frustration. Had he, when he led his men out to fight, carried a private hope that this would be the last time he would be obliged to leave his quarters to put down an incursion that had likely come about in retaliation for some act of Senuthius?

Had he, perhaps, looking into the future, had his mind on his long-cherished hope of which he made no secret: that with an end to raiding from within the empire and some diplomacy, added perhaps even to a proper treaty, lasting peace and security could be brought to both banks of the River Danube?

'The Bishop Gregory is here to see you, Master Flavius.'

Flavius turned to acknowledge the slave who had been sent to tell him of this visit, realising that he was one of those whose manumission he had this very morning examined. This was not the time to tell him; that must wait for a formal reading of the testament.

'Be so good as to ask Ohannes to attend upon me?'

As the slave went to do as he was bidden, Flavius, with some difficulty and a serious amount of pain from his shoulder, slipped out a hand from his sling to retie the bundle as tightly as it had been on discovery and reseal the letters in the oilskin pouch. Lacking a place to hide it, for he felt by instinct it needed to be kept as undisclosed now as it had been when his father was alive, he slipped that into the black sling that once more held his arm.

CHAPTER FIVE

The youngster was determined to avoid wearing his emotions on his sleeve, to present a calm demeanour when within he was seething with hate and a desire for bloody revenge. How easy it was to imagine behaving in that fashion, given his lack of years and a quite natural apprehension in dealing with a man many years his senior and one his father called a natural and practised dissembler. In deep and resonant voice, Gregory Blastos offered his condolences for both his loss and that of his absent mother.

He then made an enquiry as to the state of his damaged shoulder, very obvious in its sling, but no remark followed regarding the equally evident blemishes on his face, now two proper black eyes. His tone then became that of a man of position and maturity, addressing what to his mind was no more than a callow youth and one, moreover, who had quite seriously sinned against God and his church, much being made of that funeral pyre.

The cleric, given he glanced several times, was obviously wondering at the presence of Ohannes, who was standing just inside the door, silent and stiff of face. One reason was the trust now reposed by Flavius in his father's retainer, added to his fear that he would be unable to control his desire for revenge; the old soldier was there to stop him committing violence or even murder.

Added to that was the fact that he would never allow himself to be alone with a known pederast, a man who had, by repute, trouble controlling his hands. The Belisarius brood had been a handsome lot, none more angelically so until puberty than Flavius and even that had not rendered him ugly: he was tall for his age and well proportioned and he worried that under the clerical pomposity and strictures there might be a degree of unwelcome attraction.

'What you did was blasphemous, if not idolatrous, and it is only sympathy for your understandable grief that stops me from acting to chastise you as I would another, though I must insist that you do suitable penance when your period of mourning is complete.'

Flavius replied with a blatant lie, one accompanied with violently shaking knees, which he reckoned was plain to see under the embroidered smock that barely covered them. Likewise his voice, hoarse anyway, seemed to have within it an added and obvious tremor, which he sought to cover with a bowed head.

'I thank you for that, Your Eminence, I acted in haste and heartache.'

'Understandable,' the bishop murmured softly, smiling, lips now shiny and wet. He moved a couple of paces closer, a hand held out towards the good shoulder, which made Flavius shift quickly to one side to keep a space between them.

The youngster was not in the least sorry for what he had done but it would be folly to challenge the divine who represented the authority of the patriarch in this part of the province, a man who, with no father to protect Flavius, could bring down on him a punishment he would have no means of avoiding. At a word from this slimy Greek, Flavius could spend the rest of his days in a salt mine.

Why had Blastos waited so long to come calling? Was it to emphasise his own standing in relation to the status of a mere imperial centurion? In the two days since he had set light to that pyre the youngster had received a whole host of citizens expressing sympathy, some the smaller landowners who had been part of the militia gathered to repel the barbarians.

In times past the same men had often come to the very room in which he received them to complain about some act of Senuthius that diminished their pride or their purse; now they were keen to make plain they had only acted on the field of battle as that same figure dictated. In accepting their condolences, as well as their excuses, Flavius had wondered how much of what they said was true conscience and how much a mere pretext to salve their guilt.

Now he felt, in some cases, a sense of embarrassment; within the list his father had sent to Constantinople were the names of people who had come to offer him their condolences, which had Flavius castigating himself for his notion of them being false in their feelings. He could not prevent, at that point and with those thoughts, his good hand straying into his sling to feel the outline of the pouch of documents secreted there. If he saw the movement and wondered, the mind of Blastos was elsewhere.

'Numbers obliged us to bury the victims of the recent incursion in a communal grave and they have had a Mass said for their salvation. But we must say another for the departed souls of your father and brothers that are, thanks to your actions, in deep peril of eternal damnation. Now, as it is my duty, I will confess you and grant you absolution.'

If Flavius had been nervous prior to that he was rendered doubly so now: could he in confession, before taking in the blood and the body of Christ, fail to tell when asked of what he had found? Would he, in failing to be utterly truthful, damn his own soul?

'Leave us alone,' Blastos hissed at Ohannes, there being no need to explain why.

Dread of God's wrath disappeared somewhat, Flavius wondering if he had things other than damnation to worry about. In truth such fears were misplaced; Bishop Gregory Blastos carried out his clerical duties impeccably, listening to the young man's filleted confession without interruption, imposing upon him as penance a strict regime of prayer and repentance, before producing a small box containing bread and a vial of consecrated wine, both properly administered.

The bishop then began praying sonorously above his kneeling body and bowed head, asking that he should be granted forgiveness, yet all Flavius could hear throughout was his father's voice cursing this man, his blasphemous depredations and filthy behaviour. It was necessary to hold to the truth that if God was omnipotent and could see everything and everyone, to the innermost thoughts of their soul, a blessing from Gregory Blastos might well be meaningless.

One hand dropped from where it had been placed, on the top of his head, to softly caress his cheek and then seek to cup his chin. Flavius shot to his feet and looked the bishop in the eye, which must have contained a measure of his fury at what was being inferred. His glare was greeted by a smile and a shrug added to a soft injunction that to a troubled youth sounded like a threat.

'I am sure in time we may be friends, Flavius, closer than your grief allows us to be at present.'

Still wary, Flavius moved to the doorway and called on Ohannes to return, to take up his position by the doorway, wearing the same unfriendly expression with which he had previously fixed their visitor. Both the act and the look seemed to mildly amuse the bishop, who had begun to relate how busy his church had become since what he called 'that unfortunate event of two days past'.

'So many victims, you understand. Many of those who have come to pray for the souls of those we lost have also asked that the Lord bless you with the means to overcome your sorrow.'

'For which I am bound to give them thanks.'

'A goodly number are curious as to what you will do now.'

'What can I do but take my mother, if she comes here to grieve, back to the place of her birth. There is family there, after all, and given my father's appointment is no more—'

'Ah yes,' Blastos interjected, taking hold of the large and expensive cross that adorned his chest. 'We will sadly need to send to Constantinople to have another come to protect us, as well as the men to do so, perhaps in greater numbers than we have hitherto been granted.'

The word 'sadly' struck a totally false note; Flavius could not believe Blastos cared a sliver for the men lost of whatever rank or relation, so again he was left fighting to stop himself from raining curses down on this swine's head. When he did speak, he croaked a question he had been dying to ask since the bishop arrived, not that he anticipated an honest answer.

'Do you feel that Senuthius acted as he should?'

That brought a deep, almost animal growl from the throat of Ohannes, which got him a look of utter disdain from a man who thought the views of such a fellow to be worthless. The bishop then looked at Flavius, eyebrows raised, as if he was surprised to be in receipt of such a question.

'I mean as commander of the militia.'

'How is a mere priest to know? Such things are

the province of fighting men, which my calling dictates I cannot be.'

'You were present.'

'In the capacity of my office, no more, to bless those going into battle.'

'Which was as good as over before Senuthius sounded the advance.'

Up came the hands in a gesture of futility, added to a furious shake of the jowls, leaving the youngster with a distinct impression he had pushed Blastos into an area in which he was far from comfortable. It was as if such an enquiry was unexpected, yet how could he come to this house and not anticipate something of that nature to be raised?

'Yet you must agree that I am entitled to ask for an explanation?'

'I am not sure I understand the nature of what you are asking.'

'He stood unmoving when it was clear that battle had been joined.'

Blastos turned away to address a wall, thus breaking eye contact. 'Senuthius stuck rigidly to the standing arrangements he made with your father.'

Much as Decimus Belisarius hated the senator he had a need to deal with a man upon whose support he depended if any incursions lay beyond the capabilities of the cohort he led, trying as it was to do so. If nothing serious had happened for years, precautions had to be taken against such an occurrence and plans laid to counter it. Flavius could easily recall when such meetings had taken place, they being ones from which his father returned in a foul mood, making little attempt to hide from the family his frustration.

'Then why did those plans fail?'

The already deep voice dropped an octave. 'My son, only God will ever know.'

'Yet surely you, of all people, know the mind of Senuthius Vicinus?' There was flattery in the way Flavius said that, as if it was too obvious to be denied, yet more spooned on as he added, 'Are you not also his very close friend and confidant, indeed his confessor? I find it impossible to believe he would act in a way he had not yet discussed with you.'

The reply was yet again addressed to the wall and the voice, for the first time, showed a hint of real uncertainty. Blastos was pinned by his own vanity; he could not admit that he had no knowledge of the thoughts of a man who was his patron and one he wanted everyone to believe was his equal and friend. If the truth was not obvious to the bishop, it was to anyone with eyes to see; he was in no way the senator's equal, more a lackey than a companion.

'I do not say that your father and Senuthius always saw eye to eye, but in this matter they were in full agreement. I seem to recall, though it's some time ago, four years if am a-minded right, what was planned. That should there be another serious attack, the imperial cohort would seek to get between the intruders and their boats to secure the riverbank and hold it while the militia under Senuthius drove them onto their swords, though, of course, knowledge on what was intended had to be kept to the very few who needed to know, so you would not have been aware of it. I doubt your father told anyone, he being a man who knew how people gossip and was well able to keep things close to his chest.'

Having delivered this statement Blastos turned back to face the youngster, looking him full in the eye, which caused Flavius acute discomfort: Belisarius senior had certainly never told him what was planned and as for keeping quiet about things? Blastos missed the sense of that reaction, concluding very quickly that his listener was unconvinced, that more was required, so he carried on, his voice sounding less than wholly confident.

'If I understand little of war, I do know it is all confusion once battle is joined. Something took place that could not have been foreseen, something that caused your father to alter his tactics. It saddens me to say that if you look for the cause of this unfortunate event, it is there you must go.'

The temptation to scream was near to overwhelming; how could he so blatantly lie? Sound alone would have told Senuthius what was happening and that he needed to react. Even with his lack of years it had been obvious to Flavius, so why was it not obvious to him?

Gregory Blastos now fixed him with a steady look, of the kind that was meant to imply enough had been said on the subject and that he was too young to understand the ramifications of matters better judged by his elders. It was time to move on, Blastos demanding to know if he had sent word to his mother.

Such an abrupt change of subject threw the

youngster; obviously the bishop was keen to get away from a discussion he found awkward, and much as the son wanted to pursue it, there was little point. His mood, after that last insult to the memory of his father and brothers, was so far from collected he could feel his heart pounding in his chest. The short pause before he replied in the affirmative was necessary to steady both his racing pulse as well as his bitterness.

'Have you asked her to return?'

'I must leave it to her to decide. If she wishes to gaze upon the very spot of our misery then I will go and fetch her, for it would be unbecoming that she should travel alone with her grief, and that I have told her. What I have written will provide a poor substitute for the truth.'

'Truth?' Blastos asked, as if such a thing was untoward.

'How bravely they died.'

That got a nod, but not one that seemed to acknowledge the sacrifice. 'When do you think you will depart to join her, for you will have no reason to remain in Dorostorum?'

There was something about the way that was posed, as if it was only of passing importance, that set Flavius even more on edge, the deliberate lack of emphasis added to the lacklustre look in eyes that were now fixed on a spot just above his head, implying not indifference but calculation.

Revelation came without any need to examine from where it emerged and nor did Flavius question the certainty of his conclusion. There had been less than clear hints from those who had earlier come to offer condolences regarding what had happened on the day of battle that, if they had made him curious, had not coalesced into any firm view.

Now they did: either Blastos or Senuthius had somehow got wind there was an official mission on the way from Constantinople. For men who relied on distance from real authority, aided by a wilfully blind provincial administrator, to hide from view their transgressions, such a visitation could not be other than a threat, especially when the man who had sought to have them examined for their crimes was present to not only back them up, but to do so with witnesses. Fear of Senuthius would evaporate in the face of a body representing the emperor.

The memory of those two thieves came to mind, men whose bodies had disappeared in the hours of darkness, no one knowing who had removed them or where they had been taken. Were they just casual robbers taking advantage of the empty villa to seek to rob the place of valuables? Or had they been sent to the house knowing that it would be empty?

Once that thought had taken hold there was no need to wonder why the imperial cohort had been left unsupported. Senuthius had taken a golden opportunity to rid himself of a long-time adversary who might well have found the means to be his nemesis. Such contemplation made it hard to keep going, but Flavius knew he must reply, it being even more vital now that he do so in the same manner and tone that he had struggled hard to maintain. He must give no hint of his thinking!

'There are matters to clear up here and it will

not surprise you that is a task for which I am, at my age, unprepared.'

'Of course, I merely wondered if you might wish to join your dear mother quickly and persuade her that such a journey is unnecessary. The travelling is arduous enough, ten times more so bearing such a burden.'

'That is a decision I must leave to her.'

'Young as you are, Flavius, you now stand at the head of your house. Perhaps it is a duty you should assume and act to spare your dear mother any more unhappiness. I would tell her to remain where she is and draw comfort from your presence. I feel I must, as spiritual adviser to you both, strongly counsel that such a course is the one you should adopt.'

They want her and me out of the way! Why? In case my father confided in us? His mother probably knew, for they were very close, a fact of which Blastos, having observed them from the advantage of his office, could not but be aware. He is also uncertain about me; much safer that neither she nor I are still in Dorostorum when...

'Nevertheless,' Flavius insisted, 'you know my mother well enough to be aware that even with the unwanted elevation of myself to which you have referred, she will do as she wishes and not what I tell her.'

'A pity,' Gregory Blastos responded, in a sour tone. Then, taking a deep and what was intended to be a meaningful breath, he turned suddenly brisk. 'Now, a second duty intrudes and we have other matters to discuss. It devolves upon me, on behalf of the *magister* Conatus, to oversee some of the duties undertaken by your late father until a replacement arrives.'

Was that true? When it came to defence, untrustworthy as he was and without any official position, Senuthius seemed a more fitting candidate, added to which the bishop would not make such a claim without his consent. The whys and wherefores of what arrangement they had come to would remain a mystery so there was little point in dwelling upon it, though Flavius could not avoid letting loose a pointed dart.

'Even if you are not a soldier?'

'I am assured I will not want for support in that area,' came the testy reply. 'What it means, of course, is that I am required to take into my possession the treasury your father held on behalf of the empire as well as any correspondence in which he might have been engaged.'

Correspondence! The time had come to prevaricate, to say the great coffer that held such things was bolted to the floor of the room Decimus Belisarius had set aside as his place of work, with the addendum that anything pertaining to his family he had to retain, given his father's personal papers had been kept within the same chest and – the lie came easily – he had yet to go through them anything like methodically. He held his breath till he was sure that Blastos had swallowed the falsehood.

'Of course, and I am happy to allow you to separate anything private but I must insist you do so in my presence, for it may be that you will not know one from the other.'

'Perhaps in a day or two, Your Eminence, when

78

my grief has receded somewhat.'

The fleshy hands spread once more, as if in an expression of deep regret. 'Alas, that cannot be. I must act with haste for the sake of such responsibilities, even if I find it uncomfortable. I have a party of men without the atrium gate waiting for me to take possession of anything deemed official.'

'You wish to go through it now?' Flavius asked, affecting genuine surprise.

'If I had a choice...' That lie was left unfinished.

'One more day, perhaps?'

'Sadly no, my duty is clear and I doubt the *magister militum*, once I have informed him of my actions, would thank me for delay.'

There was silence as each examined the other, Flavius sure that, just as he was trying to disguise his true feelings, Blastos was doing likewise: if Senuthius was threatened by any hint of an imperial enquiry then so was the Bishop of Dorostorum for, though their sins were of a different nature, they acted in concert.

Having read the last letter from Justinus more than once, he knew that Constantinople had gone to great lengths to keep secret what was to be visited upon this border city, hence the decision not to inform anyone in Marcianopolis. Flavius could plead but it would be to no avail, so with obvious reluctance he stood to one side and indicated the open doorway, still guarded by Ohannes.

'Then I have no choice.'

Blastos smiled and the lips were shiny again as his hand went once more to that heavy cross on his chest, as he sought a pious excuse for his behaviour. 'Sometimes a man is forced to act against his better instincts. I hope you believe that I am obliged to do so now.'

CHAPTER SIX

If the request for access to the chest had been put with a contrived air of regret the perusal and removal of its contents was carried out in a very different manner. Blastos, even if he could not miss them, made no remark regarding the deep, fresh cuts around the lock, in itself an act that underlined the suspicions of the new head of the household. The bishop merely stood to one side as Flavius opened it, before relieving him of the keys.

He had each despatch – those received and copies of those sent over the years – brought to the desk, set by a south-facing window, to be brusquely examined. Some, probably complaints regarding his own behaviour as well as that of Senuthius, made the bishop suck on his teeth, even if the contents could be no mystery.

They were then cast, like the rest, into one of the small canvas sacks fetched for the purpose of removal, and once filled, taken out by one of the quartet of servants the bishop had fetched along, he presumed to whatever conveyance Blastos had used in coming here.

Flavius was gratified to see they were his church servants and unmilitary, not those who formed the bishop's armed bodyguard whenever he travelled to the limits of his diocese, necessary given how few of his flock agreed with his stance on dogma. He was consulted regarding anything pertaining to the family: deeds of possession for properties purchased as well as a ledger containing a list of domestic accounts; in addition there were two sacks of coins that amounted to a limited spendable inheritance.

Those objects over which he had so recently grieved were put to one side for Flavius to do with what he wished before Blastos turned to the ledger that related to the centurion's duties and obligations. Likewise, this had a list going back years, of payments and credits. Blastos, after a quick glance and yet more sucking of teeth, tucked that inside his own tunic, the leather bag containing the residue of the imperial funds – a small sum of money indeed – staying by his side.

Increasing frustration was clear to an acutely sensitive observer: much as the bishop tried to disguise it, Blastos was looking for something and not finding that which he sought and it was far from hard to guess what that something must be. Once the chest had been emptied Blastos went to kneel before it, leaning in to tap the sides and the base, even the arched lid, as if in search of some secret compartment, before finally getting back to his feet and looking the youngster right in the eye.

'Are you sure you have not been through the contents of this chest?'

'A glance, no more,' Flavius replied, for to say no would create, not dissipate suspicion. 'To find my father's testament.'

81

'And where is that now?'

'In my chamber.'

'Nothing else?'

'No.'

'You are sure?'

'Certain!'

The cross was in his hand again, this time held out from his chest and aimed at those blackened eyes, the tone of his voice a rumble from deep within his frame. 'It pains me to remind you that a lie given to me is as blasphemous as one given to God himself.'

That could not be anything but uncomfortable, Flavius being acutely aware of what he had inside his sling. Not only an official despatch but the name of who would lead it, an F. Petrus Sabbatius, as well as when it was intended they should set out from Constantinople. That being a date already past, it could be close to arrival if not actually imminent, something that depended on the eagerness of those tasked to carry out such enquiries.

'Are there any other places where your father kept papers?'

The way the clerical eyes ran over him, top to bottom, sent a shiver through the youngster; it was as if he was hinting at a personal search, not only of his bedroom but of himself too. Inspiration had him turn to Ohannes, standing by the doorway. He approached the old soldier, seeking by the look in his eye to alert him to what he intended, for he could not chance his voice lest it betray him. Coming close he put his good hand on the older man's shoulder, while slipping his weak arm just enough out of the sling to show the end of the oilskin pouch.

'This fellow served as *domesticus* to my father. Perhaps he knows.'

To get the pouch out of his sling unseen was a risk Flavius felt he had to take. Ohannes must know, given how he acted as the centurion's body servant and was with him as he carried out his duties, that everything being requested was in this very room, the place from which his master had discharged his duties and one to which, when he set out to face the barbarians, he fully expected to return.

The youngster was holding his breath, released when he discovered he had a shrewd fellow conspirator who, if he was not sure what was going on could, at the sight of the edge of that pouch, make a guess. In an act of pure theatricality, designed to cause a distraction and take the clerical eye off the exchange, the old man tapped his forehead with a pointed digit, as if he was a numbskull, this as his other hand took what he was being given.

'Master would not have trusted me, young sir, for I am unlettered. He kept his private matters close. Only person who might know is your mama, to whom he was given to share his concerns.'

Spinning round Flavius used his body to mask the Scythian, giving him time to conceal the object in his own smock. He found himself looking into the face of a worried cleric, suddenly contemplating that what he sought might be a hundred leagues away. Then Blastos shook his head, implying that if such a scenario made no sense to him, he was at a loss to know what to do about it. If, as Flavius now supposed, his father's enemies had found out there was a commission of enquiry on the way, they were obviously in the dark about the make-up of the members as well as when it might arrive.

The sooner it came the more dangerous it would be to both. With time, having disposed of their chief accuser they could, through bribes and threats, so muddy the waters that no one would dare to witness against them and that would mean no allegations could be proved. An even more disturbing thought occurred: they might try to shift any blame for what would appear to be a false set of grievances onto the complainant.

'There has to be another place your father kept papers,' Blastos insisted, his expression no longer calm, for the first time overtly flustered, so much so that he was required to be more open. 'I happen to know that he had a certain amount of correspondence with the imperial capital recently on an important matter.'

'What kind of correspondence?'

Flavius made this enquiry with his brow furrowed, not sure that, if he was taking a spiteful pleasure from the clerical discomfort, he should be. Whatever, it made Blastos even more uncomfortable and forced him into a hurried and unconvincing excuse.

'It relates to certain matters we discussed in the sanctity of the confessional, which leaves me unable to tell even you. But I know of their existence as well as of their significance, which leads me to insist that they must be kept in another place.'

'Then I am at a loss to know where that is,' Flavius responded, with a catch in his voice that gave veracity to his continued lying. 'Perhaps my brothers would have known and, as Ohannes here said, my mother, but they are no longer with us and she is far off.'

'I fear the villa will need to be searched.'

Flavius protested immediately and vehemently. 'This is a house in mourning.'

'And I have the good of the empire to consider! You of all people, being your father's son, would not surely stand in the way of that? I have my men still with me, and so I am able to carry out the task at once.'

Flavius took a deep breath before responding, finding when he did the means to sound very adult. 'I must refuse, Bishop Gregory, until the proper period of mourning has passed, for my dear mother's sake if no other.'

'You cannot refuse.'

'I do not wish to be difficult but I am, as you were keen to point out, now master of this household. Unless you can show to me an authority that gives you such a right, I will not accede to such a request.'

'I am here on behalf of the *magister militum!*'

'Who will have to give you written permission to act as you suggest.'

Flavius knew he had got it right by the confused expression that engendered; Blastos had no actual authority to act. If there had been the time to send a report of what had occurred to Marcianopolis, and to stand down any support that might be on the way, no reply had come back giving Blastos the powers he claimed, in what was at least a two-day journey on fast mounts with regular changes.

'His need is enough.'

'Forgive me, Bishop Gregory, but you must know that no one can act in such an arbitrary fashion. If I learnt anything from my father, it is never justified to exceed the bounds of the law, and he stayed true to that even when he had the unquestionable authority of his command.'

'I have God as my authority.'

Flavius crossed himself but the look he gave the bishop told him that too was insufficient. Blastos tried bluster but he could not carry it off for he lacked the means to be convincing and, realising that to be true, his expression became increasingly concerned as he sought a solution. No doubt Senuthius was waiting for the successful finale to this visit.

'Then I must seek what I need and will do so.'

If they exchanged a mutual glare both knew one fact so obvious it needed no airing: Flavius could be allowed no freedom of movement.

'Until then I command that you stay within these walls and that you touch nothing you may find. I will leave people here to ensure that is obeyed, and as a precaution I will also take from your stables what mounts you have.'

'There is only one now,' Flavius responded with a look of gloom. 'Mine.'

'A fine beast, I recall, which will serve to cover the first stage of my messenger's journey.'

Bishop Gregory Blastos did like to think of himself as the equal of Senuthius Vicinus; only rarely was he disabused of this comfortable notion, so when he arrived at the villa of the man he held to be an associate and equal he was, even if concerned, ill prepared for that which he ran into: a torrent of highly personal abuse for his very obvious failure to find any evidence that either had cause for concern.

With anyone else he might have stood his ground, but not with the senator, who, despite the girlish pitch of his voice, never had trouble in making the cleric wilt. With his height and girth, he oozed power enough to match his temper.

'No doubt you were too busy slavering over the Belisarius brat to properly carry out what you were sent to do. All that would be needed to put you off the task you were sent to carry out is a flick of those long, dark eyelashes of his and you would be billing and cooing like a pigeon.'

'The lad has two black eyes and a damaged shoulder...'

'As if that would stop you! It probably added to your dribbling.'

This dressing-down did not end there; Senuthius went on to list the ways in which his sexual preferences and inability to disguise them made him a fool, to point out that as a representative of God he was an embarrassment to his entire flock, delivered in a voice loud enough to carry throughout the largest dwelling in the borderlands. Worse for the clerical pride, it was done in front of the children of the house, a boy and a girl, golden-haired, plump and well-fed twins, who had not yet seen ten summers, their mere presence made doubly galling by the way their expressions seemed to mirror their father's disdain.

'It may be there is nothing...'

Blastos got no chance to plead that excuse; the large senatorial frame actually shook with irritation, and given Senuthius had a belly large enough to testify to his prosperity, it was obvious even under his richly threaded garments.

'My cousin smells a rat in the imperial court and Belisarius has to be the cause. When he says I should be on my guard, I am not fool enough to ignore his advice, even if you are!'

'But he has no idea what we have to guard against.'

'We?' Senuthius growled. 'You, Blastos, have only to concern yourself that you do not end up in a remote dungeon for pederasty and the selling of forgiveness for gold. It is I who is at real risk and by that I mean everything I own, and for what – acting as my duty as a father and a citizen dictates?'

The senator then waddled over to embrace his children, standing between them and laying his hands on their shoulders, his voice becoming soft and mournful as he spoke. It was well known he doted on his offspring, which stood in sharp contrast to the way he had treated their late mother, a woman who had needed all her skills with paints and powder to hide the regular bruises inflicted on her by her violent husband. Sometimes she was so badly beaten as to be unable to appear in public for weeks and there were those prepared to readily believe that her death had not been from any natural cause.

'These two innocents could be left as paupers by the malice of that Belisarius swine, and that I will not allow to happen.'

Quickly Senuthius bent to kiss each plump child on the head, before quietly telling them it was time to be about their evening studies, so as to be ready for their schooling come the morning. He watched them depart the main room of the villa with a look most men reserved for a favourite mistress and only when they had gone did Senuthius bellow for his *domesticus*. His senior household servant came scurrying into the room within seconds, to find his master talking to the bishop in a less irate tone, a haughty gesture having the man wait by the door.

'We know letters were sent out under the Anastasius seal and not from the office of the imperial scribes. Some other hand composed them and in such secrecy that the only fact my cousin could glean was that they were to be delivered by a special messenger to Dorostorum, and since they did not come to you or I, they had to be for Belisarius. He would not throw them away, therefore they must be in his house, unless they went up in that stupid pyre his son built.'

The thought that they might have been consumed by the flames cheered Blastos up somewhat, until Senuthius dismissed the notion as not only fanciful but too risky to assume. The man rambled on as he waddled back and forth with that particular gait all men use who have been heavy from birth, the feet splayed wide to accommodate thighs that could not easily pass each other.

If he was telling the bishop things they had discussed before, Senuthius was in reality talking to himself and not without a dose of his habitual self-pity, based on the notion that the malice of lesser creatures would ever see his actions in the wrong light.

For all his strength and prominence locally and his ability to buy gubernatorial silence in what was a distant and little regarded corner of the empire, Senuthius knew that he operated too often outside the laws to feel entirely secure, hence his ongoing feud with the man who had the task of enforcing imperial edicts. If he had seen Centurion Belisarius as an irritant, the man had, until recently, been no more than a flea to his great beast and one moreover without influence where it truly mattered.

If that had changed, due to the shifting nature of power in the imperial palace, as related to him by the same relative who had hitherto nullified any complaints against him, it could leave him exposed. The emperor was a man to be swayed by the last voice that had his ear, and in many ways that had been an asset in the past: the people who had counselled him, when contacted by his cousin, were easily won over either by conviction or bribery. The former came from the feeling that as long as the border was kept secure at low cost, how peace was maintained seemed of little account, the latter requiring neither explanation nor principles!

What had hitherto been simple had grown more complex and the foremost cause was religion, or to be precise the interpretation of dogma, and that was fuelling a division that had existed since anyone could remember, made really serious by the action of Anastasius in promulgating the

90

supremacy of the Monophysite position. If rumour came slowly to the borders of the empire, those that had recently emerged were worrying indeed.

The only substantial force of soldiers in the Diocese of Thrace, indeed between Dorostorum and the capital, barbarian *foederati,* were under the command of a general called Vitalian and he was threatening revolt to overturn the imperial edict. If that came to pass, the first city to feel the brunt of insurrection would be Marcianopolis and the *magister militum,* Conatus, a serious part of the Vicinian network of support.

But it was in Constantinople that such things really mattered and there too they had taken a less than encouraging turn. Conflict at court between the soldiers of empire, who had to fight its battles, set against civilian courtiers who had as their prime concern the costs of doing so, was endemic. Military campaigns against powerful enemies required the hiring and feeding of mercenaries, the empire having centuries ago lost the ability to man its forces with its own citizens. The preferred method of the palace officials, seen as a cheaper one, was to buy peace in ingots of gold where a threat could be considered serious; outside that parameter, as on the northern border at Dorostorum, trouble was ignored.

The military had acquired increased influence recently, thanks to their victories in the recent war with the Persians, and in the febrile politics of the Byzantine Court that had brought several of the commanders into positions of increased weight. If the conflict had ended, there was an uneasy peace

on the eastern border and a major fort being constructed at Dara, meaning the soldiers, being still
needed, constituted a substantial body of power.

Fighting men being no more upright than their
civilian counterparts, the senator's cousin had
assiduously sought to find out whom he could
bribe and whom he could either sideline or
diminish by the kind of base rumour that swirled
around such a shifting polity. Yet the admission
was open: there were those who might be beyond
such attempts, and a further concern came from
the fact that the centurion Belisarius, having
served so long and in so many campaigns, could
have a bond with some of these soldiers that
might be unbreakable by any means.

This was then fuelled by the rumours of secret
communications. Uncertainty created anxiety
and with good reason; to fall from favour in the
empire was not just to lose land, wealth and
power – it just as often meant a loss of your very
life and if not that, a public blinding that would
leave the victim a begging imbecile with nothing
but a gutter in which to exist.

The thought of such a fate, added to the notion
of his children being rendered destitute, so
terrified Senuthius that Blastos was subjected to
a stream of sorrowful self-indulgence as his host
went from listing what he saw as his virtues,
through a paean to his qualities, followed by a
lament as to what he would forfeit.

The bishop had been subjected to such tirades
before and so he knew what was coming;
Senuthius was working himself up to a pitch in
which he could justify whatever action he deemed

necessary to protect himself. It had been the same when the hint first came of some kind of unknown imperial communication with the centurion, culminating in the only safe course of action, which was to eliminate that part of the threat within his reach.

The voice went from whining through to firm resolve and then rose as it had on previous occasions to a solution. Senuthius always started quietly until anger began to take over, to go through growling then protestation before rising to what was a spitting crescendo of bile. He would not be brought down, would not see everything for which he had striven eaten up by imperial wolves on the word of a man like Belisarius, consumed with nothing but malice and jealousy for his position.

It ended with him screaming imprecations on that name, one fist thumping into his other hand with increasing force as he worked himself into a frenzy that had the imperial centurion lambasted as a traitor and an ingrate, a liar and a thief, quite missing the paradox as he damned with equal vehemence his public probity. Finally red of face and perspiring, Senuthius stopped, took several deep breaths and coming close, addressed the bishop in a soft voice, though not one without a degree of tension.

'The Belisarius villa must be torn apart, stone by stone if need be, and that brat who survived can be racked and his flesh charred until he reveals what he must know. You must go to your pulpit and damn the whole family as heretics. Use that stupid pyre the boy built as a sign of their sacrilege, Blastos. Tell your flock of the rituals carried out in secret within the walls of that house, of blood sacrifices to pagan gods and the desecration of the symbols of Christ our Saviour. We know, do we not, how they will react?'

'You wish to engineer a riot of the faithful?'

The question was posed without passion; if the notion of what was being proposed troubled the bishop he made no mention of it, just as he had so recently acquiesced in the plan Senuthius had hatched to rid himself of the imperial centurion. Desperate times required remedies to match.

'Led by men I will provide,' Senuthius replied, gesturing to his *domesticus*, a witness to the entire exchange. 'But we must ensure that, in any confusion, they and only they get within the walls.'

'To search?'

'To find! Let that brat wish he had died along with his father and brothers if he does not lead them to it.'

CHAPTER SEVEN

Having turned to give instructions, ordering that the requisite men be gathered from his outlying farms, Senuthius allowed Bishop Gregory time to think – really the first since he had arrived, so passionate had been the mood of his host – a short break in which the bishop could begin to calculate the outcome of what was being proposed, so that once the senator was done and the *domesticus* had departed, he could point up some possible difficulties.

'It will ill serve our cause if we leave the Belisarius boy a gibbering wreck.'

Senuthius could not resist the barbed response. 'Perhaps we should hand him over to you to do as you wish.'

'Tempting,' the bishop replied calmly, deliberately declining to rise to the slur, while being sure that the storm of abuse had subsided and he could address Senuthius as an equal. 'But that will not serve either.'

That got him a questioning look; traduce him as he might, and often did, Senuthius knew that the cleric had a devious mind, added to a peasant cunning which came from his low birth and impoverished childhood. He also knew that the memory of that straitened past was both the spark that animated the ambition of the priest as well as the cause of his anxieties; having ascended so far in the only institution, outside soldiering, that permitted such an elevation, he had a deep fear of loss.

'Whatever has happened in Constantinople it would be unwise to heighten the risks, which the broken body of the centurion's son must most certainly do.'

'If they hear of it, Blastos,' Senuthius barked. 'Remember, there is no swine sending grievances any more.'

'If Flavius is alive...' The bishop paused and spread his hands; he had no need to elaborate on that. Even with his tongue cut out and his eyes gouged the boy could write. 'But to just kill him might be worse, and since we are unaware of the nature of what we face, it may make matters more difficult.'

'While you are busy creating difficulties, I hope your mind is working on a solution.'

'Why would I need to, when your outstanding genius has already provided one?'

Senuthius brightened at that: he loved flattery and in Blastos he had a man well versed in the art of sycophancy.

'If we brand the boy as a heretic and so inflame the righteous against him, how could anyone be expected to prevent, say, a crucifixion?'

'He must speak before that!'

'Perhaps he will do so to avoid such a fate and you will have no need to take hot irons to his flesh to get him to talk. I will promise him the protection of the Church if he confides the whereabouts of what was sent to his father from the capital.'

'And when he has divulged what he knows?'

The cross was once more in the priestly hand, as if by holding it he could be absolved of any sin he might commit. 'Try as I might, I cannot protect him from the anger of those who would burn any heretic they could find...'

'Perfect.'

'And then,' Blastos added, 'I can write to the patriarch, who knows me to be a loyal Monophysite, and tell him I have found and contained a dangerous spread of something much worse than Chalcedonian heresy, that I have uncovered pagan worship, which being on the border with barbarians, we must most assiduously guard against. I am sure such a thing will please him.'

'Don't go seeking higher elevation, Bishop Gregory,' Senuthius said in a piping voice, the eyebrows lowered over a penetrating gaze.

'Would I desert you after all you have done for me and my church?'

That got a nod, even if the man giving it was unconvinced; Senuthius had paid to repair damage done to the basilica of Dorostorum by an earthquake, one that had occurred decades before and rendered the city a diocese that was not one to which many men of the cloth aspired. Far from rich, and in a ramshackle condition, Blastos, lacking influence to get a prized appointment, had taken it as the bishopric he could get, rather than the kind for which he craved, a see in which money flowed easily into his coffers without the need for underhand appropriation.

'Be assured I will do more, much more,' Senuthius responded.

This statement was at total odds with his thoughts, those being that even an ally can be a danger. Was he reposing too much trust and therefore his fate into the hands of this man? Since arriving, Blastos had held under one arm the ledger of the imperial centurion and this he now held out to Senuthius, who took it and ran an eye practised in figures over the columns.

'The monies left over?'

'In my saddlebag, which if you wish, you can send someone to fetch.'

'No need, you may keep it,' the senator replied, holding the book open and out. 'But this I will have my scribes go over and they will make some changes, even compose a complete new set of ac-

97

counts. Let us ensure that, if examined, Decimus Belisarius is seen to be nothing but a liar and a thief, seeking to lay the blame for his own crimes at the door of others.'

'It is necessary to allude to the man's wife, who may at some time in the future be on her way here, almost certainly if her only surviving son comes to any harm.'

Senuthius did not seem to see that as a problem. 'If her husband and her sons were heretics, how can she be anything but the same? It will be perceived that what happened in that raid was nothing but divine retribution for their family apostasy. Perhaps, once we have dealt with that which needs to be seen to, we should send to her a message that says it would be unwise to return to Dorostorum. Why would she want to anyway, just to gaze on the rotting skeleton of her youngest on a cross and perhaps face a similar fate?'

'If we are done, Senuthius, I should return to the city.'

'It is near dark, Bishop Gregory, stay and dine with me and together we can compose the sermon by which you are going to damn the Belisarius name.'

Flavius never knew the identity of the person who gave him warning of what was about to be visited upon his house, only that it came through the narrow slats of a shuttered window, the voice was male and it spoke heavily accented Greek. When he offered to open the shutter and light an oil lamp the suggestion was vehemently dismissed.

'I don't want you knowing who I am.'

Having been awakened from another set of troubling dreams he was far from being in the best frame of mind to react. 'Then how can I trust what you say if I cannot see you?'

'You can believe me and happen to live or think I am a liar and die.'

'At whose hand?'

'You know who and if he does not do the deed himself, it will be his need behind it.'

The tale told was not strictly coherent; the person giving it was breathless, either from exertion or fear of discovery, yet it did not lack for verisimilitude. If what Flavius suspected regarding the deaths of his family was true, added to his suspicions of what Bishop Gregory had been seeking, then what he was hearing made perfect sense. It also induced a degree of real terror.

'And how do you know all this?'

'Man has ears. Some, not many, have a sense of right and wrong.'

'What am I supposed to do?' Flavius demanded.

'Flee, if you have any sense, for by this time tomorrow you will be nailed to a cross if you don't.'

'Flee to where?'

There was no reply, just the sound of scrabbling and heavy breath. Flavius flung open the shutters to reveal nothing but a dark and hooded shape heading away from the villa, his hissed call to stop going unanswered. The clouds that had partially obscured the moon parted to show an eerie view of trees and bushes, as well as the roofs of other houses that lay beyond the walls of the garden. When he looked straight down he saw, lying on the ground, the outline of the ladder his messenger had used to get up to his window.

He needed to talk to Ohannes, but one of the people left behind by the bishop was, on the cleric's instructions, sleeping across the outside of his chamber door; others, he suspected, were placed at the villa exits like the atrium and the kitchens. It had been years since the mischievous child had clambered out of that very window to avoid the parental constraints but Flavius knew well it could be done, knew that it was possible to drop down onto soft ground close to the wall, where his mother planted vegetables that required the warmth of the afternoon sun to prosper and grow. In her absence it had been tended and watered by one of the servants.

He had one leg over the sill when he paused, reprising what he had been told. If even half was true, it was obvious that whatever happened subsequently would oblige him to vacate the family home if not forever, certainly for the succeeding days. Where to go and for how long was a problem that would need to be solved, but not at this exact moment.

Going back into his room and using what moonlight filtered through the open window, Flavius dressed slowly, silently and not without pain, in his military garb, breast and backplate, knowing his sling would have to be discarded. He strapped on his sword, gathered up his shield, his spear plus his helmet and cast them out to land on the ground, taking care to spread out the places where they made contact so they did not clash and cause a noise.

Lastly he gathered everything that had been given to him by Gregory Blastos, his father's testament, papers and most importantly the family money. The rolled-up document he loaded in a canvas satchel and put over his good shoulder, the twin sack of coins he tied tightly to his belt, and once sure there was nothing left he could safely take with him, he went back over the sill and slowly, relying on his good arm, let himself down until it was at a full stretch.

There is always an odd feeling in dropping, doubly so in the dark, for the clouds had once more cut off the moonlight, and unlike in his past escapades, he could not see where he would land. As he hung there, Flavius was assailed by a deep fear, not just that a fall of twice his own height might land him on a rock and cause him to sprain or break an ankle, but of that which awaited him even should he succeed without mishap.

The sob that came from his throat he had to suppress but he was a boy again, near to fifteen summers now, no longer pretending to be a man, as he had been before the Hun raid, and the feeling was uncomfortable. What kind of fate was it that left him to care for himself and what kind of destiny was it that put him in such imminent danger when just days before he had lived a normal life?

Flavius opened the hand that was holding on to the sill and fell to the ground, giving with his knees and mouthing a prayer to what seemed an indifferent God as he did so, for he had landed on soft ground.

Weapons, helmet and the canvas sack he left under a tree halfway between the villa and the servants' quarters, these being set in a low building that adjoined and ran at right angles from the kitchens of the main house. No ladder was required to get in but it was necessary to maintain silence, not easy with a shutter inclined to creak, even less so when, once inside and away from that opening, very little light penetrated to aid him. That he should have only a sketchy notion of who slept where in this part of the villa was hardly surprising: he had not wandered into this area since being a curious toddler.

Flavius reasoned that, in the hierarchy of the household, Ohannes must rank quite high, which would indicate that he would be one of the few with a cell of his own in which to sleep, as well as one close to the main house. The lower the servants, be they slave or free, the more crowded was their space, so in an annex without doors, it was possible to silently pull to one side the canvas screens and listen for the breathing of more than one soul.

In the end it was the old soldier's preference for a cooling night breeze to aid his slumbers, plus the snoring of an elder that identified him to the youngster, or more importantly, the tip of a resting spear catching the light from an open shutter.

Flavius's hand had barely touched the shoulder when one of Ohannes's shot out to take hold of his throat, the grip immediately so tight the boy could not speak his name, only croak and hope it made sense. He was never sure of what got him release and a chance to breathe; perhaps there was enough light to see his face. Nor did he make much sense as he gabbled in a whisper what had been told to him, which had the old man, now sitting upright as Flavius bent over him, reaching out to shake him gently and hiss that he should both slow down and sit.

Without going into detail, Flavius first told the Scythian the gist of what was contained in that oilskin pouch, hidden now in this very room, and why it was so important that it be kept secret from Blastos, before going on to the tale of his recent visitation. This was heard in near silence, the only sound being growls of outrage from Ohannes on hearing what Senuthius and Blastos intended.

Then it came to the solution proposed by the messenger that Flavius must flee, given that if he knew a commission of enquiry was coming, but had no idea exactly when, he would likely be dead before it arrived. As he talked and with eyes now adjusted to the low light, the youngster could just make out the slow nodding of the head, followed by the whispered reaction that flight should be for more than just the youngster.

'I am not sure they will torture the slaves and servants but they might, there being no power to stop them. Me? They have seen we are close, as I was to your papa. I have no more notion to feel the hot pincers Senuthius has in store than you. We must go together.'

Flavius felt he ought to protest, to say that this old man had done enough, yet such was his relief that he would not be alone that noble sentiment died in his throat. 'But where? I have good friends who might aid me, Philaretus and Asticus, and there were folk prepared to witness against Senuthius.'

'No, you will only put them in danger. The only place that fat sod will struggle to lay a hand on us is over the river.'

'Can that be safe? Romans are not much loved there.'

'Maybe not safe, but when there are two evils it might be the lesser, since we must flee on foot. Senuthius will have mounted men out as soon as it is light, maybe even sooner. He has to reckon on us going south, which might just give us the time to get a boat and make the crossing.'

'I have no notion to end up as a barbarian slave.'

'Better that than hanging on a cross to be pecked at by carrion,' Ohannes growled.

'How do we get out of the villa unseen?'

That got a reassuring chuckle. 'Same way as every servant your papa ever employed, who wanted a wet or a woman without him knowing.'

Flavius was sent to fetch that which he had left under the tree, with Ohannes, now fully armed, on hand to take them from him and help him back across the sill, the oilskin pouch containing the roll of letters joining the others Flavius carried in his canvas sack. He was led along a corridor to the very end of the servants' quarters, the increasingly foul odour a sure indication they were heading for their privy.

It was a windowless enclosure, which accounted for the strength of the smell, but it had a low hatch by which the night soil could be removed of a morning to be taken to the general midden that served as fertiliser for the kitchen garden. They went through that hatch on hands and knees, emerging into moonlight so strong that it had Ohannes insist they wait.

'I have no notion of the numbers that priest has set to watch or where they are. In this light a man can see a good distance, and picking up movement is easy. We need a bit of cloud.'

'What do we do if we're seen?'

'We kill, young sir, for there be no choice, in silence if we can manage but without if not.'

'Then we will truly be outside the law.'

'The law, sad to say, died with your papa. The only justice left is what Senuthius decides and Blastos carries out.'

The moon was strong and high, the light of it great enough to wash out the stars, which threw everything into sharp relief. Flavius leant his back against the wall of the building and dropped his head, suddenly overcome with a feeling of weariness. If a sense of terror and excitement had animated him it was ebbing fast, to be replaced with creeping despair.

'We must be here when that commission arrives, Ohannes.'

Since that got a grunt, it was not possible to know if he agreed or thought him mad. Nor was there time to ask; as soon as a large cloud began to obscure the moon they had to move, using the rapidly fading silver lining to guide them before it disappeared completely, plunging the whole area into Stygian darkness.

What aided them was knowledge; this was home to both and Flavius, especially, knew it like the back of his hand. The faintest outline of a tree branch or the smell of a pungent plant was enough to tell him exactly where he was. That got them to the outer wall and a gnarled and ancient olive tree, a spot where the youngster knew they could climb, just as he knew that one outer bough went towards that enclosing wall, albeit the limb had been cut and sealed within so as to avoid an easy point of entry for intruders.

With a field of wheat on the other side, Flavius cast his spear and shield over the wall then donned his helmet, finally setting his canvas bag on his back where it would not interfere with his efforts to climb. Even with a less than fully useful arm, those ancient and twisted branches gave him enough purchase to haul himself up; the problem of Ohannes's painful and inflexible knees posed more of a difficulty, which meant the youngster was required to lodge himself for support, then with one hand help the old man up from one crooked resting place to another.

The next predicament, once they had reached the height they needed, pressured Flavius; to crawl along that truncated bough one-handed was to risk falling off so, with a quick prayer and a welcome sliver of cloud-edge light, he stood up, balanced himself, then skipped along the branch to straddle the outer villa wall.

That flash of moonlight had aided him but it had also allowed one of the bishop's servants to see his silhouette, judging by the shout of alarm that came from the main part of the house.

Ohannes, not trusting to his balance, was inching his way along that same length of wood by bestriding it, pushing with his hands, in one of which he had his spear, able to move only a couple of inches at a time, cursing as he did so the limbs that would not behave as he wished they should and once did.

'Hurry, Ohannes,' Flavius called, as more shouting came from the villa itself.

'As if I ain't doing the best I can!'

The light of half a dozen torches appeared, Flavius quick to calculate the distance between them and the house, set against how much time they had. Though Ohannes was looking away from those waving lights he could tell by the accompanying noise that they had a difficulty.

'Get going, Flavius,' Ohannes called, 'I will seek to hold them at bay.'

'Never. Pass me that spear.'

Ohannes held it out at full arm's length as Flavius raised himself up to stand on the wall, grabbing the shaft to turn and raise it for throwing. There was no precise aim, just as a target a clutch of torches, getting closer and closer, into the middle of which he cast it with all the force he could muster, less than full he being so precariously balanced. It was sufficient; a high-pitched scream rent the night air but more telling was the way those flaring centres of light stopped, wavered and then retreated with haste. Only one torch was left where that spear had made contact and it was on the ground.

'If I have not killed someone, Ohannes,' he hissed, as he helped the old man make the gap between bough and wall, 'I have wounded them badly.'

'Care not for him, care for us, for those fellows who have run away are set to fetch help. So let us get down from here and away.'

CHAPTER EIGHT

The wheat, if not yet ready to harvest, was grown to near-full height, tall enough to make finding the thrown spear difficult, which had Ohannes fuming that it should be abandoned, an injunction ignored. To be without that and his shield, especially now that the older man's weapon was beyond use, would leave them both at risk. The next difficulty was soon apparent as they made their way through the stalks; a black moonlit line of crushed corn stalks that marked their passage.

'If we cannot avoid it, we must use it, Master Flavius, by heading south but away from the villa, which is the way we would be expected to go. At the field's edge we will double back behind the hedgerows.'

The sense of that was immediate; they would leave a clear trail then no sign of their progress at all for, in any field where the planting ran up against a high hedge, the seed would have failed to take so they could move without leaving a trace. There was only one question; did they have time? It was with a heavy sucking sound that Ohannes responded; if marching was purgatory to a man his age then running was hell.

'Them servants have to get to the bishop's palace, then they have to rouse him out. Blastos, God rot him, is no more a fighting man than those he left to keep an eye on you, so he will need to get out his bodyguards and that will take time, even more to alert that sod Senuthius. It's him we have to fear.'

'The bishop's men will have dogs to aid them,' the youngster added with a sudden chill to his spirits.

The Scythian responded with a hissed curse, which told Flavius that he shared the apprehension such a factor produced. Copying Senuthius, Blastos had a deer- and bear-hunting pack, big ferocious beasts, and the house they had just departed had any number of articles that would give the dogs a scent, bedding being the most obvious. The notion of being tracked down by such creatures was enough to make his heart pound; blood up they might drag a human down as they would any other living creature.

Ohannes had to stop to get his breath, which allowed Flavius to look back over the field. The sky was clear once more, the moonlight so strong he could even pick out the movement of the corn tops waving in the breeze. A brief flash of orange made him look back to the villa, a blink of torchlight to indicate that one of the men Blastos had left was in the top branches of that olive tree. Never mind the line of their progress; perhaps those same eyes could make out the immobile silhouettes of their fleeing quarry.

'I think it best to keep going in the same direction until it clouds over, Ohannes, if I can see the walls...'

The old man was bent over, puffing. 'A pause, Master Flavius, till I can get my wind again.'

'Not master now, Ohannes,' came the gloomy reply, as Flavius hitched up his satchel. 'I am in possession of nothing more than I carry.'

'Much more of this,' Ohannes wheezed, 'and it may be you will need to carry me.'

'Which means we must move at a pace that will not see you crippled.'

Still wheezing the old man responded. 'Before we move at all we must seek to put any dogs off.'

'How?'

'By leaving them a smell so strong they will be confused. Time to get your pecker out, Master Flavius, and do as I do, create a circle of piss.'

Was it nerves that made it near impossible to comply? Whatever, it seemed to affect Ohannes less, for he sprayed his urine around with seeming abandon, shaming the dribbling of Flavius who had trouble obeying the other instruction, which was to avoid wetting his sandals, since that would leave a trace for dogs to follow.

As soon as the light faded they moved, this time at a walking crouch, easier for Flavius than Ohannes, but less tiring than jogging, the only impediment the odd overgrown bramble stalk that, having outgrown the hedgerow and invisible to the eye, caught their garments on its spikes. On the north side of the wheat fields it was well-maintained woodland and once in that both men could move freely and at a suitable pace as long as there was moonlight, keeping an eye on the position of that orb to guide their way to the very road they had traversed on horseback two days previously.

Without the moon, which disappeared with frustrating regularity and plunged the woodlands in complete darkness, progress was impossible. Even when they could move they were obliged to stop and let die down the distant barking of farm dogs marking their progress, being as they were in the area that had escaped the recent battles, and that constrained them until they crested the rise that overlooked the area where the barbarians had carried out their killing.

The smell of burning was still in the air, pungent and sickly, either from gutted farmhouses or maybe even from the funeral pyre, as once more an obscured moon halted their progress, making hellish what had been so far disturbing. The sounds now were the faint ones of wild beasts, from feral cats to wild dogs and wolves tearing at rotting flesh, ghostly shapes that emerged in the resurgent moonlight, as did that upon which they were feeding.

Bishop Gregory Blastos admitted he had not seen fit to properly bury the casualties the barbarians had caused, be they the men who had fought under Decimus or those who had succumbed to the massacre before flight. So much for his claim of a communal grave: they had been given no more than a shallow trench and a covering of loose earth, easily scrabbled out by eager claws. In daylight it would be the vultures that fed here, which had the youngster talking about the worst scavenger of all, for this land, with few if any survivors, was now without the families that once tilled and tended it.

Ohannes spat loudly at the mention of the Senuthius name. 'Word is that he will give any abandoned farms to his men. How can he do that?'

'By falsifying the titles he can erase any presence of the previous owners. And making his followers tenants buys the loyalty of those he favours and he also gains from their rents.'

That caused the old Scythian to issue what had to be, in his own tongue, a venomous and blasphemous curse not unlike the blasts of spleen that had been issued by Belisarius Pater at any mention of the Senuthius name. That particular bit of chicanery Flavius had read about in that cache of letters.

'He did it before, Ohannes, with the help of the provincial governor, just before we arrived here as a family. It was the first complaint laid against him after my father took up his duties.'

There had been several big raids that year, followed by loud complaints to Constantinople demanding protection, that being the reason for the appointment of Decimus Belisarius to his post. It had, since that day, been his view that some of those loud in their pleas had got more than they bargained for when the new centurion discovered what was going on. He, in turn, got less when he came to realise he was powerless to stop such officially authorised thievery.

'The Sklaveni took the farmers as slaves, Senuthius took their land, sure they would never return, but just in case he stole it by legal means.'

Flavius looked ahead to the wide silver glow of

112

the River Danube, dotted with the odd glim of a lantern where some local was out night-fishing and that had him thinking of another one of his father's grievances that could be laid at the door of Senuthius, an occasional dip into piracy, for the river was a major trade route from the interior to the Euxine Sea and beyond.

If the thieving of Senuthius was rare, it was always of a valuable cargo, for he had contacts upriver with the means to alert him to worthwhile objectives. It was a hard crime to stop too: the imperial centurion had no ship with which to patrol the river and nor could he tie himself and his men down on the riverbank in the hope of a surprise intervention.

If he found out about what had been pirated, and sometimes he was aware he did not, it was too late to do anything. The ship and crew would be at the bottom of the river, taken out and sunk in midstream as soon as the cargo had been unloaded, to then be dispersed and sold in places beyond the reach of his authority. Given the barbarians, too, indulged in such activities it was easy for Senuthius to protest his innocence when a ship was found to be missing and accusations were laid against him.

'Hard to get a grip on a man who coats himself with oil,' Ohannes moaned at the mention of this further criminality. 'Known a few of those in my time.'

'None as slippery as Senuthius,' Flavius responded, as he began to list for Ohannes many of his other crimes, these too culled from the letters in his canvas satchel.

113

Some were only alleged, yet the list was long: it seemed there was nothing to which Senuthius would not stoop in search of profit. Stockpiling grain to create scarcity and up the price that must be paid when the harvest was poor. Adulterating both the wine and olive oil used by the poor and needy on a regular basis. The outright theft of land had already been mentioned, as had raiding across the river for slaves.

But added to that was the intimidating of lesser landowners by crop burning or physical beatings if they dared to stand up to him, demanding the payment of bribes to ensure they did not suffer more than once. Any less subservient neighbours, those who would not bend the knee, usually ended up selling him their farms rather than put up with endless harassment. He added to that downright fraud when it came to trading in any of the myriad commodities he now controlled.

Not that he participated in any criminal act himself; Senuthius always acted at one remove. He had willing lieutenants to do his bidding, the same men who had protected him from a furious Flavius, as well as too many folk who sucked up to him out of fear or merely because of his deep purse. Also plain was the simple truth and one that had frustrated Decimus above any other: the more he transgressed the more powerful Senuthius became in terms of wealth, influence and followers. Not all the citizens of worth were wholehearted in their regard for him, but they were men who looked to their own interests and could see clearly where power lay and with it their own prosperity.

These thoughts induced once more a sense of

creeping despair. Swear vengeance he might for the blood of his family but there was only one power in the land that could create for him a situation in which he might kill Senuthius, something he had determined upon as he watched that funeral pyre burn. If he could not bring to the commission the truth of what had occurred, would they even find they could uphold any of what had been sent to them?

'Ohannes, we must stop!' The injunction was obeyed but Flavius could sense it was unwelcome. 'If I cross the river who knows what it will lead to?'

'Have I not already said...?'

'Even if we remain free to act as we wish on the north bank, we will have no idea if the people my father was expecting have arrived, have no knowledge of what they will hear and no way of putting before them the accusations that he listed.'

'Something I will be willing to talk about when my backside is sat in a boat and we are more'n the length of a cast spear out on yonder water.'

'Don't you see, Ohannes...?'

The response was a furious hiss. 'I see my flesh rotting on a cross if what you say they are about is true. I can see too that your mind might be working at ways to bring down Senuthius, Master Flavius, and that is to be expected. But think on the time your papa put into that and no result to show for it.'

'I cannot stop you from crossing if that is what you wish...'

'Don't you dare take that tone with me,' Ohannes spat. 'You have your birth but recall

115

your years.'

That checked Flavius completely; the Scythian had rarely spoken to him with anything but respect, yet here again was that stance he had adopted when he used his spear to threaten the stallion. The recollection of that produced near-equal irritation.

'Am I only to be indulged when what you want marries my thinking?'

If he hoped to dent the older man's ire he failed miserably. 'Your papa is dead and so are your brothers, but were the centurion able to speak from beyond then he would ask that I keep you whole, and even if the words were never spoken that is what I shall do. Stay on this bank of the river and you will die, for certain, an' me too for I will not leave your side.'

'You do not know my thinking.'

'Crossed over the river you can do as much thinking as you wish. Now it is fleeing that matters.'

'We can find a place to hide on this side.'

'With dogs on our trail?' Prepared to be stubborn, the notion that he could was taken from Flavius by the sound of baying hounds, faint but unmistakable and carrying a long way on a still night, which allowed Ohannes to add, 'Only thing that will keep us from them is water and as for the men handling them, lots of it.'

It was time to move at speed, and luck and good moonlight soon set them on the riverbank at a spot where an inundation created a small strand of pebbles, the water lapping it deep enough to break the spoor. That would not last long: the bank rose and protruded out into the river, the water becoming too deep through which to wade, so it was back to dry land and a patch of thick untended woodland. It did not need to be stated that such a dipping of feet would last only minutes; the dogs would be sent to both ends of the strand, so still making ground was essential.

Ohannes, even if he was wheezing again, showed no sign of wishing to do anything other than hurry along, although he had enough puff to curse when once more the moon was covered by cloud, killing what little light came through a thick overhead canopy. Forced to stand still, it occurred to Flavius that it had been an error to come to this part of the riverbank, albeit not having thought of it himself beforehand, he reckoned it would be churlish to point out to Ohannes why: they were within the area of the recent raid and the barbarians had taken every boat as they retreated.

They needed to get beyond the old watchtower that lay to the north, where there might be craft still beached, and that was going to be made difficult in what was now continuing pitch dark. Either the moon was obscured or the woods they passed through were too dense in the overhead cover to permit any light to penetrate, obliging them to find once more the riverbank, where they sought out another small inlet with its strand of pebbles and stopped, Ohannes stooping to splash his sweating face with water, the word spat out when he stood again.

'Look.'

The crest of the hills that overlooked the river

was dotted with tiny spots of light, numerous torches too far off to be seen as flaring, while faint on the air was the sound of the pack of dogs, which produced a sobering conclusion. Cloud cover and deep woodland would halt them but it would not hinder the pursuit of these men, let alone their beasts. Only when the sky cleared again and in open country could they move on at a pace sufficient to stave off capture. To escape would be a miracle, for they could not outrun the dogs once they were left free to take the chase on their own.

'Take off your armour.'

'Why?'

'Do as I ask,' Ohannes growled, working at the straps of his own. 'Perhaps if we leave them here they will think we swam for it.'

'Only a fool would do that.'

'Or a man desperate to escape and with no other choice.'

Loath to part with a possession he prized, Flavius did as he was asked, fingering, once his breastplate and back protector were off, the shaped leather as well as the gilded metal decorations mounted on the front. The design was Roman in origin, the same as would have been worn by an imperial tribune in ancient times and elaborate enough to cause envy amongst his peers. The smell of warm leather was strong, that mixed with the sweat coming from his own body.

'My father gifted me this.'

'Then he will look down and see the sense of what we are doing with it.'

'No mere centurion for you Flavius, was what he said as he gave it to me.' There was a distinct catch in his throat as he bent down to pick up his spear.

'We are going to have to wade along the river-bank and hope it is not too cold or deep enough to drown us.' Sensing rather than seeing doubt, Ohannes was quick to add, 'We can't hope to outrun them and no stretch of pebbles is going to put them off for long. We need deeper water.'

'But they know the direction in which we are going.'

'With luck they will reckon we have tried to swim the river or at least to get to one of them boats out fishing. Whatever, if we stay in the water they will have to cast around a long way for the dogs to scent any spoor.'

'And when we come ashore again?'

'We will be dripping so much there will be nothing to pick up and that, if we can fool them, will oblige the sods to wait for sunrise. Time, Master Flavius, is our only friend.'

While he was willing to acknowledge the truth of that, the youngster's mind was more on the canvas sack he was carrying, as well as its contents, the writing on which would scarce survive immersion in water, even those in the oilskin pouch. As for his father's testament, that would be rendered pulp. The thought of hiding them foundered on the time it would need to dig a deep hole and one well enough hidden to avoid detection – again dogs with his spoor on their snouts would easily root out anything he had held close.

He moved back into the woods, the sound of a cursing Ohannes in his ears as he sought out a tree that he might again be able to recognise, blessed by the outline of what appeared to be an ancient oak, wide at the base, climbable if not easily so and in full leaf judging by the sound of the wind rustling its foliage. A soft call to a less than contented companion got him a leg up to one of the lower branches where he again found further progress impeded by the pain from his left shoulder.

That had to be ignored and up he went until he felt sure whatever he left here would not be visible from the ground. With a silent prayer he put his lips to the sack then tied the loops he had used to carry it tightly round a branch before tucking the body into the joint of the main trunk. Getting down was easier and Ohannes was there to aid his final descent. The thought of slicing the oak with a couple of sword cuts, so he could find it easily again, had to be discarded; if he could see them so could others but the location had to be marked in some way or he might never again find it.

Flavius fetched half a dozen pebbles from the riverbank and, by the tree, arranged them in a small mound, fiddling until an impatient Ohannes dragged him once more to the edge, he wading into the silver, rippling water, hissing his worry, given he was taller.

'Keep your head above the water, Master Flavius, we can't have you drown.'

'Ohannes, I can swim.'

'Good, and I hope it is enough to save me from going under, if God is with us.'

'Hard to believe after what has happened that God has any time for a Belisarius.'

'Well cursing him won't do us much good,'

120

Ohannes barked, his voice holding a catch of breath as the river water came up above his groin.

Flavius, realising that his backplate would float and before he followed the Scythian, picked it up and threw it out onto the river, far enough to hope it would drift downstream and still be visible; to his mind leaving it on the bank would only tell the pursuit that they had been on this spot and fix their chase. Then, carrying his breastplate he waded in with his spear above his head, following Ohannes into water that was icy cold, barely warmed by the sun and still with some of the glacier melt or underground springs from which it and its tributaries emanated many hundreds of leagues to the west and north.

The breastplate he jammed into the tangled tree roots that stuck out of the first stretch of high bank he encountered, decorations to the fore, something that would at least be visible from the river if hidden from those on land, another indicator of where he had hidden his sack. Progress, easy to begin with, was made awkward by the way that those outcrops of ground jutted out from the bank, obliging the pair to risk deeper water, this compounded by the odd depression underfoot. Risk also came in the regular shallow little inlets, for these had to be traversed at speed and in full view of the shoreline, having made sure the men pursuing them were not within sight.

In this their use of torches became an aid; they would not move without them for fear of ambush and the glare was a sure indication of their location: likewise the noise of the dogs, still on leads, much more prominent now, was an indicator. When that baying sound rose to indicate the pack was close, Ohannes called a halt and had them take shelter under an overhang where the water came up to their necks, the trailing branches of a tree above their heads. To counter the glare of the moon reflecting off the water the Scythian grabbed some damp mud and began to smear his face, Flavius following suit.

'We will stay here and let them pass,' came the whispered suggestion, before he added a touch of gallows humour. 'Try not to let those teeth of yours chatter, Master Flavius, for it will be as loud as a drumbeat to a hound.'

CHAPTER NINE

Flavius and Ohannes were never to know what saved them from capture: the fact that Bishop Gregory Blastos was asleep at the villa of Senuthius and even when roused out by a message of what had occurred, neither man reacted as they might. The corpulent senator was sure that the escapees could not get far with a pack of hounds on their tail, the bishop being less sanguine but not prepared to dispute the conclusion drawn: that the innocent did not flee, so what had happened was positive, for it told them Flavius knew what they needed to find out. It was also an act that would only increase the sense of terrible sins committed, the very thing needed to excite the populace.

'There will be many who doubt that of which we will accuse young Belisarius – after all, the family appeared upright, even if they were minded to worship in Chalcedonian blasphemy.'

Blastos was tempted to add that so did most of those who made up his flock but he stayed silent, there being no need to remind his host that in supporting the imperial edict they were in a minority within his own diocese as well as the greater one of Thrace. Not that there was much opportunity anyway; Senuthius was thinking on his feet again and talking fast.

'The fellow he has fled with is the same one who looked after him when he was tipped off his horse and attended the cremation, is he not? Let's blame him for introducing Lucifer to their household and throw him to the mob for his devilish corruption. God knows by the look of him he could be a pagan shaman.'

'No crucifix for him, then?' yawned Blastos.

That act set off his host, who replied after a mighty yawn of his own. 'Why waste the timber? Let the faithful tear him limb from limb and feed what's left to their pigs.'

'Then I would be grateful to be allowed to go back to bed, I am weary.'

'That slave boy I sent to you must have pleased you?'

Blastos pulled a face. 'He stank, Senuthius. Would it be possible to bathe your gifts first?'

The fat man was already leaving the room. 'Don't tell me the smell of the creature stopped you.'

The second factor that aided the escape was

fear; the reluctance of those set to pursue them to admit they might have failed. Someone would have to tell their master and that was bad enough, for the bishop was not shy of the whip. Worse than that, to do so meant one of their number going to the home of Senuthius and that induced terror, he not being a man to tolerate any level of failure. A lash could be a welcome punishment compared to what he might see as fitting.

As a group they had set out full of determination, a commodity that faded somewhat as time went by and both legs and minds grew weary, the same applying to animals denied the raw meat they had anticipated when taken from their kennels. Given there was no natural leader, dissension broke out as to the best avenue to follow, one dimwit even insisting that Flavius would have gone south and their whole endeavour on the riverbank, despite the spoor followed by the dogs, was false.

If Ohannes and his young companion had no real idea of the nature of the dispute, they were close enough to the hunters as they passed along the riverbank to hear what sounded like a lack of harmony. As the sound of voices faded, and it became clear that the Blastos servants were still moving away from their position, the Scythian hissed it was time to move, which they did at the slow pace such a passage through water would allow. Finally he led the way back onto dry land and broke into an immediate jog; if he and Flavius were also fatigued they had their fears to sustain their efforts.

'Look, Master Flavius.'

Ohannes wheezed this when they had covered good ground, coming to such an abrupt halt that the youngster, head down, not really looking where he was going and himself straining for breath, bumped into him.

The old man had spotted an approaching boat. One of the people who had been out night-fishing was coming in with his catch, his position very obvious by the lantern on his stern pole, there to both attract the fish and to show any other vessel on the river of his presence. The fisherman had beached his boat before they came upon him; he was tying it off and taking out his oars and his catch when he heard the noise of their approach, wet sandals squelching on pebbles.

It never occurred to either to wonder at what kind of apparition they presented in what was still pale moonlight. They had been in the water and if they had avoided a true ducking their hair was soaked and straggling; Ohannes particularly, with his height and the slight stoop of his gait, looked like some kind of ethereal wraith. Sensing lost souls the poor fisherman let out a cry of dread and sunk to his knees, hands clasped before him.

The voice that rained down hellish curses made even Flavius wonder from where it came, so warbling and ghoulish did it sound, before he realised that Ohannes was playing the mischievous sprite in his native tongue to terrorise a fellow who would be prey to such fancies. Before they got close enough to be seen as human the man had got to his feet and fled, leaving the Scythian to quietly chuckle in a way that annoyed Flavius.

'I have money, Ohannes,' he said, tapping the

leather pouches still tied to his belt, 'we could have paid him for his boat.'

'And have him boast of the gold he got all over the place, a fellow who rarely sees a copper coin from one month to the next. How long do you then think it would be until Senuthius got wind of that? And what then of the poor fellow? He would be roasted till he told the truth.'

The response was defensive. 'It is what my father would have done.'

'And noble as he was, he would have been wrong.'

'You would not have dared tell him so!'

That got a bark of a laugh. 'How little you know of real soldiers. When it comes to letting the men who lead them know they are being dense, they have their ways.'

'My father—'

'Never had much cause with him, God rest his soul, but that does not signify. Now we have a boat, however we have come by it, are we going to use it?'

Even if he too had concluded there was no choice, that Ohannes was right, the response was far from immediate. Flavius felt that he was being too much led, indeed pushed, and he resented it, added to which, what Ohannes had just said – the notion of his being less than wise – he thought of as diminishing.

His companion must have sensed his mood. 'I would hate to go on my own, but go I will.'

'The catch?' Flavius asked, as Ohannes picked up the oars.

'Take that as well, for even ghouls have to eat.'

126

There was some reassertion of balance when they were on the water, Ohannes being no oarsman, unlike his young companion who had spent many a summer's day fishing these very waters and so found himself issuing instruction, given he was unable to row himself due to his shoulder. Despite the strictures to avoid doing so he and his friends had also passed the midpoint of the river many times to cast an eye on the northern bank, not so very different from its southern counterpart but exciting merely because it was forbidden territory.

Given the run of the Danube, added to the width and the lack of rowing competence, they drifted steadily downstream to make a landfall in a patch of woods, something accomplished just before sunrise, an added plus since they managed in the grey light of the predawn to do so unobserved. Then came another dispute: Ohannes was all for casting the boat adrift, Flavius insisting they would need it to get back across. In the end the youngster prevailed and they dragged it far enough inshore to hide it in some bushes.

'We can eat the fish.'

'Only if we can cook it, young sir, and I would be unhappy about doing that afore we have found out how far off we are from company.' There was daylight enough now to show the crestfallen look of a very weary youth. 'But let us, now we have enough light, gather the means to light a fire.'

They set off as soon as the sun was over the horizon, for low in the sky the angle of its light allowed them to hold to a course that would bring them back to the point from which they set out. Added to that Ohannes knew how to use the terrain to guide his way and tired as he was, Flavius found himself learning some useful skills of movement.

The path of the sun lay to the south of where they were, so moss that showed on the bark of a tree indicated north, since it never saw enough sun to burn off the greenery. Likewise the mere shape of a sapling or a bush could help, for they too inclined towards the sun.

To avoid any risk of getting lost in what was quite dense woodland Ohannes left cuts low down on trunks, arrows pointing in the direction from which they had come, these disguised with earth rubbed in to take away their bright and too obvious appearance. There was game in the forest, deer and birds, obvious by the noise, and care was needed to avoid boar sows who might be raising young, for they would attack anyone and anything that threatened their piglets; at any sign of rooting the Scythian became very wary.

Bears he thought unlikely so close to the river on which there were a string of settlements, likewise wolves, and, after some time casting about, Ohannes pronounced himself satisfied that they were far away from humanity. They returned to their landing point and lit a fire under a large tree in full leaf, for the smoke would hang in the branches and be dispersed before it topped the canopy. Part of the fisherman's catch was gutted and cooked, then consumed by two very hungry souls, the fire doused as soon as they were finished.

'Smell of woodsmoke carries too.'

'I know that,' Flavius retorted, in a less than

truly civil manner.

'Well, you will forgive me for my instructing, Master Flavius, given I have no notion of what you do know and what you don't. All that sword and spear play you and your companions got up to might be one part of soldiering, but it is only that, and all your wrestling is nothing but sport. Most youngsters I have met and fought with needed a lot of telling about what was right and what was stupid, an' if they failed to listen then they died.'

A hand was rubbed across a face still bearing much of the mud with which it had been previously coated. 'Forgive me, it is weariness that makes me talk so.'

'Then it's time you got your head down.' The look that got was a protest, but not a fulsome one; Flavius was near to exhaustion, as much from the strain on his emotions as his body. 'You need sleep if you're to think clear, though God only knows what you can do. You rest and I will stand watch.'

'We must take turns.'

'And we shall.'

'Somehow I must get word to Justinus of the death of my father,' Flavius said, through a stifled yawn, 'as well as how he met his end. We cannot leave that to the likes of Blastos.'

'Well, right now he will be doing what you should be – sleeping.'

Flavius Justinus had been a soldier for exactly the same number of years as Decimus Belisarius – they had enlisted together – and he was inured to the habits of his profession, high rank and regard for his abilities making no difference; he woke with

129

the dawn and rolled immediately off his cot. If his limbs, sixty-five summers in age, now creaked it was an act still carried out in one swift movement, to be followed by a morning piss and a wash in the bowl of water left by his side overnight.

The room he occupied was barren, again as befitted the old campaigner he was. Justinus had declined a bed of comfort in one of the many beautifully furnished chambers in the imperial palace, electing instead to occupy something more akin to a hermit's cell; to the courtiers he now mixed with it was a space both barren and ridiculous and he suspected the men he led, the excubitors, successors to the praetorians who had guarded previous emperors of Rome, thought him either foolish or a man inclined to braggadocio. In truth he liked simple things and straightforward people.

For Justinus his room had two advantages; the first was a single entrance, a stout oak door that once bolted would take a real effort to break down. The second was a window, the bars of which could be removed, which overlooked one of the canals that fed water to the imperial palace. With these attributes he felt he could sleep in peace: anyone seeking to harm him, and he was sure such creatures existed in a court full of competing factions, would have difficulty in doing so. The killing of the *comes excubitorum* was a prerequisite to the assassination of the emperor.

Making his way to the door he undid the bolts and upon opening he was met by the rigid back of one of the men who had been set to guard it. There were four per night, each chosen from amongst his troops at random, given a token only after all the other sentinels, several dozen in number, had been set at various key points under junior officers to protect the imperial apartments, they chosen by the same method as a protection against plots.

He had known before he ever took up his present duty what were the responsibilities: to keep his master alive, the best way to achieve that being to ensure anyone seeking to harm him would struggle themselves to survive. If others thought him overcautious then he would reply that the history of the palace in which he was employed had seen enough purple blood expended as to make his precautions worthwhile.

Never a man to take anything for granted, Justinus walked the halls of the palace as the sentinels were being changed, to observe that the first act of the day was carried out with proper discipline and secondly to ensure that the officers who took up their stations were from the cadre he commanded and he knew them all; if he could not identify every ranker by face – the imperial guard was a thousand strong – he always gave the impression of doing so, in some cases, where the faces were memorable, able to greet them by name.

That done he headed for the garrison barracks to eat breakfast in the company of the rest of the corps, electing to sit at a different board and with a different hundred-man *tagma* each morning to thus break bread with an unfamiliar group he led, conversing with and hearing, if they were so minded, their concerns and complaints. Word soon spread that caution was unnecessary; a man could speak his mind to the Count of the Excubitor as long as he spoke with honesty.

Justinus would also watch in silence as, fed and equipped and under their unit commanders, who tended to be the sons of the well-born and thus prone to dissipation, his men went about the duties that had been allotted to them on that day's orders. If much of what he did was seen as outward show it served a serious purpose; he wanted all to know he was vigilant, to have them think he could see into their souls and sniff out any threat to his primary duty, as well as being a man who, appraised of a genuine grievance, would see it addressed.

He would also, on occasions, turn up and partake in their training in swordplay and spear work, as well as the drills they practised for ceremonial occasions, and given no quarter was asked for, none was given; he was as likely to depart bruised and weary as any other.

Justinus knew as well as anyone that in an empire depending on mercenary rank-and-file soldiers for its security, quite a number of whom came from well without the imperial borders, loyalty was personal, not to the state. He would, as he had sworn, be faithful to Anastasius, and the emperor would be secure as long as his men were loyal to him.

Any breakfasting and organising was completed before the palace, as a centre of governance, came fully to life. Then it became a hive of bodies, hundreds of people from high officials to common scribes needed to run the realm, with messengers coming and going endlessly from all corners of the empire. Every province had its committed representatives just as the satraps who ran them sought support to bolster their personal positions, which were not always in concert with either imperial policy or those they were set to rule over.

The wealth of the Eastern Roman Empire was stupendous. No goods could enter or leave any one of two hundred plus ports or cross a thousand-league border without paying custom dues, nor could land change hands without a duty being paid, while tax farmers ensured that where the imperial bureaucracy ended, the reach of the government did not.

Given the gathering of huge sums of gold over such a large area and through so many different harbours and markets, corruption along with intrigue was endemic, ranging from the petty squabbles of the palace, with servants numbered in the thousands, to the near blood feuds of those who held higher office and sought to sway imperial policy, differing on what that should be either from genuine principle or in search of individual gain, and that included blood relatives – three competing nephews of a man with no children of his own.

At the head of the whole stood the elderly emperor himself. Anastasius had once himself been a high palace official and had come to the diadem from, as it was termed, without the bed sheets. When his predecessor Zeno died, his empress Ariadne had engineered handsome Anastasius's elevation over the heads of the more obvious candidate, Zeno's brother, and had then married him. Having worn the diadem for many years now he was well encased in the ceremony and grandeur of his elevated rank.

Only those with whom Anastasius was intimate, and they of necessity had to be few, were able to discern that he suffered all the frailties common to the merely human; he fretted and was often indecisive, swayed by powerful voices, as well as being so mean he was a byword for parsimony. Of necessity close enough to observe his master, as many others could not, his *comes excubitorum* knew of his many weaknesses as well as his few strengths, though it would have taken hot tongs to get him to reveal them.

If Justinus slept in the surroundings of a hermit, the rooms from which he exercised his responsibilities reflected more the position he held, a set of sumptuous apartments that controlled access to those of the imperial couple. While care had to be taken not to offend powerful officials, he always made sure they understood his function, which was to keep Anastasius and his ailing wife, the Empress Ariadne, safe from harm.

To do that he had to earn and keep their trust, a problem when he thought Anastasius often ill advised and one particular plank of their policy totally misguided. It was a subject to be avoided, for not adept at telling falsehoods, Justinus might be forced into an honest reply if asked for an opinion.

'Highness.'

Justinus bowed as he presented his emperor with the overnight reports of disturbances in the city, the first personal duty of the day, not that Anastasius would read them; nor could Justinus recite them to him, for that, reading and writing, was an area in which he utterly lacked the skill. The nephew on whom he depended being absent he presented a summary given to him by a literate servant, though there was very little to report from that sent in by the *praefectus urbanus;* the previous night Constantinople had been quiet.

'A dispute in the docks between sailors from Alexandria and others from Latakia, a few wine shops destroyed and heads broken, but no reported deaths.'

The old man nodded, which upset the barber trying to dress his hair, not that the fellow let his irritation be known to the subject of his attentions; Justinus picked it up because he saw the eyes flash for a second. Like all functionaries he cared only for his own role in palace life; it mattered not to him that a fear of riot was a constant in the mind of the emperor and with good cause. The capital was a feverish melting pot of many races and, though underground, any number of outright criminals as well as creeds that refused to adhere to official edicts on religion.

Anastasius himself had experienced how dangerous this could be, and all due to, as was the case in Thrace, his stance on religion. He had, in the year '12, been massively troubled by uproar, had seen his statues cast down as well as those of his predecessors, the homes of his relatives set on fire, and the disturbances only snuffed out when he offered himself before the febrile mob in the Hippodrome and proposed he stand aside if they put up another candidate. Fickle as ever, they cheered him to the heavens!

135

Then there were the factions called the Greens and the Blues, originally supporters of the rival teams of charioteers, now more a pair of groupings representing different parties in the city. Loosely they were low-class mobs controlled by either the old Greco-Roman aristocracy or the bustling merchant class. The leaders would happily bring their supporters onto the streets in pursuit of some policy that suited their interests, naturally opposed by the other side which had them engaging in an endless ritual of tit-for-tat and bloody violence.

With the members of these factions numbered in their tens of thousands no one could be sure the troops quartered in the city were numerous enough to contain the danger – they were certainly too few to crush either community – and emperors were frequently obliged, like Anastasius, to appear before the mob in the Hippodrome to placate them over a policy inimical to their interests. Often it was politic that they should consider fleeing the capital and more than one emperor had faced being deposed; God help the man who aspired to rule who did not have some kind of approval.

'Enough.'

Anastasius issued this command in a voice as soft as the wave of his bejewelled hand, which was sufficient to send packing the man attending to his hair. Another command cleared the chamber of others waiting to attend upon him, which made Justinus curious, for it implied that his master wished to converse with him without being overheard. As an extra precaution he spoke in the Illyrian dialect common to both, Anastasius being

136

a native of Dyrrhachium on the Adriatic coast.

'You have seen the reports of how matters fare in the Diocese of Thrace.'

'I have had them relayed to me, Highness.'

'You know Vitalian as well as any man in my service, Flavius Justinus, do you not?'

The use of the full name had the commander of the guard stiffen, for it seemed too formal. He did indeed know Vitalian, for he had served under the general during the recent Persian War and helped him to put down the Isuarian risings that had plagued the early years of the present reign.

'I need to be aware,' Anastasius continued, his voice still low and even, 'before I attend the council, if the threat he presents to us is real or sham.'

There were always times in the life of a court official, and Justinus was that, when a choice had to be made as to whether to be truthful, as against others, or whether it was more prudent to tell the emperor what he wanted to hear. No position was safe; every appointment was in the imperial gift and could be removed at a stroke, albeit such an action in certain cases was not without risk to the emperor: some men were too powerful to just dismiss, and if a ruler wanted to be sure of success it was safer to kill the person in question, sometimes including his family.

'General Vitalian is not a man to issue a false challenge.'

'A threat, then?'

'I would say it would be wise to treat him so.'

What he could not say was that the policy enacted to give him cause to rebel was foolish,

137

doubly so when Vitalian, a committed Christian and strong in his support for Chalcedonian beliefs, commanded the only decent-sized force of soldiers on the European side of the capital. Added to that, camped as he was in a region that supported his views on dogma, he would have no trouble in recruiting others to his banner.

'Given the difficulty that Vitalian is creating, I cannot see it as wise to alienate what support we enjoy on the Danube border.'

Justinus now knew why Anastasius had cleared the room and spoke in dialect, this being a subject that when discussed, his guard commander had requested be overheard by no one. He also suspected he knew what was coming.

'Given the possibility of serious disturbances, I suggest that you give instructions that the commission headed by Petrus Sabbatius is to be recalled for the time being. He will not have got far I suspect. Dealing with the complaints of your old comrade...' That got another waved hand, until Justinus provided the name. 'Belisarius will have to wait.'

'We are all yours to command, Highness,' Justinus replied, making sure that whatever anger he felt was well concealed.

'Be so good as to call back in my attendants.'

Which was, without the need to say so, a dismissal.

CHAPTER TEN

If sleep brought welcome relief and restored both Flavius and Ohannes it did not bring comfort, but they had a whole day with enough of that fisherman's catch remaining to feed themselves and to begin to think how to proceed, which would not be easy. That did not become any more simple after a second peaceful night, when the only threat came from others fishing too near the shore for comfort. Daylight brought back to the fore the real concerns.

To camp on the northern bank of the Danube for any time without their presence being observed was impossible; even in deep woods they would be seen by someone and that was if they stayed still, not an option if there was a need to hunt and fish in order to eat. They would be spotted, too, from the river trying to tickle their supper, for they lacked the means to cast a line. Snares would have to be set and a certain amount of movement had to be undertaken to put those in place, as well as to seek out larger creatures.

Easily edible food to steal, like chickens, were more likely to be found where folk were settled than in the wild, but too much theft of that kind would soon result in a reaction. In order to eat what they caught, a fire'd have to be lit so it could be cooked, all of which put them at risk of discovery and from folk unlikely to be overly friendly.

'If they don't cut our throats straight off,' Ohannes intoned, sat on a fallen and rotting tree trunk facing the river and Flavius, 'they will find out who you are and that will mean a bit of gold for selling you to the Huns. Worse still, they might sell you to Senuthius.'

When Flavius showed an immediate impatience to recross the river, Ohannes had the task of restraining him, on the very good grounds that it was not yet safe to do so; indeed, the old man was far from sure it would ever be that.

'And what if that commission from Constantinople comes and goes without our even knowing?' Flavius demanded.

'You put too much faith in that, to my mind.'

'And where else would you have me place it?' That got the youngster a look; it also got the older man an apology. 'I did not mean you.'

'Never thought you did,' came the less than convincing reply, followed by a sigh that hinted at understanding. 'You want revenge and that is only natural, but it might be in seeking blood you end up as dead as your family and what good will that serve?'

'I must somehow contact my mother and I cannot do that from here.'

'Aye, that is a worry. If they had a cross in mind for you, I fear they might have something of the like for her should she choose to ignore your request and arrive at a time inconvenient.'

'Which would be any time before the commission arrives.' Flavius looked to the trees under which they sat. 'I might be able to see something from the upper branches. Make out if the coast is clear. Men still searching I could not miss.'

'With that shoulder of yours, you might just as like end up with a broken neck.'

That got a slow swing of the arm and a wince. 'It's getting better, good enough to row.'

'Give it the time it needs, Master Flavius, for if you do go back, an' I cannot see how I can stop you, then you best be fully fit for fighting.'

'My sword arm is good.'

'That's not enough in a real scrap, young sir,' Ohannes hooted. 'Folk would have you believe that battle is all pretty sword and spear work, but it is nothing like. It's gouge, bite and kick as much as anything, with the need for trickery to make sure you don't fall and the fellow afore you does. I once needed to crush one head with a stone.'

'If a sword is used properly...'

'And who says you'll get the chance? I used to watch you and your fellows being instructed, thrust here, parry there, how to use your shield. Never saw anyone tell you to put the boss of that hard into the groin of the boy you were contesting with, wouldn't be proper that.'

There was a scoffing tone in the old man's voice that set Flavius on edge; he considered himself the best of his group – only rarely did he ever have to give ground to another – and he felt it was incumbent upon him to say that if Ohannes had been watching their practice he would have observed that.

'Very lively it was too, but as much use to you in a true contest as a stalk of corn. I say that, and if your papa were here he would say so too.' That saw the young head drop, and brought forth an apologetic hand from Ohannes, to tap his good shoulder. 'Didn't mean to pain you, lad.'

'Remind me, Ohannes,' Flavius insisted, unable to hide the fact that he was close to tears again.

'Recall the way we fought those two thieving sods that tried to rob your house, Master Flavius.'

'I wish you would stop calling me that, it makes me sound like a child.'

It was a good job he was not looking at Ohannes then, for he would have seen in the old man's eyes a reaction which indicated that was exactly how he saw him; there was, however, nothing in the voice to let the youngster discern that opinion.

'What I am saying is this, that from what I could see, an' I admit it were not much given I was far from looking at what else was happening, for I had my own concerns, you fought real foul.'

That allowed Flavius a smile. 'Which would have got me a swipe of the vine sapling from those who instructed us.'

'It gets praise from me!' came the empathic reply. 'Them fellows were there to teach you to look and act noble-like. Yet there's not one of them ever saw it as the right way to be going on.'

'How I wish we could ask them.'

Ohannes crossed himself and murmured a blessing for men who had died fighting with his old and now deceased master. Yet his voice was strong as he continued and he picked up and made a mock threat with his spear to drive home the point.

'All that fighting fair is nice for an arena and a crowd content to do without blood. It will not serve where it's a choice between you and another. Fight dirty I say again, 'cause winning is the only thing that counts.'

'Put up the spear,' Flavius said in a soft voice, looking over the old man's shoulder.

'Trouble?'

'Lots.'

'Too much?'

Flavius nodded and the spear was laid gently on the floor of fallen leaves at his feet, Flavius wondering why Ohannes spun it first so the point was aimed towards the trees at his back. That done he turned, at no greater pace, to see on the edge of the small clearing in which they had made camp, a line of men in amongst the trees, several with bows already strung with arrows.

'Best stand,' he said, 'arms well out.'

Flavius did as he was bidden, moving to one side so Ohannes did not mask him in any way. Making a quick judgement based on their clothing, he issued a greeting in the Sklaveni tongue, nervous that there would be some kind of reply, for it was very close to all he knew of their language, a few common words. As it was, all he got was a look of deep curiosity from a man who stepped forward, his stance and attitude, or perhaps it was the way the rest looked to him, marking him out as their leader.

Flavius put him as older than any of his brothers, over thirty summers, and he was well built, with a broad pair of shoulders and hands hanging loose at his side, yet still they looked capable of action. Bareheaded, the face was broad, the nose flattish, the eyes a deep brown and steady, and while his non-archer companions had their swords out he did not. The silence did not last long, even if it seemed so, and what followed was a set of guttural words that neither Flavius nor Ohannes would understand, before he changed to good Latin.

'I have had to lie to my men about who you are.'

'And who am I?' Flavius asked, feeling a knot in the pit of his stomach.

'You are the son of Decimus Belisarius and there is a man over the river, a senator of the empire, who sent a message not a day past, willing to pay handsome for your body, dead or alive, if you are found.'

'And if I say I am not?'

That got a laugh, head tilted back, though not a very humorous one, more the kind that enquired if he was taking him for a fool. 'Flavius Belisarius is who you are, even down to those two shiners of yours, which those who took the message were told to look out for.'

'Not much point in denying it,' Ohannes hissed, which if it was too low to be overheard, still drew the other man's eye.

'In the company of a slave, too.'

'I'm no slave, nor ever likely to be!'

'Like to hear you say that to a Hun with a whip.'

'I might prefer death to that.'

The man nodded and glanced at the spear that lay at the feet of the old soldier. Given their eyes were locked, the youngster could not help but look from the one to the other, the Scythian determined, the other fellow slightly amused. Yet it took

144

no great imagination to understand the meaning of the exchange; Ohannes was implying he might just have time to lift and cast that spear before he was taken by arrows and there was no doubt at whom it would be aimed.

His possible target spoke quickly in his own tongue, which had several bows lifted, the arrow points lined up on the Scythian's chest. 'Even if death is certain, something tells me you might still try.'

'Spare the boy if I do.'

'No need to kill him.'

'If you intend to hand me over to Senuthius,' Flavius croaked, his hand going to the hilt of his sword, 'then I would rather you did.'

'A noble death?'

'Better that than what the senator has in store for me.'

'Take out your sword slowly, and if you have a knife that too, then lay them on the ground. No one is going to die here and nor will it be decided what is to happen when we leave this glade.'

'Ohannes?' Flavius asked, unsure what to do.

'Obey, Master Flavius, there's no choice.'

'Why did you call me that?' came a hiss.

'Look into his eyes,' Ohannes replied as he stepped away from the spear, Flavius drawing out his sword and dropping it. 'He has no doubt who you are.'

Without another word the Sklaveni leader spun on his heel and began to walk away. There was no need for him to actually say they had to follow nor did either think it prudent or useful to ask. The others fell in alongside and behind them, a couple staying to gather up their weapons. The way the party moved told Flavius these people knew these woods well, there being no deviation from a course that paid little attention to thinning undergrowth. The man merely barrelled his way through bushes and ferns, with Ohannes softly counting off the number of paces.

'Never know,' came the whispered reply, when the youngster asked him why.

The hut they came to was well hidden by foliage. Made of sods of turf interleaved with rough strands of wood, it was roofed in evergreen tree branches that had it blend into the surroundings. It had to be a hide for hunting, a place in which a body of archers and spearmen could wait until the forest forgot their presence. As they were ushered in under an opening, only the Latin speaker followed them, the rest remaining outside, and the first thing he did was to take from Flavius the small sacks of coins tied to his belt.

'I dare not take you to the town. I must leave you here and under guard, for if I do not, word of your capture will get across the river before the sun dips tonight.'

'You are not going to hand us over to Senuthius?'

'The decision is not mine. Food will be brought to you and I advise you not to try for an escape, because the men I leave behind will have orders to kill.'

'Am I allowed to know your name? You know mine.'

'No harm in that, Flavius Belisarius, my name is Dardanies.'

'And who are you, what are you?'

That got a wry smile. 'Am I not a mere barbarian?'

'You speak good Latin.'

'One day you might find out why.'

As soon as he exited the hut a wickerwork panel was placed across the entrance, plunging the interior into darkness, the only sound Flavius could hear the breathing of his companion. He was dying to ask what they should do now, until he concluded that would be useless; they were trapped and prisoners. Slowly, as his eyes adjusted, he realised there was some light coming in through the gaps in the roof, not much, just enough to see the outline of Ohannes, who spoke in a low and incensed tone.

'Didn't take Senuthius long to set these particular dogs on us, did it? Happen that boatman set the riverbank afire, spreading alarm with talk of evil spirits. I should have killed him.'

Flavius did not want to dwell on that, or to say that had Ohannes tried he would have endeavoured to stop him. Why kill a man for the mere fact of his being in the wrong place?

'I wonder what has been offered for our heads.'

'It will be a price hard to resist.'

The movement was felt rather than seen, that and the sounds of Ohannes tapping the walls, the injunction soon issued that Flavius, like he, should look for something loose, a thick branch or a stone that they could employ as a weapon.

'If we are to be given food, then it will be handed over by one of the men he has left to guard us.'

'Who will be expecting us to try something,'

147

Flavius replied, the pitch of his response less than encouraging. 'It might be best to wait and see what that Dardanies discovers.'

'You would put your fate in the hands of a Sklaveni?'

'He does not know what to do with us, which means that even if Senuthius has offered a sizeable reward, there are people unwilling to take it. My father dealt with these people–'

The interruption was sharp. 'That I know! Did I not accompany him?'

'I never heard him claim them as bad and I doubt you did. To his mind they were more sinned against than wicked.'

'If he'd had the men he needed your papa would not have crossed the river to talk.'

'If he'd had the men he needed he could have reined in Senuthius.'

The wicker panel was pulled aside, flooding the hut with light, but only long enough for the pair to see a wooden board with bread and a hunk of cheese upon it thrust in, then sent across the packed earthen floor by a foot, that followed by a hand setting down a jug right by the entrance. Then it was back in place and they were in darkness once more.

'Might as well eat,' Ohannes said, the gloom in his voice obvious. If that was the way they were going to be provided for, the chance of catching the giver off guard was near impossible.

Time soon lost all meaning, even if they could see through the gaps in the roof, and the shifting brightness, the way the sun moved in the sky. Having found nothing that would aid them to

148

escape, both sat on the floor in quiet conversation, Flavius learning more of the older man's past and the service he had seen with his father than he had been gifted hitherto, it being a story, he suspected, replicated all over the fringes of the empire.

Life could be harsh for the folk that lived within its borders, yet Ohannes was sure it was worse without. As the youngest son of a large brood, and with uncles who were less than fond of anyone that might split what little the family owned, horses and cattle, there was nothing for him to inherit when his father died, which left the choice of labouring for others or crossing into the Roman Empire and once there taking service as a soldier.

'For your citizens are too soft to do what fighting needs done on their own.'

'Tell me about serving with my father.'

'What's to tell, Master Flavius? That he was a good soldier, yes, that he did not rise as high as he might, that he had occasion to use his whip on my back more than once?'

'He whipped you?'

'As he did to anyone who deserved it, an' there were many of that ilk.'

There was a sense in the tone of Ohannes's voice that had Flavius ask him if he was smiling.

'I am, as I ever do when I recall some of the mischief I got up to when I was a young buck. What man can resist women and wine, Master Flavius, for I never could and the fellow who had to keep us up to our mark was the likes of your papa. He was only a *decanus* then, mind – once he got a leg-up to a higher rank using the sapling

149

himself did not go with his dignity.'

'You sound as if you hold no grudge.'

'Why would I, me being the sinner, as all soldiers are, given half a whiff. Your papa was fair, and there is not much more you can ask than that, for there were others of his rank who used the whip for pleasure and there was many another punishment they could mete out if they were so minded, which meant they had to worry about a spear or a sword in their back when we got into a close and busy fight.'

'Their own men would kill them?'

'Didn't happen often, but happen it did.'

Ohannes kept talking and Flavius kept listening, for there was nothing else to do, and given his years, not much for the youngster to relate. The pitch of the voice changed, depending on whether Ohannes was talking of fond memories or things that had upset him. He did not object to being questioned, as when he related the fights he had taken part in, Flavius eager for detail on the two major campaigns in which he had served.

'What can the likes of me tell you? We are told to march, so we march, we are told to camp so we make camp. If you're in the front rank as you assemble for a battle you see your enemy right enough, into his eyes as you close, but most times you don't know what you're doing or why. It's what I said to you afore. Staying alive is what matters and let the folk that have to worry about what it's all for...'

The hut was again flooded with light as Dardanies entered, followed by a trio of much older men, who judging by the torques and ornaments with which they adorned themselves, were of a higher tribal rank than the man who had taken them captive.

CHAPTER ELEVEN

What followed was a very obvious argument and one in which neither Flavius nor Ohannes were part; there were clearly divided opinions about what to do and the disagreements were fierce, all carried out in their native tongue. The only indication of which way matters were swaying came from the looks aimed in their direction by Dardanies. Sometimes they were gloomy, at other times curious, the sole exception being when he became part of the discussion and was seen to be protesting.

'These people must be able to speak some Latin,' Flavius whispered: that had to be the case, based on their having lived so long and in such close proximity to the border.

'Daresay,' Ohannes replied, his voice normal, as Dardanies shot him an irritated look for having the temerity to speak, 'but why should they? Satisfying us is not what this is about. They are seeking what is best for their own tribe.'

Back and forth it went; sometimes it seemed to the pair watching as if one or two of these tribal elders might come to actual blows, so fierce were the physical gestures. At times hands shot out pointing in different directions, which Flavius

151

interpreted as the choice between the Huns and Senuthius, while seeking to work out what option was gaining ground.

On it went until finally it seemed two of the trio had worn down the arguments of the one most voluble and dramatic in his gestures, another turning to Dardanies to bark at him, which had the recipient shaking his head, not in any kind of refusal. Their captor looked, if anything, miserable and it was, naturally, he who spoke.

'A decision has been reached.' He paused and addressed his superiors once more in his own tongue, giving the impression of wishing to confirm something before he spoke. 'They are not as one.'

'Tell that in any language,' Ohannes hissed.

Dardanies responded furiously. 'It would do you well to hold your tongue.'

'Best obey,' Flavius responded, nudging Ohannes and giving Dardanies a look of understanding, before adding, 'He does not wish you to think he is fearful.'

'Just as well, for he has no cause to be, not that I think what has been decided is right.'

'It would be a kindness to tell us what that is.'

'You are to be taken back over the river.'

'No kindness there,' Ohannes spat.

'Not to be given over to Senuthius Vicinus, which is the course I would adopt, but to be sent on south to a point where you can make your way without fear.'

'Not the Huns?'

'No.'

'Am I allowed to ask why?'

That got a sigh bordering on resignation. 'Our elders think it beneath us to send you back to a certain death and a painful one, while to just sell you into slavery would demean the memory of your father, who, even if he was Roman, tried to keep in check the worst instincts of those who wished to profit from our weaknesses.'

He gestured to the trio of elderly men, still scowling, but from time to time, as Dardanies spoke, including him in their disapproval. 'You will not know this, but many times, when our hotheads disobeyed the decrees of our tribe and crossed the river, they fell into the hands of your family.'

'I know that,' Flavius replied.

It had hardly been a secret in his house when the cohort had some success, just as it had been acknowledged that the achievements had been against numbers insufficient to really trouble a body of professional soldiers.

'It was said your father only killed when he had to.'

'No Roman would do otherwise.'

The reply was sharp and it was clear by their expressions that the elders did speak some Latin, certainly enough to understand the statement made by Flavius, as well as the pride with which it had been delivered.

'How little you know of your own kind, but boys, I suppose, must be allowed their dreams.'

Two nods, one furious shake of the head, then a remark from one of the elders that was clearly an instruction to get on with it, possibly that explanations were not necessary. Dardanies, how-

153

ever, seemed determined to keep providing the rationale for what had been concluded.

'Sometimes, when he could, your father sent them back to us as a gesture of peace.'

That Flavius did not know; as he tried to disguise his surprised reaction, he was sure the Sklaveni, all four of them, had picked up on it. Somehow it seemed to please them.

'So, it would be dishonourable for us to choose a way of proceeding that would harm you.'

'And me?' Ohannes demanded, still with a tone of defiance that was not appropriate.

'You matter only in that Flavius Belisarius is too young to be set free without help.'

The youngster glanced at the Scythian to see if he was rendered grateful or annoyed; there was no evidence of either and he was required to look away. Dardanies was still speaking, this time in a tone of voice that utterly lacked cheer.

'For the same reason I have been given the task of seeing you to a place of safety.'

'How will you deal with Senuthius?'

'It has ever been our approach to deal with that swine as little as is possible.'

A stream of instructions issued from one of the elders, to be countered with objections by Dardanies, yet as an argument it lacked any vigour until, abruptly, the older men left. That they did not go far, or that their dispute was far from laid to rest was obvious, given they could be heard still arguing through the soft sod walls, this as Dardanies explained what they had planned.

'The longer we wait the more chance that word of your capture will get back to Senuthius. Therefore we will cross the river as soon as we are sure it is safe, with enough of an escort to deal with any patrols the senator has out. That done, I will carry on with you until you are well away from danger.'

'Where will we cross?' Flavius asked.

Dardanies seemed surprised by the question. 'Where it is safe to do so.'

'There is something on the southern shore I must collect.'

It was Ohannes who objected. 'There's no time for searching.'

'If there is not time for that then I will not go until there is.'

'You will go,' Dardanies snapped, 'when we say you will go.'

'I will not!'

That produced on the face of the Sklaveni warrior a smile larded with curiosity. 'If I tell that to the men who have just departed it may alter their decision.'

'So be it.'

'Best tell him what it is,' Ohannes said with a sigh.

Which Flavius did, starting with the letters he had found and what they portended, which could not be anything other than beneficial to the Sklaveni: the possible impeachment of Senuthius and not only an end to his raiding for slaves but a warning to others not to take up what the senator might be damned for. He made no mention of his father's testament, given that would do nothing to sway Dardanies, but to him it was something just as vital that he recover.

'And where is this sack?'

'Hanging in an oak tree, high in the branches and out of sight from the ground.'

The eyebrows went up. 'An oak tree where?' The lack of a response from the youngster was eloquent enough to have Dardanies actually burst out laughing, for it obviously implied ignorance, Flavius responding quickly that he had left more than one sign as to the location.

'Visible in the dark?'

Tempted as he was to lie, Flavius had to tell the truth, which he did with a shake of the head. Even with a full moon and complete starlight he had no certainty that the sign he had left, his breastplate, would be visible and nor did he know if the group of pebbles had been found and either disturbed or removed.

'Do you know how many oaks there are on the banks of the Danube?' Another shake of the head: to even guess would be foolish, which explained the mordant tone of what came next. 'If I blindfolded you, cast a javelin full force into a hayrick, then asked you to find it, what chance do you think you would have?'

'It is vital that I have those letters.'

'Being vital does not make it possible.'

'I do not ask that you accompany me, what I do ask is that you give Ohannes and I the time to seek it out and recover it.'

'Have you thought to ask me, Master Flavius?' Ohannes snapped.

'I hope you will aid me in this, as you have in everything else, Ohannes, but if you decline...'

The Scythian produced an expression, the one with which he had responded to statements like that from Flavius before, aiming to tell him he was getting above himself. Stubbornness won out over being respectful.

'If need be I will go on my own.'

'One of these days, Master Flavius, you are going to issue that threat an' I am going to let you do as you wish.'

'But not now?'

Ohannes looked pointedly at Dardanies. 'Not for me to decide now, is it?'

They exchanged a hard mutual stare for a second, before the Sklaveni exited, his voice soon joining those of the elders who were still in disagreement.

'They're off again,' Ohannes scoffed, as the voices went up a notch.

'How can I convince you that those letters are vital, Ohannes?'

'You can't, 'cause I don't see things the same way as you. It's all very well seeking to preserve the memory of your papa, Master Flavius, but it makes no sense, as I have sought to tell you more than once, to get yourself killed in the process. That is my opinion and has ever been. Matters will take their course an' if you can affect them all well and good, but to do that you must have breath in your body and blood running through your veins. So staying whole is the most important thing and that is what you must set your mind to doing.'

The two were staring at each other – it seemed as if they were silently seeking some truth as yet unstated – when the light that permitted this was doused by the re-entry, through the doorway, of

Dardanies and the elders.

'They wish to question you.'

Which they did, showing that in at least two cases their Latin was of a standard that did not require Dardanies to translate. Only one struggled and he seemed the least inclined to think the letters of any importance. Yet it was obvious the other pair saw matters differently, very much in the way that Flavius had sought to persuade Dardanies. As the questions flew back and forth the youngster realised just how right his father had been.

These people wanted peace and security and it was not from fear. Along with the decorations they wore there was clear evidence that these grey-hairs had been active warriors and they had the scars to prove it. The notion of a body that might impeach and bring to a halt the depredations of Senuthius was as attractive to them as it had been to Decimus Belisarius. Finally, questioning over, they left the hut again, to once more continue their discussions outside, until a peremptory command was issued for Dardanies to join them. He was gone for not more than a minute and on returning he gave Flavius a look, accompanied by a miniscule shaking of his head that lifted his spirits.

'These letters of yours are things my elders wish to see.'

'So we must find them.'

'Sadly yes, which means we must risk our bodies by seeking out the spot where you hid them, for that must be undertaken in the light of day.'

'I have not felt that God was on my side since the day my family was cruelly slaughtered...'

Flavius paused then, suddenly aware that he had made no enquiries as to how many of the Sklaveni tribe had taken part in the raid that led to their deaths. 'Were you part of that?'

'Part of what?' Dardanies asked guardedly.

'The majority of those who raided across the river were, I think, Huns...' He had to pause; Ohannes had gifted him with a sharp jab in the ribs, but he was not to be put off. 'But not all. How many of your tribe took part?'

'Some.'

'And you?'

'It matters not,' Ohannes insisted.

'It matters to me,' Flavius said, looking right at the Sklaveni, 'especially if I am to put my trust and my life in your hands.'

If Dardanies was made uncomfortable, which he seemed to be, he soon found a way to deflect that with a question of his own. 'Does it not occur to you, Flavius Belisarius, to ask why such a raid was ever mounted?'

'Hun greed.'

'Truly they are that, but was it enough?'

'I do not follow.'

The reply was given in a mordant tone and one that implied some kind of knowledge. 'No, you do not.'

'You have yet to answer my question, Dardanies,' Flavius said, his mind too fixed on his own preoccupation to pursue any other avenue. 'Did you join with them?'

'It was too good an opportunity to let pass.'

'A chance to kill Romans?'

'You praised my knowledge of Latin. How does

159

a warrior of the Sklaveni get that?'

'By being captured?' That got a nod. 'Were you a slave?'

'Perhaps you are not a fool after all, Flavius Belisarius. Perhaps one day I will show you the scars you get from a Roman master who takes pleasure in punishment. And let me tell you, before I do, that I have never met anyone so devoted to the God you just sought to invoke when you spoke of your family.'

'How close were you to my father and brothers when they were...?' He could not finish, could not say the word 'killed'.

'Nowhere near, but do not doubt if I had been I would have used my weapons in the same manner as the Huns who did cut them down.'

'And you have been chosen to get me to somewhere safe.'

'I have been commanded to do so and it is not a duty I relish.'

'Perhaps I might have to pay the price for your hatred of Rome?'

'No, Master Flavius,' Ohannes interjected. 'This man will not harm you.'

'I might, fellow, but only if we meet after I have discharged the task given to me.'

'How can you be sure, Ohannes?'

'Perhaps he will tell you.'

'Better coming from you, Greek.'

'Neither Greek nor Roman,' the Scythian replied forcefully. 'Not that it makes much odds, since I was a soldier of the empire.'

Then he turned to Flavius. 'If he was minded to cut your throat, Master Flavius, he would have taken on the mission he has been given with glee. I might not know a word of his tongue but I can read a face and what I saw was a man in despond.'

'Enough,' Dardanies snapped. 'If we are to take a boat out on the river and be in plain sight of the southern bank, you Flavius Belisarius need to be disguised and that includes hiding those bruises on your face that make you look like an owl.' He laughed then, a loud hoot. 'Might be best to dress you up as a woman.'

There was sheer pleasure for Dardanies then, provided by the reaction those words received; Flavius, on the cusp of manhood, was deeply offended.

The disguise was flour mixed with water and plastered around his eyes, added to a hooded smock that, pulled well forward, hid much of his face from view. It was less that he might be spotted from the riverbank than that they were bound to pass other boats on the constantly fished-upon river, where a sort of truce existed. Each person seeking to cast a net, whichever side be they from, was, unless open conflict was in progress, left in peace.

Much of the day had already gone so, with the sun beginning to sink towards the level of the treetops and using the boat Ohannes had acquired by terror, they set out, Flavius laying low in the bow. Dardanies and the Scythian did the rowing, harder against the flow of the river, the latter with his previous cack-handedness until instruction had him working his stick with competence if not skill.

161

The Sklaveni knew the river well and was good at identifying landmarks on both banks, asking a stream of questions about the time they had taken to cross. That neither knew, just as they had no precise idea as to from where they had set off. With little to aid him and the light fading and it being useless to search in darkness, that first evening produced no result.

Once more beached on the northern shore, they made their way back to the hut, Ohannes and Flavius to spend the night under guard, Dardanies going off to wherever it was he resided, returning before dawn. They were soon once more out on the river, working from the point at which they had previously abandoned the search. Spotting one of the watchtowers that had lined the river since the time of Hadrian, Flavius knew they had gone too far, so they reversed their course.

'It would aid us to be closer to the shore,' he suggested.

Dardanies was wary and with good reason, given he did not know what Senuthius had set in motion – everything he could muster, he supposed, given that, according to his young captive, he might stand to lose the same should Flavius Belisarius survive.

'He must know by now that you did not go south but either crossed the river or are in hiding on his side. Why else would he seek to reward us for your capture?'

'We have seen no one looking.'

The reply was brusque, with a sharp nod towards the densely wooded shore they were pre-

162

sently passing. 'That does not mean they are not there.'

It was a flash of sunlight, suddenly breaking through a gap in the tree canopy, that caught one of the decorative motifs on Flavius's breastplate – a glint, no more, and in time a blink of the human eye. This had the youngster pointing, his voice less excited than his motion as he nailed the contradiction in the Sklaveni's reservations.

'How are we to get possession of it if we do not land?' Flavius said, as he cast his eyes up to examine the trees, several of them oaks, prepared to exaggerate what he could see and identify. 'I think I see the very tree there!'

The oars being swiftly backed, the boat came to a standstill, the sticks used to keep it in place as the wooded bank was examined. They were searching for any movement, acutely aware that if they had been spotted, to observe any would be unlikely; anyone wishing them harm would stay still until they landed. It was also true there was little choice, so Dardanies having checked with Flavius, at a word the oars were lifted and dipped, and very gently employed to take them close to the shore.

'Take up my spear,' Dardanies said, he being armed, obviously directed to Flavius since he was not rowing.

The youngster lifted it and for a moment he exchanged a look with the Sklaveni and it was one full of meaning. Were you really nowhere near my father and brothers when they were cut down, it asked? Will you keep to your task when taking Ohannes and me south or will you seek to kill us as soon as you are out of sight of your

163

elders, and thus get vengeance on Rome?

'Ever thrown a spear from off of a boat before?'

'No.'

'Then brace yourself well and aim high, for it will move under your feet.'

Those words broke the spell, which had Flavius, spear on his good shoulder and feet braced by the timbers, looking hard at the shore until he used the point for a second to indicate the now visible breastplate stuck in the roots of the riverside trees.

'There!'

'Pull hard on my word, then lift clear!'

Dardanies snapped this command to Ohannes which, when carried out, propelled the prow towards a strand of pebbles. He immediately shipped his oar and took out his sword to leap ashore as soon as the keel ground on the stones, there to stand ready to fight if anyone appeared. After a pause he turned to put his finger to his lips and to show them the palm of his hand, thus ordering silence and stillness, a pose he held for what seemed an age, until some birds began to sing.

They would have been alarmed at their noisy arrival, but with the boat and its occupants still, their tweeting sent a sign to tell all three that no one else was moving within the woods, that driven home by the sudden silence as soon as Flavius came ashore to look for his pile of pebbles, his feet crunching on the stones. He found them quickly and gestured to Dardanies that he had done so.

'Then find that damned sack,' the Sklaveni growled, relieving him of the spear. 'And be quick.'

Which Flavius did, climbing as quickly as pain

allowed, the sack grabbed from his hands as soon as he came back to the ground; he also waded into the water to retrieve his breastplate.

CHAPTER TWELVE

Justinus had heard no more of what the Emperor Anastasius had imparted to him nor did he show either by gesture or voice that he was in any way put out by the decision, merely sending word by fast messenger to his nephew that he should return to the capital. In the words used there was no expression of approval or regret and he went about his duties as if nothing had been said.

It was axiomatic at court that the suppression of any personal feelings was the only safe way to behave and if he felt sure that their conversations on the subject had been just between Anastasius and himself he could never be certain: no man could keep such a throne without being himself an intriguer.

There was rising tension within the imperial palace, growing daily, with news coming from southern Moesia of the activities of Vitalian, who had within the areas he controlled – those within reach of the army he commanded – removed several Monophysite bishops despite a direct instruction from the *magister militum per Thracias* not to do so. Not that the writ of that official, un-popular both as a satrap and a person, carried much weight with a count of the *foederati*, general to a strong body of mounted barbarian mercenaries.

Justinus was present in his official capacity as the council gathered to discuss what action to take and it was with a creeping sense of disquiet he listened to men who knew nothing about a man like Vitalian propose solutions that could only inflame matters. Chief among them were the three nephews of Anastasius – he had lost his only bastard son to a Hippodrome riot – who tended to compete with each other in order to ingratiate themselves, each vying to be named his successor.

It was instructive to watch such born courtiers – patricians by both birth and habit – deploy their arguments, each one showing a sensitivity, not to the problem under discussion but simply seeking to discern the effect their words had on their uncle and thus a reflection of their standing. The emperor had the unusual physical trait of different-coloured eyes, one being blue the other green – which had earned him the sobriquet *Dicorus* – said by some to be a sign of the devil, by others of divine approval, these in a face now lined with the ravages of age, loose flesh on the neck and jowls, the nose grown more prominent as had the sagging ears.

Yet it was an expressive face, so the slightest intimation that anything they put forward met with disapproval brought an immediate switch of tack; if a rival seemed to have struck a chord then that was the line taken by all. The rest of the imperial council – dozens in numbers and all men of shifting principles and profound self-interest –

tended to let these nephews make the running until they could pick up which way the wind was blowing; it was then time to advance an opinion.

'If the *foederati* cannot eat, Highness, they are scarce going to rebel,' claimed Hypatius, the nephew Justinus reckoned most likely to succeed his uncle.

'You suggest we deny them rations?' Anastasius mused, in a way that showed it an idea that appealed to him, for while it would irritate Vitalian, it might not inflame matters to the point of a complete break.

'Or the funds needed to purchase them,' added the younger brother Pompeius, who had been advocating a totally different and more drastic point just moments before.

'Not deny, Highness,' Hypatius remarked, giving his brother a sideways glance full of bile. 'Restrict. Empty bellies will provoke them, occasional hunger may not.'

'And what if you are wrong?' argued nephew three, the youngest and the dimmest. Probus was obviously thinking that clear blue waters between his cousins and himself might serve him well. What he got from Hypatius was a sneer and a winning rejoinder.

'I cast only an opinion, Probus. I leave our emperor to take a decision that falls to him and I would not so traduce his wisdom to even suggest he might be in error.'

'I meant–'

'His Highness knows what you meant.'

'We cannot be seen to give ground,' Pompeius interjected, seeming to be clear now which way

167

matters were likely to proceed, 'to any general who opposes imperial edicts.'

Anastasius nodded very slowly, then looked around the glittering audience chamber, at his dozens of non-related courtiers, none of whom had as yet voiced an opinion and it looked as though none would, which Justinus found curious. Within that overstuffed body lay every vice known to man, but if they lacked sexual or financial morality they did not want for a degree of dexterity. It seemed obvious to the *comes excubitorum* that Anastasius was inclined to accept what was being proposed by Hypatius, to his mind like throwing a flaming torch into a vat of heated oil.

Sense dictated that some of them oppose such a dangerous policy but they seemed, by their lack of expression, to be in some way endorsing it and it was not difficult to find a reason why. For some, they knew they might be looking, in Hypatius, at the next emperor, so to rebut him was unwise. For others, who would reckon the nephew to be foolish, letting him have his head with a futile policy might be a good way to diminish him, given they would have views of their own on the succession, in several cases candidates from their own family.

Thus it was in the Roman Eastern Empire and it was no different in the West, now ruled by the barbarian Ostrogoth Theodoric, a man without an ounce of Rome in his being. There was no certainty to succession here or in Rome and even being strong militarily was not enough, so mere blood ties offered no guarantee. Any number of conflicting centres of power came into play on the death of an emperor so that it seemed more sheer chance than guiding principle decided the succession, Anastasius himself being a prime example.

'Let it be so,' declared the emperor after a long pause, indicating that he had given it due consideration. 'It will do good to let the *foederati* be reminded of who it is who provides their meat, be it on the Persian border or in Moesia. If they do not like it let them go back from whence they came, where they will likely starve.'

That decided, a cacophony of noise erupted, as each man present sought the floor to propose to the emperor their full support, following on to advocate some project or point of their own outside the main discussion.

Lanterns were brought to the gloomy hut – if it was still day outside little light penetrated – and with them came that same trio of elders, this time with a monk in tow. Religion on the northern bank of the Danube was diverse, folk worshipping both their own pagan gods in a form of animism and Christianity as they chose, with no overarching authority to tell them who was right and who was damned. Fear of the latter and no certainty in either was inclined to have many of them worship both.

This divine, a disciple of St Basil, had for his faith travelled all the way from Syria across the empire, to preach to the pagan Sklaveni, while also administering to those he and his predecessors had converted, for this was a land the bishop of the southern bank left alone. He could read and write in both Greek and Latin, as well as now speak in

169

the local tongue, so it was to him that the contents of Flavius's sack were passed, read out to men who were probably not literate.

'I could have done that for them,' Flavius said when he realised what was happening.

'Who says they would believe you?'

'They would only have to look into my eyes to see I am telling the truth.'

'Not those eyes,' Ohannes jested, with a circular roll of a finger.

The testament of Decimus Belisarius was immediately handed over to Flavius, as soon as the monk had told the elders of its contents. Such things were of no interest to them, in stark contrast to the information contained in the letters to and from Justinus, evidenced by the noises emanating from the tight listening conclave, loud enough, given Flavius and Ohannes were sitting well away from the gathering, to cover a whispered conversation.

'I think at least one, if not two of them have recognised their own names. My father listed those with whom he had dealings.'

'Happen,' came the laconic reply.

Yet again a question occurred to Flavius, one, like so many others, he realised he should have asked before. 'Do you recognise any of them? You said you came over with my father when he dealt with them.'

'I was never part of their talking, Master Flavius, that was done out of my sight. All I recall is that they were too mean of spirit to feed me even a bowl of meal.'

Voices were being raised. Flavius once more

sensed dispute and Ohannes was in agreement, for both could guess there was more than one way to take advantage of what these barbarians had acquired. How much, for instance, would Senuthius pay to have a list of the charges against him as well as those who might bear witness in his possession? What if they gave him both the letters and the youngster who had spirited them away?

Throughout the ongoing arguments the monk sat silent – having finished his reading his opinion was not sought – yet both prisoners perked up when they heard him interject, softly but insistently, mentioning a very recognisable name to both prisoners, that of Bishop Gregory Blastos.

That the monk was held in some regard was clear by the way he was attended to, no one interrupting, but it was doubly frustrating for Flavius not to be able to understand what was being said. Here was a man he did not know and he had heard that, as a breed, monks could be just as saintly or just as venal as any other person who took to preaching the Gospels. The name Blastos recurred time and again but so even was the voice it was impossible to make out from his tone either approval or condemnation.

Then the discussion opened out, once more encompassing those tribal elders, voices rising and falling as views were expressed and countered, with the monk now listening in silence for what seemed an age, as if weighing up the case. Finally he spoke again, crossing himself as he did so, what he was imparting being received with nods from his audience. Eventually Dardanies, who had taken no part at all in the discussions, was spoken to and sent over to talk to them.

'It has been decided that these letters must stay with us.'

'No!'

Dardanies shook his head. 'You do not have a choice in this, it has been decided.'

'Why?'

It being Ohannes who had asked, the Sklaveni turned to him. 'There is more than one reason. In your possession and once over the river...?' That unfinished remark was followed by a shrug.

'We might be taken?'

'Which means that for us these letters are lost and so is any use they might be to the tribe.'

'What was that monk saying?'

'That the crimes of your bishop are greater than the crimes of your senator, for he has sinned against God and his holy vows.'

'You don't agree,' Flavius said, 'I can sense it by your tone.'

'Senuthius is a greater threat to us than Blastos, who is in truth no threat at all. But men steeped in religion only see things as eternal. Yet it is he who advised they be retained by us and in that he is right.'

His mind working furiously, Flavius could think of no way to counter this and it was beyond maddening. If he had not formulated any definite plan, even before they had crossed the river, it had been his intention to somehow be present when the people sent from Constantinople arrived in Dorostorum, ready to provide his father's evidence and encourage those who had intimated they might stand witness to step forward and do so.

Primarily he needed to be there to see the downfall of the man responsible for the death of his family. In his imagination he had pictured himself as the person who, hammer in hand, nailed Senuthius to the stake at which he would be burnt, able to see the terror of the forthcoming conflagration in his eyes. In his mind now he could almost hear the flames licking the spitting lard from that oversized body but even more vital than the satisfaction of that, he would have fulfilled his father's mission and sent to hell his enemy.

Such dreaming had survived being captured, strengthened by the decision of the Sklaveni tribal elders: he would get back to the southern bank with their aid, and yes he would head south. But he had then envisaged a point at which he would be free to act to his own dictates and if the means had been vague his intention had been definite. Added to that he needed to tell to the commission the truth of what had happened to his father and brothers and how they had been deliberately sacrificed.

'Would it be possible to have them copied?'

The pause was long before Dardanies replied. 'I will ask.'

Another clash, more waving of arms and then Dardanies was back again. 'No, but it has been agreed that should you return to Dorostorum in a position to make use of them, and they are still unknown to our enemies, then they will be given over to you.'

'Take it, Master Flavius,' Ohannes said forcibly,

as he saw the youngster was set to once again protest, effectively silencing Flavius, who looked far from pleased.

Dardanies spoke quickly. 'Now it is time to eat, for we cross the river tonight and we need to be well away from the southern bank come daylight.'

'Are you going to eat too?'

'I am, and at the same time I must say goodbye to those who will miss my presence.'

'Children?'

A nod, then a grimace. 'It would be mocking the gods to say to them that I fear to die saving the life of a Roman.'

Flavius puffed out his chest. 'It might be that it is I who will save you.'

There was a terrible feeling of remembrance when Dardanies replied and he did so while exiting the hut doorway, using precisely the same words as those employed by the armed and ready to fight brother Cassius. 'You're too young.'

When he returned Dardanies brought with him a sack of food of the kind that would be of use on a journey; dried and smoked meat as well as three skins containing rough wine, enough for several days. He also brought the money he had removed, giving the purses back to Flavius.

'We will need to buy food, not that it will last with three mouths to feed.'

'Take one,' the youngster responded, touching a face now washed. 'It cannot always fall to me to buy things, especially if my face can be recognised.'

'Those black eyes will fade in time.'

'The sooner the better,' was the opinion of Ohannes.

'Recall how they came about, friend.'

'Friend?' the Scythian remarked.

'What else could you be?' Flavius responded, his voice cracking and not from his age. 'There is no Belisarius house now, so what need of a *domesticus?*'

'There will be again, take my word on it.'

'You can see into the future, Ohannes?'

For the first time Flavius saw the older man cross himself. 'If my prayers are answered.'

'The monk has returned with me,' Dardanies said, indicating the open doorway. 'He wishes to bless our journey.'

Standing, Flavius picked up his leather armour and in the lantern light the decoration on the breastplate flashed, which got him a hard look from Dardanies, returned in good measure by the youngster. If it was a silent exchange it was to make a clear point: such an article was like a beacon by which, never mind his face and the blemishes that still disfigured it, he could be recognised. Stubbornly, Flavius was saying that to him it was vital he take it.

'I know where we will find some sacking in which to wrap it and keep it hidden.'

The trio filed out to find the monk waiting outside and at a sign both Flavius and Ohannes fell to their knees, the Sklaveni remaining apart and upright. The monk mumbled prayers over the pair and again a flash of memory assailed Flavius. Gregory Blastos had been the last person to do this and it was an unwelcome image to

175

conjure up when seeking divine intervention on what was found to be a journey full of hazard.

With much effort he pushed that out of his mind and tried to concentrate on the faces of his father and brothers, so that his prayers should be for their souls and not just for his survival, though he quickly remembered to include Ohannes. Should he also do the same for Dardanies, who clearly did not believe in a Christian god? It seemed churlish not to do so; one day he might see the light of revelation.

The route they took to the shore was different to that by which they had come to the hut and when they got to the riverbank there was a boat waiting with two other men beside it. Obviously they would row them across and come back, which would obviate the need to leave a strange craft on the southern bank or hidden in the trees, where it risked being discovered and setting off a search.

'Do they know who I am?' Flavius asked.

'They will guess, but they are my brothers, so will say nothing for fear that I might come to harm.'

'You are lucky to have brothers.'

'Not all the time,' Dardanies replied. If he picked up the catch in the throat from Flavius he ignored it, too busy looking up to the sky, now growing increasingly dark as the last of the light faded on the western horizon and the stars that littered the sky began to glow. 'Sometimes brothers are a trial.'

'Never enough to wish to be without them.'

'Time to go and no more talking till we are well into the woods. There is some sacking and rope in the boat, wrap up that armour good and tight.'

They pushed the boat into the river and clambered in, the brothers of Dardanies taking the oars and plying them with strong and effective strokes. Flavius, as he bound what had come to be his prized possession, making a sling by which he could loop it over his back, sought to catch their eyes, there being enough reflected light off the water to make their faces visible. They made a point of avoiding looking at him; it was as if to do so was to bring down on them and their brother some kind of curse.

The crossing was near to direct and was obviously to a place previously selected, the boat eventually grounding on one of those pebble strands that had been so useful to both he and Ohannes when they had been running from the dogs. Once out, Flavius and the Scythian stood while Dardanies embraced his brothers, then he reached into the boat and produced two swords with sheaths and belts, these quickly tied around their waists, that followed by two spears, all wordlessly handed over, Flavius being sure he saw a shake of the head from one brother, to say that arming he and Ohannes was unwise.

At a gesture they set off, each with a food sack over their shoulders, straight into the seeming darkness of the woods, yet it was not as Flavius first thought a foolish move. The canopy above their heads was quite sparse and so let in, if not light, a view of the mass of stars and, hard on the heels of Dardanies, he knew the Sklaveni was following a route, one that he and his kind had taken before. He gave the impression of having passed along this way often, which had Flavius wondering how many times the Sklaveni had come across the river to use this very path, prior to a lightning foray of the kind that had been commonplace. If he was dying to ask he could not, both for the sake of silence and the notion that it would be an unwise question to pose. Better not to comment, just to remember.

CHAPTER THIRTEEN

It was impossible to stay out of sight forever; once within the confines of the empire they were in a land of settlement and cultivation, where forests had been cleared centuries before and where the peasantry tilled long-ploughed land either for themselves or as tenants of someone wealthy. Having made good progress in the dark, not without the odd scrape from a wayward thorn, or an ankle risked from some hole in the ground, they stopped at the forest edge to eat and let the dawn come up, this so they could observe what lay ahead.

'I wish to stay away from the established paths as long as we can,' Dardanies said, addressing Ohannes, his manner suggesting that to include his main charge would be a waste of breath. 'Once we reach the road south it is to be hoped it will be busy enough for us to pass unnoticed.'

'Not easy,' Flavius responded with some force and obvious pique. 'No farmer will bless you for crossing his fields.'

'Good way to get seen too,' the old soldier

added, as Dardanies produced a look of doubt. 'And if they see us as a threat they are bound to raise some kind of unease outside their own land.'

'How far before we get beyond you being recognised?'

'Several leagues, I occasionally rode round with my father when he visited the outlying settlements.'

'Me too,' Ohannes said.

That had Dardanies looking to the sky, as if seeking a divine answer to an intractable problem. Here he was in a province where to be discovered might, after the recent raid, end up with him being flayed alive and he was in the company of two people who stood a chance of being recognised all over the district. Flavius was still wearing the garment he had donned to search the riverbank for his canvas sack and the Sklaveni referred to it now.

'Pull up that cowl and keep it well forward over your head, look at the ground as you walk. If anyone talks to us, let me answer.' Then he produced a knife and moved closer to Ohannes. 'That long hair of yours is too obvious, best we cut it off.'

'Been better to have done it afore we set out.'

'Which I would have if I had thought on it, but I didn't.'

Even with a knife sharp enough to fillet a fish, such a thing could not be carried out with anything approaching neatness, so Ohannes ended up looking like a badly shorn sheep, with bits sticking up in some places and near bald patches in others.

Added to the lack of shaving for several days, it made him look older, though Flavius thought that an opinion to keep to himself. He knew from past experience such comments were unwelcome, his late maternal grandfather a prime example, he having been proud of his bearing. Vanity did not diminish with age.

'How long before you have a beard?'

Ohannes felt his stubble. 'Four or five more days.'

Then Dardanies looked at Flavius, leaning closer. 'Be a couple of years for you, though I do spy a touch of fluff.'

'How's the shoulder?' Ohannes asked, before the offended youth could respond.

Flavius swung an arm, and if he winced, the pain was nothing like as bad as it had been, saying it was better before posing a question to Dardanies. 'How far south do you go, assuming we can pass out of the orbit of Senuthius?'

'Somewhere between here and Marcianopolis, it has been left to me to decide.'

'So you could leave now?'

'I could but I won't, and besides, if I arrived home too soon...'

'You might be punished?'

'I do not do this for fear of punishment.'

'Then why?'

'You would not understand.'

'You could try me.'

That got a shake of the head so firm there seemed little point in pursuing the question. The grey dawn light went as the sun rose, to allow the trio to see much further across the ground they

180

would need to traverse, split as it was by hedge-rows. There were already people out and about, at this time of year, women and small children seeing to livestock or picking vegetables close to their dwellings, men further out in the swaying wheat, which they were beginning to harvest.

Flavius pointed out a high-framed hay cart, empty now, and a distant line of scythed men, some twenty in number, tramping forward in a bent-over row, their implements cutting at the stalks, before turning to walk upright and away for a goodly distance, the classic way of using their blades while also saving their backs.

'We cannot avoid being spotted by them,' he contended. 'Whoever is taking the sheaves onto the cart can see any unusual movement for half a league.'

'They will be youngsters, boys and girls.'

'With eyes like hawks as well as voices to tell men armed with scythes what they have seen.'

Ohannes spoke next, there being no need to say that a man with such a cutting blade would be a dangerous foe on his own; in numbers they could be deadly. 'We could wait here till the day's work is done and move when the sun goes down.'

'Best to get away from here, and you would say that too if you knew who these fields belonged to.'

'I do know,' Flavius replied, 'just as I know that over those hills you can see to the west of us, the ones lined with vines, lies the villa of Senuthius Vicinus.'

'Who might venture out to see how the harvest is progressing.'

'Never!' Ohannes snorted. 'If he wanted to know he would send a lackey.'

'Who will be on a horse, able to set off a swift hue and cry,' Dardanies insisted. 'I say we cannot stay within the boundaries of any land he owns and the sooner we are clear of anywhere where his writ has a presence the better and, since it is to me the task has been given to get you to where you will be safe, it is my decision that we gather up our things and go now.'

'So you can get back to your own people as soon as possible?'

'Yes, Flavius Belisarius, and if I am stuck with you, never ever suspect that it gives me pleasure to be so.'

When they did move they sought to mask their profiles by always having a hedgerow as a back-drop, yet to keep to that constantly was impossible, just as it was impractical to seek to get past every dwelling and the folk close to it at any distance. Spears were trailed along the ground to keep them as much of possible out of sight. Working their way through an orchard, too, brought contact with others, those tasked to trim the trees and seek out and dispose of the pests that loved to feed on them.

They passed under one fresh-faced young girl up a ladder, so close they could see the sparkle in her eyes, or at least Ohannes and Dardanies could, for Flavius kept his head down. But he too heard the blessing she shouted down and he was made just as curious by it as the others, a loud cry taken up by those working nearby but out of sight.

'What did she mean by that?' Dardanies asked, when they were out of earshot. 'What did all those cries mean? How could we be on our way to doing God's work?'

'I have no answer to that,' said Flavius, lifting his cowl so he could look the Sklaveni in the eye. 'But she told everyone in earshot that we were soldiers of Christ.'

'She favoured us with a smile too,' Ohannes responded, looking uncertain.

'Well, there's no time to ask and she's bound to tell everyone she comes across that she has seen us, so let's put a good stride in and get well away.'

As they came out of the orchards it was possible to see that line of scythe-bearing men once more, still in the distance, as well as the hay cart now halfway to being full with the sheaves. There were a couple of lads on the top who could clearly see them for they waved, which obliged Ohannes to wave back despite an instruction not to do so from Dardanies.

'Make 'em more suspicious not to respond,' the old man insisted, which got a growl from their escort.

It was not long before they were on a hard earth track, the route by which those hay carts would bring their wheat to the mill, a stone building just visible through a surround of high pines. Home to a great stone driven by oxen, it had to be given a wide berth; Senuthius was the owner and such a valuable resource would be operated on his behalf by someone he trusted, as well as having an armed guard, given it was a prime spot for a bit of pilfering. A sack of milled wheat was worth real money.

'Trusted to cheat any freemen farmers,' spat Ohannes when this was mentioned. 'With a threat to their gizzard if they question the weight.'

'There are few of them left, friend, just as there is nowhere else to take your ears of corn to be milled. Senuthius owns them all for leagues around and has done for years.'

'How did he get so much power?'

'He's a senator and the son of a senator,' Flavius replied, aware that his voice had ceased to occasionally squeak, to produce that unwanted whistling sound and was now, if not even in tone, at least deep in tenor. 'He began as a rich man and has become much more so by his crimes.'

'There are no rich men in the Sklaveni,' Dardanies responded with evident pride, as they left the track to take a wide circular detour round the mill.

This got a raspberry from Ohannes. 'There will be plenty of folk scratching to stay alive, just as there are those who have meat on their table every day. Never met a tribal elder without a belly on him and by the look of your lot they were no different.'

'That's all you know, old man.'

'An' I do know,' Ohannes scoffed, 'for where do you think I was raised? In the same kind of kinship as you. There's those that prosper and those that scratch an' don't you go telling me it's something else inside the empire than out.'

'The Sklaveni are different.'

'So you say, but I take leave to doubt it.'

'One day I will show you,' Dardanies insisted,

obvious resentment in his tone.

'You'll have to drag me by the hair to do so,' Ohannes hooted, 'an' since you have shorn me that will take a mite of doing.'

'Look ahead,' Flavius said quietly, which killed off what was likely to be a long argument, as well as a futile one. 'Do they look like soldiers?'

The mill was well behind them now, easy to avoid being sighted from, thanks to those high pines, but if the trees had hidden the stone building they had also cut off any sight of what lay on the other side and that was a clutch of men, the weapons over the shoulders of some of them very obvious, one high point of what looked like a pike occasionally catching the sun. Other weapons looked to be spears and they were heading in the same direction as themselves, though not at a similar pace.

'Maybe we should seek some cover.'

'If we match their stride,' Dardanies proposed, 'we will not overtake them.'

'If they are armed and on the senator's land they are bound to be in his employ.'

'And if they glance backwards,' Flavius added, 'what would you do then?'

'Wait or have a look,' Dardanies acknowledged.

He was clearly unhappy that they might have to do as Ohannes had said but there was little choice; the last thing they wanted to face was a group of fighting men employed by Senuthius when they were on land he might own. In the end he nodded.

'Let's find a hedge high enough to keep us hidden from this track and we will shadow them.'

Just then, one of the men up ahead skipped forward to turn and, walking backwards, relate something to his companions. In doing so he could not fail but see them, which had him pointing and speaking, the words they could not hear. The effect was to have all five of the others spin round, to stop and stare.

'We keep walking now,' Dardanies said, in a soft voice as if those up ahead could hear him.

'No choice,' Ohannes agreed.

'Be a hard fight, two men against six.'

'Three,' Flavius growled.

'I've seen him fight,' Ohannes barked, before Dardanies could scoff. 'Saved my skin too, so don't you go reckoning on his being a dead weight. I have seen him put a spear in a man at distance too.'

'Well just keep your face hidden, Belisarius,' the Sklaveni barked. 'If they spy you and know your face they will be ready for a fight before we get close.'

'You mean to fight?'

'It's that or run and where are we going to run to?'

'Might be able to take them by surprise,' Ohannes suggested.

'We'll need to old man, if we're to have any chance.'

'Old I might be, but I have seen more blood than you, so pick your man and tell me who, so I can pick mine – you too, Master Flavius.'

The closing gap seemed to last a lifetime, with the men ahead standing in a very unthreatening way and awaiting their arrival. No weapons were made ready, no swords unsheathed and once close enough they could see that several of the men were smiling as if they were long-lost friends. They could also see that what they had taken to be spears were billhooks on long poles, the kind used to trim trees, not proper fighting weapons, but deadly in a close contest. The pike turned out to be a pollarding tool, a saw on a pole long enough to reach the high branches of a fruit tree.

'This is like that girl on the ladder,' Ohannes whispered, 'makes no sense.'

'It's still dangerous,' Dardanies insisted. 'Hold your weapons loose till we are close enough to cast. Spears will even the odds.'

Flavius was aware of the wooden shaft in his hand, as well as the sweat of his palm upon it, which threatened to make it slippery. Added to that his mouth had gone completely dry and much as he tried to work up some saliva he could not. He had picked the fellow on the end opposite him – they were moving forward abreast and the men they were approaching were spread over the track – and his heart was beating furiously as he worked himself up to carry out something he had never yet done and that was to cast a spear at his victim when not himself feeling threatened. There was no sign that his chosen target intended him any harm.

He was back in his own home again, facing those two robbers, but wondering now if he could do what was required in cold blood, as he had done in reaction to the danger facing Ohannes. Under his breath he was murmuring, telling himself that these could be Senuthius's men, people who at their master's bidding would not hesitate to kill him, or indeed strip him of his skin with hot irons at the senator's command.

'Hail friends,' called out the fellow in the right centre with the pollarding tool, speaking in common argot Greek. He was taller and more bulky than his companions and up close slightly better clad, his clothing a padded jerkin in good condition. 'Do you come to join us in the cause of Jesus?'

'We do indeed,' Dardanies called back, revealing that he knew Greek as well as Latin, before dropping his voice. 'Another ten paces, then we cast.'

The weapon they had supposed to be a pike was then raised, but aimed at the sky. 'We have a long march till we join with General Vitalian, but it will be a cheerier one in company.'

'Vitalian,' Flavius croaked.

'So?'

Flavius ignored the enquiry from Dardanies and called out quickly, for there was no time to explain. 'You are joining the man who commands the *foederati?*'

'What man would not, who cares about one day ascending to paradise?'

'Keep hold of your spears,' Flavius insisted, his voice a hiss.

'We must act.'

'Look at these men, do they threaten us?' Then he called out again. 'We are on the same purpose.'

'Then a blessing upon you, young sir, and a tribute to your years.'

For a moment Flavius thought he had been recognised and he tugged at his cowl to make sure his face was partially hidden.

'By your throat I know you are not yet a man but there's not a right-thinking soul in Moesia of any age and who can fight that does not rally to the general's banner. By the time all are assembled we will be a mighty host. It is time that old fart and skinflint Anastasius was kicked out of his palace and sent to live in Egypt amidst those heretics he is so keen on siding with.'

'Time to decide,' Dardanies spat.

There was even less time to explain now than hitherto, added to which he had no idea if Dardanies would even understand; how could a pagan comprehend those who advanced the Chalcedonian dogma and were prepared to rebel against a Monophysite emperor to kill off the rival creed they saw as heresy?

Did he even know that Monophysitism existed? Was he aware that this had been brewing for decades and had been a bone to be gnawed at in the Belisarius house? If there was to be an uprising in a cause in which his father believed, should he leave his post to join it? If he had never served under Vitalian he held him to be both honest and upright in his faith.

'Just do as I say,' Flavius insisted.

'You're giving orders?' Dardanies demanded.

'You got the right of it, Master Flavius?'

'Yes.'

'Certain, are you?'

'Keep your spear down and for the love of the Lord smile.'

Ohannes hissed at Dardanies. 'Best do as he says.'

'You might, I won't.'

'Six against one, I think you may well just.'

They were within easy throwing distance now, so close they could barely miss. Yet there was still no hint of a threat from those standing before them and they were grinning. Maybe it was those looks that persuaded Dardanies, Flavius never knew. He just had a certainty that the way to get clear of any threat from Senuthius was in the company of men going south to fight for General Vitalian. That way they could, instead of skulking from hedgerow to hedgerow, walk the open road without fear.

There was only one question remaining and that would make all the difference, one that made him take a tight grip on that spear shaft again. With his other hand and holding his breath Flavius threw back the cowl to fully reveal his face. With six pairs of eyes upon it, and the same number of faces to examine, there was a gap of several seconds before he could exhale with relief; there was no exclamation, no flash of recognition in those faces. He was to them a stranger.

CHAPTER FOURTEEN

The exchange of names that followed was the usual blur of words and greetings, carried out when they were moving again, meaning not many would be immediately recollected, though when Flavius gave his given name – he did not add the

190

non-peasant Belisarius – that raised an eyebrow, such a clearly Roman tag for someone who appeared to be a *rusticus* being unusual in these parts, this quickly covered by the excuse, albeit a true one, that his father had been a soldier.

The name Dardanies was accepted, given many a barbarian crossed into Roman territory to live and work, while Ohannes being Greek raised not an eyebrow, though it occurred to Flavius, and it should have done previously, that the old soldier must have adopted it at some time, which led him to wonder what he had been called at birth.

The spokesman of the group was the one with the padded jerkin, the imposing belly, the loud voice and the long pollarding saw. Called Bassus he was very much the leader, either by sheer force of his personality or some position he held yet to be established. As they walked and conversed it was necessary to be very vague about from where they had come, as well as many other matters that would naturally occur in conversation.

'How did you come to be fully armed?' had been one of the first and most awkward enquiries, though men who had only farming implements posed it in envy not suspicion.

Flavius responded quickly, conjuring up a handy lie, aware that the others were struggling to think of an answer; they were, after all, masquerading as peasants.

'I am the son of a soldier and he was able to equip us all.'

'He must be a man of means, then?' Bassus boomed.

'He is a man who hoards weapons, friend, for

191

he has long been eager to be on the enterprise in which we are engaged.' The question that hung in the air was quickly dealt with by another hurried bit of invention. 'He is too old, himself, though he will scarce admit it.'

'Ten years on me,' Ohannes added, picking up on the falsehood and proving yet again he was no fool, 'but still with fire for the love of God in his belly.'

'Praise be to that,' Bassus responded.

His look of satisfaction communicated itself to the others, the subsequent talk they exchanged amongst themselves establishing the names in the mind of Flavius and he assumed the others. There was a Firmius, confusingly two men called Gregoras, a Phocas and the youngest, not much above the age of Flavius, called Rogas. They came across as simple and easy-going folk as were others they encountered, like the inhabitants of a clutch of dwellings that lay close to the track, who rushed out with fruit and bread with which to feed them and praise their purpose.

The glue of the cohesion of all was religion, which required to be explained to a sceptical Dardanies, something carried out away from the rest of the group – who, finding themselves amongst like souls, country people who shared their concerns about crops, weather and the price of the harvest, were engaged in comforting conversation, consuming the gifts they had been given while batting away the questions of eager and numerous children who darted around them demanding attention.

Ohannes seemed the most indulgent of the

brats, allowing them to play with his weapons and pretending to terror when they threatened him, the babble of these excited urchins allowing Flavius to give an outline of the dispute between emperor and citizens without any risk of being overheard, not that he received the impression his explanation made, to his listener, any sense. On examination, did it really do so for him? In seeking to clarify the point of disagreement he had been obliged to examine his own words as he delivered them, which raised in his mind a lack of his previous certainty as to the rightness of the cause.

While he held that the Chalcedonian dogma was the correct reading of scripture, that Jesus could be both human and divine and be born of a woman, he did wonder if it was a belief that justified conflict that might lead to bloodshed. Not that he was prepared to allow the Monophysite position dominance, but he did wonder why the two could not coexist, in mutual tolerance if not harmony.

'If you had many gods, as we do, every man could worship those that mean most to him,' Dardanies responded, 'and leave others to find their own way to consolation.'

'To think so is to condemn your soul to perdition.'

'You believe in what you call hell?'

'I do, but you may call it Hades if you wish.'

'One day we might meet in the afterlife and carry on the argument.'

'Make it too loudly in this type of company and we will be there soon.'

'You are good at telling lies, Flavius Belisarius,

193

is that a Christian virtue?'

Sensing the mockery, the youngster was close to an angry reply, but he bit back on it. 'It is story-telling and necessary and it would do you well to take more part, as Ohannes does, for your silence and distance might make them suspect you.'

'The first one to do so will die, so be on your guard for I will need you to aid me with the remainder.'

If Dardanies was smiling he was not joking and that was a worrying thought, which produced a possible solution. 'With these fellows to accom-pany us we have no more need of your protec-tion.'

'The day will come when I feel that to be true, then you will wake the next morning to find me gone.'

'But not yet?'

'No. We could still be on land owned by Senu-thius and he has a presence well to the south here.'

Flavius nodded; he knew as well as Dardanies that though they were passing out of the senator's properties they were not yet clear. Ownership of land was as nothing to the extent of his influence; those feeding and praising them now might be his tenants or, if freeholders, senatorial clients. Be-tween Dorostorum and Marcianopolis he would have like-minded magnates who had no doubt been requested to look out for Flavius, the same kind of message and for the same kind of rewards he had sent over the river to the Sklaveni.

It had been another block to any attempt to curtail Senuthius. He had clients all over the pro-vince, people who would, like him, have armed retainers. So to get beyond the very furthest limit of his reach was a distance too great to calculate. In truth, given the number of fighting men Senuthius alone could muster, added to the danger that could be visited upon Flavius if that imperial commission arrived, was there any number of leagues that would guarantee safety?

His mind was diverted from these worries when Bassus called out, he having assumed a sort of leadership of the whole, that it was time to move on. It suited the trio not to dispute his assumption of authority or to question his opinion.

In making their way Flavius and Ohannes would engage in conversation with whomsoever they found themselves alongside, Dardanies less so; indeed, he kept a worrying distance and what Flavius feared with growing certainty came to pass as Bassus, having made a point of getting close and out of nearby hearing, pointed out, in a low voice larded with suspicion, that he was a quiet one.

'As ever was. His mind wanders and he has had much grief in his life.' That getting a sympathetic grunt, Flavius was quick to add, 'Not that he talks of it, he keeps his pain to himself.'

'He will have faith in the Lord to see him through.'

That was not a question but a statement and one with which Flavius was happy to concur, but, he did add that Dardanies had an unpredictable temper, one triggered by any allusion to that which troubled him, with an added aside that it might be politic for Bassus to pass that on to his companions.

'It would be sad that our cause should suffer, even in a slight way, for any dissension.'

'I'll pass the word.'

Before the sun began to dip they came across another band, a group of four souls again armed with various farming tools, all capable of damage to flesh and bone but not in any way military. They too were heading to join General Vitalian, which had Flavius covering his head until the greetings were complete and he was sure that recognition was unlikely. Another even more confusing round of introductions followed, added to additional curses aimed at the emperor and even more declarations that he needed to be brought to see the error of his ways.

The night was spent in a barn provided by an eager-to-please-them farmer and a prosperous one. He had slaves of both sexes and while the males fetched water with which to bathe weary feet, the females brought food of a quality that probably few of those present, judging by their comments, normally enjoyed. Flavius had, and in consuming it his mind was taken back to his home and his loss, so that he needed to turn away his face so that none could remark on his evident discomfort.

In imagining what had taken place by the banks of the Danube, he could see his brothers slash and cut with their swords, hearing his father's voice as he issued commands that would close the ranks of those he led, to cover for the fallen as they re-treated step by step. They had rushed into battle with the certain assurance of support, only to find none coming and themselves isolated. Had the creeping knowledge that they were being betrayed slowly sapped their courage?

'Easy, Flavius,' Ohannes said, very softly and with a gentle hand on his shoulder.

'You do not know what is on my mind.'

'I can guess, for you were grunting and cursing.'

'I can see them fighting, Ohannes, and I can see them cut down, feel their pain as well as their despair as the truth dawns.'

'They died fighting and if your brothers were like your papa, and from what I knew of them they were, all would say to you now, if they could, that they would rather die in combat than in bed of old age. What they could not have lived with was to run from danger.'

Flavius knew it to be a comforting fallacy, the stuff of imaginings common to him and his peers as they wielded their wooden weapons and dreamt of glory, but he could not find it in himself to challenge Ohannes in a cruel way.

'You have many years on you and still breathe.'

'For which I thank the Lord.'

'And I thank him too,' Flavius replied, crossing himself.

A sort of commotion in another part of the barn distracted them, the sound of a squealing female and the raised voice of one of the men they had met late in the day. Standing, for to do so was to take his mind away from his troubled thoughts, Flavius saw that the fellow had hold of the girl's wrist – and she was that, not much more than his age and slim of figure, no match in strength for the fellow troubling her.

The movement of Dardanies, much closer to him, he caught out of the corner of his eye. He was feeling for his spear and Flavius guessed it was a desire to protect the girl that would animate him; she was a slave and very likely she was like him, a barbarian and a pagan, perhaps even one of those taken by Senuthius in one of his raids on the Sklaveni and sold to this well-to-do farmer.

'Dardanies,' he hissed.

Flavius was shaking his head violently as he stepped out into the centre of the barn, glad to see that his action had stopped the movement of the hand. It had not changed the look on the face, which was still one of seething fury, and that deepened as the girl squealed again and twisted to try and get clear, the action producing laughter, worryingly from more than one throat.

'Ohannes, help me deal with this.'

Flavius stepped forward without waiting to see if his request had been met, moving towards the point of nuisance, unhappy to note that Bassus, who acted the leader in everything else, was not willing to do so now. The voice over his shoulder calmed him.

'Best leave that wench be, friend,' said Ohannes.

That killed off the laughter and changed it to something more troubling. After a moment of confusion the face of the man holding and pulling at the girl's wrist altered completely. When he spoke there was not a trace of affability in his voice.

'And who would be telling me what to do and what not?'

'I would,' Ohannes said, stepping past Flavius.

In a straw-filled barn lit by oil lamps, placed carefully to avoid starting a fire, the old soldier looked grim, ten times more so with his badly cut hair than he had before.

'And who might you be?'

'A Christian, brother, as are you and one that would feel it a sin to taunt.'

The eyebrows went up and he tugged at the held wrist. 'This? She's a barbarian, man.'

'So you would treat her as a plaything?' Flavius asked.

'Jealous are you, youngster?'

'Disappointed that anyone marching on the Lord's business should act as you are doing now.'

That made the fellow sit forward, the action dragging the still-held girl with him, bringing from her throat a whimper of pain. 'Careful I don't box your ears, lad.'

Flavius was dying to look behind him, to see what Dardanies was doing, but he dared not; he needed to hold this fellow's eyes, even as he jeered at him.

'By the look of your mug that's been visited upon you not long past.'

'And,' Ohannes barked, 'the man who did it is dead.'

'What, this mite a killer?'

The miscreant looked around his companions and laughed, far from encouraged by their less supportive response – his insult aimed at Flavius was being seen as wide of the mark, for if he did look young he was tall, showed decent muscle, while the glare on his face left no one in any doubt he was serious. All of these factors, when he did speak again, made the fellow sound sullen.

'Man wants to have a bit of fun with a slave girl and suddenly...'

He did not finish, his eyes moving sideways, which told Flavius that Dardanies had joined him. As his look ranged over them it was clear he saw the threat the trio posed and so did those he could call companions.

'Game's not worth the candle, is it?' Ohannes asked.

The moment of danger seemed to last longer than the actual time, the tension being something Flavius felt he could almost touch. The girl's wrist he let go of and she ran out of the barn, an act followed by a stillness as the odds were assessed, not least how much support the man who had held her had from those with whom he had taken to the road. It was the lack of certainty there, Flavius thought, which produced the response.

'Please yourself,' he said half turning to break eye contact, 'but I shall keep one eye open as I sleep. Strikes me you three might want that wench for yourselves.'

The final shot was aimed at Flavius and accompanied by a barked laugh intended to amuse his friends. 'Not that you would do her much good, lad, with what you have to gift her. As for the ghoul at your side, well I doubt his years would see him the stallion.'

Ohannes turned his back on the voice, to whisper in the ear of Flavius. 'We have made an enemy there.'

'My friend,' Flavius called out, blushing at the way the fellow had insulted his manhood. 'If I

200

interfered it was for the sake of your soul, not from any desire for my own gratification.'

'Hark at him,' came the response to his facility with words. 'Lord of the manor or what?'

'We are all engaged in an enterprise that we hope will raise us in the eyes of God. What a shame it would be to sully that.' He turned to Bassus. 'I suggest that prayers would be in order, to thank the Lord for what we have received this day and what we hope to achieve in those to come.'

That being a hard suggestion to gainsay, the whole assembly were soon on their knees, Flavius throwing Dardanies a meaningful look that forced him to comply, though not without a cynical smile on his face. As others mouthed the words of their prayers, he stayed head down and silent, which caused no comment at all, it being commonplace. Naturally, given the hour, what they had just done and a long day's march on the morrow, the next act was to settle down to sleep, and exhaustion was enough, in the case of Flavius, to compensate for the loud snoring that filled the barn and barely relented until they were woken by the crowing of the cock.

Those who needed to used the back of the barn to relieve themselves then joined the rest at the horse trough to duck their heads and get the sleep out of their eyes. Their host, a well-fed fellow of a hearty mien, arrived in person to wish them well on their way and to pass on food for the journey, which had Flavius haul on his cowl, hiding as much as he could, using others to shield him from view.

If he did not recognise the farmer that did not

mean he would not be spotted in turn. They were no more than a day's ride from Dorostorum and here was the kind of citizen who might well turn up there to the local assembly, a talking shop naturally dominated by Senuthius as well as Gregory Blastos and, according to his father, utterly useless when it came to reining in either the senator or the bishop. Even so, it was held to be instructive to his sons as an example of the Roman way of conducting politics and many times Flavius had sat with his friends in the old Greek amphitheatre to watch the debates.

In the event he got away without being seen and he stuck close to Ohannes and Dardanies, one shielding him on either side, as they continued on their way south, the old soldier, whose aches brought on by marching he was vocal about, slowing the pace so that a gap opened up between them and the rest of the band. This allowed him to begin to lecture the youngster.

'What you did last night was noble but foolish.'

'It was not. Tell him, Dardanies, you were reaching for your spear, were you not?' A nod followed, given with a look of renewed fury at the memory. 'So you see, Ohannes, I stopped that fool from being killed. What would have happened if I had not?'

'Well, that's as maybe,' came the reply, from a companion very reluctant to concede, even after a decent pause, that he might be mistaken, 'but you don't get what I'm driving at.'

'Which is?'

'You seem to have it in your head that all these men marching to join General Vitalian are fired

202

by a love of God.'

'If not that, what?'

'Plunder,' Dardanies suggested.

'That's the right of it,' the old man agreed. 'Oh, they'll spout their faith at every turn, and I daresay amongst the gathering host there will be those that truly believe in the cause as it is stated, Bassus, I would say, being one and maybe, too, those he leads. But just as many sense the chance in this to get their hands on the kind of riches they can only dream of.'

'You cannot be sure of that.'

'If the *comes foederatorum* raises his standard where is he going to take it to?'

'Constantinople, to face down the emperor.'

'And what's in the city?'

'I have said – Anastasius.'

'As well as his palaces, along with those of the patrician class and rich traders, citizens who eat off gold plate. There are rich churches, too, and best to not mention the women. There's no good asking that fellow you challenged last night about what his purpose is, 'cause he will only respond with a load of pious blether. But it's my guess, judging by the way he got hold of that lass, his faith is closer to his gonads than his soul.'

Dardanies had started to laugh, a low chuckle to begin with, growing heartier as he thought on what was being said.

'It's not a matter at which to laugh,' Flavius cried, the certainties with which he had been raised sorely dented.

'It is,' came the reply, the laughter stopping abruptly. 'At least we pagans are honest in our intentions. We fight for treasure, slaves and to make free with enemy women. We do not cloak our acts in false godliness.'

CHAPTER FIFTEEN

Of all the glories of the Roman Empire their system of roads was the most enduring, as well as being a prime asset in times of trouble, there always being strife somewhere. If Emperor Anastasius was known to be tight-fisted with imperial income – he had raised massive sums in taxes in his years in office and spent as little as possible – he never stinted on the prime means of communication throughout his domains.

By this method he kept in touch with the Ostrogoth Theodoric in Ravenna. He could be told within days what was happening from the coast of Illyria or the deserts of Egypt and all points in between. Most vital was the threatened frontier shared with Persia, an enemy with whom he had just concluded an unsatisfactory peace after a less than conclusive war, which on balance had not favoured the empire.

Likewise he was made swiftly aware of the results of the agreed policy towards Vitalian and the omens were far from good: the champion of Chalcedon, which is how the general increasingly saw himself, had reacted with fury to the cutting off of supplies and money and in this he had only reflected the stance of the *foederati* he led, barbarian mercenaries from every far-flung imperial border. Conatus, the *magister militum per Thracias*, had been immediately deposed; it was rumoured he had been executed, while those officers who had served him and had not defected to the rebels were subject to the same fate.

That same system of roads and messengers had brought news that the mission to Dorostorum was no longer a viable one, which rendered its recall fortuitous and any future enquiry unlikely. Justinus certainly did not doubt that the list of crimes against the local magnate warranted investigation, but the despatch stating that Decimus Belisarius had foolishly engaged a vastly superior enemy without waiting for support and had died for his folly, along with all his men in the process, rendered it near to pointless.

The story as related did not ring true to a man who had known the victim since childhood; it was not the action an experienced old soldier like Decimus would risk – if anything he was prone throughout his career to caution – and that made it suspect. Added to those reservations was the nature of the person who had sent and vouchsafed the information. Bishop Gregory Blastos was one of the twin villains listed in the original exchange of complaints. Whatever the truth, Decimus must most certainly be dead and with his demise went any chance of bringing meaningful charges against his enemies.

When the council gathered once more it was to debate the outcome of General Vitalian's reaction – the fate of a centurion and his cohort on a distant border would not rate a mention. If the reports were far from good, no one present would have sensed any alarm in the imperial breast; Anastasius was calmness personified, going through the ceremony of arrival and enthronement as if nothing had occurred to disturb his equilibrium.

Watching him, Flavius Justinus was impressed, even if he suspected it was all a performance, a point he made to his nephew, Flavius Petrus Sabbatius, recalled and swiftly returned to Constantinople.

'The tiger he has by the tail is one of his own devising, Uncle,' Petrus murmured. 'Perhaps someone should remind him of that.'

Petrus had been halfway to Marcianopolis when he received the cancellation of his commission and was able to report just how little there was, militarily, between Vitalian and the capital, though only to his uncle, not to the court.

'Telling him so would be a swift way to forfeit your head.'

'I doubt he needs me to inform him. You, perhaps?'

Justinus acknowledged that with a nod but no response, this as the emperor's nephew Hypatius took a step forward and began to speak. Having been the progenitor of the policy now causing alarm he was in no position to withdraw his previous advice, so he was strong in his opinion that an army should be immediately raised to counter any threat.

'From where?' Petrus whispered.

'The Persian border, there's nowhere else.'

There was no need to continue the exchange,

neither uncle nor nephew needing to allude to the risks attendant upon that. Move troops from the east and the enemy might be encouraged to take advantage of a peace known to be very fragile.

'And if you, Highness, will permit,' Hypatius was saying, 'I will undertake the duty of leading it.'

'But is he capable?' Petrus asked.

Justinus replied to him in a caustic tone. 'Of the three nephews, he is the only one who might be.'

'How much time will that take?' demanded nephew Probus, following on from a very flowery and self-abasing paean to his uncle's sagacity. 'If Vitalian marches swiftly he will be outside the walls long before my cousin can bring forth a host to confront him.'

'Not perhaps as dim as I supposed,' Justinus muttered.

'No great ability of thought is required to draw that conclusion.'

Justinus smiled, the tone used by Petrus being full of disdain, an attitude he applied to all three of the imperial nephews, indeed to a majority of the functionaries who made up the emperor's council. Few, he thought, had any brains at all but they did have desires and he was adept at sniffing out the wellsprings of their actions. What did they stand to gain from their advice to the emperor? Who were they secretly allied to, set against others with whom they were locked in concealed conflict? A natural intriguer himself, Petrus had the nose to sniff that out in others.

A glance sideways showed Justinus that his nephew's expression matched his thoughts and

207

reminded the uncle that the youngster of whom he had become fond was, if clever, far from skilled yet in dissimulation, which he had many times sought to remind him was a necessity in the bear pit of the imperial palace. They were so unalike in many respects, Justinus a soldier with a friendly manner when circumstances allowed, Petrus utterly unmilitary, indeed scholarly by inclination. It was that which had brought him into his uncle's service until he now acted as his confidant.

Their differences extended just as much to their physical appearance; where the older man was broad and muscular, made more imposing by his armour, with an open countenance and a ready smile – many would have said he was bluff and hearty – Petrus, if of the same height, was slight of frame with narrow shoulders and an awkward gait that gave the impression of a man sidling, not walking. He seemed to wear too often a pinched expression, as if he was ever crossed in his thoughts, inclined to bend his head and tug at his untidy reddish hair, inherited from his patrician father, as well as bite his tongue when called upon to think.

'I ask permission to challenge my cousin Hypatius for the leadership of any host gathered to counter the renegade Vitalian.'

'God come to their aid if Pompeius is their commander. You could put yourself forward, Uncle. Anastasius trusts you.'

'To lead a failed enterprise? I think not.'

'You do not fear Vitalian, do you?' Petrus asked, a degree of surprise in his murmured tone, to which he hastily added, 'Not that I think you fear anyone.'

Macedonius, the Patriarch of Constantinople, gorgeous in his ecclesiastical robes, was speaking now and what he was saying brought a grunt from Justinus, he being a pliant individual, entirely subservient to the imperial whim. He was insisting that no concession be made in dogma to any rebellion, be it by Vitalian or any other malefactor, which finally brought from Justinus an angry if quiet rebuttal, one for his nephew's ears only.

'The way to deal with Vitalian is to modify the stance on dogma, accept that each man has the right to worship in his own fashion. That is what animates those who follow him; take away that and you remove the threat.'

'And that, Uncle, is where you are wise and our esteemed emperor is not.'

If the atmosphere while marching south was now slightly strained within the group as a whole that ceased to matter when they came to the *via publica* from Marcianopolis to Dorostorum, block-paved, well drained and kept in decent repair by a local levy on the surrounding landowners. There they joined with other bands heading for the same rendezvous, called forth on the same purpose, which allowed the trio of Flavius, Ohannes and Dardanies to detach themselves from the others by increasing their pace to meld into the increasing throng, Flavius especially eager for news of the imperial commission, who would have been bound to travel this route.

He knew just where to enquire: every *via publica*

had, at five-league intervals, government funded *mansios,* places of accommodation reserved for non-military officials or imperial messengers. If they were sparsely spread, at least for anyone on foot, and not open to all and sundry – to get in required official endorsement stating your name and business – the first villa they encountered was fortuitously close to the point at which they had joined the highway.

Flavius quizzed the watchmen at the gates, asking for news regarding any substantial official body that had come north recently and used the accommodation, or merely stopped to refresh themselves, change mounts and eat. With no need for discretion he was able to describe what that of which he was seeking news might look like: a number of court officials perhaps, of high calibre and bearing and most certainly a priest, travelling in some style.

Slipping the man at the gate a copper coin, not that it produced anything positive, eased the habitual reserve of all watchmen; no body fitting the description Flavius gave had passed this way in recent times and further gentle interrogation produced nothing that might even remotely point to that which he sought, while the name F. Petrus Sabbatius was met with a shrug.

Carrying on he tried the public houses in which a common traveller could get sustenance and even a bed, now crowded out with the men sharing the route – raucous and uninviting places to Flavius, but entered to make the same enquiry and met every time with universal and blank incomprehension. The owners made their living by selling food and wine, an excess of the latter, judging by the sounds of singing coming through the open doorways of every one they approached, what words that could be understood far from spiritual in their composition and rendition.

'No point in getting distressed by it, is there,' Ohannes opined, as they passed another crowded establishment where lyrics being sung were particularly blasphemous. 'It's as I said to you prior, not all who are on this road with us are assembling for God's purpose.'

'Neither are all of we,' growled Dardanies.

If the majority aiming to join Vitalian were farmers or labourers, such volunteers were leavened by a small number of men bearing proper arms, who by their bearing and swagger, as well as their easy camaraderie, gave the impression of being ex-soldiers. Ohannes, who sought to see from various bits of their apparel where they might have served, sized them up quickly and approvingly.

'Stuck for a crust after the end of the Persian War, many were, and took to serving the wealthy as watchmen. Now they are happy to up sticks and come to join the uprising. Once you have soldiered proper it's in your blood.'

Such admiration did not extend to more numerous armed individuals, men who had taken up positions of employment in which guarding property required that they possess swords, spears or both. Ohannes would manoeuvre close enough to get to talk to them too, happy to report back that first impressions were accurate: they would struggle to make true soldiers.

'Might be fit to stand guard over a farm, but not up to a real fight.'

'And all from north of where we now are. I should be home now, given it would be a good time to pillage, with so much protection missing.'

Flavius looked at Dardanies as he said this, realising he was jesting, albeit the comment had within it a strong element of truth. What might happen on the Danube border now, especially now; following on from the massacre of the imperial cohort, there was no organised force to oppose raiding and no support could be expected from Vitalian's army, now wholly intent on another objective.

'Serve them right,' was his sharp opinion, when he outlined the risks to the citizenry of Dorostorum. 'They should have held to their bond.'

'Trouble is, Master Flavius,' Ohannes responded, 'it is not the guilty who will pay.'

Dardanies cut across what looked about to become a lament. 'If I have not said it before, Ohannes, I say it now. It is time to drop the tag of master and start addressing our young friend as Flavius. You put him at risk every time you address him so.'

'Habit,' the Scythian replied, in a grumpy tone.

'A bad one can get you killed.'

'What will do for me is all this marching,' the old man said, rubbing at his shoulders, then easing his knees. 'Every bone I possess aches.'

Flavius laid a concerned hand on the man's back, his voice carrying the same tone. 'Then, since we are under no one's command, let us rest awhile.'

Leaving the road was not immediate; they waited until they spied a fallen tree trunk big enough to use as a communal seat, Ohannes being strong in his belief that if he was to sit on the ground they would struggle to raise him up again. Before they ate some of their provisions the old man disappeared into the woods at their rear to relieve himself, leaving Dardanies and Flavius alone.

'You are fond of him, are you not?'

'As was my father, and he saved my life, so why would I not be?'

'Odd that,' Dardanies smiled, 'he told me you saved his.'

'He exaggerates, I acted by instinct and if it aided him it was by chance.'

'I have observed you are much given to modesty.'

'Honesty is the word I would prefer.'

The return of Ohannes did for that conversation and after he joined them the three sat eating, which curtailed much in the way of talking, this as a stream of men passed them by, few with any interest. On a hot day and feeling far enough away from recognition Flavius fretted at still wearing the cowl, which he eased back as much as he dared, while tending to gaze at the ground before his feet, constantly checking himself for that which he could not help, looking up as some fellow on the road called out to another.

To say Flavius was troubled was well off the mark, for he had a whole cart of worries, and not just his present preoccupations. Would his mother, once she received the news of the death of her husband and sons, do as he had asked and await his arrival, or would she rush back to the family home? He felt the need to prevent her, given the strong possibility her welcome and treatment wouldn't be any different from that envisaged for him, though Senuthius would need to be careful how he treated her.

If his father had been less than wholly popular through the needs of his responsibilities, she had been the reverse and was held, particularly by the poor of the city, in high regard, due to her selfless consideration for their welfare. To accuse her of sorcery would surely not be believed by folk whose illnesses she had medicated and whose poverty she had worked tirelessly to relieve.

That thought checked him; who would believe that anyone in his household had indulged in pagan rites? No one with eyes to see or a brain to think, but a mob fired up by lies and fed with free wine was of a different nature. Senuthius would expend gold to damn anyone named Belisarius, and Blastos would use his office to aid him!

If that was not an immediate dilemma, it would become that once they reached Marcianopolis, where there was another *via publica* that joined that city to the main road west, the *Via Egnatia*, which would take him to Illyricum and in doing so impose a choice. What would his mother want him to do, seek out the imperial commission and go with them to Dorostorum or look to her security? He was looking at his own feet once more, thinking that she would insist on the former, when another pair appeared.

'Can you spare a bite, friends?'

To avoid looking up was impossible. The man

214

before them, with a spear in his hand, a sword at his waist and a plain leather breastplate on his chest, was clearly a one-time soldier, covered in dust, as were the trio he was addressing. With the butt of the spear shaft resting on the ground he was leaning on it in a way that indicated he was as weary as Ohannes, who was the one who replied.

'Been on the march long, brother?'

There was a pause, as if he found the question obtrusive. 'All the way from Axiupolis.'

It seemed the name of that city made no sense to Dardanies, but Flavius knew it lay well to the east of Dorostorum, it being the nearest fortified town in that direction, as would Ohannes. Many times his father had gone there to confer with his opposite and equally under-strength counterpart and mull over their difficulties.

'That's many a league,' Flavius replied.

'And many more to go, I think.'

'Not as many as you have behind you, friend; Marcianopolis will be not much more than another day's march.'

Flavius was wondering why Ohannes was growling, but he was in no position to enquire as the fellow spoke again, the expression implying he was impressed. 'You know the road well?'

'Well enough,' Flavius responded. He looked around, to the sound of the old man growling even louder. 'Are you on your own?'

'I was with a party, but I seem to have got separated.' He smiled, showing broken teeth. 'Too much time spent talking to others on the path to salvation, but I can catch up with them if I have

215

the strength to put my best foot forward.'

'Have some bread and wine, then,' Dardanies said.

He held out a torn piece of his own round of bread. Ohannes immediately proffered his wine flask and the man drank from it with the requisite constraint, not consuming too much. Still chewing he wiped his sleeve across his face before speaking again.

'Why, that is kind of you, I feel right restored.'

'Glad to provide for a fellow Christian.'

'And where have you come from?'

Flavius was about to reply when Ohannes spoke to cut him off. 'What matters where we all hail from, friend? It is the cause in which we make our way that matters.'

'True enough, brother, true enough.' A hand went to the soft cap on his head in a sort of salute. 'Well, I say God's blessings upon you and I will be heading on – with luck and your kindly sustenance I will come upon my comrades.'

'You should not have spoken so freely,' Ohannes hissed, as soon as the man was out of earshot. 'And happen you should not have spoken at all!'

'In what way do you mean?'

'What lad your age, and at best a labourer, speaks educated as you do, has knowledge of the roads of the province, as well as how far it is to Axiupolis and can tell how far we still have to go to the general's meeting place?'

'Any number of folk know that, and you must have gone there with my father!'

'I take leave to say they do not,' the old man insisted, before addressing Dardanies, sat on the

216

other side of Flavius. 'You heard of Axiupolis?'

That got a shake of the head and a shrugged reply from the Sklaveni. 'What's done is done. Can you be certain talking to that fellow is a risk of any sort?'

'Likely not,' Ohannes replied, though he seemed far from mollified. 'But best not to take a chance, best to keep a tight lip.'

'You worry too much,' Flavius murmured, his resentment at being checked obvious.

'Thank the Lord someone has the sense to!'

As they had sat eating the air had grown heavy, as clouds rolled in from the north-west to first cover the sun, trapping the summer heat, then to thicken and darken, which was enough to let all know they were in for a downpour, and soon the first roll of thunder came rumbling to their ears and that meant lightning. With every post house full to bursting and likely to get even busier there was scant chance of shelter.

If it was known to be unsafe to shelter under a tree in such circumstances there was mutual agreement that it was better than standing out in the open and being lashed with rain. The clouds were turning black now and the thunder was regular, soon followed by the first visible flash of lightning cracking brightly across the sky.

'Oh, for a shield,' Ohannes called, 'best thing going to keep your head dry.'

'I have heard men being struck on the boss by lightning and killed,' Flavius said, as the first drops of rain began to fall, large enough to bounce off the paving blocks from which the road was constructed.

'Who's to say it would not have done for them anyway.'

Dardanies had his sword out and was heading for the trees. 'Time to build a shelter.'

Once into the woods, he began to slash at the thinner branches of the trees, soon aided by the others, who knew what he was about, just as they knew they had left it late to act. It was not long before they had a frame of sorts as well as the evergreen foliage with which to cover it, under which they could take shelter even if they were damp by the time it was up.

They sat huddled within this as the rain beat down, much of it caught in the trees above, yet enough falling to drip through their canopy and all the while the heavens rumbled and spat. To peer out was to see bolts of heavenly fire striking the ground, while all around the noise of thunder assailed them and the wind the storm whipped up had those under cover grabbing parts of their makeshift shelter to keep it in place.

'Those are my gods speaking,' Dardanies said. 'It might do you well to listen.'

'Never did much take to anyone shouting, divine or otherwise,' Ohannes hooted, 'an' who would want to bow their head to such a temper?'

Flavius thought it politic to say nothing, especially when he saw the way the Sklaveni took the old man's jest; it was not well received. So there they sat in silence until the sounds began to fade as the storm moved on, the rain easing until it eventually stopped. They stepped out to find steam rising from the paving, water dripping from the trees and the air still heavy and damp, with grey clouds filling the sky.

Others, who had taken similar shelter, began to emerge and if they were to a man far from dry, neither were they too concerned; it was summertime in a part of the world where clothing could dry out quickly, the only concern Flavius expressed being that the delay made it unlikely they would make the military camp near Marcianopolis before darkness.

'Though we should keep going as long as we can, even after dark.'

'Not with all that cloud,' Dardanies contended. 'Won't be able to see hand before our face when the light goes.'

All around them parties of men were settling down for the night, disappearing into the deeper woods looking for timber still dry enough to make a fire, kindling being no problem. Flints were being plied to the small mound of still-dry leaf mould that would be the first to flame, they carried on as the light faded and the road emptied.

'Can't go much further than this,' Ohannes said, holding up a hand to show that it was barely visible. 'Let's make camp.'

CHAPTER SIXTEEN

It was not the dawn chorus of birds that woke Flavius, but the point of a knife at his throat, in a light so dim that he could not make out the face of the man holding it, even as he leant forward to

219

whisper in his ear, telling him to stay still and say nothing. The threat that others would die in their sleep if he did not was enough to ensure silence. Two things registered: the smell of stale wine on the fellow's breath and the fact that, having chosen to sleep quite a distance from his companions – really from the snoring of Ohannes – he had rendered himself vulnerable.

The free hand grabbed his smock and hauled him into a sitting position, before it was laid on his back to push, a signal to stand up, which he did, all the time with the cold steel pressing on his flesh. The cowl with which he had covered his head was used now as a drag to get him away from his companions, this as shadowy shapes now emerged from behind trees to surround him.

'What do you want?' he croaked.

'You, Flavius Belisarius.'

It was still warm, even in the predawn, yet he felt a chill at the use of the name and that induced silence without the need to be told to maintain it. More hands were on him now, as if seeking part possession of his being as he was hustled deep into the woods, so deep that if the light was increasing it was barely doing so here.

'Who are you?' he asked eventually, trying a louder tone.

'Can't you guess?' came the reply, likewise no longer a whisper, which was worrying for it established how far he was from any hope of rescue. 'We were the fellows who tipped you off that horse of yours, and those two black eyes, even if they are near to faded now, were a sure sign to any with eyes to see. Not many youngsters on the road south, even fewer with such marks on their face, who can't keep from looking up time to time.'

'Couldn't help showing away, either, could you?' said another, more authoritative voice. 'Telling me how far I had come and what was left to go in that high-born Latin of yours, as if one of your years and a *rusticus* would know of such things.'

'You are in the employ of Vicinus?'

'Were, but the smell of coin was stronger with Vitalian. Hankered to visit Constantinople again too, only this time to come away with something to show for it instead of an empty belly. No need now, the senator will pay handsome for you, and why bother to weary ourselves marching or fighting?'

The man reached out and detached the purse Flavius still wore on his belt, smiling as he tossed it and weighed it in his hand. 'We even have a ready reward here, not much of one, I'll grant, but it will pay our way in wine and food when we head back north.'

There was a moment when Flavius considered appealing to their Christian principles, only to put that aside. These would be men of a stripe that Ohannes had spoken of, ex-soldiers who had taken service with Senuthius because that was where they could employ their skills in a time of peace; they had set off to join General Vitalian with nothing but plunder in mind, so what came out was an expression of his desperation.

'My friends will search for me.'

'Only to find your body if they get too close, boy, for Senuthius would like you alive but he will take a corpse if that's all we can provide. Now shut up and walk.'

Which they did for some time, and in silence, until they reached and began to cross a small clearing, providing light enough for Flavius to see that he had five men – they were no longer mere shadows – to contend with, not that he had any notion of how he was going to do that. They were armed, he was not, his sword and spear now lying where he had left them, beside the rough wood frame he had made so he could sleep off the still-damp ground.

He was not yet fully a man and they were armed, were bound to have experience and certainly had the muscle to defeat any attempt he made to overcome them. How could they have crept up on him so easily when he should have been safe? If he was apart from Dardanies and Ohannes the whole edge of the forest was dotted with like-minded souls sleeping off the toils of the previous day. That lifted his spirits just a little, for though he had been taken captive he was a long way from Dorostorum and the way back was on a road full of folk to whom he might be able to appeal.

It was as if the leader, always supposing he was that, read his mind, for he spun Flavius to look him in the face, revealing himself as the fellow to whom bread and wine had been gifted the day before.

'We need to stay here until the road clears, a day or two happen, so I will tell you now that we are going to remain in this forest. Your mind will be set on notions of escape, so I say put them away, for any one of us will kill you if you try.'

'Hard to carry a body all the way back to Dorostorum.'

That got a cackled laugh. 'Your head will do.'

'Best tie him up, Nepo, and lash him to a tree for he is strong for his years. If he runs he'll be a bugger to catch.'

'Had that in mind, didn't I,' came the abrasive reply; it was a voice that hinted at annoyance. 'You think me as dense as you?'

'Just suggesting,' came the quick rejoinder, in a tone designed to deflect any offence that had obviously been taken.

With a mind acute to any possibilities, Flavius registered that: the fear the man had of the one he called Nepo, added to the response from a fellow who did not worry if he offended in turn. There was something, too, in the way the others did not look at Nepo as if fearing to catch his eye and perhaps the edge of his temper. If there was any respect there was unlikely to be any love and perhaps that was something he could exploit.

Not that such a feeling lasted; they had made a makeshift camp on the far side of the clearing, rough-framed cots similar to the one on which he had slept, and the pile of wood they had gathered and laid off the ground to keep it dry hinted at their intention to stay put for some time. There were dead birds and a couple of rabbits hanging from a branch, so they had food too, as well as the ability to set snares for more; these men, experienced at living off the land and in a forest full of game – he assumed there had to be water somewhere nearby – could stay here for an age if they felt they had to.

Pushed against a gnarled tree, one with several growths rising from a very wide stump, his hands were hauled round to the back and lashed together on one of the thinner trunks. There was no need for such a constraint to be tight – it only had to be secure enough to make it impossible for him to untie – so at least he could still feel his fingers, for which he was grateful.

Slowly Flavius eased himself down to the base of that sapling till he was sitting, his eyes alert as his captors went about their tasks, looking for anything that might gift him an opportunity, while fighting the waves of despair with which he was assailed, countering these with silent prayer. He had got clear of the clutches of Senuthius once; surely there would be a chance to do so again.

Nepo was clearly the leader, established by the way he set errands for the rest, sending them to check the snares they had reset before nightfall, or to gather more wood, not hard in an age-old woodland with much decaying timber on the ground, this while he barely moved, instead helping himself to wine from a skin that went regularly to his mouth. There was no need to light a fire, it being summer; that would only be set during daylight hours in order to cook, and like he had seen done by Ohannes, it would be smothered and extinguished as soon as that task had been completed. At night it would be used to keep at bay any animal or human threats.

Would they untie him to allow him to feed himself? And if they did could he make a run for it and hope to outdistance a spear cast at his back? What were his chances of getting hold of one of

224

the weapons they carried, which had to be set aside to allow them to carry out the tasks set by Nepo? All of these thoughts rushed through his mind, one tumbling notion after another, the only one he was quick to discard being any appeal to clemency.

Listening to their talk did not bring comfort, concentrating as it did, even if it was disjointed, on the rewards that Senuthius would grant them for the youngster and how they would spend it. This seemed to encompass drink and women, they being very partial to the former – Nepo was not alone in employing the wineskin, for none seemed able to pass it without helping themselves to a wet.

When not talking of drink and carnal pleasures they indulged in much speculation, increasingly ghoulish and seemingly a source of much raucous humour, of the various tortures the senator might visit upon him, all of them severe, and how he would squeal when they were applied, the increasingly outrageous opinions causing much laughter, this listened to by Flavius in silence, though his thoughts were far from sanguine. Could he create some kind of diversion that might get him free?

'How long have you been employed by the senator?' he asked Nepo.

'What's it to you?'

'I wonder if you trust him.'

That got another of Nepo's barking laughs, enough to tell Flavius he was doing the same up a useless tree.

'No need – when he does not pay us in hard coin he lets us loose to plunder and is handsome with his rewards when we cross the river to take

Sklaveni slaves.'

'Hard copper coin, I suppose?' Flavius asked. 'Should be gold, given his prosperity.'

'Matters not the colour, as long as there is enough,' Nepo responded, lifting the wineskin to his lips.

'He robbed you during that Hun raid, did he not, if you think of the captives you might have taken? He held back the militia and you, his own fighters, just so he could see my father and my brothers dead.'

'Worked, then,' came the reply, through a sleeve wiping at wet lips. 'As you that set them alight know.'

'Does it not occur to you to ask why he would do that, sacrifice the whole imperial cohort?'

'Why would it? Senator's business is his and as long as he treats us right...'

'I can tell you why. There's an imperial commission on the way from the capital to look into his crimes – it may well be there at this very moment.'

That got him an amused look. 'So?'

'So maybe by the time you get me back to Dorostorum, Senuthius will be in no position to reward you for handing me in. It might be his body hanging and rotting above the city gates and not mine.'

'Have to hope the beam holds then, won't we, him bein' such a weight.'

'And if they come along too late for me and examine what you have done at his bidding, they might just take the rope to you.'

'Enough!' Nepo snarled, his mood of humour

evaporating. 'If you don't stop wittering on about what can only be tall-tale telling, I'll have you gagged.'

'They will draw and quarter you, as well,' Flavius shouted, his voice desperate, 'all of you, if you harm me.'

Nepo got to his feet and turned away to shout to his companions, going about their allotted tasks, the wineskin swinging in his hand, head back and his call seemingly aimed at the higher branches of the trees.

'Hear that lads, we are all for the butcher's table...'

If he had intended to say more that was made impossible by the near removal of his head. The blade on the pollarding tool was serrated and as sharp as any sword, so it ripped through Nepo's gullet as if it were an overripe pear. Flavius had barely registered the way the shaft had been employed, only seeing it at the point where the end made deadly contact.

The sounds from around the perimeter of the clearing went from loud shouts of alarm to screams, some of severe pain, one a plea for mercy, swiftly cut short. The man who stepped out from behind the tree to which he had been tied did not look at Flavius until it had all gone quiet.

'Bassus!' he cried, just as Dardanies appeared from the side of the clearing, then Ohannes, both with blood dripping off their swords, this while someone cut his hands free. Falling forward onto his knees – he had been straining at his bonds – he found himself looking into the dead eyes of Nepo, staring from a head that had ended up near to his feet.

'God be praised,' said the man who had killed him, crossing himself, this as Flavius began to weep tears of relief. 'We must say prayers and thank him for your deliverance.'

Which the whole party did, all nine kneeling to say thanks to God, Bassus employing a deep bass voice to call on his maker and theirs. No attention was given to the souls of those departed and neither were they moved from where they had fallen, merely stripped of their arms and any armour, which would now adorn the men Bassus led, and divested of their clothes to look for concealed valuables, Flavius's purse being returned. When they departed, the rabbits and dead birds went with them.

The cadavers remained, food for creatures of the forest.

'I think the Lord knows he owes you some good fortune,' Ohannes said, as they made their way back to the highway. 'For it needed his hand to see this done.'

Having woken to find Flavius gone, they had assumed he had just wandered off to relieve himself, the truth only dawning when he failed to return. That he was absent for any time without his weapons and his still-sacking-wrapped breastplate, as well as his bag of documents, led to a search of the nearby ground and that showed evidence to a hunting man like Dardanies of many feet having trodden down the leaf mould.

By the time they had concluded that Flavius must have been abducted – and there could be only one cause in which that would happen – the roadway was once more full of those making their way south. Amongst the throng were Bassus and his original band of five companions, they being more than willing to take part in a search for folk Ohannes informed them were rabid Monophysites, working for an evil bishop of the same persuasion.

Nepo and his companions had been careless too; following the previous day's rain, which had dampened the forest floor even under the highest trees, they left sections of trail fresh enough to follow, although with many a break that had the searchers casting around to pick it up again. When it came to closing in, Nepo and his men made that easy: they were far from as alert as they should have been, trusting in the security of the deep forest and thinking there was only a pair of companions with any interest in rescue, a number they could deal with. At the very last his rescuers had been able to close in the last few paces before beginning the killing without worrying overmuch about noise.

'I got to the back of that tree without being seen, young fellow,' Bassus said, patting his ample stomach to indicate that the width of the multiple growths had hidden even him from view. 'That heretic I killed was too busy with his wineskin to keep a proper watch, and the rest, well he took their eye with his bellowing.'

'Heretic?'

'Your companion Ohannes told me he was that and are we not on our way to put such vipers in their place? If only we could have done the same for the apostate who sent them.'

'I told him of the nature of our bishop,' Ohannes added quickly.

'They will not be reasoned out of their foolishness,' Bassus boomed, 'and that leaves only one way to damn their creed. They are no better than pagans.'

'You would kill them too?' Flavius asked.

'I would give them a chance to come to God, but if they refused his blessing, well...'

Dardanies had the good sense to cross himself when he heard those words, though if his expression looked pious to the likes of Bassus, Flavius knew better. In time he managed to sidle over to Ohannes while also distancing himself from Bassus, the point to be made in whispers that it was dangerous for the Sklaveni to stay with them; it was time for him to depart.

Separating from Bassus and his band would be impossible now and for Dardanies to remain in company was to risk his true beliefs being discovered, Flavius sure that even facing death he would not accept the Eucharist. Expecting an argument, he and Ohannes were pleased when, having got enough distance away from prying ears and stopped for what should be the last night before joining Vitalian's host, Dardanies concurred.

'Though I was tempted to stay with you all the way to Constantinople, which must be a sight to see. Perhaps one day...'

'You would not believe the evidence of your own eyes if you gazed upon it,' Ohannes replied.

'How will you depart?' Flavius asked.

230

'Easy in such a crowd, which will grow greater the closer we get to the camp of your *foederati*. I will get lost among them, then slip away and do what that fellow Nepo intended, stay hidden in the woods until the road returns to normal and a man can go north without being questioned as to his faith.'

'Then I should give you my thanks now.'

'Mine also,' said Ohannes.

'And I should give you back your second purse.'

'You may need it, so keep it.'

Dardanies shook his head and pressed the small skin sack into the hand of Flavius. 'You will need it more.'

'You're a good man, Dardanies, hard as you try to come across as being not so.'

'The gods forbid we should meet north of the Danube – I might give you cause to change your mind.'

'You still have not told us why you accepted such a task as this.'

That got Flavius a jaundiced look. 'Does it matter?'

'To me, yes.'

As he sat on the other side of a fire, the flames caught the Sklaveni's eyes and there was in them a sort of sadness. Given he stayed silent so did the others, for it seemed to speak would not get him to open up, quite the reverse, so they waited while he considered his response, Flavius wondering if he was considering giving one at all.

'It was a punishment,' Dardanies said finally.

'For what?' Flavius demanded, which got a glare from Ohannes, a clear indication to shut up

231

and let the man take his own time, which he did, not speaking again for what seemed like an age, the light from the fire reddening his cheeks.

'It was I who encouraged members of my tribe to join in with the Huns, I who led them across the river.' The eyes were focused on the fire now, the expression fixed, as if the memories were unpleasant. 'When your father got between us and the river, I thought we were doomed, thought of the family I would never see again...'

'But you were not.'

'I could not fathom the way the Hun leaders behaved, for they did not panic when they could see plainly they were trapped. Instead they went about their task of killing the imperial cohort as if there were no militia within ten leagues to threaten them.'

Ohannes interjected, clearly confused. 'If they did not panic, why did they kill those they had taken captive too?'

The eyes lifted and looked right at Flavius. 'The Huns were not there to take slaves, they had no need of them and they had always intended to just kill rather than capture.'

'In the name of God, why?'

Dardanies paused for a long time and when he spoke it was slowly, deliberately and with a sense of discomfiture. 'They had been well rewarded beforehand.'

Flavius experienced a cold feeling in the pit of his stomach as Dardanies spoke on, describing the way they had prepared for the raid and executed it, for he knew that if the Huns had been paid to undertake it there was only one person with the means and the need.

'Senuthius bribed them, in many pounds of gold I suspect, to come through our lands and cross the river. The Huns knew we would be unable to prevent it without much loss of life, so they asked for passage and gave us solemn promises not to trouble any of our people. They even handed over hostages who would forfeit their lives as a sign of good faith, so it was agreed to let them pass. A troubled Rome is better for our safety than one susceptible to raid themselves.'

'It seems they came only to kill my father!'

'If I know that now, we, the Sklaveni, did not beforehand.'

'When did you guess the truth?' asked a damp-eyed Flavius.

'Once back on our side of the river the Huns were eager to boast, if not to share any of the senator's gold.'

'That man is Lucifer,' Ohannes moaned.

'I asked you before if you took part in the killing of my family and I ask you again.'

'And I said no, just as I told you if the opportunity had been put before me I would not have hesitated.'

'What about this journey we are on?'

'I found myself out of favour with the tribal elders for allying myself to the Huns, but what disturbed them more was what had happened to your father, the only man on the other bank in whom they had any trust.' The voice hardened. 'Not that the trust was boundless, you understand, but they believe we cannot fight Rome, that to exist alongside the empire in a sort of peace is the best for which the tribe can hope.'

'You do not?'

'I did not,' he sighed, 'maybe now I do.'

CHAPTER SEVENTEEN

As good as his word, Dardanies disappeared the following day, with no more words exchanged, even easier than Flavius had supposed, given the increasingly crowded nature of the road on which they were travelling. If there was only one major highway, it had a large number of less well-maintained tributaries, *viae rusticae*, and from these volunteers were filtering in to swell the numbers.

Abreast of another government *mansio* Flavius once more quizzed the man who guarded the gate, a fellow even less forthcoming than his predecessor, probably due to his irritation at the number of men begging him for either a bite of food or a drink, many of the volunteers now without any means of sustenance. Thus the bribe had to be larger, which was a waste given the response was just as negative; there was no sign of this F. Petrus Sabbatius!

The encounter left the youngster with his thoughts, even more troubled now than hitherto, the information that had been imparted to him by Dardanies gnawing at his innards, his imaginings filled with punishments of increasing bloodiness to be visited upon Senuthius, none of which seemed to be enough to satisfy his anger.

The why was a point simple to conjecture with; the how, when he thought on it, eluded him for he was on the wing, letting circumstance carry him forward without any clear idea of where it would lead. The notion that they should find a way to detach themselves from this mass of believers and extract his vengeance foundered on one question: to where would he and Ohannes go that would advance his cause?

To seek to get back to Dorostorum without the presence of this Sabbatius and those with him was too dangerous to contemplate, and Flavius had no idea how far they had yet progressed from the capital – all he knew was that logic demanded they should be on this road. And there was another consideration: would they seek to continue on their task in the face of Vitalian's declared rebellion? Ohannes doubted it.

'If I was them an' got a sniff of this, I would set my horses for the Bosphorus and use the whip too.'

'General Vitalian might let them pass through.'

'In a pig's ear, Master Flavius – they come on the business of Anastasius so the least he would do is hold them, worst he might cut off their heads.'

Frustration made Flavius lash out. 'Can you not think of anything to say that might bring me cheer?'

'You're alive, be grateful for that,' came the gruff response, before the old man nodded and added, 'Bit of a hold-up on the horizon.'

They were making a final approach to the encampment to which Vitalian had called for his co-religionists to assemble. Instead of a flow of

235

bodies it now became a sort of jostle, then a heaving near-stationary mass, the cause only established when they finally made it to the camp entrance.

There some of the general's officers were trying to sort out and direct to the right place those arriving, particularly trying to assess who had the right kind of weapons, as well as single out any who might have previous soldiering experience, set against peasants fired by religious fervour and armed with every kind of farming tool that could double as something to fight with; such people had a purpose as numbers, but as soldiers they would be a military asset of questionable value.

'Do we want this, Master Flavius?' Ohannes asked. 'For there is little time to decide.'

Flavius had gnawed on that problem every time they passed a *milus* stone; now he was being forced into a decision: the source of his hopes and his only chance of justice for his family lay in either Constantinople or those who had been sent from there to undertake an enquiry. If Vitalian was going to force the emperor to change his religious edict that could only be done by force, which meant marching on the capital.

'So it is in that direction we must go, Ohannes, and hope that somewhere we will meet up with those we need to aid us.'

'Hard to get clear once you join an army and painful if you're caught.'

'Then tell me how we can get past this point and carry on ourselves?'

That got a shake of the head. 'Even less safe, happen.'

236

'Then we are, as we have been for a time now, in the lap of God's mercy.'

'Amen to that.'

Even with his years and thanks to his very obvious sword and spear – Flavius was sure his bad haircut had an effect too – Ohannes was spotted as a potential warrior. Questioned, he was quick to relate his military service and since he would not be parted from Flavius and he was equally armed, both were directed to the area set aside to form up proper units, centuries in the old Roman pattern that the leaders hoped might be able to perform like a proper army.

The shouting and the swishing of the short *flagellum* reminded Flavius of the vine saplings employed like whips by the men who had sought to train him and his friends in arms. But now he was under a breed of a different stripe; those issuing orders were tall and muscular, very fair of hair, with striking blue eyes and light skin that tended to peel, or at least go very red, in the sun, added to various adornments about their person of gold and silver.

'Gautoi, I reckon,' Ohannes informed his young charge, when he had examined them closely, adding that they had come down from the north in the last few years, providing a new source of mercenaries for the empire. 'Worse than Germans, I hear.'

The Gautoi claimed kinship to that race, but came from a land separated from Germania proper by a large inland sea. Flavius was thrown back on his histories, to recall from his studies that all the tribes north of the Rhine tended to be numerous and formidable as enemies. The fate of Varus in the Teutoburger Wald was still told to frighten children. In that deep forest, during the reign of the Emperor Augustus, three of his legions had completely disappeared along with their eagles, every legionary assumed to be horribly mutilated or burnt alive in wicker baskets.

Since those far-off days the Rhine had been breached time and again and Gaul overrun, though each barbarian incursion eventually led to settlement. The Ostrogoths, another Germanic tribe, had, halfway through the last century, over-run the old Roman provinces of Italy, which Constantinople had feared lost to the empire for good.

After much bloodletting, a chieftain called Theodoric had taken power. He proved to be an admirer of the Roman way of life and, independent merely because of distance and a lack of any desire for reconquest, he had taken up residence in the imperial palace in Ravenna. Then he sent to the previous Emperor Zeno a message to acknowledge that he acted only as an imperial subject; in short, he did not claim the title of Western Emperor.

'Don't like 'em much, whatever German band they come from,' Ohannes added, when this was recounted to him, the fate of parts of the empire not something to hitherto trouble his thoughts. 'But, by the Lord, can they fight!'

'Which we might see evidence of,' Flavius crowed happily, receiving from his companion a jaundiced look when he added, 'Maybe we'll get a chance to test our skills against them.'

He then found himself looking into the face of

one who had come close and it was not friendly. The blond hair under the man's helmet was plaited and hanging either side of a face dominated by a huge moustache of the same colour, while the glare he was emitting left the youngster in no doubt that he would happily employ his whip. He barked something in what presumably passed for Latin amongst these mercenaries, but it made no sense to the people at whom it was aimed, which made the fellow, already red-faced, go puce and start bellowing and gesturing with flailing arms.

'Think he wants us to form up,' snorted Ohannes, making no attempt to hide his amusement.

This led to a great deal of shuffling as the group of which they were part sought to get themselves into some form of order. Partly achieving this task, revealed to them a person of higher rank, evidenced by the nature of his good-quality apparel, his fine helmet and, most of all, his chest armour, a breastplate decorated in much the same fashion as that of Flavius, though the devices were different. He also had a thin, leather-covered baton, edged with gold top and bottom.

A strong arm took hold of Flavius and pushed him to and fro until he was level with the man on his left, the Scythian getting an appreciative nod as he got himself in line on his own and helped others to do likewise. That occasioned a call to the finely clad fellow who had to be in command and he stepped over to stand before Ohannes, asking him where he was from and, if he was an ex-soldier, with whom he had served.

Flavius listened to a list of campaigns and generals under whom the old soldier had fought until finally Ohannes mouthed the name of his father. The sound of that, rarely mentioned in these last days, had the youngster hanging his head and working hard to hold back the tears, while at the same time wishing that his companion had kept that information to himself.

Then he heard Ohannes say, 'As fine an officer as I ever served under, sadly no longer with us.'

'I am minded to elevate certain people to the rank of *decanus*,' the officer said in clear and good Latin. 'You are clearly a man of experience...'

'And years, Your Honour, happen too many to be leading others.'

'Let us see how this century forms up, but I have marked you.'

The tip of the baton was used to lift Flavius's chin and when his head came up he found himself looking into the unblinking glare of someone who probably matched his late brother Cassius in age, with smooth features and penetrating blue eyes, the question that followed a demand to be told the youngster's background.

'I am the son of a soldier,' he replied, in what he hoped was a less elevated argot than that he had been taught to speak by his pedagogue Beppolenus, holding his breath until that got a nod. 'Dead now.'

Expecting to be asked to explain further, Flavius was grateful when no enquiry followed; he did not want his identity to be known. He had half turned away when another question occurred and he spun back. 'Can you ride?'

'No,' Flavius replied.

'Pity, we are in dire need of cavalry.'

'Why do you lie?' Ohannes asked in a whisper, when the officer had moved off and was far enough away to not hear.

'I want to stay close to you.'

That required no explanation and nor did the *flagellum* that struck Flavius's arm, followed by the barely comprehensible instruction to stop talking. The blow delivered, the moustached face was thrust forward to gloat over the reaction caused by the pain, only to look confused by what came back from a pair of eyes nearly free from the blemishes that had disfigured them. Flavius gave him a stare of total blankness, which he held as the sapling was lifted again – his attitude was clearly being seen as defiance – but no blow followed, for the intended recipient did not flinch.

In an established military encampment the units of ex-soldiers and those who had their own weapons were allotted proper huts in which to sleep and to store their possessions. The rest were put into tents, which was less of a problem than it might have been given the weather was dry, as was the ground after a day of sun.

Most important of all they were fed, Vitalian having lopped off the head of the *magister militum* – the man who had delivered the message from Anastasius cutting off his rations – and purloined his treasury in order to buy food to supply his putative army as well as pay them. An added tax on landowners in Moesia was imposed so he could continue to do so, as well as distribute small sums to his new recruits: if many might have come for

241

religious reasons others had not, and they would not stay without some kind of reward.

To say the camp was in chaos was an understatement; for every man present who was aware of the basics there were ten *rustica* who had no idea. As the head of an established fighting force Vitalian had good men capable of issuing instructions but pitifully few able to obey them, added to which, fired only by religious fervour, these farm and field labourers were not of the type to respond to the harsh discipline necessary to make them truly effective.

'Such numbers will look good at a distance.'

'Not, Ohannes,' came the mordant reply from Flavius, 'if the men examining us have good eyesight.'

They too had been drilled, but with a tenth of their century having served before, old habits came back and others had at least the wit to follow their lead, so if they were bellowed at it was with instructions to march this way or that, to wheel as a body, to form various combinations in which they would be deployed to fight, added to the method by which, should they be forced to retire, they could do so in good order.

There was no training in actual fighting, mock combat, which came as a severe disappointment to Flavius, added to which he was beginning to get frustrated at the time it was taking for Vitalian to move; he needed to be on the road. Halfway through the several days this drilling took, Ohannes was given the rank of *decanus*, responsible for seven plus himself.

If what he commanded was less than perfect,

Vitalian knew how to inspire even the rabble, this evidenced when all were called before the oration platform, in front of which he had lined up his formidable-looking *foederati*, to be told that soon they would march on the capital and give the emperor a choice of two outcomes: either he would have to reverse his position on Chalcedon or face being deposed and thrown to the mob in the Hippodrome. The cheer this received was loud enough to chase every bird in the region away from nest and perch.

It was instructive to observe the reality of a military organisation as opposed to that of which Flavius had so copiously read. In recounting the nature of successful campaigns, historians, even when they were in personal command, never referred to the toil visited upon the common soldier. They wrote of manoeuvres and battles as if those involved were mere fodder to their ambition, nothing more than an asset to be employed.

Camp life at the level at which he was living was very different and he had to suppose that once they moved the obvious lack of overall cohesion in the host must get worse. Flavius saw the sense of Vitalian sticking to the Roman model of organisation, which had the advantage of simplicity for a range of recruits who would struggle to adopt the way the empire was now restructuring its army; his father, given the number of men he led, had stuck to the description 'cohort' and the title 'centurion' when it had long gone out of use in the main imperial forces.

He was also acutely aware of the change in

243

Ohannes in the coming days; for a man who claimed he had been short on obedience himself and who had been reluctant to take promotion, he came down hard on any of his *contubernium* who showed any inclination to question his orders. He wanted the barracks clean and the men who served under him that too.

'Don't go getting used to this, which is comfort,' he growled. 'It will be tents once we are on the march and nowhere to shit either. We cook our own grub and keep ourselves up to the mark, for I have no craving to feel the centurion's rod if any of you lot are slack.'

And that eventually came to pass, as it had to, for endless time was not a luxury Vitalian could afford. There had already been desertions, either through a loss of desire to continue or a hatred of discipline and the punishment that went with it. So finally they marched, and if those at the head, the mostly German and Gautoi *foederati*, both mounted and on foot, looked impressive, what came in their wake did not. The better centuries marched in reasonable order but, still armed with that which they had brought from their farms, the *rustica* looked and were a motley horde.

Worse was their inability to carry out swiftly and effectively the very necessary tasks that must be performed when setting up a temporary camp after the first day. Tents had to be erected and in regular lines all centred round the general's headquarters. Each century had to dig a latrine fit to serve the eighty men in the unit, and that was often a cause of dispute, as was whose turn had come to fetch the food as well as who should gather the wood to cook it.

When it came to guard duty – which, outside those before his own quarters Vitalian quite wisely left to those bodies of men he thought he could trust, while sparing and favouring his barbarian *foederati* – Flavius and his ilk found themselves lumbered with more of that than was strictly their due. But there were other evenings when the duty fell elsewhere, allowing a small amount of freedom to do other things: look for friends in other units, find the leather workers and see to repairs of footwear or scrounge for extra food.

For Flavius, given they were now marching down the main imperial highway, the *Via Gemina,* and they always camped somewhere within walking distance of some reasonable-sized habitat, a town or a large village, it gave him a chance to go and ask his most pressing question. In Debellum they had camped around a proper citadel, it being a city, and so he took to wandering the streets and that was when the name of F. Petrus Sabbatius registered.

It only raised his hopes for no more than a few seconds; the man who answered in the affirmative, if he did not know what the imperial envoys were about, did know that when the city was told of Vitalian's rebellion they headed south, not north. They were on their way back to Constantinople and it was a glum Flavius who returned to the camp that night, to toss and turn, seeking to decide what to do.

'Continue as we have,' was what he said to Ohannes in the morning, as they bathed in the lake that abutted the city. 'What choice do I have?'

Progress, which was laid down at five leagues a day, proved near to impossible and the mustered force lost much potency through the inability of many of the peasant levies to keep up the pace. As a positive, the further south they went, they were greeted as they passed through any town by crowds wishing to bless their cause, although the gifts of food and wine did nothing to speed progress; the combined factor of both often had them trying to make camp after sunset instead of the full light of day.

'Seen it all before, Flavius,' Ohannes would say, when some act of insubordination or stupidity was obvious enough to be observed. 'Including being showered with flowers and kisses. Same lot will hurl curses and stones at you if you have to fall back.'

It amused Flavius, the way the old man now addressed him: he seemed to have taken to his rank and was more than happy to no longer address his young friend as a superior being. Not that he was hard on the lad, able to take the joke with which Flavius responded, that if Ohannes laid on with too much chastisement, then he would decamp to join the *foederati* cavalry.

Long days melded into a week and if there were losses in numbers due to illness or desertion, what was left was growing leaner and better as good habits took over from petty confrontations. Those chosen to lead the mass of *rustica* were asserting their authority and the men they were in charge of were wise enough to see where their own interests lay, for if they behaved they were fed. Added to that, there were priests along to encourage them

246

and to press them to recall their purpose.

For a youngster who had read avidly about marching armies and bloody battles what he was engaged in was a cause of ceaseless fascination. If he could see the faults in Vitalian's hastily gathered host he could also begin to work out the remedies, not least that this army would have been much improved by a longer period of training and by actively divesting itself of some in the ranks, perhaps even reforming into the more modern formations of *arithmos* and *numeri*. Easy to say, hard to do and dismissed out of hand by Ohannes, who thought that handling soldiers in units of eight was hard enough; to expand it into the up-to-date and three-to-four-hundred-strong numeri would result in havoc.

Added to that, just holding such a body together was far from straightforward and only possible because most of the harvest was in. The general only had such numbers until the spring, when the need to undertake planting would take most of his volunteers away, added to which there were those who would just break down from the sheer toil of being in any army.

While Ohannes was full of beans at the outset, Flavius became increasingly aware, even if the old man tried to hide it, of the toll endless days of marching was taking on him. Ohannes had done his twenty-five years already, bore battle scars and carried the recurring aches to go with his long service. The fact had been obvious long before they had joined Vitalian, but now the pain Ohannes was feeling began to manifest itself in an irascible and sometimes downright offensive

247

manner, which did nothing to endear him to those he led, not a true soldier amongst them.

Flavius was not the only one to discern the cause but it was not something the others would discuss with him, he being seen as too close to the man driving them towards something approaching defiance. The words Ohannes had used about unpopular officers came to mind; if they got into a fight, some of these men might be tempted to spear him in the back.

So he began to take on as many of the duties as he could, using the excuse of youthful exuberance to cover for what he saw as a necessity. He would go round Ohannes's charges every time they broke the march to ensure they were fit to continue, leaving the old soldier to take his ease; showed eagerness when anything had to be communicated to Forbas, the centurion who led them; was ever out in front once they had been directed as to where to camp, to take from the commissary the tally needed to draw their food and wine – acts which were seen in a far from flattering light.

'Grovelling little shit.'

Flavius had just overseen the marking out and erection of the tent, one of the tasks Ohannes was duty-bound to perform; instead he had stood back and let the youngster get on with it. Was he meant to overhear what the speaker was calling him, was he meant to see the nods the insult received from several others?

Tent up, Ohannes lay himself down on the floor, the way he made it to his comatose position, with suppressed moans at the pains in his joints, evidence of the strain he was under, every groan getting from his soldiers lifted eyebrows or an under-the-breath curse. There was no harmony in this group and any fellow feeling, if it existed, did not include Flavius or Ohannes, made doubly obvious by the way their supposed comrades sought other company and separate campfires as soon as they could.

The centurion Forbas, a leathery veteran who, if not as old as Ohannes, had done nearly as much time, was no fool. He could see what was happening and was wise enough to also be aware how easily discontent could spread, it being a disease to an army as deadly as the plague. In doing his rounds he had seen Ohannes stretched out and early asleep too often and it was not a position anyone of his rank should be observed in.

Forbas was setting the camp guards and the *contubernium* of which Flavius was part were due to mount part of it, this while the man tasked with ensuring they stayed awake and at their posts was, having wolfed his food, flat out, fully dressed and snoring his head off. His equipment was clean, but only because Flavius had taken care of that.

'You, outside,' he barked. Obliged to comply Flavius left the tent to be confronted by a less than sanguine countenance. 'What's going on?'

'I don't know what you mean, sir.'

'Don't fanny me, boy. I have been watching your friend the last few days.'

'He's my *decanus*–'

'Don't interrupt and more importantly don't lie to me, or you'll find yourself strapped to a wheel and hard leather stripping the skin off your

249

back. I have eyes to see, so I know you are close. Question is, can he do the job he has been given and accepted?'

There are times when you look into another pair of eyes and know that a lie will not serve; in the case of Flavius it had always been those of his mother. But Forbas replicated that now, which obliged the youngster to respond with the truth.

'Five leagues a day would tax any man.'

'No excuses, boy,' came the response; if the tone was softer it did not seem much less threatening. 'Even if we struggle to manage the five and might be forced to do more.'

'He is feeling his years.'

'For which I can have some care, but my task...'

Forbas paused; he did not have to say that if he had sympathy for another old sweat he was in no position to indulge it. Being seen to be soft with anyone in the century would lead others to take advantage and that was made doubly so by the rapid assembly of a host in which discipline was fragile.

'I can do what needs to be done, sir.'

'Carry out his duties?'

'Only those that do not diminish him in the eyes of others.'

'It's a noble notion, boy, but it won't serve. Who else is there to take his place?'

The reply was as much a defence of Ohannes as the truth. None of the men he had so far marched with had impressed with either the qualities to lead or the desire to replace the man who did, added to which none had soldiered before; all they were good at was moaning.

'Then you must undertake the duty, since you're practically doing it already.'

'At my age?'

'Wouldn't be tolerated in a proper army, but something tells me that you don't need to be told how far this lot is from that.'

'But will the men follow me?'

'They will, for if they do not, they will have to deal with me.'

'And Ohannes?'

'I will tell him and if it eases your mind I will be kind about it. Now find out where your lot are and get them ready for guard duty. As for your old friend, he is excused for tonight. But on the morrow, like everyone else, he will march.'

CHAPTER EIGHTEEN

The night was a nervous one for Flavius, who should have slept but dared not. The method of ivory tallies used to ensure the sentinels were at their post and awake kept him on tenterhooks, for if any of the men he was now nominally in command of fell into a slumber it might not only be the miscreant who paid a price. The centurion on duty, a man unknown to the youngster, made his rounds and handed out his tokens to all who were alert; woe betide any man who could not return the requisite number come daybreak.

He had to see them changed at intervals, so that each man had four full glasses of sand with

251

his head down and only two split shifts of duty on the section of the outer encampment ring for which they were responsible. Such was his worry, and his fear that he would not be woken by a disgruntled inferior, that he kept himself awake by seeking to recall how his father had handled his role as a commander and how he could apply it now, thoughts that were as daunting as they were enlightening.

Dawn brought little relief, though the night had passed off without alarms; the men, Ohannes aside, were in a foul mood and it was moot as to the cause. Lack of rest or the notion of being ordered about by a lad just turned fifteen and a voice that occasionally cracked to prove his adolescence; he suspected the latter but what kept at bay outright and vocal complaint was the proximity of Forbas, who was never far off and obviously willing, a message sent by many a glare, to intervene if anyone was insubordinate.

They breakfasted, struck their tents, loaded their personal possessions and the tent onto the cart that served the whole century and once they were blessed at Mass it was time to be back on the road, marching four abreast. Flavius was in the front of the two files and on the right, Ohannes beside him, and had a chance to quietly put to them what he could not do in the hearing of anyone of higher rank: that if they were so disgruntled by his elevation and annoyed by having to obey his commands he would happily step aside for anyone they proposed, albeit such a person would have to be approved by Centurion Forbas.

'Suits me,' Ohannes declared, somewhat restored after his slumbers and marching with seeming brio. 'Who would want to care for this lot?'

'You took pleasure in it,' came a loud reply, from a fellow called Helias, the Greek name for watchman, which was backed up by a loud 'Aye!' from two of the others. 'Not that I saw much care.'

'So you might think,' the Scythian shouted, clearly stung, 'but if I took it, it was to get out from being under the likes of you.'

'Must have slept well,' came the call from another. 'Let's hope his legs are as strong as his voice.'

'That's past now,' Flavius declared, looking behind to see if anyone in the ranks to the rear had heard the Scythian bellow, only to find he was staring at a row of blank eyes; if they had heard, and they must, all were pretending not to. 'And Ohannes, keep your voice down. Helias, if you want the position of *decanus* speak up, the rest too for I will not put it to you again.'

'Only fit for those that grovel,' cawed Tzitas to some suppressed laughter.

'You'll eat those words, mark me.'

Flavius caught Ohannes by the arm and growled at him. 'Be silent, for the love of God, or you'll see us all at the wheel.'

That his old friend was hurt was clear, his expression left no doubt, but Flavius was not willing to soften the look that went with his admonishment. In truth he was conflicted, aware that his new rank would cause him many problems and not least in his relationship with a man to whom he owed so much. But if he was to be a *decanus* then he must act like one and the first rule was no favouritism.

It was not a very elevated rank, to be sure, but just to be lifted from the mass of ordinary foot-sloggers and have some status, even if he sought to disguise it, was pleasing, especially to a young man who had dreamt, not so very long ago, as he read the histories of successful campaigns, how he would one day command armies and win great battles. His next words were a whisper.

'I need you to aid me.'

'Which I will,' came the reply, though not in a tone that eased the mind of the person at whom it was aimed.

'A mite less talking will be welcome.' The gravelly voice of Forbas, who had come back from his position at the head of the century to see what was going on, stiffened every back and had eyes rigidly looking ahead. 'Save your puff to move your feet.'

At the first rest break Flavius made a point of sitting slightly away from Ohannes, so as to establish to the others that he was not going to be over-partial to his interests. Whether it worked or not was hard to tell, given there was none of the relaxed talk that might have been exchanged in a *contubernium* at ease; what it did do was leave him with no one to talk to and a period of time to think.

Almost one of the first lessons Flavius had ever received on fighting had been when he overheard his father lecturing his brothers. Decimus sought to drum into his boys that if you fought for the empire or for the legion of which you were part, such notions evaporated when it came to actual combat. He could hear him now driving home his point, that you fight for only two people, the man on your right and the other on your left.

'Keep them alive and they will do likewise for you.'

Listening, Flavius, if he had not actually dismissed it, could not see himself as a mere soldier in a line of the same; he was, in his imaginings, a commander, a person directing the fight as much as taking part in it, albeit he was out in front inspiring those who followed him by his martial prowess. When he dreamt of such engagements, all of them were furious, all of them successful, every one, when it ended, with Flavius Belisarius standing in amongst a slew of dead enemy bodies, just before he was cheered to the heavens by his soldiers.

This was reality; seven men alongside whom he must go into battle and not in some grand position. Now he was recalling the truths Ohannes had sought to impart, that at this level you would see little and know less, so what mattered was the spirit that animated them as a group. Calculation, the number of leagues covered multiplied by the days they had been marching, told him they could not be far from Constantinople now and what would happen then? Would they be thrown straight into a desperate fight and if they were—

'*Decanus!*'

He shot to his feet and slammed a fist into his plain leather breastplate, looking over the heads of both Forbas and the well-dressed officer who had lifted his head with his baton that first day; it

255

did not do in the Roman army to look a superior in the eye.

'Come with me.'

Both spun round and walked away, obliging Flavius to move swiftly to get on their heels as they headed towards a covered wagon with a good-looking and well-caparisoned horse tied to the wheel, his eye drawn to the elaborate saddle, edged with adornments in silver, the accoutrements of a rich individual.

He had known just from his dress that this officer was of the equestrian class at least; indeed, by his smooth cheeks, calm look and easy air of authority he might be a born patrician. The tailgate of the wagon was down and on it sat a stone flagon and some beakers, to which the officer pointed with a lazy finger.

'Help yourself to some wine, *Decanus*.'

Forbas had already picked up and poured himself some, smacking his lips after a swallow, which produced on the officer's face a fleeting look of aversion and one that amused Flavius. Not that he showed it, indeed he was wondering if he should decline the offer of wine, sensing this might be a test of some kind, unaware that his hesitation was noted.

'Don't hold back, it will wash the dust out of your throat.'

'A fine pressing, Tribune Vigilius,' Forbas said, after another deep swallow.

A thin smile: was it genuine? Vigilius removed his helmet to reveal short-cropped fair hair. 'From my father's own vineyard, Forbas.'

'An ancient one, sir?'

256

'Planted in the reign of Constantine.'

Definitely a patrician and from an old family, Flavius thought, an easier assumption to make given he could observe the easy manner and the innate confidence while not himself under scrutiny. Vigilius picked up a goblet, poured some wine into it and handed it to him, the stone of the cup cold in his hand, the wine it contained made more pleasant, and it was of good quality, by being served in such a material.

'Centurion Forbas informed me last night of his action in promoting you.' The raised eyebrows – the eyes were startling and blue – seemed to indicate that Ohannes and his demotion were not to be mentioned. 'I make it my business to know all of my inferiors who have responsibilities, so I am bound to ask if you are comfortable being in charge of the men in your *contubernium*.'

He had to disguise his voice again as he replied. 'It is too soon to say, Your Honour.'

Another fleeting smile. 'An honest response, I like that.'

'How much time do I have to gain their trust, sir?'

'A good question,' came the response, followed by a pause in which Vigilius was working out if the person asking was worthy of an answer. 'We are two days' march from the capital. What happens when we get there is as yet not known.'

'If we are still long enough, Tribune,' Forbas insisted, 'we might be able to beat some discipline into them.'

'Beat?'

'Beast, I meant, work them till they drop. Some

257

hard training and mock fighting with sword and spear, which time has not allowed us to work on. I have not seen any of your lot do more than march. That tells you little of how they will behave in combat.'

'Perhaps the emperor will throw open the gates of Constantinople and abase himself at our feet.'

Flavius looked at Vigilius, only to realise that he was mocking the very notion, before he poured himself some wine and addressed him. 'What are you like in mock combat, *Decanus?*'

'I expect to hold my own, Your Honour.'

Tempted to boast, for he had shown genuine prowess in such activities, Flavius held back. Let his superiors find out from observation rather than his own lips.

'You must do more than that,' Vigilius replied, for the first time in a voice that was firm. 'You will need to ensure the men you lead can hold not only their own, but the enemies we face.' Those blue eyes lost that lazy look and went hard. 'I am no great lover of the whip, but I urge you to see it employed at any sign of insubordination.'

He looked at Forbas, as if to include him in what he was saying. 'You are young, very much so, and the men you lead all older by many years. They will seek to exploit that, *Decanus*, and if they do you must report them to Centurion Forbas who will put them right. Do not seek to be popular, seek to be respected and then should we come to fight you might survive it. If you fail, then...'

Vigilius drained his cup and gave him a look that said the talking was over. Flavius fisted a salute and marched back to where his men sat.

It was easy for a man of the background of the tribune to say he must gain respect, something he would get from rankers, as long as he was competent, merely for his birth. It was not so for Flavius and at the root of the problem was Ohannes, who, as the day went by, began once more to show signs of serious fatigue: the previous night's rest had restored him for the morning; that did not hold once the sun had passed the meridian.

Instead of looking ahead his chin was from time to time meeting his breast and his breath was increasingly laboured. He had to be nudged to keep his spear upright and his shield in the correct position and was prone to a very occasional stumble. To favour him in any way would be fatal and Flavius knew the rest were waiting to see what he would do, hoisting him on the horns of a real dilemma, not made easier by the knowledge that they still had a whole league of marching yet to do. Ohannes might well collapse!

'I have never asked you, friend,' Flavius whispered, 'how many years you have?'

'Lost count,' Ohannes replied, which implied to Flavius he was no more skilled in numbers than he was in writing, 'but I was full-grown when I enlisted.'

Twenty-five years of service, Flavius calculated, maybe twenty summers old when he joined the army and in three more he had served as the Belisarius *domesticus*. Coming up fifty, which was old, too old to still be soldiering. The last league before they made camp was spent in encourage-

259

ment and the odd helping hand, every time he touched Ohannes bringing a snort from those to his rear.

They got to the chosen field and Flavius was quite brusque to Ohannes when it came to setting up the tent, only relenting when it came to tightening the ropes that would hold it down by passing over the food tally and sending him away to draw their supplies. The rest had to gather timber for their fire and get it ready to light before they buffed the dust off their equipment and stood to for an inspection by Forbas.

'At least we have no guard duty tonight,' Flavius said, once they had been dismissed.

'Not that we'll sleep,' Helias moaned, to Flavius his natural mode of behaviour, 'with our ancient goat snoring.'

Aimed at Ohannes it had the old man beginning to rise to his feet – he had been lighting the kindling and it was clear there was going to be a confrontation, which got a bark from Flavius that made everyone freeze.

'Permission to take that piece of shit to some place quiet and teach him some manners,' Ohannes growled.

The word 'Denied' from Flavius melded with the response from Helias, which was, 'In your dreams, old man.'

'Get the fire going, Ohannes, and let us eat. We will all be better placed after a meal.'

The reply was defiant. 'I'm not goin' to take much more from him, Master Flavius.'

'Master?' Tzitas demanded. 'What's that about?'

'Slip of the tongue,' Ohannes snarled.

It might have worked if Flavius had not looked away, avoiding any eye contact at all, for if Ohannes's slip of the tongue had made them curious, his reaction only engendered suspicion, not that a word was said; it was all in the looks. But the mode of address had not gone away; as they ate it cropped up in all the most inappropriate places to tell the *decanus* that it had registered. The butcher who had cut their meat was a 'master' at his craft. Would they 'master' the enemy when they met them? Emperor Anastasius was far from a kindly 'master' to his subjects.

To get away from it and think, Flavius took a tour of the camp, something he had done many times, passing the eight-man *contubernia*, each round their own fire and seemingly at ease with each other, not the case with his. It could not last; Ohannes would not back down and if he struck any of the others Flavius would be obliged to punish him

Moving out from the lines of properly pitched tents he wandered into an area populated by the numerous, non-combatant camp followers, some of them the 'wives' and children of the men who had joined Vitalian. In description they fitted any known type, from bent old crones to bustling and sprightly young women who busied themselves about the camp. Here they cooked for their *rustica* menfolk and washed their clothing, no doubt supplying comfort as well, Flavius supposing that with a wage earner on the move – so very few of those who had joined owned anything but their labour – the women had to move too.

It was probably a mistake to make his way right

through the middle of the area where they had pitched their makeshift coverings, for this exposed him to sights he would rather have not seen; they did not conceal everything that happened within. If the men were allotted their own part of the camp that did not mean they stayed there and it was some time before the *nummi* dropped and Flavius realised that the term 'wives' covered more than connubial attachment.

As a result he was also exposed to many a ribald comment; that he was tall for his age and good-looking only increased the banter as he was invited to 'dip his wick' and have 'a roll on the straw'. It was enough to have him quicken his step and in doing so he bumped right into a young girl carrying a bucket of water, the contents going flying.

'If he won't spill his seed,' came the raucous cry, 'he can tip out water.'

Through the laughter that engendered, emitted by a dozen harpies, he heard the follow-up comments. 'Bet he's got as much juice in his pouch as he has cast on the ground.'

'Too mean to share it with us.'

'Shame, with enough to go round.'

'Please forgive me,' he said to the girl, who was on her knees righting the bucket and did not see how much he was blushing.

'Of no matter, sir,' she replied just as a loud bellow sounded from a male throat.

'What are you about, girl?'

Flavius turned to see a fat fellow approaching, unshaven and bearing a heavy black growth, a sweat-stained leather cap on his head, the garment he was wearing open so his belly hung out

262

to droop over the top of his filthy culottes. He pushed past Flavius and raised his hand to strike the girl, now cowering.

'Hold!' Flavius cried, grabbing the hand. 'This is my doing.'

The hand was pulled violently away, the other used to push Flavius in the chest and send him stepping backwards, coming with that a barking command to, 'Stay out of things that ain't your concern, brat.'

The slap then delivered only skipped past the girl's tied-back golden hair, which did not satisfy her assailant as punishment since he raised his hand again. There it stayed as he looked down at the point of cold steel that had pushed against his flesh, so soft that the sword point could make an impression without making a cut.

'Stay that hand.' Flavius pressed gently to force a retreat, aware out of the corner of his eye that the intended victim was gazing up at him and that she had a fearful look on her face, so he said, 'Hand me the bucket.'

The rope was put in his hand and as it was he realised those who had been ribbing him had gone very quiet. Not so the fat one.

'That's my girl an' I can do to her what I like.'

'She did nothing wrong, I did,' Flavius replied, looking at the face; the fat man was still looking at the sword point and Flavius was sure he detected a tremble. Certainly the tone changed; now he was pleading.

'Respectfully, Your Honour, you do not know her. She is ever clumsy.'

'Stand up,' Flavius said, with a sideways glance,

'there is no need to cower there.'

Looking at her, he missed most of what the fat man was saying, only afterwards recalling that he claimed to be her father, that she was a trial to him, forever rebellious and always had been, while only his hand, oft used, was of any service in controlling her. The reason he was distracted occurred immediately; she was beyond pretty even in a shapeless smock, had rosy cheeks in fair skin, if not entirely clean, and a pair of striking blue eyes.

'Where is the well?' he asked in Latin, and when she looked confused he repeated it in Greek.

'Right by the road, sir.'

'I am no sir,' he grinned, taking her hand and lifting her up, before withdrawing his sword and leading her away.

Freed from the fear of instant death, the fat fellow started to bellow at him as an interfering arse of a jumped-up nobody who might learn better if he was not careful, the litany of abuse killed off the instant Flavius spun round, though once he carried on again he could hear the father telling anyone around who would listen what he was going to do to the barely-out-of-his-soil-cloths sod who had insulted him.

'Did you understand that I said sorry?' They were by the well, so Flavius put in the rock used to make it sink, hooked on the leather bucket and began to lower it. 'You have no Latin?'

All it got was a shy nod and a reply so soft it was impossible to hear.

'I have got you into trouble, have I not?'

Another nod and this time she did speak, yet still without looking up. 'I thank you for staying

264

his hand, sir.'

'It was only right,' he said as he felt the way the water slightly checked the bucket, 'just as it is fitting that I make amends.'

He began to pull, raising the now weighty bucket out of the well, and once it was above the rim he hauled it over to the parapet and unhooked it, retrieving the rock. 'Why do we not take it back together?'

With each having a hand of the rope they made slow progress, actually stopping when Flavius asked her name, which he was pleased to hear was Apollonia, seeing her rosy cheeks go bright red when he added that it suited her.

'If I tell you my name is Flavius, will you remember it?'

The 'Yes' was emphatic and for the first time she looked directly at him, right in the eyes, and Flavius felt a need to take an extra breath.

'Is he your father, as he claimed it?'

'Timon took me in, and my mama.'

'Not blood, then. Does he treat her as badly as he seems to treat you?'

'Worse, sir.'

'Worse, Flavius,' he corrected her gently, which caused her to smile, that requiring another deep inhalation.

There was no need to ask what would happen once he was out of sight. Whatever punishment this Timon had intended would be multiplied by a dozen to cover his shame at his own cowardice. Flavius allowed her to lead him to where the water was required, disappointed that there was no sign of that fat belly, but the women who had ribbed him were still around so he spoke to them, for they must know Timon.

'A message for Timon,' he cried out, in a voice now turning rich and deep, 'that I will come by each night we are camped, and if I see so much as a blemish on Apollonia's skin, I will use my sword to remove from him what he no doubt considers his jewels, in short I will make a eunuch of him, and a hand on Apollonia's mother will earn him the same fate. Have a care to pass that on for I will not warn twice and should he think to overcome me by numbers, I am a *decanus*, so he will need many and armed.'

Despite the distractions to his thoughts, he knew he needed to concentrate on the problem that had brought him to tour the camp in the first place. Walking had ever aided his thinking and as he went on his way he passed the various people that supported the army by their employment, the butchers, the armourers with their lit forge, the storekeepers with their wagons of grain, peas and pulses, men who required to be rewarded in coin for what they did.

An idea began to form in his head, a possible solution that would kill two birds with one stone. It would also leave him free to act with only consideration for his own needs. By the time he got back to the tent it was a resolution, not a notion. His fire was nearly out and he needed to stoke it, the old soldier emerging from the tent as he was throwing on the logs, coming close to talk.

'I humbly beg–'

Ohannes was not allowed to finish his whispered apology, Flavius physically stopping him by putting his fingers to his lips.

'It matters not, old friend, and what is done is done. If the others are curious that is all they are. I have no intention of satisfying their noses and they will not ask anything of you, so it will be forgotten in a day or two.'

'Happen,' came the unconvinced reply.

'More important than that, I am going to ask that you be shifted to a duty with which you can cope.'

'I have that now.'

'No, Ohannes, you do not. I daresay you will be sprightly in the morning but it will not last and you know it. What happens if you collapse?'

'I won't!'

'And I cannot take the chance that you will. I would strap myself to the wheel rather than hand you over to Forbas for punishment, which I must do in my rank.'

'I've felt the lash before.'

'Not by my reporting you.'

Ohannes was still defiant, but now he was sounding like a petulant child. 'I can take it.'

'But I cannot hand it out,' Flavius said in a weary tone, rising to tower over his still-seated friend. 'So I either have to put you out of harm's way or ask Forbas to find another *decanus*.'

'Don't take it amiss, Master Flavius, but if he had to promote you, there cannot be a rate of folk he thinks fit of the rank.'

Flavius grinned. 'I don't, which is why I want you somewhere in which you can have it easier. All you will do if you stay is show me up as useless.'

'You're not that an' never will be.'

'You can see into the future?' Flavius joked, still grinning.

'I knew your family, all of them. I served with your papa and watched the way your brothers grew to manhood. If there is a God in heaven, then everything they had which was to be admired is now within you.'

'What a burden that is, now they are gone.'

'No escaping it, is there, more's the pity.'

'If you have so much faith in me Ohannes, then trust me in what I am about to do, which is plead with Forbas to put you in a place where you can ride one of the carts.'

'Not a fighter?'

'I did not say that, did I, but you are for certain no good at marching.' Flavius adopted a deliberately hard tone; he was resolved to act and there was no going back. 'No more argument, I have decided and you will obey.'

CHAPTER NINETEEN

'Two days there, maybe, no more, and we will be outside Constantinople,' said Forbas. 'I have that on the authority of the Tribune Vigilius.'

'Is he as rich as he looks?'

'Richer, father a senator and was something at court till this brewed up. Seems he has retired to his estates till it all blows over.' Which was as good a way as any of saying that he was Chalcedonian. 'Anyway, what do you want?'

Flavius outlined his problem with Ohannes as well as the solution he had come to, which the centurion took surprisingly well.

'As it happens I am about to break up what remains of one unit and distribute them throughout the century, too many are a man or two short.'

Sensing the enquiry Flavius was about to make Forbas just added the rate of desertions.

'Hard to keep an eye on everyone, be better when we have a settled camp. The centuries we can watch, but the peasants are a nightmare, what with no real discipline or marching formation, and we have lost a rate of them. Caught a few and strung them up as examples, though they got a priestly blessing first. We're not barbarians.'

'What happened to the *decanus* who lost his men?'

'What usually happens, Flavius, a bout at the wheel and no skin on his back, a lesson to all that if you lose a man, you pay the price. He lost three and bled for it.'

Flavius was thankful Forbas was not looking at him, for he went white. He was also thinking, if this is what happens with volunteers, what was it like in a proper army?

'So Ohannes can be shifted?'

'Why not, if it sorts a problem? Can't see him being much use in a fight at his age and he's no good as a *decanus*, though there's not many soft stations, that's for certain.'

Not much use at his age, Flavius thought: that's all you know, Centurion Forbas; he could probably give you a good bout.

The centurion was deep in thought, tilting his

269

head to consider the options. 'The *forestarii* are light on numbers and you can get him put with them.'

'They ride in carts?'

'They do, with their timber.' Forbas then barked a laugh. 'Arse full of splinters, I shouldn't wonder.'

His visitor was not laughing, he was considering, that being far from an undemanding area of labour. The woodcutters had to hew and gather enough timber for the nightly fires lit by a whole camp of what Flavius had roughly reckoned to be around six thousand men, from the great blaze that burnt before General Vitalian's tent down to the cooking pot of the meanest peasant volunteer. It was a blessing they were not in anything like enemy territory; that made it a doubly heavy task involving the fighting troops as well: the host needed to throw up a nightly stockade. Did it serve his deeper purpose?

'Permission to speak to the *curator* in charge?'

'You don't need it from me.'

Another salute. 'I am obliged, Centurion.'

He was halfway out of the tent when the question was thrown at him. 'What's this "master" joke that seems to be attached to your name?' It forced Flavius to turn and compose his face into a look of confusion, added to an exaggerated shrug.

'No idea.'

'It's all over the camp,' Forbas growled, 'and if it is set to take you down a peg I need to know so I can nip it off.'

'If I find out I will tell you.'

It was all over the camp; any man he passed who recognised him called out 'Master', and gave him a thumped chest salute accompanied by a grin. In other circumstances it would have been harmless, just gentle ribbing. Had it been wise to deny any knowledge of the reason to Forbas? He was not a man who would take kindly to being lied to, but that was for the future.

The *curator* who led the timber parties was likely as strong as an ox; he certainly looked like one, nearly as broad as he was long, with forearms as thick as a normal man's thighs – they were like the trunks he was required to saw through. He had a wide body and a square head, completely bald, lacked teeth and that lent his talk a whistling quality at odds with his stocky appearance. If his eyes looked dull to begin with they soon lit up when Flavius offered him one of the coins bequeathed to him by his father to ensure the new recruit to his gang was not overburdened with work.

'A half *follis*,' he said, his eyebrows rising as he took, with his gums, what had to be a useless bite of the twenty-*nummi* bronze piece. 'What am I taking on, your mother?'

'A good friend, an old fighter, whose knees are not up to a seven-league march each day.'

'What about his arms?'

'Good,' Flavius replied, looking meaningfully at the coin, 'if they are not overtaxed.'

The coin was examined once more. 'Might be able to let him just gather and carry if this comes regular.'

'How regular?'

'Each Sabbath day?' Flavius had only one thing in mind so he nodded in agreement. 'Where'd a

271

youngster like you get this kind of money?'

'That's none of your concern, the only thing you have to worry about is anyone asking where you got it.'

'Something tells me you're no soft touch even if you're short on years?'

'Never was and never will be. I will bring my friend to you and if you look after him right, I will do the same for you.'

Did he take that as a threat? He might have, for his reply was a growl. 'I can take care of myself, young 'un.'

Flavius nodded and left, his route taking him past the line of the officers' tents and being a warm night the flaps were open so he could see in. One belonged to Vigilius and within he saw what was carried in that covered wagon from which he had been given a cup of wine: fine furniture and hangings to make the interior luxurious, as well as carpets to line the floor. There was a low campaign cot made from well-fashioned and polished wood, with hangings on the sides to keep out prying eyes.

The tribune was at a table, his back to the flap, so Flavius was afforded time to stand and envy the tribune's comfort, which included an obsequious fellow who appeared to pour him wine, only it was no stone cup this time but glass, established when Vigilius lifted it to drink and it reflected the light from numerous lanterns. If anything established that he was rich, it was that. Not only that he could afford such an object but that he must be unconcerned about the loss or damage to it on campaign.

'What you hanging about for?'

Flavius spun round to face one of the barbarian mercenaries, who at least spoke comprehensible Latin. Like his compatriots his face was framed in pigtails that might be blond, but could also in the light of the torches be grey, for the face was deeply lined. The man had a spear and shield so was obviously part of the men guarding this part of the camp; only the *foederati* were trusted to bear arms so close to the senior officers, wary as they were of assassination by agents of Anastasius.

'I was thinking I might have such a tent one day.'

That got a derisive grunt, not that the person in receipt really noticed. The conversation made Vigilius look round, Flavius wondering if he could see and identify him. There was no sign that he had; the tribune merely turned once more and went back to whatever it was he was engaged in, so the dreaming youngster moved off as he was commanded to, egged on by the barbarian's jabbing spear. Back at the tent he found the old man alone, asleep and needing to be shaken into wakefulness.

'Pack up your belongings, Ohannes, you look destined to be a Gideon.'

That did not register at first; Ohannes needed to be reminded that the saint was the feller of trees. 'He was a mighty warrior, as well, so that fits you like a well-cut smock.'

He moaned of course; it was not fitting, and someone who owed him much was taking him down a proper peg. The youngster made it plain, yet again, there was no choice.

'I'm sure they are friendly,' Flavius said as they

273

made their way through the camp. 'Or at least better than what you have shared with so far.'

'Master Flavius...' The youngster sucked in his teeth to hear that word from Ohannes within earshot of anyone they might be passing, which got him another quick apology. 'I have found myself with strange companions many times in my years and if it is stiff at first it ever settles, it just takes a bit of time. The sods you now command are no different and had they seen me fight, well happen they would have changed their refrain.'

'When we get to Constantinople, maybe they'll get the chance.'

'And you might get sight of the folk you are so keen to talk with?'

'Perhaps.'

'What about your mother?'

That got Ohannes a sharp glance, but he was looking away. 'She will be expecting me any day, I should think, given the time that has passed.'

'You should send her word.'

The response was so terse it was wounding. 'If you can find a way for me to do that, then tell me. If not, do not mention it!'

'Seems to me you have taken to your new rank very well,' Ohannes growled, putting Flavius on the back foot, something he was well able to do.

'I had hoped at one time to be destined for higher things, remember.'

Was it the tone of that Ohannes picked up, or was it that he felt the need to take the sting out of his previous remark? Certainly his tone was emollient. 'Got to start somewhere, unless you're a patrician, but you will make your way, which I have said before.'

'Why are we in dispute?'

That got a humourless laugh. 'Nature makes us so.'

'Before I hand you on, Ohannes, know I will come by tomorrow to see how you are faring.'

'For which I thank you.'

The introductions to the *curator* passed off without trouble and Ohannes was shown to their shared accommodation and he and Flavius said their farewells. Stood outside the tent, wondering if he was doing his friend right, he heard Ohannes introducing himself to those he would work with and he seemed easy with it, bringing home again that he had lived, since probably he was Flavius's own age, a transient life. Was that now his lot?

His next port of call was to seek out Apollonia, sure he caught a sight of Timon disappearing at his approach. If she was glad to see him it did not show, which he put down to shyness, and when he asked if she could walk with him it seemed that she was reluctant to oblige. While he could think of many reasons why that might be, the one that did not occur was that she did not like him and with much effort he slowly broke down her resolve and she finally spoke a little.

Flavius feared he was interrogating her, but without him posing questions there was only silence. She came from a village he had never heard of, and asked about the province it was in she had no idea. Prior to this campaign, in which Timon hoped to make money from the army by washing and mending clothes – not that he toiled himself – she had never been more than five hundred paces from their hut.

Age? She had no idea and if he put her near his own, then Flavius could not be sure so unrevealing was her clothing. When she began to seek to count on her fingers, Flavius noticed how raw were her hands, reddened from the work Timon had her along to do, washing for small payments. In normal circumstances he might have told her all about himself, but the residual reserve he had formed around his identity he kept to, for it made no difference to her who he was.

In the end they just sat for a while, he feeling as tongue-tied as she, which had never been the case with girls at home, where he and his friends had moved on from taunting them to seeking to impress them; it had not, in his case, gone as far as any kind of intimate physical contact, though others had boasted of matters he could only imagine.

'Timon has left you be?' he asked and she nodded. 'Your mama too?'

That suddenly animated Apollonia; she looked right at him, clear fear in her open-wide blue eyes. 'She is terrified of what he will do.'

'But I have let it be known what he will face if he harms you.'

'And how long will you be present to protect us?'

'As long as is needed,' he lied.

Flavius realised, with a sinking feeling, that armies form and armies disband, with the elements dispersing, and that would apply as much to camp followers as soldiers. Unless he was present permanently, Timon would have his way.

276

'You must not worry,' he added, lifting her unresisting hand and kissing it, aware that the touch of her skin was affecting more than his fingertips, which had him shift uncomfortably. 'I will take care of you.'

That was a statement he later lived to deeply regret.

The man from the disbanded *contubernium* joined at dawn and the words used about new comrades being stiff was borne out by his cold reception. Named Baccuda he was a fellow with no real jaw and protruding upper teeth who proved, on further acquaintance, to be a real dimwit. Any question posed to him took an age to elicit an answer so Flavius gave up seeking to establish from where he had come and what was his fighting background, given there was no time for lengthy interrogation.

They were on the move again, now marching through a string of hamlets edged by tilled fields, or those given over to pasture and full of sheep and oxen, produce that fed the great beast of Constantinople. Halfway through the day the blue of the Sea of Marmara became visible to their right, sparkling in the sunshine with many a sail, some red, most a dull brown, dotting the ocean, either beating up to the port city or sailing away on a firm breeze.

The barbarian *foederati* were, as usual, to the fore of the host, ready to do battle, even if those scouting ahead could espy no enemies waiting to contest the ground before them, news that rippled through the marching columns. The emperor was, it seemed, content to rely on his walls, for if he had any soldiers they had been withdrawn into the city, which sent a plain sign that God was on their side.

There was, it was assumed, one more temporary camp to make, the last, everyone hoped, before they could settle into something more permanent, which would see those with an eye for a bit of coin setting up shops and taverns at which the troops could take their ease and also their pleasures, be they alimentary or carnal – another fact of campaigning never mentioned in the histories and one Flavius only knew because it was being discussed and anticipated.

As promised, he went to visit Ohannes, to find him aching as much from felling timber as he would have done from marching, only in different places, a fact he made plain to Flavius in no uncertain terms. When the youngster led him away from his part of the camp he followed, producing a litany of moans to let it be laid down, and no dispute about it, that he was a fighter not a saw man.

Flavius spotted a little copse of trees, an area outside the lines of campfires, seemingly deserted, and indicated that was where they should go to talk.

'I have seen enough wood for a lifetime this very day.'

'Oblige me, Ohannes.'

Which he reluctantly did. They stopped on the edge, where there was enough starlight with which to see each other, and when Flavius issued an apology, that engendered another litany of complaint, which he had to stop quite brusquely.

'My friend, it was done for a purpose, so please be quiet and let me explain.' That got a grunt and a far from happy one. 'What chance do you think you would have of getting away from here as a member of our *contubernium?*'

'Get away from here?'

'You have a sharp mind, old friend, so I ask you to think on what might have been my motives for arranging your present posting – one, I might add, I had to pay a bribe to secure.'

The wait for an answer was long, evidence that Ohannes was thinking it through. 'Do I sense it was not just to get me out from under your feet?'

'You are halfway to the truth.'

'Not much good when only you know the other half.'

'I have a task I would like you to perform, though I cannot command it and would not even if I had the right.' Ohannes did not respond, leading to an extended silence that forced Flavius to continue. 'I want you to leave Vitalian's army.'

'To which there would be a purpose?'

'I must go on to Constantinople and I have no idea, even if I can succeed in what I need to do, how long that will take and, while I am engaged in that, how my mother will act if I do not go to her and there is no message to say why.'

'Which you could have asked for before you had me shifted.'

'But...'

Ohannes came out with a definite chortle, as he hit on the conclusion. 'Had I left prior it would have been desertion, for which I could have been strung up if caught and you would have felt the hurt of a proper lash. This way I can go and you are not at risk.'

'Forgive me if I misled you.'

Not the truth, really; Flavius had worried that a man who could not stop referring to him as 'master' might, if included in his thinking, say something to render it impossible; better Ohannes only find out now why he had chosen to act so.

'You're a sly one and no mistake, Master Flavius.'

Was that admiration or astonishment? Hard to tell.

'If you go missing from the *forestarii* it will not rebound on me, and added to that it has to be easier to go missing from a forest than a march on the *Via Gemina*. I want you to slip away and go to my mother to tell her in what I am engaged.'

'If the folk you seek are inside Constantinople, which I take leave to suggest they will be–'

'Then,' Flavius cut across him, 'I must find a way to get within the walls and I hope I am with a body of men who might achieve that.'

'And if they don't?'

Flavius ignored that and produced a small slip of parchment, on the obverse of which was one of his father's roughly composed letters to Justinus. 'I have written down the place where her family villa is located.'

'Which I cannot read.'

'But which I will tell so you can recall it – the writing is to show anyone local who can aid you. I have done a drawing of the way from the *Via Egnatia* to her family farm as well.' Flavius pressed a purse into the hand of Ohannes, the one Dardanies had returned to him. 'With this you can rest in the post houses and be fed. I ask only that you do not tax yourself; proceed at a pace that suits your bones, but make your destination.'

'And what am I to say?'

'Stay where you are until I come for you.'

'Will she take such a message from me?'

'My father trusted you, Ohannes, and I have as much faith in you as I have in God. Go, if you can, to my mother and stay with her, protect her. A snake like Senuthius will not rest if he thinks she has the means to bring him down, any more than he will be content until he is sure that I am dead.'

'And if I do not succeed?'

'Lap of God, Ohannes, is it not? How many times have you told me to trust in that?'

'Seems I will miss a battle.'

Flavius put his arms around Ohannes then, as much to hide his emotions as to demonstrate an affection which had deepened so much that love was not too strong a word to explain it.

'I will fight for both of us.'

The clutch from the old soldier was just as tight and his voice was as cracked as that of Flavius had ever been these last months. 'Then I pity those you face.'

'We cannot be seen together again, Ohannes, it will smack of—'

'No, I understand.'

'Choose your moment with care, friend.'

The laugh was hearty, intended to reassure. 'No need, this lot can't see the wood for the trees.'

'Till we meet again, then.'

The clasp then was the same as he had ex-changed with his school friends, a grab of each other's arm in a tight and truly Roman grip.

Flavius could not return to his tent without again visiting the area set aside for the camp followers and, of course, Apollonia. From that first tender touch of fingers he had moved her on to a hold-ing of hands, able to ease her away from whatever duties she was required to perform in order to walk with him.

Yet her reserve made any attempt to take matters further difficult. Only in later life would Flavius come to see how selfish had been his actions, for if he had been asked he would have denied the truth, that he was fixated on only one goal, natural for his age, but utterly lacking in consideration for the consequences.

They ended up in the same woods in which he had talked to Ohannes and that led to a first out-of-sight kiss, followed by hands eager to explore and a diminishing resistance that they should. If what followed was a great deal of inexperienced fumbling there was a moment of which Flavius had dreamt too many times without realising the pleasure to be felt.

How soft it was, warm and so welcoming; the immediate tingle he felt and the sensation of flesh against his flesh and pubic hair entwined when he thrust forward made what followed seem the most natural and beautiful thing in creation. To add to this was the way Apollonia seemed to take equal enjoyment and employ matching physicality to their encounter, even her gasping and increasingly recurrent cries adding to their mutual pleasure, which had they timed it, would not have seen many grains of sand filter through the neck of glass.

Sated they lay together, letting their breathing subside as Flavius let himself be subsumed by his sense of wonder, until discretion demanded, after more tender kisses, he take Apollonia back from where he had fetched her. Did those who looked at them guess what had taken place? Certainly the harpies had a glint in their eye but no act of either let them have a hint, their parting acted out in such a chaste manner.

It was only when walking back to his tent with a real spring in his step – he had climbed a mountain this night, killed a lion single-handedly with a spear, swam the Inland Sea and conquered the Medusa as well as the Minotaur of legend, in short he had become a man – that Flavius realised that one thing his father had sought to advise him of had not happened.

Decimus had counselled a son sprouting spots and fluff on his chin of what was to come to him in time and of his family's hopes, the first night with a new bride and the accepted pain he would inflict, which had to be borne and would lead to many a happier repeat. Why had Apollonia not cried out in pain? Why had she been so forthcoming in her responses? Who had penetrated where he had been so thrilled to go before him?

It could have been anyone, Timon, a companion of her years, some other soldier, but if it was enough to raise a question, did he care? With his thinking fixated upon more of what he had

283

just enjoyed, he put aside any consideration of how Apollonia had been deflowered and by whom.

CHAPTER TWENTY

What was heading their way was no mystery to anyone in the imperial palace; the emperor knew from his advisers that the forces of Vitalian were close and would be without the walls of the city in a day, two at the most. The composition of his army and the numbers were likewise acknowledged, including the old-fashioned way it had been structured, not seen as a reason for any concern, quite the reverse; such things as centuries were thought of as not fit for the requirements of up-to-date battle. The only unknown was what Anastasius intended to do to counter it.

In terms of fighting strength, Vitalian had the numbers but Anastasius had the quality. To protect his person he had several four-hundred-men-strong *numeri* in his palace guard, commanded by Justinus, a man he trusted. To secure the city and its walls there were twenty more, formed into two *numerus* brigades and commanded by tribunes that would each man one of the seven landward gates, the three others set to protect the long sea defences that ran along the Bosphorus to the Golden Horn.

Justinus, carrying out his daily ritual of reportage, was able to say that according to the *praefectus urbanus* the populace seemed sanguine and not in the least restive; there was no evidence, even if many of them were strong for Chalcedon, of any move to support, by untimely rioting and threats to the imperial person, the aims of Vitalian.

Justinus had naturally been asked for a private opinion on what should be done to counter the rebellion. Unable to say what he really thought, that the imperial religious policy was misguided, he stuck to matters purely military. The number of troops in the capital he insisted, not including those he commanded, which numbered five full divisions, could hold the walls. How to counter Vitalian? As far as anyone knew he lacked any kind of shipping so the units allotted to the defence of the sea wall were spare. They should be sent out to disrupt his progress, retreating in front of him, though stopping to present occasional battle, so as to break the spirit of what must be a hastily assembled host.

That delivered, Justinus could not help but wonder from what other sources the emperor was receiving advice; his own had been acknowledged and from subsequent imperial reactions he assumed had been ignored. Anastasius was gifted with any number of people to tell him what he should do and by reputation he listened to them all. One was his wife and then there were his personal valets or his barber and the thirty courtiers who formed the *silentiarius,* tasked to ensure that no untoward noise disturbed the imperial repose.

Petrus Sabbatius, who was busy writing out orders for his uncle, came out with a sneering aside when this was relayed to him. 'I would not be surprised to find the man employed to sponge his arse after an evacuation is his most important counsellor.'

'Then it would be a patrician,' Justinus replied, the person designated to attend upon imperial ablutions being a much sought-after role. 'Not that such is always a good thing, high birth does not always come with brains.'

Petrus passed him a completed Order of the Day, which the uncle wrote on using his signature stencil, his reply acid. 'Half of them struggle to wipe their own backside.'

That got a laugh; if they were equally unimpressed by the standard of the patricians of the Roman Empire, it was ever Petrus who came up with the diminishing invective. Not that those who had risen to high office through long imperial service were much better – all were self-serving – which made the task of the ruler a balancing act.

When the common people complained that Anastasius was a weathervane on policy, they did so without knowing of the competing interests he was required to deal with. He might be an *autokrator* in Greek but few could rule in any way they wished without facing the risk of being bloodily toppled and the most fearful enemy was within the city walls, not without.

'I dined with a good number of your officers last night, Uncle.'

'I can imagine where.'

Petrus shrugged; he had a well-known taste for seeking entertainment in the less salubrious parts of the city and in that he had much in common with the inferior officers of Justinus. The whole *excubitorum* corps was in receipt of better pay than common soldiers of the empire, as well as better rations, but in terms of officers it had become, under Emperor Zeno, a sinecure for those with means of their own and with money never a consideration they were liberal in their spending.

Like every port in the world, the area around the Constantinople docks was full of brothels and places of entertainment where morality was not on offer. Justinus was no prude; he had visited such taverns and coarse establishments himself but Petrus was drawn to them like a moth to a flame. Polite dinner, of which he was obliged to be a part as the son of a wealthy patrician noble, bored him rigid and so did court formality. To many an observer he was an unsuitable helpmeet to a man seen as upright but that took no account of his very telling suitability in one vital regard: the trust engendered by blood.

'I wonder when they speak highly of you, if it is only because they are in my presence.'

'Very likely not the case, for in all my years I have learnt to have faith in soldiers who are not afraid to tell me they are discontented, while those who remain silent and husband their grievances are not the ones on whom it is wise to turn your back.'

Training schedules were handed over for each company and the stencil was employed once more. 'How happy you must be in the field compared to in the palace.'

'Why?'

'There is not a soul here on whom I would turn my back,' Petrus replied, with some venom.

'Not even me?' Justinus asked, grinning.

'That is not a question deserving of an answer. All I will say is, that if your inferiors were telling me their true feelings, I am humbled by being related to a paragon.'

'Humility does not suit you, Petrus.'

Said humorously it was not entirely taken that way, causing the nephew to hunch his shoulders and begin to tug at his hair. Justinus knew Petrus to be by nature an intriguer, which he was not. He was not a fool and had the means to survive in the hothouse of imperial politics, but there was no notion to become deeply involved in that quicksand, with its shifting alliances and deep feuds.

Petrus loved it; he was a mine of information on everyone who mattered and a great number of those who probably counted for nothing at all. Every thought he had passed on to Justinus, who was grateful, given it saved him from expending too much energy on the subject himself. In a place where no one person seemed to trust another, these two, very different in age, outlook and personal habits, through ties of blood as well as affection, had an unbreakable bond, which if it had started as an older man educating a young aspirant, had moved on from there to a point of near equality.

'And what do you take from all these paeans to my character?'

Petrus stopped pulling his hair and looked directly at his uncle. 'I take it they are deeply loyal to you.'

'Good,' Justinus replied, having a good inkling of what lay beneath that statement. 'Then Anas-

288

tasius is safe.'

'It is as well to add to that, Uncle,' came the cooed response, 'that he is also very old.'

'As a refrain, Petrus, that is tending towards the tiresome.'

'Forgive me for bringing it to the fore again, and I will cease to mention the emperor's age or his declining health if I have a necessary aim to lean on. Just tell me under which one of *his* nephews you think you will be able to survive and prosper and I will bend all my wiles to help secure his elevation.'

'I wish you to pen me a letter, Petrus,' Justinus said, in an abrupt change from what was an uncomfortable subject on which to speculate, for he distrusted them all. 'It is to be one of condolence to be sent to the widow of my old comrade, Decimus Belisarius. She has lost much.'

'Do you wish to mention you are distrustful of the report on the engagement in which he perished?'

'Does it matter? He is dead. All his sons died too, Petrus, one of whom Decimus named after me. Four of them, is that not a tragedy?'

Petrus shrugged, he being less affected by what had happened, having no personal connection to the family. When he had penned the replies to Belisarius, he had seen it as his duty to point out to his uncle that the main subject of the complaints had a powerful relative at court, a man whom it might not be politic to upset.

Justinus had waved such considerations aside; the senator and ex-consul Pentheus Vicinus, now holder of the title of *magister praesentalis* – the

289

palace had as many designations of rank as people – would never know how the commission had come into being, it being a secret between his *comes excubitorum* and the emperor. Petrus had felt constrained to argue that in a palace where secrets were rarely kept for long, no matter how hard they tried to keep it so originally, the truth would emerge as soon as the commission took effect and that there would be repercussions.

'If only a half of what Decimus has accused this Senuthius Vicinus of is true,' had been the reply of Justinus, 'then he would be better advised to pull a cowl over his head to hide his disgrace at sharing blood with such a villain.'

Tempted to tell his uncle he was being naïve, Petrus had kept his counsel.

On the last day of the march, Flavius had an odd feeling of freedom, added to the waking sensation of triumph, for which he chastised himself. Yet it could not be gainsaid that having only himself to be concerned about induced a feeling of relief, rapidly countered by conscience: he had to set against the emotion what he owed to Ohannes and, after him, Dardanies. Then there was Apollonia, to be looked forward to when they made their next camp.

The sun shone on the army of Vitalian, while a cool breeze came in off the sea to make pleasant what could have been sweltering and the whole host seemed in good spirits, which held until they espied what it was they would have to overcome, the walls of Constantinople being enough to chasten the most fevered pilgrim. The host was called to Mass, as they were daily, but this time to show anyone watching from the battlements that this was a pious army marching in God's cause.

For those who had never seen the walls, and Flavius was one who had only heard of them, their size and magnitude was both astounding and sobering and that was at a distance. He knew from his father there were more defences behind these great multi-gated and turreted edifices, walls built by a string of emperors to protect an ever-expanding city that had been Roman long before Constantine named it his eastern capital.

Once they had fanned out and made camp, with no sign that anything of a warlike nature was about to occur, Flavius took the first opportunity he could to examine them more closely, trailed by a couple of his men, who listened as he explained that what they saw before them presented, to an attacker, no more than a fraction of the problem.

These were the walls of the Emperor Theodoric, with forward battlements twenty cubits in height protecting an intervening moat overlooked by another set of even higher defences, great blocks of stone capped by arched red and smooth tiles that made getting over the very tops impossible; the only way onto the parapet behind was through the crenellations and each one would have at least one defender to hold it.

Massive square towers butted out at each great gate to create a zone of death before the heavily studded and massive oak doors, while behind them lay a narrow bottleneck entrance sealed off by a protective portcullis. Along the seaward side of the city the curtain wall was too high and continuous to be overcome from ships.

'How do you know all this?' asked Helias, the question accompanied by a look of suspicion.

'My father served here and he told me.'

'Did he tell you how to overcome them?'

Flavius produced a wry smile. 'No, he reckoned it impossible.'

The next question, querulously posed, came from Tzitas. 'Then how are we to manage it?'

He nearly said they should pray for an earthquake, which if strong enough would bring the walls down, or, as he had been told, forty days of rain, for if the River Lycus, which fed the teeming city, flooded, that too could undermine the foundations. Instead he invoked Joshua.

'He succeeded at Jericho, we must do likewise here.'

Blowing horns sounded just then, and for the first time Flavius shared a genuine and fulsome laugh with these two at the coincidence. Not that there was too much time for mirth, for that was a call to assemble and had them rushing back to their lines, to find Forbas in no mood for their dallying. A training field had been prepared, as well as a raised platform from which what went on could be observed. His century was to be gifted first use, with short wooden staves to act as swords, longer ones with a blunt end to replicate spears.

'Get your helmets and shields and let us see what use you are!'

The whole was split in two, thirty-two men each, for it was under-strength by two whole *contubernia,* and they were set the task of showing their

292

prowess. First the centurion and his *decani* had to get their men into lines to oppose each other, which showed many had either never engaged in proper battle drill or had forgotten anything they had been taught.

Flavius's first command was to instruct his lot to stay tight to each other, to advance or fall back as a complete unit and to always face the enemy. These were the same exercises in which he had participated in the sand-filled enclosure in Dorostorum, the same place where his father had regularly exercised his men.

If he knew what was required, it was not the case with all; too many men flew at each other with gusto and the air was loud with stick hitting stick, impressive in terms of zeal but actions that would be useless in real combat, and that was not confined to the ranks – several of the *decani* were equally inept.

It took all the strength Flavius could muster to restrain buck-toothed Baccuda, who was swinging his stave like a man possessed, in no way like he would employ a proper spear, his shield held away from his body, the fellow he had chosen to fight just as stupid; if either had faced a decent opponent they would have been battered to the ground. Worse, they were unaware that such behaviour in a real fight would endanger everyone on their own side; at all costs the line must be held!

Forbas should have been beside himself observing this, but when the horn blew to separate the competing factions he looked surprisingly calm, calling his junior leaders together.

'Now we can see clearly what we must do and a

start has to be made with you lot, who seem to have lost any skills you might have had. You cannot lead if you do not know how to fight yourselves, so fetch your spears, form up in a line and listen to what I say.'

For a man held to be short on temper, Forbas was surprisingly patient, arranging them in line and even personally adjusting their shields and spears to the correct position. When he came to Flavius their eyes locked, for there was no need to touch his equipment: it was where it should be, shield slightly angled to cover his neighbour on the left and once Forbas had sorted out the man to his right, a gap through which he could employ the weapon he carried.

'Shield rims at eye level and look at me.' He then called on them to advance one pace at a time, ordering that they keep a firm grip on both their weapons and their protection. 'When you move forward stamp, get your lead foot down hard and brace yourself. Remember there will be an enemy trying to either kill you or force you back, so the move must be as one. Once it is safe to do so take another pace forward.'

They went through it several times until it was, if not perfect, enough to satisfy Forbas, who now had them do the same with swords, which required a different shield position so it was possible to properly use the weapon.

'You need to be stabbing not swinging, for that will expose you. Get your weight right and your body behind the blow.'

It was all in the manuals and histories Flavius had studied, the classic fighting formation of the legion, whose success rested on tight discipline and total solidity and that had not changed even if the army had been reorganised in different-sized components with new names. Everything must be done as a unit and once Forbas was satisfied, the *decani* were sent to instruct their own men.

'If they don't do as you say, give them a swipe of your stick and if they are really bad you have my permission to stick your spear up their arse, the real one too.'

The training went on until, despite the cooling breeze, every mouth was dry and filled with dust and all were soaked with sweat. Forbas then called a halt and directed his charges to wooden vats of water, cool, fresh and fetched from a nearby spring. Flavius was enjoying his scuttle when a hand on his shoulder had him turn to face Forbas and a raised and crooked finger.

'You, with me.'

There was no choice but to obey and throwing the scuttle to another he followed the centurion across to a spot just below the raised platform where there was some shade from the sun, now well past the zenith.

'I think you are going to have to tell me who you are.'

'Flavius.'

'Which is the given name of half the folk in the whole empire and something tells me it is not all of yours, so out with it. And why are all and sundry now referring to you as "master"?'

That got a shrug. 'A jest, no more.'

'I watched you today, as I have watched you since we formed and you are not as the others around those water butts. You knew what to do without being told, which means you are fully trained and if that's the case at your age...'

'We used to practise at home.'

'Home is where?'

'North of here.' That got raised eyebrows, being clearly insufficient. 'North of Marcianopolis.'

'That's a lot of ground.' Flavius nodded and Forbas growled. 'Do I have to beat it out of you? For I will. You'll wish you had never been born!'

'Dorostorum,' Flavius conceded after a long pause, mentally berating himself when he observed the way Forbas reacted, eyes narrowing and taking on a knowing look.

'Where there was a fight not long ago, a bad one.' When Flavius declined to take that up, Forbas added, 'There was a big raid from over the Danube, one we were told the locals might struggle to hold. We were all set to march, to put aside thoughts on this place, when news came that the raiders, who turned out to be Huns, had run away, so we were stood down. The sad bit was the fate of the imperial cohort, who were led to their deaths by some fool who–'

'Not true!' Flavius exclaimed, protesting at what could only be a lie concocted by that viper Senuthius, but the news of such a disturbing falsehood opened him up more than he wanted and he could not stop the wetting of his eyes, which did not go unnoticed.

'How would you know that?' Forbas asked, in a low voice, and when he got no answer he added, 'Listen, lad, I am not trying to catch you out and you're clearly distressed, but I like to know who it is I am dealing with.'

The implication was slow to come, but it was an obvious point Forbas was making. There had to be imperial spies in Vitalian's host. Was he one of them?

'Settle for Flavius,' he hissed, a last try at obscurity.

That got a shake of the head. 'Is that old friend of yours a servant? If he is, a lad with an armed servant is no ordinary spear, is he? He will have been schooled, perhaps?'

'I came to join the cause and to fight to see Chalcedony restored. Why does anything else matter?'

'You're not like the rest of them out there. Tribune Vigilius said there was something about you that didn't smell right, something about the way you spoke and I thought he was spouting shit. Now I don't.'

'If I wish to keep things to myself–'

'For what, fear of an angry father coming to fetch you for running from home?'

'Not that.'

'You said what we were told of that Hun raid was not true. How can you say that with such certainty?'

'Because it is a lie.'

'So tell me.'

'Only if it goes no further.'

The response to that was a long time coming. 'You have my word.'

That night he took Apollonia to the same little copse, only this time with impatience. In having his way he was confused by her lack of joy and no enquiry seemed to elicit from her what she found troubling; had they not just repeated what had occurred the previous night? He tried words, but they seemed to have little effect, and he attempted to sulk like a thwarted lover, only to find she went silent.

'Tomorrow?' Flavius whispered to her before they were within the hearing of anyone close to where she laid her head for the night.

'If you wish it,' she replied.

'Of course, as much as you.'

She was gone in a flash, with not another word, leaving Flavius with views and opinions that came from his peers his own age, not his parents. Girls were strange creatures, unfathomable.

CHAPTER TWENTY-ONE

It was rare for a meeting of the imperial council to go on after the setting of the sun. Anastasius being a man of strict habits and receding levels of energy he liked to retire to his private quarters early to eat and drink, take his ease, talk with a very tight circle of chosen friends and then sleep. But the lamps were lit as the Scholae *Palatinae* guards were changed under the watchful eye of their commander, activities which only held up the discussions for a short time.

If not crowded, the audience chamber held sufficient courtiers, scribes, guards and servants to make it, on a summer night, uncomfortable and over time the multiple lines of advice had fallen into two camps, those both military and civilian who wished to appease Vitalian, in short men who had some sympathy for the right of free worship, up against those who were in outright favour of the emperor's edict. They thought it best to destroy him and his beliefs while he was within easy reach.

'Justinus?'

He was obliged to step forward, surprised to be asked to do so. It was obvious Anastasius was about to ask him once more for an opinion, which given the presence of other generals, some of whom were superior in both age and experience and had commanded armies, came as a surprise and as he hesitated his nephew just had time to whisper in his ear.

'The wily old fox is up to something.'

Justinus bowed his head. 'Highness?'

'What would you advise now that this rebel is outside my walls?'

'Do nothing.'

'That is hardly an option,' cried Probus, his least mentally favoured nephew. 'It insults the dignity of the emperor as well as the state. We should get out from this cowering and drive him away.'

'Into the sea if we can,' cried another courtier, an old man with flowing near-white hair, using the kind of flowery arm gestures seen in old drawings of the Republican Senate.

Justinus was tempted to tell the first speaker to stick dignity up his rear; in his experience, standing on that in a war tended to get men killed and

299

armies defeated. With the other he could use that theatrically upraised arm and put it in the same fundament.

'The possibility was aired that we harass him on the march, but that was not seen to be viable and would, in any case, only have slowed him down.' He made a point of not looking at the throne; the emperor knew that had been his advice but it had been proffered in private and would stay that way unless Anastasius chose to reveal it. 'We sit behind walls Vitalian cannot breech, with a port open to any amount of food we need to bring in.'

'While Vitalian eats the food from our nearby fields,' Probus added, 'feeding his army on what should be feeding the populace of the city. There will be shortages and that could mean rioting.'

'If you send the city divisions out to fight men will die to no purpose. Let him, like an unsweetened grape, wither on the vine and in time he will go away.'

As Justinus stepped back another stepped forward with Petrus whispering again to identify the speaker, a man who had hitherto held his counsel.

'Senator Pentheus Vicinus.' That got a nod from his uncle and he added, 'Well versed in intrigue.'

'Who in this room is not?' came the equally discreet reply. 'And is he not cousin to the criminal named by Decimus?'

With his nephew at his back Justinus did not see the look he received, which implied in no uncertain terms that there was *one* person not well versed in intrigue in this chamber and it was the uncle. Vicinus began to speak, employing a very rhetorical mode of address, which to a soldier

300

smacked of going round the houses. It was full of references to the glory of the empire and the sagacity of its present ruler. Finally he came to the point: surely wisdom dictated the first thing to do was talk. Once he got on to the real point of his intervention his language was a lot less extravagant.

'Invite Vitalian to attend upon you and let him set out his grievances.'

The hiss from Petrus was right in his uncle's ear. 'If he comes through a gate he will be killed.' A pause. 'Which is not such a ridiculous notion.'

Justinus shook his head as the speaker continued. 'It may be that a few small concessions will satisfy, if not Vitalian himself, then those he leads.'

'You think there are those ready to betray him, Senator Vicinus?'

'Unlikely. As you know, Highness, I have met Vitalian. He is a man who inspires loyalty among those he commands, for, if his opinions are skewed, his nature is not. He is a zealot for his cause, but it may be to others his views are towards the extreme. Perhaps those closest to him could aid him to modify his demands in order that no blood needs to be spilt and peace can once more be restored. It is fitting that it should. Might I also add that should any of his officers aid us in this, it would be appropriate that they should be well rewarded.'

'Bribe them, sound thinking,' murmured Petrus, before another pause and a question. 'Do you think all of this spontaneous, Uncle?' That got no reply; the senator was speaking again, explaining how this could be achieved.

'If it pleases Your Highness, since I know Vitalian, I am happy to convey such an invitation to him.'

'He might not take benevolently to that,' Probus cried, as he saw his policy being swept to one side. 'He might send us back your head.'

'If my head is forfeit in the service of my emperor,' Vicinus responded, in a sententious tone, 'then so be it.'

Anastasius raised a hand palm out to command silence and then gave his consent. 'An offer I cannot do other than accept, Senator.'

'Too pat, far too pat,' said Petrus. 'It has the stink of being arranged beforehand.'

He moved alongside Justinus who replied with a sigh. 'I do not have your nose for subterfuge, nephew, but no rat would have trouble smelling this.'

The details took little time; it was agreed that the senator would take an invitation to the rebellious general and his senior officers to attend, under a safe conduct, upon their emperor, where it was hoped common ground could be found that would still the need for any conflict.

'He will kill him,' Petrus said, 'he has to.'

'I fear he might ask that I do the deed.'

'You would decline?' Justinus emphatically nodded his head, but Petrus had a solution handy. 'One of your officers would I am sure oblige, in fact I may know the very fellow.'

'One of your drinking and whoring companions?'

'Who else?'

Which told the uncle that if he had hoped to shame his nephew for both his way of living as well as his tranquil attitude to assassination, he had singularly failed.

The spirit that had animated the host and carried them all the way from Moesia had begun to wilt; faced with such a barrier as the Walls of Theodoric, what had seemed both divine in inspiration and attainable by sheer faith evaporated. It soon became evident that to achieve their stated goal was going to be neither easy nor rapid, a fact bound to dent the fortitude of those who had seen the task as being over long before the spring planting.

Flavius did not set out to be an extra-knowledgeable naysayer, but he was too wedded to logic and too well read in the history of siege warfare to do other than point out to his own group and anyone else prepared to listen the very palpable difficulties, which, if it had not infected the lower ranks, he suspected would command the thinking of those who led them.

'They will know that even if we had enough men to close off every gate, you still need to have a fleet of ships to blockade the port and keep food from getting into the city.'

'What about attacking the walls?'

Helias asked this in a hoarse voice, his mood grumpy. He seemed to have slept little or drunk too much, having gone off in search of entertainment the previous night, and was now struggling to eat his breakfast of bread and figs.

Those wishing to take advantage of a new source

of custom had wasted no time in setting out their stalls between the walls and the camp and all must have come from within the city, which turned some minds to a quick raid that would get them inside the gates. Flavius was damp on that too; he suspected the guards would not be slack: anyone exiting would be allowed out by no more than a small postern, easily secured by one soldier, and would probably have to, on re-entry, use a password of some kind.

'To attack the walls you need siege engines,' said Flavius, replying to not only Helias, but also to a committed group of listeners. 'Ballista and the like, and even then what kind of rocks would you have to fire to breach those structures? They are four cubits thick.'

'There has to be a way, surely,' insisted another fellow of no name; he came from a separate group. 'Or why have we come all this way?'

'You make it sound a waste of time,' added Tzitas.

'There are only two ways to get into Constantinople,' Flavius replied, unaware that he was sounding smug, 'that is, short of a miracle.'

That had them all crossing themselves, as though by doing so they could bring one on. Flavius was halfway to telling him that from what he had read miracles rarely came along when they were required. He did not because he was not prepared to admit he could read and even more reluctant to list what those histories had contained.

'Possibly you can undermine the walls by tunnelling underneath them.'

Helias snorted derisively, before noisily coughing up some phlegm. 'You, maybe, me never, I like to see the sun.'

'How far out would you begin?' asked Tzitas.

'Beyond a cast spear,' another soldier called Conon said, which was surprising, given he rarely spoke.

'More than that,' Flavius insisted. 'You have to begin digging where it cannot be seen.'

'That would take forever.'

'It would, and the defenders will not just let it happen. Even if they cannot see it they will know.'

'How?' demanded a chorus.

'Don't think all those folk Helias went to see last night are honest traders.'

Helias cut in, with an angry growl, 'Rogues and cheats, that's what they are!'

'You should have kept to our tent,' Tzitas crowed, 'serves you right.'

'Like our leader?'

Flavius had no interest in what Helias had got up to the previous night or how much he felt he had been dunned and nor was he going to respond to his jibe; so someone had blabbed about him and Apollonia, hardly surprising since it seemed you could not take two steps in an army camp without someone gossiping. He was lost in his imaginings of sieges and battles and relating his opinions with the eagerness of his age, which carried with it a lack of sensitivity.

'The other way is starvation, a siege that stops any food getting in, even better if we can cut off their water.'

'But you just said that needs ships...'

'I did, Tzitas.'

'So knowing we lack those, how does our general hope to do what you say is not possible?'

Flavius was so lost in his enthusiasms he did not pick up that his way of talking to them was beginning to grate. Now his voice had that quality that implied to his listeners that only a fool would not be able to deduce the truth.

'By stirring up the population of the city, of course! There must be many within the walls that are Chalcedonians. My father was always harking on about how prone the people of the city were to riot, and what better cause could there be than the one we are fighting for?'

The sun, which had created a golden sky, rose from behind the city of Constantinople, silhouetting in sharp relief the many spires and also warming their bodies. Unaware of how he was beginning to bore his audience, Flavius began to explain what he knew of the Blues and Greens and how much trouble they could cause. He did not get far, interrupted as he was by a set of blaring trumpets, the sound coming from the same direction as the shining sun, making it impossible to see anything.

Much to his annoyance all his unit stood and walked forward, shading their eyes, and they were not alone; it looked as if the whole host had reacted in a similar fashion, and looking along the line, once he too had joined them, Flavius could see Forbas and Vigilius acting with the same curiosity as every man they led, only the tribune had a servant strapping on his breastplate.

'What does this say?' asked dim Baccuda.

'It's a call for you to take up the diadem,' Helias

joked, coughing and spitting again. 'You from today are to be emperor.'

'Me?'

'Does anyone have the wisdom to deserve it more?'

The half-suppressed laughter was enough to let the numbskull see he was being practised on, which made him glower and brought to mind for Flavius the character of Thersites from the *Iliad*, so ugly did that make him appear. Tempted to say so, he thought better; this lot would know nothing of Homer.

'I'm sure that gate before us is opening,' called Tzitas, well in advance of the others.

All the while they had been watching, those trumpets had continued to blow and the rising sun, now illuminating the battlements, began to flash off the metal with blinding streaks of light. Tzitas had the right of it, the great gates had swung open and from within them came a body of men on foot, all in startlingly white robes: closer to they saw the broad purple stripes with which they were edged.

'A delegation from the senate,' cried Helias.

'What use is that?' Flavius enquired only to be utterly ignored, which piqued him enough, after several seconds of total silence, to add, 'Suit yourself!'

Did they not know, these ignorant *rusticae* that the senate mattered not a scrape on a wax tablet since the time of Augustus and had lost even more power since? It might talk, it rarely even met to do that now, but it did not decide: only the emperor had that right.

Horns began to play to their rear and from that direction came the pounding of hooves, soon to reveal the mounted *foederati*, led in person by Vitalian. He had them fan out before their own encampment with the general at the centre, under his personal banner, an attendant rushing forward with his helmet, that quickly donned, which had his companions looking to Flavius to explain, which he did, feeling his standing restored.

'A precaution,' Flavius replied in what was in honesty a guess. 'He fears a surprise sortie by cavalry.'

'Gates are being closed again.'

'You have good eyes Tzitas.'

That got a rare smile from a fellow not accustomed to praise. 'Have to.'

Vitalian had been joined by his tribunes, all now mounted and clad in their armour, Vigilius included, and they lined up just to his rear looking straight ahead at the approaching embassy, for that was all it could be, given there was not a weapon in sight. Nor were these senators in any rush, walking forward at no great pace as suited their dignity, their servants trailing them bearing trays piled with food.

Vitalian dismounted too and walked forward, lifting off his helmet and picking out the man who led the arrow-shaped delegation. When he was a few cubits distant he threw wide his arms, that replicated by their general, a man he clearly knew, and they came together to engage in a tight embrace, before they thrust apart to stand, arms on each other's shoulders, deep in what was obviously friendly conversation.

'Christ be praised,' cried Helias, 'I think we have won. Happen they'll make you emperor after all, Baccuda.'

'Oh, to be a fly buzzing round that exchange,' Flavius said, thinking that if Helias was right, he would be within the city by the time the sun went down and once there he would somehow contrive to find his father's old companion.

'Try it,' Helias suggested, 'they might do us all a service and swat you.'

Flavius glowered as he observed Vitalian take the lead senator's arm and walk him back towards his own tent, the line of his soldiers melting away to create a path through which all could proceed. The horsemen had been stood down and returned to their lines, likewise the tribunes had dismounted, their mounts led away by grooms, and they now trailed their general as he led the whole into his tent.

Forbas, sensing that any talks would take an age, began to bellow orders that would see his men once more on the training field, but to engage in mock battle when it was clear their leader was talking, as well as knowing that whatever was concluded would affect them all, was purgatory. If that was true of the majority, it was doubly so for Flavius. As time went by, the sanguine hope for a resolution faded somewhat, to be replaced by growing doubt; if they were negotiating and taking so long about it that did not hint at agreement.

The youngster so wanted to be in that tent; growing up in the home of a man in command, he had been privy to, if not everything that happened, a great deal of what went on. As a child he had wandered into meetings to be greeted by his indulgent father and have his chin chucked by those with whom he was in discussion. Older, and certainly in the last few years, he had been able to listen to such exchanges and understand what was being decided, for only very rarely had his father shut the door on them.

Irritated at the time, he realised now that he had been allowed to hear things of no consequence. When the door was closed Decimus must have been in conversation with those he wished to witness against Senuthius, or perhaps laboriously penning his letters to Constantinople, neither of which he wanted to share.

The *flagellum* carried by Forbas hit him a stinging blow across the shoulder, followed by a meaningful look and a command to concentrate on what was happening; the centurion did not need to ask where the youngster's mind was. It was within that tent and in his head Flavius was engaging in any number of imaginary conversations, ones in which his sagacity naturally triumphed.

'You're not a general, Flavius, nor yet a tribune. You are a *decanus,* so for the love of Christ behave like one. Now let us get properly formed and we will start again.'

Flavius looked at those he led; expecting sympathy he could not comprehend why they seemed pleased to see him a victim of Forbas's whip, a notion which troubled him for a while, until everyone was distracted by the senatorial delegation emerging from Vitalian's great tent to return to the city.

Curiosity was now at fever pitch; had the talking

310

failed to achieve what everyone now hoped for: a way that would see their aims satisfied, allowing them to return home? For the gloss of soldiering, the excitement that had animated nearly every man when they left their homes, had been rubbed off by experience.

It was an aid to deep curiosity that officers had servants, and like that breed they, with few exceptions, were the kind to adopt a superior and knowing air so that they could draw flattery, or even some kind of gift, before they revealed what they knew. The senior officers would go on the morrow to meet and negotiate in person with Emperor Anastasius, but General Vitalian had declined to join them.

No great imagination was needed to discern why; the emperor was not to be trusted and once inside the city their commander and the champion of their cause might never get out again. As dawn broke Flavius was up and watching, his hopes riding on the half-dozen officers he saw depart, dressed in finery that he had not seen before, clothing fit for an imperial audience.

CHAPTER TWENTY-TWO

The delegation from Vitalian would be met by a mounted escort and brought along the Triumphal Way, no doubt an object of much curiosity to a crowd of citizens. Justinus had been ordered to parade the entire *excubitor* corps in order to greet

311

the delegation, which meant his soldiers had spent hours in special preparation and all were inspected before they were deployed, not only lining the avenue that led from the Triumphal Way to the palace gates and the portico of the entrance that also served as that for the imperial senate house; inside the building they were spaced along the corridors, their breastplates freshly oiled and polished, the plumed-ridge helmets gleaming, especially the silver decorations that marked them out as bodyguards to the emperor.

The even more gorgeously accoutred officers were there at intervals, and thanks to the duties they had been obliged to undertake to ensure their sections were up to the mark, none were bleary-eyed from a night of debauchery. Their commander had taken station on the portico steps and was there to greet the rebels, as was Pentheus Vicinus. The very obvious fact of Vitalian's non-presence was already known, which had caused Petrus to praise the general's wisdom for not, as he put it, 'Laying his head in the lion's cage, with a beefsteak for a helmet.'

Anastasius was likewise dressed for the occasion, the sparkling jewel-studded imperial diadem upon his brow, the garments he wore purple, the devices upon them traced out in heavy and awesome amounts of gold thread. His throne, of worked precious metals surmounted by imperial eagles, sat on a raised dais, as did he until the embassy from Vitalian entered the audience chamber, at which point he stood and stiffly descended the steps to greet his visitors in a show of friendship and seeming humility, that

312

answered by deep bows.

'How did we come to this?' he asked, his old voice, rather reedy now, full of sorrow.

'Because you are an aged dolt,' Petrus whispered, so low no one could hear him.

'We shall talk,' Anastasius continued, 'and being of goodwill I am sure that what divides us can be bridged.'

He followed that by a clap of his hands, which brought into the chamber servants bearing trays on which there were gifts, objects of gold and silver, cups, chains that had talismans and medals attached, these distributed by the emperor with his own hands to men for whom, judging by their expressions, such wealth was overwhelming.

'A few small tokens of my esteem and be assured that should we resolve our differences there will be much for you to take back, not least to General Vitalian, who by your presence clearly trusts you to judge if what we conclude meets the needs of those you lead. I ask you to accompany me to a less public place, where we may speak our minds freely and I adjure you to pay no attention to my imperial dignity.'

'We would never assume to offend that, Highness,' said Vitalian's second in command.

'Then let us proceed to talk, Diomedes, for I sense in you a man who is looking for conciliation.'

Petrus was whispering to himself again, as Anastasius swept out of the audience chamber, trailed by a group of courtiers, which included Pentheus Vicinus. 'Flatter one, divide from the others, who will seek your favour, you old goat.'

If there was a slur on the imperial character in

his musings, there was also a bit of admiration. It had been a fine gesture to get up from his throne and come down to meet Vitalian's representatives, but where they might have seen humility Petrus saw nothing but condescension.

It was telling no one else departed from an audience chamber now cut off from what was being discussed, a place that became a buzz of useless speculation. Every possible outcome was aired, including the notion that all that waited in private for these men was a bloody execution. This had many an eye searching for the *comes excubitorum*, who by his absence added fuel to that kind of conjecture.

Justinus had departed but in the other direction, to stand down those troops who had no need to maintain their station in the heat of a day that would, as the sun reached its zenith, turn unbearable, with the caveat to his officers that they must stay fully dressed and be kept standing by in the cool of their barracks, given he had no idea when they would be required to parade again.

'And change the men in the corridors every double glass. Added to that I want a messenger outside my quarters and one to keep watch on the room in which they are talking. If anyone emerges I need to know, and if the emperor leads it will be everyone back to their stations.'

'You do not see, Uncle, that is one of the things your officers esteem you for, your attention to the well-being of the guard.'

'Only one thing, Petrus?'

His nephew smiled, which reminded the older man that when he did so it was not an expression

314

to warm many a heart. With its sideways lift it tended to look like the precursor to something sly or insulting.

'If I was to tell you all of what they say it would bring you to the blush, given you so hate anything that smacks of flattery.'

'As long as they do as they are commanded I rest content, I need no more.'

'I am sure they will obey whatever order you choose to give them, now or...'

That got Petrus a hard look, for it hinted at the future not the present. 'Perhaps I should gift a few with a good lashing, just so they know I am not easy prey.'

'I know one or two of your officers who take pleasure in such things and are willing to pay for the service. Give it to them gratis and they will be yours forever.'

'Has it ever occurred to you to mix with people with a higher set of morals, or indeed any at all?'

'It has occurred, Uncle, but then I recall how dreary such people are, and so I do not seek their company.'

'Your mother complains to me often that I do not rein you in.'

'Do you wish to?'

Justinus smiled. 'We are all judged in the final accounting by God, Petrus. If you wish to go to perdition in your own way, who am I to prevent you.'

'For which I thank you: having one father is bad enough, two would be ... shall we settle on Hades, where perhaps I will be allowed to atone and then proceed, cleansed, to paradise.'

There was jocularity in that, but Justinus knew that underneath the displayed cynicism his nephew could display the attributes of the deeply religious. Given that sat uncomfortably with the way he lived his life, his uncle could only assume the young man was conflicted, wishing to stay pure but unable to resist temptation. Also Petrus was ambitious, though that too tended to fluctuate between what he saw as his duty set against those moments when the seizing of opportunity became his priority, tempered by the fear of acting in a manner seen as precipitate.

The way he assiduously courted the officers of the excubitor might just be for the purposes of entertainment in what he saw as good company. Yet there was possibly another motive and his normally sanguine uncle sometimes allowed darker thoughts to enter into his thinking, the notion that if there was an altogether deeper purpose, it might not be inimical to his own well-being.

'So, Petrus, what will Anastasius offer these men?'

'You think I know, Uncle?'

'I have often thought you can read the imperial mind.'

'Difficult,' Petrus chortled, 'given the singular lack of comprehensible text.'

'Let us test your appreciation against what transpires.'

'Am I being tested?'

'You may decline to respond if you wish, I have no right to demand anything of you in this regard.'

316

Justinus, having pricked his vanity, looked down to hide his smile at a set of papers compiled by his nephew that he could not read, covering the move by reaching for his stencil. This was an object made for him by Petrus so that he could sign his written orders. Sometimes as he ran the quill through the stencil he wondered if he should employ another scribe, perhaps even just to tell him that what his nephew had written was what he had dictated, only to dismiss it – that was a route to not trusting two people, added to which a palace scribe would go gossiping all over the place, which was no way to keep hidden from anyone what he thought.

'He will seek time, offer them concessions, ply them with gold and try to convince them to persuade Vitalian that there is no longer any purpose in revolt.'

'Expensive?'

'Cheap for an old skinflint who has amassed so much gold that the treasury struggles to contain it. He must have ten times what Zeno left him.'

'Well,' Justinus replied, 'let us see if you are right.'

He reached for his *galea*, polished bronze with patterns of silver and gold, embedded with flashing coloured glass, having become aware of a certain amount of commotion, running footsteps and folk calling out. His supposition that something had happened in the negotiations proved correct when, after a loud knock, one of his officers opened the door.

'The emperor is preparing to come out, sir.'

'Alone?' asked Petrus mischievously of a man

he knew well, which got him a grin.

'No blood, more's the pity.'

'The guards,' Justinus barked.

'Are all in place in the audience chamber and the corridors.'

'Make sure the rest are ready to line the avenue.'

'Sir!'

Petrus had it to the last dot, a fact not known to the likes of Flavius for a whole day. A time in which, having seen their officers return and observed that they came laden with what could only be imperial gifts – they were hidden from sight by sackcloth – they all spent hours wondering what had been agreed, if anything.

The only distraction from that came by seeking diversions, most of his men in the temporary taverns and brothels set up between their camp and the walls, in Flavius's case by a visit to Apollonia for what had become the swift and excruciating pleasure of relief, given half his day was spent in anticipation.

'You do not seem happy to lay with me?'

'I am,' she insisted in a husky voice that was less than convincing, avoiding his eye by pulling him down in a close embrace.

He did not truly believe her; the coupling they had just engaged in was nothing like the first time. Yet Flavius was reluctant to challenge what she said by pointing out the difference between her eagerness then and what seemed close to meekness now, convincing himself that to speak would hurt her feelings. It would be a long time before he admitted the truth to himself: that his own desires and gratification were of such paramount concern as to overcome any feeling of selflessness.

'Now we know where he sneaks off to.'

The voice of Helias had Flavius jumping to his feet and pulling at his leggings to cover his nakedness, leaving a confused Apollonia on her back wondering what was going on.

Tzitas spoke next. 'Do you think he'd spare us a go?'

'He might,' was the hopeful response.

'What in the name of the devil are you doing here?' Flavius demanded, as Apollonia, embarrassed if not actually shamed, rolled on her side and pulled down her smock to conceal her nakedness.

'Just out for a saunter, *Decanus.*'

He wanted to shout at Helias, indeed both of them, for they were grinning like a pair of baboons, but it is hard to stand upon your dignity when you have just been spotted with your leggings round your ankles and your bare arse visible to the world. As he tried to speak, he heard a sob.

'Look what you have done,' he barked.

'Not half of what you have done,' Tzitas snorted, 'and even less fun.'

'This was not fun,' he cried reaching down to comfort Apollonia, only to realise how stupid that sounded. With his back to his tormentors he spoke softly to her. 'Go back to your mama. I will come tomorrow and make it up to you, I promise.'

She was up and running so quickly he could not catch her smock to restrain her, so he turned around and glared. 'I'll make you pay for this.'

'We'd rather pay for what you just had, Flavius.'

He wanted to strike Helias, they were of a height and he was unsure what stopped him. Possibly, he was to tell himself, because a superior does not physically strike an inferior; if he needs to punish him there are official ways to secure that. It did not always hold water; there was always the nagging suspicion that he had backed away from a scrap he might not win, for if he had struck Helias there was no doubt in his mind that the ranker would have fought back.

Just then the horns blew to summon every man in the camp and since Helias and Tzitas were already running he could do nothing more than follow. It was not Forbas this time – the call to assemble came from Vitalian himself and so they lined up in front of his oration platform, eager to hear what he had to say, knowing it had to do with their purpose.

On the same platform stood all of his senior officers, those who had gone to meet the emperor as well as the many who had not, and Flavius examined their faces seeking to get some kind of drift of what was to come. Then Vitalian spoke, in his strong carrying voice, to tell them that Anastasius had seen the error of his edicts on dogma and had agreed terms, which he then outlined: freedom to worship according to Chalcedon, all bishops removed from their diocese to be reinstated, a gift of money from the imperial treasury – enough to get them back from whence they came.

That made the examination of those behind Vitalian more acute, as Flavius sought evidence of disagreement; had the emperor really given way so easily, was he not secure enough behind his great walls to defy the host before them? While he was speculating on this his fellow soldiers were cheering and he realised how relieved they were and had to be open about his own emotions. For all his bluster about looking forward to battle, he had harboured no great desire to attack the defences of Constantinople and die seeking to overcome those walls.

Some of those to the rear of Vitalian looked downcast; clearly they were not in agreement and his own tribune Vigilius was one of them. How much he would like to ask him why – which would not happen, it being a good way to a flogging for his temerity. In any case, the mood of the host was obvious and it was some time before their general could make himself heard again. Eventually the cheering died away, calmed by his outstretched arms and their gestures for silence.

'If we have not fought a great battle we have won an even better victory. Collectively we have imposed upon a man the truth that citizens of the empire will not stand by for tyranny. Anastasius now knows how much we love our God and also knows how we choose to express that love. Jesus was born of man and is divine. He is the Son of God and he came into this world through the agency of his mother Mary.'

That got a chorus of amens; it was not just the priests that fell to their knees in supplication.

'Let that be proclaimed loudly as we march back to Marcianopolis, a triumphal parade that will commence at dawn tomorrow, for we have no longer any need to remain in this place. Our work is done!'

The cheers deafened again, but that last exhortation concentrated the mind of Flavius; he had no desire to go back north, unless he went with a body that would gain him justice for his family, but where to go? Then it came to him: the gates of Constantinople would be open as soon as Vitalian's host broke camp. He would enter the city and there seek out his father's old comrade, Justinus, so he could impress on him the need to act.

The assembly was not dismissed; a cart came down the road that separated the main camp from the officers' tents, filled with sacks, and orders were shouted that each century should form a line to be rewarded with several pieces of imperial copper, a gift to cement his goodwill from Anastasius himself. Judging by what he overheard, Flavius guessed that most of the coin would stay here and be spent within sight of the city; those enterprising traders were in for a profitable night.

With his two copper *folles* clutched in his hand he went in search of Apollonia. He needed to tell her of his plan and also to say that soon he would be going north again. Flavius approached her camp, only to run straight into the *curator* of the foresters and, judging by the glower on his large, round face, what he was going to tell Flavius was not pleasant.

'Did you set out to dun me you little shit?'

Flavius put a meaningful hand on his sword, to tell this squat brute what might happen if he resorted to violence, before saying, as innocently as he could manage, 'Why do you say that?'

'Don't fanny me. That fellow you paid me to employ showed a leg this morning and disappeared.'

The manufactured look of surprise and confusion felt utterly unconvincing and the voice seemed no better. 'Disappeared?' An angry nod, met with a questioning look. 'Are you certain he has not just gone for a stroll?'

'Stroll! With his sword, spear, and shield! I should have known anyone coming with that lot was not to be trusted. But if I have been slow, it was 'cause I expected to be paid for my service, which I take leave to say you will seek to avoid now. Well, if you think–'

Flavius stopped that tirade by pressing the two bounty coins he had just received into the man's hand. 'I am as surprised as you, *Curator*, but I must accept responsibility. He was a man I trusted, but it seems that was misplaced. I cannot have you suffer for my error, so please take what I have given you as my recompense, though I am sure money is of no interest to you, it is more mortification that animates you.'

Angry as he was there was no way to gainsay that and maintain any worth, self or otherwise. The ox-like brute looked at the coins in his hand and took long enough about it to allow Flavius to slip by him and flee. At the place occupied by the camp followers the news had been spread of what was to come and it was not something to make everyone ecstatic, though the harpies were enjoying a bounty. Many here lived off the existence of the host and they would march back with it to uncertainty.

Apollonia was one of those, as was her 'father' Timon and the woman he had taken in as a wife, really a pair of hands he could exploit and live off while toiling not himself. The sudden visit of Flavius caught him out; normally Timon fled when the youngster came for Apollonia. He was lying on a straw palliasse, his great gut bare as usual and sticking up, but that did not last.

At the sight of Flavius he rolled over and with some difficulty got onto his stout knees. The struggle to actually rise was too great, which left him looking up with a pleading look seeking mercy in his eyes, unable to actually speak when Flavius asked where his paramour was. That only got a finger to direct him.

He found her with her arms, up to her elbows, in water, scrubbing against the rough side of a tub to get clean some stranger's garments, her mother, stick-thin and looking like a crone, toiling likewise. The look she gave him as he dragged her daughter away was full of hate, something that again only made sense long afterwards – when he knew that she would pay the price for what he was about, and with pain.

Apollonia he led to the woods where they had enjoyed their trysts and he explained to her what he intended to do, but he told her not to fear, once his business was complete he would seek her out and rescue her from Timon, all this listened to with his eyes on the top of her blonde hair and bowed head. Then he embraced her and that stirred in him feelings that needed to be dealt with, his conduct, as he pressured her gently to the ground and indulged his pleasure, taken with the passivity that had become habitual.

Sated, Flavius rolled to lie beside her, where he reiterated his promise, and wiped the tears from her eyes that he knew to be sorrow at their parting. There, with her head crooked in his arm and talking of an imagined future, he fell asleep and when he awoke it was to the blast of the horns sounding dawn. There was no sign of Apollonia and his first thought, one that shamed him when he recalled it, was to ensure his purse was still tied to his belt and there was something within to clutch at.

He had intended to gift Apollonia that which he had received in bounty but sleep had taken away the chance to give her any of his own money in its place; now there was no time, for the camp might break and the host might begin its march to the north before he had retrieved his weapons and, from the century baggage cart, his prized breastplate, still in its sackcloth wrapping.

'She will manage till I rejoin her,' Flavius reassured himself as he ran, 'and then she will see the last of that swine Timon.'

CHAPTER TWENTY-THREE

Flavius handed in equipment he had been issued, plain breastplate and greaves, and recovered his own, placing the roll of letters that had never left proximity to his skin inside the sacking. He then watched the host of Vitalian march away with something of a sinking feeling, realising if it was not as acute as that which he had felt on returning to his empty family home, the emotion was similar, as if some part of his being had become detached from the whole.

In part it was what they left too, a field scarred by their presence, the grass where they had walked, marched and exercised bare and brown, with green patches where tents had been pitched added to the slashed black trenches of too many latrines. Long before the last soldier had upped and left, the traders who had set up their stalls had dismantled their ramshackle constructs, before heading back to a city that now had open if still well-guarded gates, they too leaving behind them the blot and filth of their presence.

Having been camped near the sea, the gate by which Flavius chose to enter was in itself astounding at a distance and even more so close to. His father had described the fabled Golden Gate and fired his youthful imagination with talk of his youngest son being granted a triumph, this being the route used by a victorious general when he entered the city. The notion had been scoffed at by Atticus, his brother correct when he insisted that things like triumphs were never granted now, emperors being too jealous to grant honours to military men who might become excessively popular.

The Golden Gate was set back from the main walls and protected by a pair of towers topped by twin statues of winged victory. There were three entrances, the two smaller openings allowing people to enter through one and exit through the other. The centre gate was the one that a new emperor would ride through in procession and in his mind's eye Flavius could conjure up the figure dressed in purple robes, a glorious diadem on his head, stood on an eight-horse chariot driven by a slave, traversing the whole of the Triumphal Way to the Great Palace that would be his residence.

If Vitalian had been a threat, no single person, even armed with a spear, was seen as such. He approached under the watchful eyes of the guards from one of the city regiments, in highly polished breastplates over red tunics, atop the battlements. Flavius passed their gaze without trouble and he was likewise looked over by men in different clothing, chain vests over green tunics whom he took to be city prefects. No one sought to impede him and he passed without hindrance, and beyond that gate the vista opened out into a great wide thoroughfare, colonnaded on each side with shaded walks lined with shops, and into the distance stretched a panorama that had him thinking he had come across one of the Seven Great Wonders.

No description of a city like Constantinople, however comprehensive, could prepare a person for the entering of it and Flavius was no exception; compared to Dorostorum the buildings were larger and more magnificently decorated, with bas-reliefs and statuary. In trying to calculate the dimensions of the Triumphal Way, marked out as some thirty paces, it was hard to be precise. His measurement could take no account of how hard it was just to cross, it being crowded with both horse-drawn traffic and humans who seemed to have no notion to give way to one another, let alone some bumpkin now dressed in rough country clothing. Nor did they do any more than disdain his apologies as he bumped into them.

Later he would say to others that it was never a good notion to look like a stranger in the capital city, to walk along, head back, to gaze at every sight that took your wondering and astounded eye. The slight tug at his belt destroyed his day-dreaming in an instant and he shot a hand out to grab that of the urchin who had just sliced through the tie on his purse with a tiny but obviously sharp knife and was seeking to run off.

The thief was not one to give up easily; he swung the knife in a vicious arc seeking to stab the hand that held him, forcing Flavius to likewise swerve abruptly, which sent the sacking-covered breast-plate swinging round to his side, that partially impeding the swipe he aimed at the fingers holding the knife, this while he pulled hard to put the brat off balance.

The combination saved him but the pause was only temporary as he realised the little toad who had tried to rob him was shouting that he was the victim of a thief, this as he tried to stab his so-called assailant in the chest. This was no time for finer feelings; using his free hand Flavius thumped him round the ear with a buffet that would have felled an adult, yet still the little swine would not drop the purse.

A crowd had begun to gather and it was obviously confused, from the little Flavius could truly make out, as to who was victim and who was felon. Another swing of that blade ended with the second wrist being held, which got the new arrival to the city a hard kick in the shins, one he had to counter by using his own boot. That took the urchin's legs and allowed Flavius to spin him and cross his arms so that he was holding him back against his chest.

Having not gotten far from the gates the hulla-baloo had alerted the city prefects and two of them came bustling through a crowd that had done no more than spectate and comment, in a situation which, in Dorostorum, they might have stepped in to clout the obvious thief as well as disarm him. As it was, Flavius felt a very strong hand on his own collar, followed by a command to let the little fellow go, vaguely noting the strong accent of the city, so very different from his own.

The boy began to moan as soon as he was released, to be immediately grabbed by one of the prefects, a fellow who also had a twang to his voice, a sort of lazy drawl as he demanded to know what was going on.

'He dropped his knife, Your Honour,' the urchin cried.

He then began to weep copious tears, either from the pain Flavius had inflicted or a sheer aptitude for drama, the streaks running down a filthy puckish face that at another time Flavius might have seen as lively. Looking down, there it was, right at Flavius's feet.

'He tried to nab my purse, cut through the tie as easy as you like.'

There was a moment then, so convincing was this childish play-acting, when Flavius saw himself being had up as a criminal, a split second when he could imagine being dragged off in chains to be incarcerated in a deep cell with water dripping off the walls. He was brought back to reality and the sun creating shadows by laughter, this from both the city prefects, one of whom responded.

'You got to hand it to the little turd, he does magic a story so easily.'

'You know him?' Flavius asked.

'Surely do.'

'But it was him, Your Honour, honest,' cried the boy wriggling to get free and failing.

'Goes by the name of Ivo and a right menace he is.' The prefect leant over to look the urchin in the eye. 'Picked the wrong mark this time, didn't you, Ivo? Fellow with a sword too, which you are lucky he did not get loose or we'd be picking your head off the paving stones.'

The other prefect spoke from behind him. 'I will accompany you to the office of the urban prefect, young sir, where you can swear against the boy. See him in the mines, if I'm not mistaken.'

'And not afore time,' the one holding Ivo added, handing Flavius his purse. 'By your mode of speech you're a stranger to the city I suspect?'

Flavius was about to say yes and, he had been part of Vitalian's army, but he stopped himself and merely nodded.

'Then have a care, lad; for every honest citizen in our capital, there's a wrong 'un to match them and if you don't keep your wits about you then you're meat for villainy. It's lucky you was on the Triumphal Way, which is patrolled. Had you been in an alley you would have been in real trouble.'

'Do I have to accompany you? I have business to attend to at the imperial palace.'

First the eyebrows went up a good two fingers, then the man before him looked up and down and what he saw did not fit with what he had heard said. Then he smiled, the way a person does when they are favouring an imbecile.

'With the emperor, no doubt?'

'No, with his count of the excubitors.'

'Really?'

'Yes.'

The amused look evaporated and he shook Ivo, who wailed. 'Well, that will have to wait a while, for if you do not come and swear that this little sod tried to lift your purse, which we cannot do for we did not see it, then how are we to have this complaint filed?'

It was amazing to Flavius the way the crowd that had gathered to witness the event obviously had no intention of hanging around to be a witness against Ivo; they dispersed as soon as the prefect mentioned the need for someone to swear.

Flavius looked at Ivo, the tears, which had now dried up, leaving clear lines on his grubby cheeks. 'The mines you say?'

'Too much of a mite for the galleys, though maybe he will grow into them if he lives long enough.'

'And that will be for life?'

'A short one, such labour kills you young.'

'Do you have a mother, Ivo?' A shake of the head. 'A father?' Negative again.

'He lives in the gutters, young fellow, can you not see that by the filth on him?'

He sensed Ivo had sniffed his reluctance, which turned the malevolent look to which he had hitherto been subjected to one of soulful supplication, that in a blink of an eye, making him think this little toad should be with a troupe of performers, so quick were his wits. Flavius reasoned that if he went along and swore against this mite, who was stunted in his growth, Ivo would die as a slave and not long into the future. He knew little of mines but they were places of toil deadly to grown men.

'Is there not a place where such children can be cared for?'

'Six feet of good earth is best,' said the prefect, 'but saving that there is an order of St Basil monks who take in urchins and bring them back to God, though not without someone gifts them the means.'

'Then let us go there, for I cannot swear as you ask me to. I could not, as a Christian, condemn this boy to the life you promise for him.'

'You are from the country,' came a voice from behind and it was not a compliment. 'Have to be.'

'I have been foolish, as you say, leaving myself exposed by my behaviour.'

Ivo had a gleam in his eye now, one that indicated to Flavius that if he was taken in by monks, he would not be with them for long. But that was not his concern – he was thinking that his need for divine aid was great and how could he ask for mercy on his aim if he was to deny it to another soul? It was also, he had good reason to believe, what his mother would have done, for she always took the side of the poor against authority and that had sometimes included her own husband.

'Soft in the head, are you?'

'Naw,' said the second prefect, 'a fellow like this can't keep waiting the Count of the Excubitors.'

Flavius let the sarcasm pass without comment. 'I would be obliged if you would guide me to these monks of St Basil.'

'Not likely,' came the response, as he was less than gently handed Ivo, forced to take his collar. 'This turd knows the way, let him direct you.'

Both prefects departed, leaving a passive boy in Flavius's hand. There was a second after he let him go in which Ivo had no idea what to do; it did not last. He made a dash for it but not before he had a last attempt at swiping the purse.

Flavius continued on his way, still wrapped in wonder at the sights, passing through the various forums built by successive emperors, all of them described to him by his father; the Forum of Arcadius, then of Bovis and on to the great open space where the road split in two, overseen by a tetrapylon. Next came the great Forum of Theodoric, he of the mighty walls, rectangular instead of round, and last that of the man after whom the city was named and the first forum built. It was the Forum of Constantine, where sat, square and imposing, with its Doric columns, one of the city's senate houses.

It was impossible to keep his eyes from looking skywards as he came within sight of the Hippodrome, trying to image it in the whole of its oval shape, which trended away for near a *milia,* as well as its tiered seats inside that could accommodate thousands. How could anything so massive be built and was there no end to human ingenuity aided by the divine hand of God? If he knew the Great Palace was at the end of the Triumphal Way that was where his memory of parental recollection ran out, which obliged him to seek to ask the citizenry how he might contact the *comes excubitorum*.

Laughter was the least rude of the responses; several times he was told where to go and none of the proposed destinations were pleasant, most being blasphemous. One soul, when he seemed to persist by blocking his passage, looked set to fetch him a blow until an assessment of the risks changed his mind. Impatience was the common denominator with the citizens of the capital; everyone seemed to be in a hurry, obviously on some business that did not allow for courtesy to an outsider.

In the end, as he passed the Milion stone, from which all imperial distances were measured, he was constrained to ask a blind beggar, sat in ragged clothes by the roadside, if he had any knowledge of the layout of the Great Palace, which got a rattle of his cup before any answer was forthcoming. Having proffered a coin and noisily dropped it in, that was checked for value by fingers obviously sensitive enough to tell how much had been gifted and the answers were forthcoming.

'Each party has their own gate,' he rasped. 'Who is it you seek, young sir?'

How does he know I'm young, Flavius was thinking? But he explained, not using the word 'count', but just the unit he led.

'Then you want the Gate of the Excubitors,

which is the entry to their barracks. That you will find by passing the baths, which surely you cannot go by without noticing, for you will smell them.'

The cup came up again and that got the fellow another *nummi* from the purse, again felt for value, followed by a nod that indicated it was just reward.

'I thank you, kind sir.'

'Kind?' he wheezed. 'Sir? Where you from, the moon?'

Flavius went on his way and the beggar began to chant his mantra, asking for alms for the love of God, the tin rattling endlessly. If he went awry once he eventually came to a gateway guarded by two men in highly decorated uniforms, breastplates with filigree silver decoration, *galea* helmets again picked out with silver, topped with black plumes, the whole over tunics of the same sombre hue.

Their square shields were black too, marked out with imperial eagles and metal edged. Not an eye moved or flickered as he approached, until he got what was obviously too close, at which point one of the guards dropped his spear, thrust one foot out to steady himself and told him to halt.

'My name is Flavius Belisarius and I have come to see your commander Justinus.'

The look that got somehow told Flavius he had caused a shock, this underlined when the guard responded with a confused, 'What!'

The request was repeated, which led to a pause before the other guard, who had not moved, began to shake, his lips compressed and his face sort of puffed up, an indication that he was seeking to suppress his hilarity. The man who had first spoken was not amused and he barked at Flavius.

'Be on your way, you witless dolt.'

'I am not witless, the count was a friend to my father and if you give him my name I am sure he will see me.'

'I'll give you the toe of my boot if you don't shove off.'

'I insist–'

He got no further; the tip of the spear was thrust forward to stop a finger width from his chest. 'Get out of here before I fillet you.'

Flavius had taken a step back and the guard did likewise, adopting once more the stoical pose that went with the duty.

'Can I pay you to carry the message?' he asked, his tone slightly desperate. 'I will write my name down and if you take it to Justinus he will be grateful.'

'Get on your way, you idiot. The likes of the *comes* does not want to talk to a bumpkin peasant.'

'I am the son of the centurion Decimus Belisarius!'

'You're the son of a whore, laddie, and if you do not get those feet moving I will have you thrown into the dungeons, where the rats will no doubt enjoy you as a meal. Now move.'

There had to be another way, Flavius reckoned, so he began to walk off, mind racing at possible avenues, the most outlandish being to break into the Great Palace and find Justinus, which was quickly abandoned as the road to a certain death. He could take station outside the requisite entrance and, like the blind beggar, use supplication

336

with those passing in and out to get his message through, yet how would he know whom to ask?

The bustling crowds, still paying no attention to his progress, were beginning to grate, yet it was looking along the Triumphal Way that alerted him to how steeply angled were the shadows. Night was coming and it would descend quickly, plunging the city into darkness. He had to find somewhere to lay his head and that became the most pressing need. Tomorrow was another day and surely he would find an opportunity to advance his aims.

Constantinople was not short on wine shops, the most obvious place to gain information about somewhere to sleep – they often doubled as hostelries, even in Dorostorum. The capital being a much-visited metropolis, it took only two attempts to find the right kind of place. Flavius got a bed, but in the process he also discovered how limited were his means; the cost of a cup of wine, necessary before he could enquire for a bed, shocked him, but not as much as what he was asked for a cot in a room to be shared with three other souls, the same to be paid in advance.

Once in the upstairs hovel, for it was not clean and stank of too much human occupation and too little vinegar used to clean it, he had to calculate how long his limited funds would last and the conclusion was not reassuring; he had little time to get to Justinus before he ran out of money and found himself sleeping in the gutter, for he had no notion that Constantinople was home to much in the way of charity.

CHAPTER TWENTY-FOUR

Sleep was not easy; if the snoring of those who shared his space was bad enough, it had been hard to get to sleep in the first place, one of them having brought a whore up from the wine shop to engage in noisy and prolonged rutting, which Flavius could not help compare to his own sweet couplings with Apollonia. His nightly prayers were delivered when lying down, he being sure that to kneel by his cot would only lead to derision, added to which, aware that every time he spoke he identified himself as a stranger, he made no effort to communicate.

There was a stinking privy on the ground floor and in there, when he had been alone and hoping no one was coming, he had taken his purse and jammed it in the instep of his boot. In his cot the other foot was pressed against that and he hoped he would be able to get through the night without moving and subsequently not risk being robbed. There was more than a moment of self-chastisement; was it Christian to assume his room-mates to be dishonest? Set against that was the sure knowledge of what would happen to him if he were left bereft of funds.

When dawn came he was up and using a street trough to wash, not an activity that apparently appeared necessary to anyone else. The city was already busy and, suspecting that he would be charged more to eat in the wine shop than elsewhere, he set off to look first for a bakery, and then perhaps a shop selling cheese, another for sausages. These he found in the colonnades that lined the Triumphal Way and with his purchases sharing the sacking of his breastplate he set off for the Forum of Constantine, where there was public seating as well as a fountain with water to drink.

Resting there, munching his breakfast, Flavius felt very alone. The population streamed by in all directions and he could have been one of the statues that lined the forum for all anyone cared. It came to him that in leaving the host of Vitalian, he was on his own for the very first time; he had no one to consult. Ohannes was on his way to Illyricum, he hoped, and those with whom he had shared a tent were marching back to Marcia-nopolis; if they had not necessarily been friends they had been human company. Added to that, Apollonia was with them and suddenly he ached for her presence and not just with carnal intent.

There was no one in Constantinople to talk to, or at least the one person he wanted to address was behind the walls of the imperial palace, so might as well be on the moon. The notion of waiting to pass someone a note foundered on the element of chance involved; a common soldier might just take his money and pocket it. Could he approach anyone of standing looking as he did, with what he wore, never fine, now showing the signs of weeks of marching, they would likely just brush him aside.

He began to walk, knowing it aided his thinking and all of his perambulations were not on wide avenues; sometimes he found himself in narrow alleyways and felt it necessary to move his sword to be ready for any assault. Nothing of a solution, other than those methods already considered, presented itself. Turning a corner that led from one of the alleys to a small square, Flavius disturbed a group of youths busy painting some message on a wall. His appearance made them go rigid, until, realising he was no threat – he smiled – they carried on with their graffiti.

Giving them a wide berth Flavius could read the message so far, which was that someone called Fronto was a dirty parasite who what? He had to stop and wait till they were finished, one of them grinning as the last word was painted on the bricks, which completed the information that Fronto was a dirty old goat who buggered little boys and should be castrated. Message complete, the group ran off down another alley.

'Where to get paints,' Flavius said out loud to himself.

It was back to the Triumphal Way but that produced no results: a place stocking such things as oil and pigments would not be there, but if the citizens of the city were rude the shopkeepers seemed less so, especially when he sought to copy their distinctive accent so as to sound local. Whatever, he was directed to a place in some backstreets where he found the requisite workshop.

'Vermillion?' asked the skeletal creature who owned it.

'As bright as you can make it, and a brush as well.'

'Best tell me what it is you want to paint, for

that affects the mix – need more lead and oil if it is outside, not that it will last, thank the Lord and our sun, or I would not be long in trade.'

Flavius, looking at him, reckoned he would not be long anyway; he had a hollowed chest, a hacking cough and translucent skin, patterned with very obvious blue and protruding veins.

'Which is cheaper?'

'Indoor,' came the surprised response, 'as you would expect.'

'Then make it that.'

'How much do you want?'

That flummoxed Flavius; he had no idea, in the end electing to have the smallest amount he could. The man mixed it for him in a clay pot; better that than trying to get the blend right himself and making a pig's ear of it. Pot under his arm, the top sealed with a bit of ragged oiled animal skin and twine, his chosen brush secreted away, he made his way back to the Forum of Constantine to sit, eating more of his sausage and cheese, while contemplating his plan.

Not having slept as much as he would have liked, it was hard, with the sun beating down, to stay awake, but on a single slab stone bench every time he started to drop off the action of his body jerked him awake. It felt like eternity till the sun dipped so that it was hidden behind the Walls of Theodoric, the sky turning from gold, to red, to copper and eventually to the first sight of starlight.

That had Flavius up and moving, making his way towards the palace, gratified to see what he suspected must be the case, that the entrances if not the outer walls were lit by flaring torches. He had contemplated having one of those for his own purposes only to discount it as likely to attract too much attention, but he needed to be near enough to them to employ the very edge of their spilt light. By now it was dark, the sky an inky black and a mass of starlight that came to his aid; not only did it cast dark shadows but where it illuminated it was sufficient to see, if not clearly, then enough.

The reports of the *praefectus urbanus,* handed in overnight and taken to Petrus, who would compose a precis of them for his uncle, made no mention of an excess of graffiti, huge red letters painted not only on the walls of the palace, but on those of the baths as well, so glaring a red they were impossible to pass by without their being remarked upon. It was not long before there was a buzz of conversational noise about what the daubing meant.

The first person to whom it was reported went white, the blood draining from his features, and if he had reacted calmly matters might have rested there. But Pentheus Vicinus had the family temper as well as a sudden grip on his heart of fear and he left his house in something of a hurry to go and see for himself, that alone causing comment among his family and servants.

That someone of his eminence should stand before the painted letters registered with the guards as damned strange. When stood down they had to go and look at what had so exercised the senator, who had been seen yelling and demanding the graffiti be removed. When later they were breakfasting they were given to asking their comrades if

342

they knew what it meant, so that when Justinus came to join them, as he did most mornings, the word was flying around the room and was overheard as he passed.

'What did you say?'

The soldier leapt to his feet to reply, the way his commander had posed the question making that seem appropriate.

'It's everywhere, sir, bright red, painted on the palace walls and those of the baths as well.'

'Anyone else seen it?'

'The guards just stood down asked if any of us knew what it meant.'

'Where are they?'

'Asleep I should think, sir.'

'You finished eating?'

'I am sir.'

'Then go and rouse them out. Then find my nephew and ask him to join me outside the Excubitor Gate, the guards too.'

Justinus was moving so fast he did not see the chest-thumping salute, nor with his mind in turmoil did he hear it either. Striding through the palace and out to the gate he was trying to make sense of something that failed to add up. What was the name of his old friend doing, as reported, plastered all over the walls and demanding justice?

The sight of the letters, roughly painted, with dripping lines running from every one, did not provide enlightenment as to the way, but it struck home. He might lack the skill to read but the name Belisarius was one he had seen many times recently, the last time as he signed the commission's orders prepared for him by Petrus.

'Uncle.'

'Tell me it says what I think it does.'

'Justice for Belisarius.'

'Now tell me what it means?'

'Unless you believe in spirits, then someone has daubed the walls with it.'

Justinus became aware of two soldiers, wearing no armour and only their tunics, shifting nervously from foot to foot and wondering why they had been dragged from their beds, as well as in what way they had transgressed, which might give them a clue as to what punishment they could be in for. The command to rouse out and attend on the count had come with no other explanation. At a gesture they approached, with Justinus pointing a finger at the wall.

'This, d'you see it done?'

'No, Your Honour.'

'Didn't really notice it till one of the senators came along and started yelling blue murder.'

'Which senator?'

'No idea, sir.'

'Had to be Vicinus,' Petrus whispered. 'That is a name and a demand that would rankle more with him than it does even with us.'

'But what does it mean?'

'It is a message, to Vicinus perhaps...'

'Could be to me?'

'Why to you?'

'You read me the reports of what happened on the Danube.'

'And I recall you chose not to believe them.'

'What if this is someone trying to tell me I am right?'

'It will make no difference,' Petrus responded, gesturing for the two guards to back away out of hearing.

'Of course it will.'

'No, Uncle, what is done is done and even if you find those reports are false, that something dastardly has been done, what can you do about it? Decimus Belisarius alive and enquiring into his complaints had a rationale. But the one thing that cannot be in doubt is that he is dead. To risk raising how that came about is to expose yourself as having championed his cause, which will make an enemy of a man who, thanks to his actions with regard to Vitalian, has suddenly got the ear of the emperor.'

'Why do you always analyse matters in terms of intrigue?'

'It keeps us alive.'

'Us?'

'You too, Uncle. I have never sought to advise you.' That got a look of disbelief; Petrus never let up with his opinions. 'But I would counsel it is unwise to rely on any popularity you might think you enjoy with Anastasius. He is as devious as an emperor must be to keep breath in his body, and not beyond sacrificing a friend if it suits his aims.

'So?'

'Leave it, say nothing and if it is in the *praefectus* report, maybe even remove it.'

'Sometimes, Petrus, you go too far.'

If Justinus had hoped to chastise his nephew, he utterly failed. 'I will not be guided on the best way to stop you endangering yourself.'

If it was not stated it was in his eyes; if you fall,

Uncle, I fall with you.

'Your Honour, there's a young fellow at the gate who says his name is Flavius Belisarius.'

The speed with which Justinus moved surprised the messenger, one of his excubitor rankers; their commandant was a measured man in everything he did; rarely if ever, outside the training arena, did he break sweat. Now, and for the second time this day, he was close to running, eager to get to the gate to first find out if it was truly the son of Decimus and secondly, if he was, to spirit him inside the palace – few as possible must know he was here, perhaps not even Petrus.

There could be no doubt whatsoever he was the one who had daubed the walls; the youth's clothing, grubby leggings and dirty smock were streaked with red paint. He had a sword, a spear resting point down and some kind of sack over his shoulder. Justinus marched up, sizing him as he went: the height, taller than Decimus, the black hair long and untidy, then there was the direct look in the eyes. The spear must have worried the men set to guard the gate for they moved to create an angle in which they could watch that weapon.

'How am I to know you are who you say?'

There was no blinking in those deep-brown eyes, just a steady gaze that hinted at self-assurance; how could the older man know that not for the first time in his life this youngster's knees were shaking?

'I need to know who it is I am talking with.'

'I don't think you are in any position to demand anything.'

'I did not think I demanded, sir,' Flavius replied, in an emollient tone. 'If you are not Count Justinus, I would be obliged if you would take a message to him.'

'Which is?'

'That his correspondence with my father, Decimus, is safe.'

Justinus stood stock-still for several seconds, before growling as he spun round, 'Come with me.' Flavius heard him mutter to the guards as he passed them not to say a word to anyone, then he had his arm taken to be bustled in through the gate and, with a sharp turn, down some stone steps into a cold, stone-walled basement. There were several heavy wooden doors with grills, all wide open, the one closest showing a bare cell with a bench and a cot into which he was shepherded.

'Wait here.'

Flavius, who still had his weapons and possessions, was confused – more so when the older man swung the door shut but did not lock it. He was gone for a short while before returning carrying a large set of keys.

'I want you to stay here, Flavius, until the palace settles down for the night, then I can take you to somewhere more comfortable. I have to lock the door, not to keep you in but to keep anyone else out. No one must know you are here and if anyone but me comes through this door I suggest you kill them, for they will be here to assassinate you.'

'Who are you?' Flavius pleaded, his voice cracked.

Justinus moved close and took him by the shoulders, looking deep into his eyes. 'I was told you were dead, that my old comrade Decimus had died with all of his sons.'

'You are Justinus?' That got a nod. 'My brothers were killed fighting bravely alongside our father and by the downright treachery–'

'Save that till we can talk properly,' Justinus interrupted 'I must go back to my own guards and not only command their silence but ensure it by threatening them with hellfire and damnation. There are currents within these walls that you will not understand, heaven knows I struggle myself, but you are in my care now and, once I fetch you from this cell, no one will harm you without they need to harm me too and I have command of over a thousand spears.'

Flavius began to cry, as a month of anxiety seemed to fall away, unaware that Justinus was mulling over what he had just said; no one was immune from harm in an imperial palace.

'I have a better idea. The door locks from the inside; you do that when I go and if I do not re-turn before dawn tomorrow, get out of here, get out of Constantinople and change your name.'

Justinus had a heavy gold chain round his neck, which he removed and handed to Flavius. 'Use this to fund your travel, sell one gold link at a time and the medallion last.'

'Am I allowed to know who would threaten me?'

'The name Vicinus will suffice and it is a prob-lem of your own making. It was he who was first alerted to your name being daubed on the walls. If I thought you dead it is possible he will know you are not, just as he will know what a threat you represent to his family.'

'I want Senuthius dead, I want vengeance for *my* family.'

'In time, perhaps, first let us keep you whole.' Justinus smiled. 'I have no sons of my own. Perhaps, if God wills it, you may come to fill that gap. Now, once you have locked the door, get some rest, for when I come for you it will take many an hour to tell me everything that has happened this last month.'

'Why was the commission recalled?'

'It was the decision of Anastasius; he feared to stir up more trouble in an area that might go over to Vitalian.'

'Can we arraign Senuthius, can I see him pay for his crimes?'

'One day,' Justinus replied, but he was no longer looking the youngster directly in the eye. So Flavius was unsure if he was being told the truth.

CHAPTER TWENTY-FIVE

Justinus had to tell Petrus what had happened and how it had come about, even if he did so with a lack of enthusiasm, certain that his nephew would object to bringing Flavius Belisarius into the palace. His reluctance extended to another truth, the knowledge that he had come to rely on his sister's son as a means of finding his way through the labyrinth of imperial politics. In the field Justinus, fighting the enemy, was a master of his craft, not least because it was easy to see who your opponent was: in his present post, outside his actual duties, he often felt uncertain.

Open recognition of friend or foe did not exist in the great palace of the richest and most extensive empire in the world, a building in which an invitation to dinner could result in a painful poisoned death, where a smile could be a prelude to betrayal or a firm embrace the act that preceded the secret knife. It was not easy to admit that, being just a simple soldier loyal to his polity, and a man who saw his word once given as binding, he lacked the gifts needed to ensure his own security and continued employment.

Being a natural intriguer, Petrus seemed to thrive in this cesspool for he enjoyed the game. With no official function other than to act as secretary to Justinus, he had ample time to observe the behaviour of others, as well as the aptitude to cultivate even people he saw as potential enemies. He was adept at evaluating motives even if they were hidden by men skilled in subterfuge and he could manoeuvre for an advantage that his uncle did not even know existed or was beneficial.

'Here? In the palace?'

'Out of sight, in one of the punishment cells to keep his presence a secret.'

Petrus wanted to tell his uncle then that there were no secrets in this building, which was as much a palace of gossip as it was the seat of imperial governance, but there was no point. He had felt a clutch at his heart on hearing that Flavius was alive and that it was he who had daubed a

350

message on the walls; a moment when he saw the angel of death hovering over his body and it had taken all his guile to keep hidden from his uncle the terror that assailed him. Thankfully, having delivered his lightning bolt, Justinus seemed lost in thought, which gave Petrus time to control his breathing and begin to think matters through.

'Who saw him?' he demanded.

'The two guards at the gate, and the man they sent with the message. All three have been spoken to and issued with dire warnings.'

'The gaoler?'

'Knows nothing, I took his keys without explanation.'

'No one else?'

Justinus bridled slightly at that third peremptory query, in what, it seemed to him, was turning into an interrogation. 'Are you aiming for the post of imperial inquisitor?'

'Forgive me,' Petrus responded, knowing it was necessary to be less aggressive. 'If I feel the need to advise you I would not like to make an error through ignorance.'

'He's a fine-looking youth, Petrus,' Justinus said wistfully, diverting his own anger and a potential point of dispute. 'Even shabbily dressed you can see his father in him.'

'Am I permitted to ask how did he survive, how did he get here?'

'No idea,' came the sighed response. 'But he is the son of Decimus, for certain.'

'You are sure?'

'He mentioned the letters, said they were safe.'

Those documents had been a concern Petrus

had carried in silence, never mentioning it as a factor he and his uncle should be anxious about. That correspondence in the wrong hands could not do other than create difficulties, how much so being uncertain. Once Petrus was apprised of the death of Decimus, his elliptical enquiries directed at anyone who might know of the matter appeared fruitless.

They had produced nothing to indicate the scheme to curb the activities of Senuthius Vicinus had become known to anyone outside those already within the circle of knowledge, yet there was a residual disquiet that someone had found out something and acted upon it. That was in the past; Petrus knew he had now to deal with the present.

'Fine-looking he might be, but his method of contacting you lacks a degree of subtlety.'

Justinus did not miss the tone of deep irony but he did think Petrus had missed an important additional cause for disquiet.

'Not just me, everyone in the city can come and gaze upon his handiwork. Pentheus Vicinus already has and, according to those who observed his reaction, he nearly had an apoplexy.'

That being far from good news, indeed it had deep ramifications, there was a pause before Petrus responded. 'What do you intend, Uncle?'

'To bring him into the palace proper, to hear his tale and to do something to make amends for our failure to protect his family.'

'Did we fail?'

'Decimus is dead, is he not, and three of his boys with him? Flavius said they died bravely, but through treachery, which I find easier to believe than what we were told, which was a pack of lies.'

The fact that they were dead and that perfidy was involved only underlined to Petrus how naïve his uncle was being. Could he not see the logical conclusion to be drawn from the words he had just employed? That somehow, someone, and he could only guess it to be Pentheus Vicinus, had got wind of what the *comes excubitorum* was up to. Not the detail, unless it was Anastasius who let slip their shared secret. They had done everything in their power to keep their intentions secure, yet enough had emerged to frustrate their intentions in a quite bloody fashion.

Someone would gossip about this Flavius, if not this day, then at some time very soon. How could Justinus keep him in the palace without the presence of a strange youth being remarked upon? If it were, Pentheus, an experienced courtier steeped in the arts of conspiracy, would deduce that it might be a threat to him. For a man who had already acted as he had that would be enough and there could only be one outcome.

How far would the senator go? Would he seek to undermine Justinus with the emperor, or would he reckon that, with his reputation for probity, such an attempt would only expose his intentions? It had ever been Petrus's way to seek to put himself in the shoes of others and he did so now, knowing that for Pentheus to feel utterly secure the death of Flavius, identified or not, would ill suffice and for a very good reason: the senator was a man who lived well beyond his discernible means.

He owned several farms, it was true, and they produced abundant crops, but not enough to support the aims of a person who wanted to be a power at the imperial court, where the disbursement of gold was a necessity if you wished to avoid being seen as of no account. It was not hard to deduce where such monies came from.

Pentheus had to be in receipt of monies from his criminal cousin in Moesia and it was those that gave him the power to bribe, the funds to lavishly entertain and the means to present himself as a man of wealth. It return, he shielded the criminal activities that had been regularly reported by Decimus Belisarius.

He would act now as he had done previously, not out of family loyalty, but for personal necessity and the best way to protect what he would be desperate to hang on to was to close off all the avenues that might threaten him. One death might give him satisfaction; three, if they could be carried out discreetly, would seal off the problem completely.

'I cannot dissuade you from the course you have set us upon, Uncle?' Petrus asked, even if he knew the answer.

'I gave my word.'

Petrus nearly broke his commandment then and spoke openly, to ask to be allowed to act as he saw fit to protect all three of them from what they might face. But it was bitten back; the less his uncle knew the better. Once made aware of his actions he would want to be consulted on every gambit and move which, if it did not kill off his intentions, would at the very least impose a check on the freedom Petrus needed to manoeuvre.

'So be it.'

That got him a hard look. 'I had expected you to object more than you have.'

'There is no point, you have made a decision and I know, if you have given your word, you will hold to it. It is what makes you who you are.'

'What do I say to the emperor?'

'Nothing! In time perhaps, but not now.'

Justinus came for Flavius after the guards had been set for the night, having brought him a cloak to hide his grime-streaked and paint-spattered clothing, telling him he must abandon his spear. He then led him through seemingly endless silent corridors, lit by flaming sconces under which stood rigid-to-attention guards, who only moved to salute their commander as he hurried by. Officially Justinus had a suite of rooms, one of which was an unused bedchamber – he preferred his barren cell – and attached to that was a bathing chamber, now ready filled with hot water.

'Take off your clothing and wash, Flavius, for you stink of the gutter. I have had an excubitor tunic laid out for you as well as suitable under-garments, and when you are clean and dressed, we can talk.'

The youngster divested himself of the cloak, which revealed the gold chain and medallion given to him that morning, immediately removed and returned.

'I will await you in the other room.'

'Which other room?' Flavius asked, for they had passed through several.

'Follow your nose.'

To divest himself of his clothes, in which he

seemed to have been living for a lifetime, was bliss on its own; to then step down into a hot bath was akin to paradise, though he did question the smell of powerful unguents that had been added to the water. He would stink of them when finished and such perfumery was counted as unmanly in Dorostorum. Pleasure outweighed concern, for there was a sponge with which to wash, a pumice stone with which to scour his skin and the whole made him feel both alert and secure.

Towelled dry he used the combs provided to dress hair that badly needed the attention of the barber slave that had administered to the Belisarius family. That made him think of those he had left behind, the same bleating sheep he had taken that day his father died to the safety of the citadel. Had they paid a price for his flight? Why had he not seen fit to think on the well-being of the family slaves up till now?

He came out and did indeed follow his nose, to enter a candlelit chamber, hung with huge tapestries of mythical scenes, somewhat pagan to his taste, plus a table laden with food and silver flagons of wine. Justinus was present and so was another younger man, sat sprawled in a curule chair, introduced to him as the elusive Flavius Petrus Sabbatius.

'We call him Petrus,' Justinus said, 'there are so many of your name in the family it distinguishes him, that is if anything ever could.'

'How can I fault such an introduction, Uncle?'

Petrus tried to hide that the slight barb stung him, Justinus being prone to the very occasional remark that was designed to remind him of his

356

place. That he employed such a tactic now was telling: perhaps he was seeking to bolster his esteem in the presence of this youngster, a youth of good height and muscular, handsome of face and looking so fresh with his reddened skin and damp black hair that the man observing him felt a faint flash of envy.

'Petrus is my right hand and I depend upon him,' Justinus added, seeking by a kindly look to make up for his earlier remark. 'You may trust him as you trust me.'

Flavius was examining Petrus with the same acuity as he was under; the fact that the nephew was sprawled in the chair made it hard to judge his figure, but it looked to be thin and stringy. The hair was red in the candlelight and the head was canted at an angle that hinted at scepticism, as if he doubted what was standing before him.

'Eat, Flavius, then I will ask you to recount what happened to your family.'

'You were not told?'

'We were told they were dead, you too, and I admit to my shame I never enquired after your mother.' The news she was safe in Illyria seemed to mightily relieve Justinus; he actually acted as if a weight had been lifted from his shoulders. 'That is good, though her grief must be acute.'

Obviously they had been fed the same false tale as Flavius had heard from Forbas and he said so, before launching into a description of both the truth of the encounter as well as his adventures since that fateful day. Both men let him speak, very rarely interrupting, this done more by Petrus than Justinus, he seeming to need to be absolutely clear of what was being recounted.

'In order to come to Constantinople I joined with General Vitalian.'

If he had been sprawling throughout, that made Petrus shift and his voice, hitherto relaxed and quite often languid, was suddenly snappy. 'You marched with Vitalian?'

'As a *decanus,* which goes far to tell us what a less than perfect host he commanded. It was not the finest, yet it achieved its goal.'

Petrus coughed and sat fully upright. He then began to question Flavius about that host, of what it consisted and why so many had flocked to the Vitalian banner. He was treated to all the reasons religious and mercenary, to which he listened with more avid attention than he had shown hitherto.

'But really,' Flavius insisted, feeling he was being drawn away from his reason for being here, 'I did not come to describe to you his motives or that of his forces.'

'You want justice,' came the slightly acerbic response, 'which you saw fit to paint on half the walls of the city.'

It was easy to let the exaggeration pass. 'I do, and it would please me if you could now tell me if such a thing is possible.'

'I said in time,' Justinus replied. 'And we will not deceive you, it could be some time.'

Now it was his turn to explain, to tell in more detail of how the rising of Vitalian had led to the recall of Petrus as well as to add that if the mission on which Petrus had been engaged was ever to be reconvened, then there were considerations of politics which must intrude. These of necessity being complex.

'I am not master of that, Flavius.'

'Is there anything I can do?'

'You must be discreet,' Petrus cut in, 'and never use your family name while within these walls.'

'You mentioned a Vicinus?' Flavius asked Justinus.

Again it was Petrus who replied, bringing home that Justinus really did rely on him. The situation was explained in full, as well as the reasoning that would prompt Pentheus Vicinus to have him killed; he did not add that the mere presence of Flavius threatened him and his uncle as well.

'Sleep now,' Justinus said, yawning himself. 'We will talk more in the morning.'

'Where, Uncle?'

'My barren cell and my cot, Petrus, where he will be safe.'

'And you?'

That got a firm shake of the older head; he was not going to say that as long as Flavius was safe, so was he, which impressed a nephew who got the drift; he had worried that Justinus had not thought matters through.

As he was accommodated in the same suite that served Justinus, Petrus had no distance to walk to his sleeping chamber, not that he went there to rest for he needed to think. Was it worth seeking the help of the emperor and trying to persuade him to rid himself of Pentheus? Not with Vitalian queering the field and the man in question the originator of what Anastasius saw as a successful if dishonest policy! Just as the senator had picked up hints of the correspondence between Decimus and Justinus, Petrus had picked up hints about what was to be done about the rebels and Vitalian.

As a person who walked the corridors of the palace when no other duty presented itself, and his uncle was no hard taskmaster, Petrus enjoyed the little surprises this turned up. Often he would hear part of a discreet conversation, at other times come across courtiers in deep discussion, sometimes encountering people in conclave who in public gave the impression of being mortal enemies. It was a game he played and loved, just as he judiciously sought to make connections with anyone that he thought could further his aims.

Naturally he was close to his uncle's officers, but they were not the only troops in the capital and he never doubted that being able to tell those commanders and their inferiors outside the magic circle of intrigue that was the palace, what was being said, proposed and indeed about to be enacted made him, if not a friend, a warmly welcomed visitor. Knowledge was power and Petrus garnered it like a fish ingesting feed.

He had suspected from the day they were promulgated that the arrangements Anastasius made with Vitalian were false; the emperor might be old and increasingly feeble but he had a core of hard metal that had kept him on the throne and it was one that brooked no opposition. He had made concessions to Vitalian to get him away from the walls of Constantinople, a city that might erupt into serious riot in his support if food got scarce; indeed the populace was so febrile they might de-

360

cide they were fed up with their present ruler and seek to depose him out of nothing but mischief, which had happened before.

Petrus knew he had to come up with a solution to the presence of the Belisarius boy and one that did not compromise his uncle's sense of honour. Added to that he had to deflect Pentheus Vicinus, who must have a full knowledge of what he, Petrus, had only picked up by rumour: that an army from Asia Minor, under the command of the imperial nephew, Hypatius, was about to land on the shores of the Euxine Sea, to then march inland and destroy Vitalian.

As he sat fiddling with the bones with which he liked to gamble he began to evolve a scheme, one full of risks, but less fraught than the potentially fatal one of doing nothing. Then he again considered if he should tell Justinus of what he intended, that discarded quickly in case, by word or deed, he let slip what Petrus was about.

The next morning, secretarial tasks complete, he sent a message to Pentheus Vicinus seeking a meeting, to discuss certain matters of mutual concern – there could only be one given those flaming-red letters on the walls – knowing the senator would have to take the bait, then he went to talk with Flavius Belisarius, which he too needed to do alone, not easy since Justinus seemed to want to hold him close. Finally duty called his uncle away and Petrus made sure, in a very obvious way, that the chamber, as well as the adjoining rooms, were clear of servants.

'Please sit, Flavius.'

Petrus sensed he was reluctant; for some reason

361

the youngster did not fully trust him, that not being a fact to trouble him.

'I need to talk to you on an important matter,' he added and Flavius finally obliged. 'I am going to say to you that it is necessary to act upon what I am going to tell you as if my uncle has no knowledge of it, even if he has.'

That made the listener shift somewhat uncomfortably.

'I doubt you can fathom the level of discretion that is required to hold any position in the imperial service when you are so very close to the source of that power.'

'Your uncle mentioned it was full of what he called "currents"...'

'And greedy sharks to gobble you up if you do not show care!' Petrus exclaimed. 'I hope you believe he trusts me.'

'I suspect it was you who wrote his replies to my father.'

'I even wrote the terms of my own commission, to avoid using the imperial scribes, yet somehow we could not keep matters as secure as we had hoped. You are bound to ask why and I cannot tell you, but Pentheus Vicinus picked up something, perhaps a sniff no more, but it would have been enough perhaps to send to Senuthius a warning. That is what it is like in this place.'

'I am surprised an honourable man like Justinus can bear it.'

'He does so with my aid. I am his eyes, ears and correspondent in all things, for he cannot himself read, or write. It is I who compose his orders and relate to him that which comes in writing. I want to add that apart from my very natural affection for him, distant from any ties of blood, I am wedded to him by interest in my own advancement. Without Justinus I would not be here and would not have the opportunity to seek for myself a place to occupy when he is no longer with us.'

Petrus paused to let that sink in, his gut feeling being that love as a motive would not wash; self-interest was so much more convincing and his uncle was long in years.

'What I am about to tell you he knows the gist of, but his position of loyalty to the emperor precludes it passing his lips, so it falls to me to be the executor of his wishes. Your recent commander, Vitalian, was fed a pack of lies, or at least his senior commanders were and I will now explain what they were and why.'

Flavius listened as it was related to him; Anastasius was never going to relent of his Monophysite edict, never going to honour his commitment to keep the *foederati* fed and paid. No Chalcedonian bishops would be reinstated and more would be removed. The real shock he kept till last: that the architect of that policy of imperial deceit was none other than the cousin of Senuthius Vicinus.

'And that is the way matters are conducted here in the bosom of our empire. Lastly, as of this moment, an army is about to land in the Diocese of Thrace to crush Vitalian, which presents you with a problem.'

'How so?' That got a shrug. 'If Vitalian is defeated, it may clear the way for my uncle to get reconvened my mission to Dorostorum.' A shrug full of negativity followed that. 'But how will we manage that when Pentheus Vicinus is entrenched as the most powerful voice in the councils of empire?'

'A problem certainly.'

'How much loyalty, Flavius, do you harbour towards those you marched with? Do you feel it is incumbent on you, with this information in your possession, to alert them to the danger?'

Sensing the confusion that induced, he stayed silent, letting Flavius gnaw on the matter himself.

'Will the crushing of Vitalian guarantee that your mission will take place?' Petrus demanded, only to answer his own question. 'No, and oddly the only person who might guarantee that is Vitalian, for if he can so pressure Anastasius that he will have to deal with him honestly, it will destroy forever any influence Pentheus has.'

'Which will expose Senuthius?'

'Of course!' Petrus exclaimed, happy not to have to explain everything. 'Then my uncle will not have any reason to hold back or anyone to stand in his way in a matter he feels honour-bound to resolve for an old comrade-in-arms, namely to provide that which you painted on the walls.'

'Justice for Belisarius,' Flavius murmured, for it had become to him a mantra.

'Think on what I have said, for circumstances have put you in a position of real importance, not just to your own wishes but to the future course of the empire.'

Petrus was pleased to see the face before him pale slightly as the enormity of what this young man was faced with struck home. Time to fix in place the final nail!

'But under no circumstances talk to Justinus about this. You have seen the precautions I took so that you and I would not be overheard. This I can do because I am familiar with the place, you are not. Think of the fate of your family and how that came about. If you are overheard discussing this you will so compromise my uncle that he too may lose his head. If that happens, any hope you have for justice will die with him.'

CHAPTER TWENTY-SIX

It was necessary to leave Flavius be, to allow him to think on what had been imparted to him: another reason was to see if he reported the conversation to Justinus, that being a vital test without which nothing could proceed. Besides, Petrus had an appointment to meet with Pentheus Vicinus at his villa in the north-western suburb of Blachernae, home to many a rich individual and well away from the stink at the heart of the city.

By taking a hired palanquin from a public square and not taking a horse – never an animal he was very comfortable on in any case – from the excubitor stables, he could avoid his journey being reported.

The house was substantial, the gardens large, well tended and watered and deeply green even now, in late summer, when all about the ground for miles around was brown and dusty. A coin

365

was disbursed to keep his bearers waiting, while under the cushion on which he had sat, Petrus had secreted a note saying who he was, whom he had visited and why; he was about to sup with the devil so needed a long spoon.

The man did not look like Lucifer; he had a smooth, round face and sparse white hair over a plump rather than fat body. When he walked there was a slight forward stoop as if he was ever in anticipation of something, but Petrus knew that underneath that avuncular exterior was a mind as sharp as his own – perhaps, and this was a worry, even sharper.

'I cannot but admire your gardens, Senator. Would it be permissible to walk in them while we talk?'

That got a thin smile; Pentheus was not fooled, he knew his visitor wanted to converse without any chance of their conversation being witnessed. He called for a servant to fetch a large parasol and, under that protection from the hot sun, they proceeded to saunter around the well-defined paths through a variety of exotic shrubs and much Greek statuary.

'It is good of you to see me.'

'How could I not do so, Flavius Petrus, since my curiosity is acute about what you might have to talk to me about?'

The response was blunt, intended to shock, which was achieved. 'Belisarius!'

Pentheus stopped abruptly and looked at him, his face contorting even if he tried to control it, then he attempted to prevaricate. 'Is it a name with which I should be familiar?'

'If you wish to deny all knowledge of it, I can leave now.'

In plotting how he would deal with this, Petrus had reasoned he must gain and hold control of the conversation, hence the need to be abrupt. He had no time for endless and banal circumlocution and his brusque approach paid off handsomely.

'And if I say it is known to me...'

'Then you might ask if finding it painted on a wall and with a demand for justice, there is anything more that you should concern yourself with.'

'The walls can be cleaned.'

'It was the slate I was thinking of, Senator. We received a despatch from Dorostorum not long past telling us that a centurion of that name, along with his entire family, had perished in a Hunnish raid.'

'Yes.'

'The information imparted to you was, I suggest, somewhat different.' No reply. 'Which means I am obliged to tell you of the identity of the person doing the daubing, though I half suspect you know it already.'

He might as well have said Flavius Belisarius, but it was more pleasurable this way.

'This person.' The question came with a vague wave of the senator's free hand; he was fishing when he should have been talking. 'Am I to act as if he is of some account?'

'It might be as well to treat him. My Uncle Justinus is an old comrade of Decimus Belisarius, who died in that raid. Friends from youth who enlisted in the army at the same time.'

367

There were several slow nods before an admission, as he sought reasons why he was being told a fact that, for the sake of the Count of the Excubitor, would have been better not stated.

'I did not know that.'

'Unfortunately he chose to become involved in the affairs of this old friend, which led to certain matters being discussed in private with the emperor.'

Pentheus was good and if he briefly lost his composure it was back in full potency once he had digested the ramifications; Petrus had just given him the answer to something he must have puzzled over but there was no sign of it affecting him at all, which told his visitor what he had suspected. The senator had lacked precise knowledge of what was going on and had acted on a vague suspicion or gossip; it would be nice to know how much of each but that was unnecessary.

'Why are you telling me this?'

'If I was to tell you I did not approve of his actions?'

'Yet you must have been party to them, I know your uncle cannot read and write.' Realising he might have said too much, given away a source, Pentheus added, 'I assume that is how they communicated.'

'Of course, and I wrote them.'

'So have you come to tell me what they contain?'

'Why, when you can guess? Belisarius threatened to cause your cousin a certain amount of trouble. If you are not privy to the details of what my uncle was engaged in then the gist will do.'

The senator tried to maintain an air of detachment and he rarely let his guard drop as Petrus listed some of the charges levelled against Senuthius, all of which his listener knew since Decimus had written many times to the imperial court to complain of them, only to have them rubbished by the senator and his allies.

'I am curious, Flavius Petrus, what this is all leading up to.'

'If I was to say, Senator, that I am wholly dependent on my Uncle Justinus, who is not in the first flush of spring youth...'

There was no need to finish, for that made Pentheus nod, if not vigorously, then emphatically enough to say he understood. He knew that the male Sabbatius parent was so addled with drink as to be of no use to an ambitious son, and nor did he seem to harbour any doubt that Petrus was afflicted with a desire for, at some time in the future, personal power of his own.

'And the Belisarius boy, given it is to him I assume you are referring.'

'My uncle wants to send him north in an official capacity. It seems your cousin paid a large sum in gold to the Huns, in order that they would raid over the Danube and threaten Dorostorum.'

'Surely a lie!'

'That is to be established, Senator, but given his past actions...' There was again no need to finish that sentence. 'During the raid he was in command of the militia, but stood off and allowed the imperial cohort to be massacred and the Huns to depart without much in the way of loss. That is treason, not theft, and I think would

369

be a hard accusation to refute, indeed it would be one that must lead to an enquiry, which if ordered by the emperor cannot be stopped. And if it turned out to have a basis in fact ... well?'

Petrus was willing him to think it through; even if it does not destroy you, he thought, you will be impoverished. No more bribes handed out, no more of your fellow senators courting you and hanging on your every word, everything you value taken away including this villa and the very gardens in which we now walk. You are angling to be made consul again, I suspect, and you can kiss goodbye to that as well, for no blood relative of a traitor will have a hope.

'I cannot believe it to be true.'

'It does beggar belief, I agree,' came the seemingly sympathetic reply.

That was like a nail in his breast and Pentheus came close to wincing; Petrus believed all right, in fact he knew it to be true!

'This mission you say the Belisarius brat is set upon?'

'Has already been set in motion.'

'Gone already?' Pentheus demanded, for once showing real emotion, for if Belisarius was on his way, the conclusions he had come to about the motives of this visitor were wrong.

'No, but he will depart soon.'

'How?' came the reply, the senator reassured, though only up to a point; he was still mistrustful.

'He will go by the *Via Gemina*, I assume,' Petrus replied, with seeming indifference. 'Then by Marcianopolis.'

'But not to Dorostorum?'

'That would be unwise, don't you think? He had contact with the Sklaveni and it was they who told him of your cousin's arrangement with the Huns. He will seek to persuade them to witness against him.'

'Are we now believing the lies of barbarians?'

'It will be enough to set hares running that would be better staying in their burrow.'

A slow nod. 'In what capacity will the boy travel?'

'On horseback and alone; my uncle has got for him the promise of a written commission.'

It was again instructive to watch the senator's face, even in its immobility; such a document could only come from Anastasius. That he believed the emperor to be so devious as to keep him in the dark came as no surprise, nor should it.

'Which you will compose?'

'Of course, Senator.'

The best bargains are struck without the parties having to enter the details; Petrus was telling him he would be given a copy of that commission as well as the other information he would need. With clever men, so much does not have to be said and that was the case now, the only thing left the words Pentheus spoke.

'I think you know how gratified I am you came to see me, Flavius Petrus.'

'If I am to look out for myself, it behoves me to also look out for those whose friendship in the future I might come to depend on.'

'Let us go back indoors and drink a glass of wine together.'

'I am at your service.'

'Hidden away?' Justinus demanded. 'Where hidden away?'

'In the city, somewhere safe, and even you must accept, Uncle, to have him stay here in the palace is to put his life in danger. I moved him for that reason.'

'You have overreached yourself, Petrus.'

'I have done what was needed.'

'Tell me where?'

'It is best you do not know.' Seeing Justinus fill his lungs with air to shout at him, Petrus cut him off. 'If you are asked you can answer honestly that you have no idea. You are never comfortable telling lies.'

'While you are!'

What his nephew said was true: Justinus was a poor liar, barely able to be convincingly false in kindness, inclined to go red and even stutter if the matter was serious. It was one of the things that made him so valuable to Anastasius, his patent honesty, indeed it had marked his career and the way he had risen within it. People trusted him and were rarely disappointed.

'Do we want to keep the youngster safe?' A nod; he had not used the name, for he did not know who could hear them arguing. 'Can we do so here?'

That got an angry sigh. 'No.'

'If Anastasius asks you where he is ... do you want your loyalties to be tested?'

'You're sure he is safe?'

Petrus could see his uncle was beginning to calm

down and so he should, for what had been done was both wise and logical. 'As far as he can be.'

'What does that mean?'

'It did occur to me that a guard consisting of a couple of your officers might make things more secure.' Seeing the question rear up he cut across that too. 'They don't need to know his name, and if you wish, I will suggest a pair who talk of you as if you are the manifestation of Christ risen.'

'Don't blaspheme.'

'Forgive me, Uncle, but I have acted for the best. If that displeases you, well, I cannot do much to make it better.'

'You sometimes take too much upon yourself, Petrus.'

God be thanked the nephew thought, before saying, in a voice full of entreaty, 'It is only out of regard for you. It is not too much to say I look upon you as a second father.' Playing on the sentimental streak in Justinus usually paid dividends and it did so now. 'Permission to write the orders detailing two of your officers to protect our charge?'

'Go ahead.'

'I will bring them to you to sign.'

'Why bother,' Justinus snapped, seeking to salvage some authority. 'You take so much on yourself you might as well do that too.'

When he was alone, Petrus wrote out two sets of papers, only one the orders that would give two of his own very good friends the task of protection. The other was a commission to one Flavius Belisarius to proceed to Dorostorum to investigate complaints of collusion in cross-border raids by citizens of the empire. It had the seal of the *comes excubitorum*, which would give the youngster the right to use the *mansios* reserved for officials and military officers on official business. A copy was made for Pentheus.

One of the other functions performed by Petrus was to manage his uncle's accounts, for he struggled with figures as much as letters. With possession of the keys to his chest he took out a sum in gold, having listed it in the book as a payment for a new set of highly decorated armour of a kind that went with a general's rank, in short that equal to a count of the excubitor, enough in funds to procure that for a junior officer, as well as a horse, with coin to spare.

'If this falls into the hands of anyone else, it will ruin my uncle.'

'I will guard it with my life,' Flavius replied.

'You look very fine in decent clothing.'

Stroking a breastplate and the devices that marked it out, Flavius asked, 'Is it not deceitful?'

'An excubitor uniform is necessary, Flavius, and it goes with that commission in your hand. No one will dare question you if you are wearing the clothing of a body who act as personal guards to the emperor.'

The room in which Petrus had temporarily accommodated him overlooked one of the harbours of Constantinople, full of shipping, and as dusk settled, light began to twinkle from many a window and deck, while from below his feet came the sound of singing, that brought on by drinking and carousing; Petrus seemed to know the place well,

374

the owners too, for they had greeted him like a long-lost brother.

'Your horse is downstairs being held by the inn-keeper's groom and with it a cloak, which even on a warm night I suggest you wear until you are clear of the city. It would not do to encounter a real excubitor and be exposed.' A purse was handed over, which Flavius weighed, hardly surprised it was quite heavy. 'More funds, I hope, than you will need.'

'I tried on my old breastplate,' Flavius said, wistfully, again fingering the one he was wearing, without knowing why he was telling this strange fellow something that could not be of interest to him. 'Before you brought me here.'

'And?'

'It didn't fit any more.'

He was surprised but pleased that Petrus got the drift of what he was seeking to imply.

'The time will come when you can put all of your past behind you, Flavius, and pray to God it is soon. Shall we do that – pray?'

Flavius was then doubly surprised by what happened next, not seeing Petrus as in any way religious. Yet he was quick to kneel, uttered his supplications to the deities in a strong voice and with passion, which was only half as fervent as those he uttered when the youngster had departed, in which there was a degree of wailing and sobbing which took time to pass, for if he sinned readily, he was much assailed by the fear of damnation for doing so.

His mental self-flagellation complete he made his way downstairs to a room raucous with people

375

enjoying themselves, where he called to the owner, asked him to engage a messenger and when that was provided, the fellow was sent off with a coin and a scroll to the villa of Pentheus Vicinus.

Flavius unwittingly rode past that same villa, exiting the city by the Blachernae Gate, and that with no trouble; people leaving the city, even after dark, were of little concern to the urban prefects. Once on the *Via Gemina* he put his mount into a canter, his mind ruminating on his mission, but also the notion that he might once more come upon Apollonia, the effect of those thoughts making his blood race. He made his first nightly stop, a government *mansio* only three leagues from the city, on a route in which he had to walk as much as ride in order not to overtire his mount, for the real pressure to hurry on his travels would begin on the next morning.

When Pentheus Vicinus received the message from Petrus, he called immediately for a covered chariot, as well as two of his most loyal retainers, men who normally patrolled the grounds at night. On this occasion they would be left unguarded, the mission they were on much more vital than looking after the senator's property.

Petrus, having seared his soul, spent a happy night carousing, in what was a favourite tavern frequented by himself and a goodly number of his uncle's officers. He particularly enjoyed the dancing performed by girls who were not too shy of exposing their flesh nor of suggestive choreography designed to fire the desires of the men in their audience. As company, Petrus preferred them to the staid and painted women that he was constantly being introduced to by his mother, with heavy hints at them being suitable brides with good dowries. He liked his women with the sweat of activity on them and little or no inhibitions.

He was in a room with two of them, sated and sound asleep when Flavius espied the twin lanterns that marked the entrance to the *mansio* where he would spend the night. How different it was to approach such a place with the means to enter, to be greeted with grovelling obsequiousness by the man on night watch and have a bell rung to fetch someone to show him to a comfortable chamber. Knowing it would not be long till it was light again he lay down to sleep, removing only those things that made it uncomfortable, his excubitor breast- and backplate as well as his silver filigreed greaves and riding boots. Apollonia was much in his thoughts as he drifted off to sleep.

The watchman, who usually enjoyed a good and quiet night, was thinking that God had it in for him when a senator turned up and demanded entry. It was then he realised he had forgotten to tell that young excubitor something, but he was no doubt asleep now so it would have to wait; he would find out soon enough. Going back into his hutch he tried to do the same himself, cursing his disturbed night.

There was a commotion within the house, but the watchman was too far off to hear it and he had retired by the time Flavius awoke, to decline a bath, grab some fruit and, in a hurry, get back astride his horse and ride away. The two naked bodies found outside the perimeter of the *mansio* in wooded countryside were not connected to him, for they lay undisturbed for three days before discovery and that only came about because, in the late summer heat, they had begun to smell.

Who they were and where they had come from was never established, not that anyone tried very hard to find out, given they were very obviously, by their dress and features, people of no account. Likewise the senator had left in his covered chariot before cockcrow, not even stopping to eat.

CHAPTER TWENTY-SEVEN

Flavius travelled faster than any official would have been required to do, almost as fast as an imperial messenger, but he had a mission, and the *Via Gemina* provided the means to move with alacrity; a constant ability to change his horse, taking one from a *mansio* stable to replace the one that he left behind and a willingness to suffer the aches of constantly being mounted. This brought him to the main *foederati* encampment in only seven days and on arrival he rode in through the gates in some style, unlike his previous encounter and, being on a horse and dressed as he was, albeit he was stopped, it was with respect.

The camp was nothing like as crowded as he recalled, hardly a surprise since many of those who had flocked to Vitalian's banner in the cause of Chalcedon had gone off to their homes, or, in many of the cases he had heard, to a life where a

378

roof over the head was seen as the lot of the more fortunate. When he asked to speak to Vitalian himself he was treated as an honoured messenger, disarmed and escorted to the timber-and-thatch structure that was part of his headquarters.

The general was entertaining his officers probably, to Flavius's thinking, dining them on the proceeds of what had been gifted to him by Anastasius, when this messenger was brought in to see him and it was obvious to the youngster that most present were drunk, especially the leaders of the Gautoi mercenaries. With, they assumed, no enemy on the horizon that was not untoward; the message they received from Flavius made it less so, telling as it did the truth, not convenient lies. There would be no concessions to Chalcedon, instead the very reverse and with an army on the way under Hypatius intent on crushing them.

'Who sends you to say this?' demanded Diomedes, Vitalian's second in command.

'A friend.'

A very slurred voice shouted out in bad Latin, 'Damn you, remove your helmet when you address our general!'

As he lifted his helmet from his head, simultaneously looking along the tables, he spied his late tribune Vigilius and noted the expression of disbelief on his face when he recognised this messenger.

'Who is this friend?'

Flavius had no idea it was Diomedes who had made the demand, yet it was one, regardless, that left Flavius in a quandary; Petrus had made no mention of who he should say had sent him yet

379

surely there was only one name that would convince those he was addressing that he was genuine, which, looking at the glowering suspicion to which he was being subjected, no one currently believed. Yet he had been sworn to secrecy, the two being incompatible.

'I refuse to say, but he is a high official and one who knows and has fought alongside the man who commands you.'

That set off a cacophony of noise, some agreement, most derision, as well of cries of, 'Name him!'

'Why would anyone of rank send you?'

The soft voice first confused Flavius until he realised it had come from Vitalian; how could a man with a stentorian voice enough to address an army have such a quiet mode of expression in private? But what to say?

'General, I know this man.' All eyes turned to Vigilius, who had spoken out loudly, the question hanging in the air. 'He was recently a *decanus* in my brigade.'

'Dressed as an excubitor officer?' someone said and uproar broke out, everyone talking at once and not, in a lot of cases, with much sense.

'If I may be permitted to explain how this came about,' Flavius shouted, trying and failing to make his voice heard.

Silence was only restored when Vitalian stood to command it and even then it was not immediate, but finally he could speak. 'Hold, my friends, there are deep currents here and I am not sure with my brain a bit addled by wine I can see it straight.'

380

'Chuck him in the latrine,' one voice shouted to much raucous laughter.

'Who will treat him as his guest tonight?' Vitalian called. 'For someone must. If he is dressed as he is then he is entitled to that courtesy.'

'And if he lies?' asked Diomedes.

'Then he has no right to retain his head.'

'I will share my hut with him.'

All eyes turned to Vigilius again, now standing, some mouthing 'fool', others too far gone in drink to see him properly.

'You forgo, then,' Vitalian responded, 'the rest of the night's revels.'

'I accept that as forfeit.'

'Then take this fellow, but be warned, Tribune, should he not be here to talk with me in the morning, when I might be able to assess the truth of what he is saying, your head is as much at risk as his own.'

The pair of Gautoi sentinels who had escorted him into the building were there to march him out, Vigilius needing to hurry to catch them, and having caught up he did not speak, merely directing the guards to his hut.

'Best take station here, one of you,' Vigilius demanded. 'The other to go and tell the guard commander. You, inside.'

Flavius walked in to find the interior of the hut containing the same furnishings he had before observed at a distance, and close to they looked even more valuable. He was also aware that for some reason Vigilius was feeing awkward, as if he did not quite know how to act.

'This,' he said finally, 'is very strange.'

381

'To me as well as you, Tribune.'

'You were a common soldier a few weeks past, a *decanus* for a brief period and now you turn up dressed as the commander of a *numerus* in the excubitor.'

'I doubt you would believe me if I were to tell you.'

'You'd better try, Flavius, if that is your true name, for I put myself forward to keep you from others who would now be trying to beat out of you the truth.'

'I am Flavius Belisarius, the son of the imperial centurion of Dorostorum,' he began, and as he continued he was aware that his listener was struggling to believe what he was being told, for he left nothing out and if Vigilius doubted what had gone before he was doubly sceptical of how Flavius concluded.

'If, as you say, an army is coming by sea, it would have had to be set in motion before we ever arrived outside Constantinople.'

'It may well have been, Tribune, but that I have no knowledge of.'

'So I am expected to believe that our emperor was lying from the very outset?'

'It would seem so.'

'If I was to say to you, Flavius Belisarius, if indeed it be your name, that your tale is too fanciful to be credited, what would you counter that with?'

'Is Forbas still with you?' A nod. 'Then ask him!'

The centurion was not happy to be dragged from his slumbers but it was an order he could not disobey. If Vigilius had been shocked by what he was presented with, Forbas was no less afflicted, but once his astonishment had subsided, he was able to remind his tribune that he had harboured doubts about Flavius from his first encounter.

'You said he was not quite right, do you recall?'

'I'd forgotten.' When Flavius raised an eyebrow, Vigilius added, 'You were not of much account to me.'

As they had talked, even before the arrival of Forbas, the sounds from the main building had grown louder, male yelling being mingled after a while with female shrieks; the officers were enjoying themselves and now it had risen to a crescendo.

'Dancing girls,' Forbas explained, when the noise rose. 'At least, that's what they term themselves.'

'That's not the cry of a woman,' Flavius said.

There was a moment of disbelief, until another cry rent the air and it was definitely male and pained. Vigilius grabbed his weapon and led an unarmed Forbas out of his hut, Flavius following, and the first thing to see was the flames of the wooden camp perimeter well alight; it was under serious assault.

'I need a sword,' Flavius cried.

'Then find a dead man who has one,' Forbas shouted, 'as I have to.'

What followed was mayhem; the officers to a man were drunk, there were half-naked females running in all directions making life, hard already, ten times more so. The assault was coming over one side of the camp and Flavius, having found a

383

weapon and fighting alongside he knew not who, entered into the fray without being certain it was in his interests to do so.

The first real battle for someone so steeped in fighting lore was a disappointment and in later life part of an education used to good effect. Confusion was rife; sometimes he had no idea if he was fighting someone on his own side, not that he had one, or one of the people trying to overrun the camp. It was not numbers that drove the *foederati* and their Roman officers back, it was a lack of cohesion, added to the surprise achieved by the enemy.

The horns that blew to sound the retreat were those which Flavius had been so recently trained to recognise and now he had some idea who was friend and who was foe, for the latter were advancing while they were retreating in a ragged line. Slashing with his picked-up sword – he had cast three found lances – he managed to form something of a line by which the falling back could avoid being a rout.

Regardless of their efforts Vitalian's force was driven from the encampment, and when the fight petered out, all they could do was watch their huts and buildings burn and, along with that, anything not worth looting.

Dawn found them, blackened and weary, in an open field, the smoke from the fires still rising in the distance to the east, with Vitalian, as grubby as any of his men, walking through the disordered ranks seeking to lift their spirits. When he came to Flavius, who had found and joined Vigilius and Forbas, he stopped and barked at him.

'You brought this on.'

'No, General,' Vigilius replied, pulling himself to his feet with some difficulty. 'Flavius Belisarius fought with us. You need to talk to him and, if you will forgive my impertinence, listen too.'

What enemy they had faced the night before was nowhere to be seen and Vitalian, having heard out the man come to alert him, was firmly of the opinion that if it was Hypatius, then it could not be the main force, given the numbers Flavius had said could be anticipated.

'If that had been the whole army this fellow claims we would all be wondering with what words we might greet St Peter. It was a raid but not a battle.'

'A damned successful one.'

'We have lost a fight, we have lost our camp and forfeited that which we possessed. Have we lost our spirit?'

Flavius, listening as Vitalian rallied his officers first and his men next, thought this the stuff of true generalship. He could not be less drained than anyone present but nothing in his demeanour hinted at it. Once he had finished his encouragement he called for Flavius.

'Tell me again what you know of Hypatius.'

'You believe him?' Diomedes demanded, still unconvinced.

'If I had listened to him last night we might not be sat here in this open field, without even a tent in which to confer.'

The tale was simple and what impressed Flavius was that Vitalian saw the solution as the same. With great effort he rallied his men to march back to their ruined camp, there to search the rubble for weapons and any recoverable possessions, in fact few; the furniture of Vigilius was charred and destroyed. Next, Vitalian ordered that the nearby settlement and farms be denuded of food, no quarter given, for he could achieve nothing commanding a depleted army with empty bellies. That completed – it took two days – he marched his men out and headed east, with Flavius held close by his side, not out of affection but a lack of trust.

They caught Hypatius when his main force was in extended order, marching from Odessus towards Marcianopolis along a narrow *via rustica* expecting no battle of any consequence, anticipating an easy victory once they found Vitalian and his disorganised and already defeated troops. But they were very much in existence, and, having taken up positions on both sides of a deep valley, they charged down on the head of the imperial columns and threw them into great disarray.

The rout inflicted on forward elements of the imperial forces was total, the middle and rear parts of the imperial army fleeing back, hoping to find the ships that had brought them from the southern shore of the Euxine. The front cadres not mown down in the initial assault were now seeking to throw themselves on the mercy of their attackers, many dying in the bloodletting that followed, as they paid in revengeful mayhem for the defeat and burning of the *foederati* encampment.

The Gautoi barbarians were unstoppable; not that much effort was made to impede their butchery and it was made plain to Flavius, not that he had any inclination to interfere, that to do so was as dangerous to him as it was to what they saw as their rightful victims. Soon the paving stones of the *via rustica* were awash with blood ankle-deep, which formed a river along the sloping valley floor, while the killers were covered from head to foot in the same gore and seemingly more drunk than he had ever seen any of their officers on wine.

Vitalian was as quick as he could be in pursuit, pressuring the enemy away from Odessus and an easy evacuation, more through their own confusion than by any hard fighting. Hypatius fell back on and barricaded himself in a small coastal town called Acris and was sure, having fortified his camp, he was safe and from there no doubt sent for his ships.

Vitalian, taking a leaf out of Hypatius's book, launched a surprise attack at night, overran the temporary defences and utterly destroyed the imperial army as a fighting force. Once more the Gautoi were let loose with their weapons to kill as they pleased. Not many of the enemy made it onto the few ships that had managed to arrive in the harbour and those that sought safety on land were lucky if they ended up as slaves.

Both Hypatius and the newly appointed *magister militum per Thracias* were taken prisoner, saved from being butchered by the personal but much-diminished cohort that Vitalian kept for himself as guards, they being too valuable to just kill. The emperor's nephew pleaded for his officers, those close to him, and they too, being high-born and fit for ransom, were spared. So it was a triumphant force that marched back towards a destroyed camp, richer now than they had been before it was looted, for they had the treasury of the imperial army as pay for their success and much labour with which to rebuild.

When they finally reached the camp, they found two officers of the excubitor with another prisoner, Pentheus Vicinus, who were seeking out Flavius Belisarius to hand him over. The tale he had to listen to seemed as fanciful as that he had related to Vigilius, for these men had been sent out of Constantinople by Petrus Sabbatius.

'He suspected that Pentheus would try to kill you. Our task was to prevent that and we caught two bastards in the corridor leading to your quarters.'

'They might not have been intent on killing me.'

'They were and said so before we slit their throats, then stripped both and left them in the nearby woods to make it hard to identify them.'

'And Pentheus?'

'If he had turned up in person to see you assassinated, we were to bring him to you at Vitalian's camp. Old sod put up a bit of a fight but we got him into his chariot and away past the watchman, who was sound asleep. If you look under that threadlike hair of his, you will see an impression of the butt of my sword hilt.'

'How did Pentheus know where I would be?'

'You'd have to ask Petrus that,' said one, not answering in a way that hinted he would be able to provide any enlightenment if pressed. But then he added something meaningful without intending to. 'He's a very sly fox, that one.'

'How sly?' Flavius asked, seeking to mask his suspicion that there were things of which he was unaware, what Justinus called 'currents'.

The second officer laughed, though Flavius did not take what he jested about as a joke. 'If he follows you through a swinging door, he will come out in front.'

'What were your orders after you delivered the senator?'

'To return to our duties.'

Vitalian called Flavius into his presence so that the appearance of the senator could be explained, as well as his own tale, and he listened to both stories with as much scepticism as had been the case with Vigilius. He and Forbas had to be called to the general's new tent to back up one part of the tale. Pressed on who had really sent the warning, given it had not been Pentheus, Flavius again refused to say and pleaded with Vitalian that since his advice had saved him from annihilation his reticence should be respected, that granted, though with ill grace.

The two excubitors departed under safe conduct and the heartfelt gratitude of Vitalian. To say he was pleased ranked as understatement, for no man so hates a person as much as one who has been a friend and then betrayed him. Hypatius had been vocal in order to ingratiate himself and keep his head on his shoulders; he had laid bare the whole of the Vicinian chicanery.

Pentheus pleaded, claimed the emperor forced him to act but to no avail, and Vitalian made him grovel before throwing him into an open-to-the-elements cage where he was assailed by anyone in the camp who had filth of which they wanted to dispose.

'So tell me, Flavius Belisarius, what it is I can gift to you that will serve as a fitting reward?'

'Would I be correct General, in thinking that north of Marcianopolis, you represent the legal authority?'

'I am not the *magister* but one is dead and his replacement is in my custody, so will do anything I tell him. But why do you ask?'

Flavius was disturbed about the way Pentheus had come to be here and concerned too that there might be a game being played in which he was nothing but a low-value gambling bone. Did he here, and with this man, have a chance to do that which he sought without relying on any sly foxes?

'Only one thing, General. I would ask that I be given both Tribune Vigilius and Centurion Forbas to act under my instructions as well as a strong unit of soldiers and the right to command obedience and the truth. I have told you how my family, my father and brothers were betrayed and who was responsible. Let that man be obliged to pay for his transgressions and to suffer whatever punishment I decree.'

'Why don't you just kill him? For that you need only your own sword.'

'To do so would sully the memory of my father. I must constitute a real enquiry, call forth those who will witness and prove to those who stood aside when they should have acted, year after year in their own regard, that justice eventually will come to those who transgress against God and their fellow citizens.'

'Judge and executioner?'

'No, I will ask Tribune Vigilius to act as judge.'

'And that slug Pentheus?'

'Do with him as you wish, he is your enemy, not mine.'

'I will just remove his head.'

'So be it. Do you grant my request?'

'Have you asked those you wish to go to Dorostorum with you if they agree?'

'Yes.'

'Then choose the men you want, and may God go with you. I will get the new *magister* to compose an order conferring on you your official status. Thus you will be acting on behalf of the emperor, God rot his lying soul.'

CHAPTER TWENTY-EIGHT

The gloom that descended in the imperial palace was palpable, no one seeming to be unaffected by it from the emperor to the lowest sweeper. Vitalian had inflicted a grievous defeat on Anastasius and was now demanding a massive ransom for his nephew Hypatius. Justinus, who had been obliged to keep his own counsel for so long found the need even greater now. How had his ruler got himself into such a mess, only by his own folly?

'You do not seem to share the present mood, Petrus?'

'I am as downcast as the next man, how could

I not be, Uncle?'

'Let us say I know you too well to believe that. I am wondering if you will pass on to me the reasons why your step seems lighter than it was before we got news of the defeat of Hypatius.'

I cannot, Petrus thought, for you would be shocked, you might hate me, you might even dismiss me. But I have done you a service, for I have removed a man who had become a potent enemy in Pentheus Vicinus, whom Anastasius now thinks, since the news of his defection was delivered, first deluded him, then betrayed him. He would have found out how we sought to secretly bring down his cousin and, unlike you, he would have seen the need to kill to stop us.

I have engineered a major loss of face for one of the emperor's nephews and the one best suited to succeed him; what hope now for a nephew who has lost an entire army, a modern-day Varus? I hope in time we will be able to satisfy the burden you carry for the deaths of Decimus Belisarius and his sons, and at no time have I endangered your standing with the man you are tasked to protect and who trusts you now more than he ever has.

'What do you think made Flavius flee, Petrus, when you had him safely hidden away?'

'No idea, Uncle, but I must say he was so animated with his desire for justice that I suspect he has gone back to Dorostorum with murder in his heart.'

'Which might cost him his own life.'

'Indeed, if only he had waited. Who knows, though, he may see sense and come back to us.'

The excubitor officers Petrus had engaged were returned but there was no sign of Flavius, for which Petrus had not calculated; he was supposed to be back in Constantinople.

'How will it all end?' Justinus sighed.

'Who is to know how anything will ever end?'

'We can pray for good outcomes, an ending in which all is resolved and everyone content.'

'In that I will willingly join you, Uncle.'

Petrus said his prayers with his habitual fervour and he knew he had much to seek absolution for; he always felt he did. He had engineered the death of some men and the disgrace of others, those who had attached themselves to Pentheus seeking cover in new alliances. He had played a dangerous game and come out unscathed and if there was pleasure in that there was, too, a residual recollection of the moments of deep apprehension he had suffered in the process; it could all, his conspiracy, have so easily fallen apart, especially because it had all hinged on an innocent and easily biddable youth!

The power Flavius had was fully proconsular; he was, in Upper Moesia, the law for both church and state and one unknown to the citizens of Dorostorum. Given the road from Marcianopolis passed by the forum square and the basilica, his first act was to bypass the town in darkness with most of his men, leaving a detachment to surround and seal off the cathedral and the buildings attached, including the residence of Gregory Blastos, no one to exit on pain of death.

This set light to multiple rumours, multiplied

when the rest of his troops headed east to the Senuthius villa, a compound of buildings he invested with near a full century of mounted and bloodthirsty Gautoi mercenaries. If they arrived without warning, their presence did not go unremarked, judging by the flaring torches that illuminated the panic caused within.

'Tribune Vigilius, please send a message to the senator inviting those men he commands, on the order of the *magister militum per Thracias,* to lay down their arms or to come out and do battle. Do not use my name.'

They heard Senuthius, so carrying were his exhortations and commands, which turned to pleas that those he paid to defend him go out and fight, in time reduced to futile threats. It fell on ears that were not deaf but wise enough to see that what was being proposed was not just fruitless but suicidal. A professional body of soldiers surrounded his villa and he could not send for reinforcements; the numerous fighters who controlled his outlying farms and stood guard on his mills were cut off from any knowledge of what was taking place.

He tried to send a messenger, one fool who did not realise that his head, once detached from his body, would be slung into the villa compound, along with a second demand, one that was timed and aimed at the men who guarded Senuthius; come out now, throw down your weapons or not only will you die, but those who carry your blood will perish likewise.

For men who had once been soldiers but had settled, who had taken wives and bred children on farms looted in legal chicanery by their master, facing certain death was a powerful incentive, the loss of wives and children too great a sacrifice for a mere stipend or a ploughed field and low rent; they came out in their entirety and with them the cowering and terrified servants.

'There is one amongst you to whom I owe a great deal,' Flavius called, once the two groups were separated, to what was now a tight knot of terrified people who had served Senuthius and in many cases felt the weight of his whip. 'I do not now need to know who that is, who saved my life by advising me to flee, but if you come forward I will embrace and reward you.'

No one moved.

'I suspect you wish to keep your identity hidden for fear that someone will make you pay for what they see as betrayal, and if that is true, then know this. I am in your debt and you may come to me at any time and lay a claim upon my gratitude.'

'How will you know?' whispered Vigilius.

'A ladder,' Flavius replied equally softly, which made no sense to anyone but him.

'Our Gautoi are itching for slaughter,' the tribune pointed out, watching them as they pressed in on and corralled the surrendered fighters.

'They are not to be killed,' Flavius shouted, making a statement that satisfied the barbarians. 'I have in store a more fitting retribution in which they will shed tears as slaves, not merely their blood on a cross.'

'Your senator is refusing to come out,' said Forbas, who had been sent with a third demand and returned.

'Then set fire to the place and see if he can hold to his refusal.'

'There is much in there to loot, the swine is rich.'

Flavius got what Forbas was hinting; the *foederati* given to him by Vitalian would be looking for plunder. 'Is he alone?'

'There are two children with him, well not quite children judging by the amount of their flesh.'

'A boy and a girl, I seem to recall.' Forbas nodded. 'Tell him they will be sold in the market at Constantinople, and to the worst of the owners he sold others to, the Sklaveni his paid henchmen snatched from their farms. It is him I want, not the innocents.'

Senuthius tried to negotiate, to secure some kind of terms, to no avail, his last request a palanquin for his son and daughter, to which Flavius replied that they would have to walk, given it was a mode of travel they would now be required to get used to. Eventually he sent them out and Flavius dismounted and went to face a man he so hated, the moment he removed his helmet and exposed his face one of pure pleasure.

'You?'

'A pagan would call me "Nemesis".'

'Your voice, I did not–'

Flavius cut right across him. 'I have grown out of what you may recall and I have come so that you may answer for your crimes, not only against my house but the empire.'

He tried bluster; he had to. 'Have a care, Flavius Belisarius, I have powers and influence you know nothing of.'

'If you refer to your cousin Pentheus, I think you will find his head adorning the gate of the *foederati* camp north of Marcianopolis. He sought to betray Vitalian and play him for a dupe; now he has paid for his mistake, as you must in your turn.'

'Then kill me.'

'What, and deny myself the privilege of seeing you plead for mercy?'

'I won't,' Senuthius growled, his whole being defiant.

Flavius smiled. 'You will.'

The fat senator cried when his villa was torched, or was it the sight of his chest of gold being ransacked? His two children had been sent packing on foot and they did not walk, they ran. Every stick of Senuthius's furniture, every statue and object of value was brought out to be stacked for later distribution and when Flavius led his men and his prisoner away they were backlit by the blaze of a house in conflagration.

There are occasions when a whole district can come to life, where a normally slow and sometimes moribund way of passing on news transcends itself, a heavy raid by barbarians being one. This was another and soon the tracks and the *viae rusticae* were full of flickering torches and very animated people. They tied Senuthius to the tail of a horse and dragged him into Dorostorum, the news that he was fallen from grace seemingly able to be transmitted without any consciousness of time or distance, so that well before they reached the first outlying dwelling, the route was lined with a jeering mob.

Sods of excrement, mostly equine but some human, were chucked at the senator to whom so recently the same people would have grovelled and Flavius found it hard to contain his disgust; this lot would have dunged his father given half a chance. Worse faced the prisoner when he entered the forum, with its missing stones and air of neglect. Hanging upside down from a hastily assembled frame was the naked body of Bishop Gregory Blastos, the red-hot poker with which he had been immolated still protruding from his anus, along with the rank smell of burning flesh.

The sight reduced Senuthius, hitherto defiant, to a jelly, the chanting in favour of Chalcedony rising and falling as an added threat to his being. This Flavius had neither foreseen nor left orders to prevent and if he hated the victim he was aware that he had failed; the men he left behind saw no reason to stop a fired-up mob hell-bent on the rights of their religion.

'Kill me now, Belisarius,' the senator shouted, and he was swung round in the centre of the forum.

'No, Senator,' Flavius replied, dismounting, 'these people have to hear your crimes listed.'

'Before you hand me over to their mercy?'

'No, if you are going to die, it will be by my hand, for you must answer for my father and my three brothers.'

'One was a fool and the others bred between a fool and a whore.'

'If I could be provoked into killing you quickly, Senuthius, I have already enough cause.'

Vigilius had taken his place on the rostrum and was reading out the commission Vitalian had provided for Flavius, not that he was heard. Before him was a baying mob intent on blood and Flavius, observing it, was full of revulsion. It was mainly the low-born but not exclusively so, there being a goodly number of well-heeled citizens in the mix. He saw his own trio of friends – did they recognise him helmeted? – screaming as many a bloody imprecation as the meanest peasant.

Many of these same people had, by either silence or collusion, thwarted his father as he sought to contain Senuthius; now they were hoping to tear him limb from limb and no doubt also thinking that to do so was to expiate their own sins. That only increased as Vigilius read out, to a roar at each charge, the indictment against the prisoner, this accompanied by a multitude of presented and repeated cries of 'I will witness'.

Flavius had to give Senuthius his due; he may have panicked at the sight of the body of Gregory Blastos but he had fought hard to regain his composure and succeeded. Knowing he was going to die, he stood square-shouldered and defiant, his eyes ranging around the forum and the crowd as if to say 'I have marked you and will be waiting to greet you in hell.' The man who had captured him was also watching those same faces and with growing abhorrence.

Collectively they could have done in a blink what Decimus Belisarius failed to achieve in six years of frustration. How many now yelling themselves hoarse had been active supporters of the man they now wanted dead? How many had known and just kept silent, while the rest, who must have at least supposed that crimes were going unpunished, hid their heads deep in their cellars?

'Forbas.'

It took some time for him to respond, so loud was the crowd. 'Sir?'

Flavius had to shout his reply, while indicating he should come close. 'Sir? Will I ever get used to that?'

'Enjoy it while it lasts.'

There was no questioning of the orders Flavius issued; Forbas rode off with an escort, while Flavius apprised Vigilius of what he intended, then formed up his remaining *foederati* in two lines so as to keep these irate citizens at bay, before tying a furious Senuthius over a saddle.

It was strange to ride the same road as he had that fateful day with Ohannes, when, if his nose was sore and his eyes blacking, his world was bright with promise. Why did it look smaller and less significant now? He crested the rise to look at what he had last seen as a field of battle; now it was once more verdant farmland and there in the distance was the blue and slow-flowing Danube.

They moved down the slope, eventually coming to the very spot, now overgrown, where he had lit the pyre for his family. There he stopped, dismounted and knelt to pray, while everyone, including the noisy, trailing crowd, as well as his prisoner, fell silent. If they joined him in his supplications he did not want them to; Flavius desired his memories to be unsullied and entreaties for their souls to be pure.

Forbas had acquired a decent-sized boat and,

devotions over, a protesting Senuthius was forced aboard, into the bottom and his bonds extended to lash him to one of the thwarts. It was plain to a person who had grown up here that such activity would not go unnoticed and he was not wrong. Long before they reached the northern shore a strong body of Sklaveni warriors had gathered, and with them, Flavius could see, were the very tribal elders who had spent so much time haggling over his fate. More pleasing was the sight of Dardanies.

'I come in peace,' Flavius shouted, 'and with a gift of great value.'

A gesture indicated he should come to land and the boat was brought to lay by a small jetty. Flavius climbed out and came face to face with Dardanies, who, after a moment's hesitation, embraced him.

'What has brought you here, Flavius, and,' he held him at arm's length, taking in the quality of the garb, 'seemingly much elevated since I saw you last?'

'A long tale and for another time Dardanies. I have a request to meet once more with that monk of St Basil who talked with your elders.'

'Best acknowledge those elders first, for they are proud.'

That got a grin. 'Then lead me to them so I may flatter their arrogance.'

'There is not enough of that in the world.'

If it was said with a laugh, there was an underlying seriousness, proved by the time Flavius spent telling them how puissant and wise they were as one-time warriors and present leaders. Finally, when Dardanies felt he had greased their conceits enough, it was he who asked for the monk, who, once brought forward – he was in the crowd – Flavius took off for a quiet talk.

'I have a man who was rich and will now be poor, a great sinner who, on this side of the river will be given little opportunity to transgress more, indeed he may die for many of his crimes were visited upon the tribe with which you live. It will take all of your blessedness to keep him alive, as well as all the power you possess to bring him to a realisation of the peril to his soul. His name is Senuthius Vicinus.'

The monk crossed himself; even to him the man was Lucifer.

'It may be you will fail and he will be slaughtered, for he has visited much harm on the Sklaveni.'

'More on you and your family, that is known on this bank.'

'My desire to take his life is strong, I grant you, but where would I stand with God if I succumbed to that temptation? I would condemn my soul in order to take as forfeit his body. I will hand him into your care, with the instruction only that he must not be allowed to escape. If it is necessary to scourge him to bring him to realise his peril then that is for you to prescribe, but no man is beyond God's grace, even the greatest villain. Will you do this for me?'

'I will do that which is my calling,' the monk replied, in a very soft tone of voice, 'not for you but for the poor miscreant of whom you are giving me charge. But if you are true in your faith, you too must pray for him.'

'That will be hard.'

'God will demand it of you, for did not Jesus say to turn the other cheek from those who offend you?'

Dragged from the boat, the appearance of Senuthius brought forth gasps from those who recognised him, followed by an outbreak of screaming not much different from what had been heard in the forum of Dorostorum. It was those tribal elders, made aware of what was intended, who saw the senator through the mob to a place of safety, this not witnessed by Flavius, who had boarded the boat once more and had himself rowed back to the southern bank.

'You will regret that,' Forbas insisted.

'Perhaps.'

'What now?'

'You and Vigilius to remain here, to sequester and sell all of the property of Senuthius Vicinus, the proceeds to be passed to General Vitalian to do with as he wishes.'

'Surely you should have it?'

'No, Forbas, it is too tainted for me; I will settle for the value of my family home, which I also ask you to undertake to dispose of for me. I will set foot in the city of Dorostorum again one more time only, if I have my way. I must go now and fetch my mother to this place so that we can properly grieve for my father and brothers and erect, as I promised I would, an obelisk to their memory at the place they gave up their lives.'

It was while riding out of the city, on the road to Marcianopolis, that Flavius recalled his father's other wish and one he would fulfil by placing a plaque on the city wall, detailing the life, titles and service of Decimus Belisarius, as befitted a proud Roman soldier. For the rest there was nothing – not even his friends – so damaged was his heart by what had happened here.

On the way south, before he turned for Illyricum, he searched for Apollonia, but to no avail; the life of a camp follower was an itinerant one and if he picked up a trace it soon went cold until finally he knew he had to leave such a thing to fortune or God. It was only years later and by chance, while on campaign, he found out she had died in delivery and when he enquired as to when it had happened, it was reasonable to suppose the child might be his own.

They had performed the obsequies by the banks of the Danube, with an obelisk to mark the spot where the other men of the family had perished. Their last act was to set in stone and dedicate, near to the gate by which the inhabitants entered Dorostorum, the promised plaque after which she had naturally enquired as to what he would now do.

'I was born to be a soldier, Mother and that is my destiny, to live like my father did as a Roman. May God aid me to prosper in my choice and I hope the soul of my father and brothers will be there to guide me.'

The publishers hope that this book has given you enjoyable reading. Large Print Books are especially designed to be as easy to see and hold as possible. If you wish a complete list of our books please ask at your local library or write directly to:

Magna Large Print Books
Magna House, Long Preston,
Skipton, North Yorkshire.
BD23 4ND